Mae shot to her feet, her rising voice echoing off the walls of the cavernous space. "I've raised my daughter to recognize the monsters in this world as strangers on the outside, Deb, people who roam the streets long after she's tucked in her bed, warm and safe for the night. When she asks me why people do bad things, I tell her the monsters inside them make them harm others. I tell her those people don't understand why they're doing wrong, that if they did they would want to get help, would beg to get the monsters out of their minds…"

She wiped tears away with the back of a trembling hand. "But how do I tell her the monster lives inside our home? That he sits across from her at the breakfast table every morning, making jokes and pouring orange juice into her favorite cup, all the while planning to get Momma out of the picture for good so she can take my place?"

Mae snatched her purse from the chair, slinging it roughly over her arm. "There are things some women never tell, some secrets we're so ashamed of we keep them close until we fall over exhausted into our graves. I knew Rick was a sick man long before he came after Lily. There were nights I'd have to bite my pillow to keep from screaming because I didn't want her to hear, couldn't bear for her to even have to imagine the inhuman things he was doing…"

She paused again, staring at the carpet as if recalling a distant memory. Her face contorted briefly into a mask of horror and revulsion, the expression clearing almost as soon as it occurred. "…and he loved it, Deb," she finished in a bitter whisper, never taking her eyes from the floor. "He loved it most when I wanted to scream…"

A PERFECT PLACE TO PRAY

I. L. GOODWIN

Genesis Press, Inc.

Black Coral

An imprint of Genesis Press, Inc.
Publishing Company

Genesis Press, Inc.
P.O. Box 101
Columbus, MS 39703

ISBN: 1-58571-202-7
Manufactured in the United States of America

First Edition

Visit us at www.genesis-press.com
or call at 1-888-Indigo-1

DEDICATION

For Mother.

ACKNOWLEDGMENTS

To God Most High: Thank You for calling me out of a dark place, for showering Your love upon me. You breathed a promise in my ear one day, and this very day the promise has been fulfilled. Dwelling Place, Refuge, Shield, Fortress, Strong Tower—You are ever my Joy and my Delight.

To Deatri: I saw your initial list of comments and thought, "Boy, I'm really in for something here." How grateful I am, though, to have had the benefit of your sharp eyes and natural editing instincts working on my behalf. Thank you for your patience, for helping me through what would have been a much more agonizing, much more confusing process without your help. I look forward to working with you on the next one.

To Granny Emma: What can I say? We've been together since the beginning. Even as a little girl, I knew in my gut we'd be soul mates. You've rejoiced with me through the highs, you've comforted me through the lows. You've been a pillar of strength in my life and an enduring example of God's love all along. Thank you for your unconditional love and acceptance. Thank you for believing in me. It's because of you I knew Mae could go through hell and back and come out of it with a testimony, and a smile.

To Vickie: We started out as friends, yet over time you've become like a mother to me. Nearly every day for three years you heard me ask, "Will it ever come?" Though many a conversation began with me venting my frustration, they always ended with your simple words of peace. Now a new partnership, a new journey awaits us in the Garden. Cheers.

To Mitza: Always so patient, always so sweet. You were the first to say "Girl, this is good. Are you going to have it published?" You always call me Angel, but you've never realized you were the true angel all along. I consider it a privilege having such a dynamic person like you in my life. The best is yet to come, survivor.

To Norren: We clicked so well when we met, we swore we must have been fellow milkmaids in another life. We've racked up more memories (and inside jokes) than we can count. We've shared tons of greasy lunches, we've rolled down our share of grassy hills. You are truly my best friend on all the earth.

To Bethany: You weren't even born yet when I created Lily, but now that you're here, I see she must have been you all along. You are my sweetheart. Don't take over the world too early, your momma still needs you to be her little girl just a little while longer.

To Jessie: You're a positive force for good, an excellent cheerleader. These things come so naturally to you. Thanks for reading my tome and reminding me I'd be a "famous writer" someday. You are too much.

To Brianna: You've read all the rough chapters, you've told all the best jokes. You remind me not to take myself too seriously. You've shown me what it is to laugh big laughs over the little things. Thanks, Sis, for making the world a brighter, much more interesting place.

To Francine: Thanks for reminding me that "Positive Thinking" carries great power, even as the ink was drying on the contract.

To Betty and Charles: You guys never forgot about this book, even during the time of long silences and endless waiting. I will never forget that. Your love and support mean more than you know.

To Bev, Marcie, Carla, Veronica, a.k.a "The Crew": It wasn't always a bed of roses for us, but thank heaven, the storm is finally over. Each of you has impacted my life in so many wonderful ways, ways I can't even begin to explain here. Thank you for the good times, thank you even for the times that weren't so good. You are dear to my heart, know that each of you will be a part of me forever. Wow, this is just the beginning! Should we throw a party or a potluck? I love you guys.

ONE

Mae threw her arms over her head to shield herself from another merciless, unforgiving blow. The blow came a lot lower than expected, a rushing, steely punch to her pelvis. Shocked and breathless, she balled into a fetal position and remained there, sweaty face pressed against the carpet. "Please..." she grunted into the nap, bursts of exhaled air blowing thick, twisted threads in every direction. "No more, no more."

A tall shadowy figure disentangled himself from the surrounding gloom and kneeled beside her. His meaty fingers brushed over the staccato beats resonating from her tender flesh. He dropped her hand in disgust, then stepped lithely over her to a nearby chair. "You had enough? We on the same page here?" He settled himself comfortably on the cushions, wiping his mouth roughly with the back of his enormous hand.

"Enough," she hissed through clenched teeth. "Enough."

He stared silently at her from his perch in the chair, an expression of mock sympathy distorting his features. Finally, he clucked his tongue, slowly shaking his head. "Why, Mae, why? Why do you always insist on making things so damn *difficult* in this house? I've told you time and again—I hate the lessons as much as you do, but it seems they're the only way to keep you in line these days."

"Rick, I'm sorry. It won't happen again, I promise," she whispered, cradling her abdomen. She groaned inwardly, knowing this would cost her another week's pay—the pain was already becoming unbearable.

He sighed and rose from the chair, heading for the front door. "You get up and get ice on that face," he grumbled, fingers closing firmly around the silver knob. "Get this crap cleaned up. I mean it, Mae. I want *order* in this house when I get back, just so we're clear." When the leather soles of his shoes connected with the hard cement porch step he hesitated; for one nerve-racking moment Mae held her breath as she watched him staring off into the dark, apparently wavering in indecision. The captive air rushed from her lungs in relief when she saw him release the knob at last. "Don't worry about waiting up. I won't be back for a while," he said as the door slid shut behind him with a soft click.

Mae closed her eyes and summoned the remainder of her strength, trying to get to her feet. A wave of nausea washed over her, her trembling legs buckling hopelessly beneath her weight. She collapsed onto the floor again, her insides heaving with the effort. Minutes passed before she made the second attempt, this time digging her nails deep into the foamy flesh of a nearby sofa arm to drag herself to her knees. She pressed her face into her hands and leaned forward, resting on the cushions as if in the throes of fervent prayer. After a few deep breaths, she stood and limped into the bathroom.

She switched on the overhead light, gasping at her reflection in the mirror hanging above the sink. A rainbow of purple and blue accompanied the swelling that nearly shut her left eye. Lip split open, her right ear a bloody mess. Holding back tears, she raised up her dress to find angry plum-colored welts splayed across her abdomen. Gripped by a sudden urge to urinate, Mae pushed her panties below her hips and hurriedly sat down. A terrified whimper escaped her cracked lips when she noticed tiny drops of blood drying on the thin cotton seat of the underwear.

She undressed quietly, slowing climbing into a tub of clear water. Even the liquid warmth seemed to attack her tired and bruised body. Aching all over, she tried desperately to make sense of the events of the past half-hour, wincing as she strained toward a box of Espom salt lying on the floor just out of her reach. Let's see, she'd been making dinner, and Rick had come home early…he was upset about things at work…wasn't he mumbling something about a promotion? *Yes*, Mae nodded against the tub's porcelain edge, ignoring the rampant pounding inside her skull. Some Detective Webb had gotten the promotion he'd been coveting for months. She'd tried to comfort him, but he'd been inconsolable.

First he started in about dinner being late. She'd tried to tell him he was, in fact, ten minutes early, but he wouldn't listen. He never did.

Then it was the dress she wore. He swore he hated seeing her in blue. She'd tried to remind him how much he *loved* that dress, had specifically told her to wear it for dinner tonight, but he'd only called her a liar.

Then it was the stew she'd been warming for him on the stove. He thought the vegetables were cut too large. He snickered each time he looked into the pot and couldn't say enough about how they reminded him so much of her "oversized ass"…

Mae broke from her reverie to run more water into the tub. The pain would fade in a day or so, but unfortunate experience had taught her the bruises and scratches would take much, much longer. She squeezed water from a tangerine washcloth and laid it gingerly over her swollen eye. What exactly had caused his angry insult to escalate to swinging fists this time? "Oh yes, *now* I remember," she said aloud to the empty room, letting out a small groan.

It had been the grocery bill. That damned grocery bill. Always fifty dollars, never a penny more, she'd been instructed, but this week her favorite ice cream was on sale. She hadn't had De-Luxe Pralines and Cream in months; Richard believed five dollars was too much to pay for her "silly extravagance." She figured she'd be within budget, but when she got to the checkout stand, $52.75 glared unflinchingly at her from the screen above the cash register, an invisible finger of accusation pointed squarely in her direction…

She'd thought nothing more of it until he'd opened the freezer after dinner and spotted the ice cream. While she was washing their plates later that evening, he'd searched her purse for the receipt and confronted her with it, telling her how stupid she was and how she needed to be trained properly. Feeling that old familiar knot of panic rising up in her belly, she'd begged him to see reason, she'd apologized repeatedly, even offered to return the ice cream…but he said by then they wouldn't give a full refund and BESIDES, he felt she'd be needing that nice cold ice cream after all. Then he'd strolled casually over to the freezer, plucked the frozen carton from the top shelf…and before she'd had time to react, smashed it with all of his might into the left side of her face.

Mae sunk deeper into the warm refuge of the bathwater. She promised herself she wouldn't cry. She knew how much he hated tears. She would go and clean up the mess they'd made, climb into bed and try to come up with another plausible excuse for missing work again next week. Her lacerated lips moved soundlessly as she offered half-hearted prayers up to an invisible God living Happily Ever After someplace far above the reach of her ornately tiled ceiling, hoping her husband would simply get sloppy drunk and stay out all night. *Then at least I'd be able to get some peace,* she thought, not having to worry about him coming home in the wee hours to molest her with his grimy, calloused hands. He would want her to submit to his desires as usual, but the spotted underwear told her she'd be making an impromptu trip downtown for an exam in the morning.

Mae sighed. Where had all this gone wrong? She had a satisfying career, lived in a gorgeous brownstone in one of the best neighborhoods in the city, was surrounded by beautiful things—but her job had become her escape, her home, a house of horrors, her wonderful things—reminders she was living a lie with a man who was more than capable of killing her. She was frightened now, and tonight's events were a clear warning she was running out of time. She desperately needed time to think…but not now. Not tonight. Tonight she would rest, praying that, with morning, her answers would come.

Mae opened the door to the small bedroom, quietly letting herself in. The room was bathed in warm peach and yellow hues, vivid frescoes of exotic safari animals grazing lazily in high grasses along the walls. She narrowly avoided tripping on a giant overstuffed giraffe as she crept closer to the bed.

"Ahem," she cleared her throat dramatically, leaning into the small lump of blankets. "Miss…you don't by chance think it's time to wake up now?"

"No, ma'am!" a muffled voice piped from beneath. "I can't. I must sleep late. I'm tired from all my flying!"

"Eh? Methinks I've misheard you, little one," Mae replied in a most pitiful attempt at an English accent. She scooped the child into her arms and swung her around before plopping back down on the mattress, ignoring the protests of her bruised abdomen. "Time to get up, little girl. It's a nuuuu day, and we get to take a special trip!" She hugged her daughter close, closing her eyes and inhaling deeply. "Uh-oh," she smiled. "Been playing in mommy's perfume again, haven't you?"

The child grinned wryly up at her mother, exposing a gap where two front teeth should have been. "How'd you guess?"

Mae laughed. "How'd I guess? Well for one thing, little girl, I can smell you from across the room. I bet even the people on the next block can smell you. Or Mr. Smith at the deli across town? I'm sure he's gettin' a good whiff. Or maybe…" Mae stood to her feet, tossing her atop the blanket pile. "Maybe even the President!"

"Ow, Momma!" the child giggled, kicking the blankets to the floor. "What are you tryin' to do, break my wings?"

"Momma's sorry sweetheart. Were you a bird last night?" she asked, crossing the room to slide a pair of heavy closet doors open.

"Uh-huh," she nodded emphatically, hugging a floppy-eared pink bunny lying next to her on the pillow. "I flew all over the world on a carpet of clouds, Momma. I even tried bringing home a star for you, but…"

"But what?" Mae asked distractedly, carefully laying a pair of over-alls and a striped blouse on the bed.

"But I couldn't get it. It was too hot." She sighed longingly and flopped onto her side, the giant pink ears gripped tightly in her minia-ture fists. "Oh well. Daddy says stars are just hot balls of gas anyway…"

Mae stiffened suddenly at the mention of Lily's father. Her face was still swollen from last night's scuffle, the storm-colored bruises clearly visible in the light of early morning. She glanced in the mirror over the dresser, then hurriedly looked away. Still ugly. *Why does he have to hit me so hard in the face?* she wondered, eyes welling with tears. *Why?* It was as if Richard knew the bruises on her face would hurt her more deeply than any other marks on her body. The scars kept her hidden away from a vibrant world moving ceaselessly outside the posh brown-stone in which she dwelled. The bruises and ugly marks covering her once-lovely face meant she would remain ensnared in her prison of soli-tude as long as she chose to stay with her husband. Fear of the world from which she'd been set apart for so long ensured his continued dominion over every aspect of her life.

Richard did much more than physically harm his wife when he pummeled her; with every "lesson," as he liked to refer to them, he succeeded in breaking her spirit further. Mae's only desire to live lay with her six-year-old daughter Lily, the only remaining element in her dark world granting her strength enough to greet the sun every morning, even mornings when the pain was so bad it kept her bedridden, unable to walk her own child to school.

On the days when Richard's "lessons" were particularly severe, he'd insist on taking Lily to school himself, using threats to deter her from answering the door or phone until he returned from work, which was usually late into the night or early the next morning. She wasn't supposed to even *exist*, he said. A veteran police detective, Richard feared the twofold disgrace of a messy, public divorce and criminal prosecution more than anything else.

Lily's voice startled Mae from her reverie. "Momma, you okay? Did you hear me?"

Mae glanced down at her, lying on the pillow with the floppy-eared bunny, and sighed, reaching out to tug playfully on one of her socks. "What is it, sweetheart?"

"I said, where're we going? I don't have to go to school today, do I?"

"Of course not, sweetie. We're just going downtown to see Auntie Deb for a little while. Momma has an appointment with her this morning, so let's get you into some clothes, okay?"

"Yes, Momma." Lily held on to her mother's shoulders as she hoisted her into the denim overalls. As Mae worked to button the metallic fasteners, she felt a slight tickle across her forehead. She looked up to find Lily touching her swollen eye, staring at her with the deepest intensity. "Daddy hurt you again, didn't he, Momma?" The tender, almost empathetic look in her eyes reminded Mae that, though her daughter was young, like most children she could sense when her world began to slide abruptly off its axis. Surely she felt it the very moment "Normal" suddenly went "Terribly Wrong."

Though it hurt like hell, Mae tried to force a smile.

"How did you know, honey?" she asked lightly, releasing the fasteners and tugging the forgotten blouse over Lily's head. "I hope we didn't wake you." Mae snapped the fasteners closed again. "You know how your daddy gets sometimes. It's those people at his job. They just make him so angry—"

"Huh-unh," Lily interrupted, shaking her head softly. "I couldn't sleep, Momma. I was over there reading to Candie," she pointed to a large stuffed panda perched precariously on the window seat, "and I heard Daddy yelling. I sneaked to the top of the stairs where I knew you wouldn't see me. You were fighting, and Daddy hit you with the ice cream. I saw him do it, Momma. I saw him."

Lily grew quiet, beginning to tremble all over. The bunny slid off the edge of the bed, tumbling to the floor without a sound. Lily hardly noticed. "I see a lot of bad stuff when Daddy's home, Momma. He has bad stuff all inside him now, all in his heart." She placed her tiny hands on the bib of her overalls to demonstrate. After a pause, she mumbled absently, "I think that's why he does those things to you and me..."

"What? *What?*" Mae felt dizzy, as if a cruel something had just yanked her world from beneath her like a threadbare rug. She sank onto the bed, gripping her child and pressing her tightly against her chest. She ran her fingers through Lily's uncombed hair, again inhaling her—the scent of her strawberry baby shampoo, the powder she usually dusted on her little body after a bath. Suddenly, she was overwhelmed by the smell of the De-Luxe Pralines and Cream that had been smashed into her head the night before; the same ice cream Richard gleefully served Lily before he'd taken her up to bed. The combination of heady scents, coupled with her dizzying bewilderment, only enhanced the sickening feeling churning in the pit of Mae's stomach. What was Lily saying? It all seemed unreal.

For five excruciating years, she'd quietly endured all of her husband's "lessons." His threats and his fists, even his grubby hands rubbing on her weary body, seeking to violate her in every way he could. She'd endured all this to prevent his harming the most important part of her life. She lived for Lily. Lily's smile and laughter were all Mae felt she'd ever need from anyone, ever. But now her child, whom she'd struggled for so long to protect, was about to reveal something she'd long dreaded hearing. It was the unthinkable, coming to life: Richard *had* hurt their child. She didn't know how, but her own intuition told her this was fact. She closed her eyes and steeled herself, a woman waiting for a cosmic hammer to deal her yet another devastating blow. "Tell me, Lily. What has Daddy done?"

Lily squirmed uncomfortably on her mother's lap a moment before carefully folding her legs beneath her, turning at last to face Mae at eye level. Her tiny hands grasping the lemony cotton folds of Mae's robe, she whispered anxiously, "You can't tell him, Momma. He told me you would go away if I told anyone. He said he'd make you disappear forever." Tears welled in her eyes as she continued. "I don't want you to go away, Momma. Who else could be my Momma besides you?"

Mae placed her hands on Lily's trembling shoulders. "What did he do to hurt you, honey? Momma needs to know. I promise I won't tell him, I promise." Lily's face was nearly lost in the blur of her own tears. "You can trust me," she added reassuringly, lightly rubbing her back in small circles.

Lily sniffled. "H-He made me pretend I was you one day. You were at work, and I was home. I was sick, remember?" Mae nodded slowly, urging her to continue.

"Daddy was taking care of me. We were playing like we always do, but then he said he was tired of playing. I told him to go to sleep, but he said he wouldn't be able to unless I took a nap with him. I was sleepy anyway Momma, so I did. I got up on the bed, and I was almost asleep when Daddy started taking his shirt off. He asked me if we could play a new game before we went to sleep. He said this game would be a big secret. He said he wanted me to pretend like I was you until you came home, so he wouldn't get lonely."

Lily's face crumpled, the tears continuing to stream down her swollen cheeks. Her brown eyes, usually so clear and bright, were now red, watery and nearly pinched shut. She sobbed for a while, burying her face in her hands as if the darkness comforted her, shielded her in a way Mae's presence could not.

She kissed her daughter's hands, still covering her face. "It's okay, sweetie," she whispered. "We can stop for a while if you want."

Lily shook her head, finally taking her hands away from her eyes. She stared dully at them now, lying limp in her lap like doll's hands. "I didn't like this new game, Momma. I didn't like him touching me that way. So I faked like I was gonna throw up and ran in the bathroom. I locked myself in for so long, it was like forever.

"When I came out, Daddy was crying. He said if I ever told anybody, he'd cast a magic spell to make you not love me anymore, and you'd go away and leave me behind forever. I was so scared, I never told anybody, not even my best friend Caroline at school.

"I didn't want to play with him any more after that, Momma. Every time it was just us at home, I stayed in my room and locked the door." Lily paused again and looked up at her mother expectantly, her eyes searching for answers as tempest-weary voyagers search for warmth and light. "Are you mad at me, Momma? Would you really leave me forever?"

Mae struggled to breathe. A huge lump welled up in her throat, and she feared she would actually scream. Instead, she held her daughter close, all attempts to hide her swirling emotions failing miserably. Hot tears ran down her cheeks, and she found after all she'd been told, she could only whisper to Lily in response, "No, sweetheart. Not ever, not ever."

TWO

"Thanks for giving up your lunch hour to keep an eye on her, Maya." Deborah gave the receptionist a weary smile. "I really appreciate it."

Maya waved her off as she crossed the office, a large, apple-green lollipop in one hand. She took a seat next to Lily in one of the empty waiting room chairs. "Not a problem, Dr. Barr," she replied, handing the lollipop to the child. "Lily and I are going to have lots of fun, just like always. Aren't we, Lily?"

Deborah turned to the little girl, content in the center of a pile of toys and books she kept on hand to amuse the children of her patients. "If you need anything honey, you can tell this very nice lady, okay?"

"Okay, Auntie Deb." Lily yawned, casually flipping the pages of a colorful pop-up book.

Deborah closed the door behind her. Enclosed in the relative quiet of her office, she listened attentively as her best friend recounted the events of the past twenty-four hours. On the other side of the desk, Mae's bruised and discolored face was a visage of misery. She paused several times to dab at her swollen eyelids as she spoke.

"So when Lily told me about what Richard had done, I could only think of one thing." Mae looked up at her, stifling a sob. "I have to leave him today, Deb."

Deborah sighed. She'd known Detective Richard Spencer for years. A decorated and highly esteemed member of the Philadelphia police force, his ruggedly handsome features frequently found their way onto the front pages of the morning papers, pasted amongst endless accounts of his radical acts of selflessness. Richard Spencer was, as her physician friends liked to say, a man on the move. "He's done more for this town in four years than the entire department's done in forty," her mentor,

Dr. Wyld, commented once after the Philadelphia Daily mentioned Richard's possible promotion to Lieutenant.

Of course she'd remained silent as to the true nature of the man she knew to be Mae's husband. To the outside world, Richard was an intelligent, charming and charismatic man who seemed to be on good terms with everyone—even some of the people he'd cuffed and jailed in the past. But at home, as Mae said once after he'd held her head under a steaming kitchen faucet as punishment for her shampooed hair dripping onto the linoleum, "When we're alone, he's a completely different human being. Sometimes I lay awake nights wondering if he's the devil himself."

This wasn't the first time Mae had come to her office in the throes of despair to describe the ruthlessly abusive nature of her husband. At the end of only their eighth year together, Richard's prescription for cruelty had managed to systematically destroy his wife in every way— physically, emotionally, as well as spiritually.

As her physician, Deborah knew she was responsible for reporting any suspected abuse to the proper authorities, but after frightened, tearful pleas from her best friend, she'd reluctantly agreed to keep silent. Though Mae repeatedly refused her attempts to photograph the bruising and scars, Deborah had insisted on keeping a detailed journal as documentation of the beatings, in the event Mae changed her mind and someday wished to reveal her secret. What Deborah was careful to keep hidden, however, was that if something mysterious were ever to happen to her friend, she would use the journal as concrete evidence of foul play, leaving no speculation as to who may have been responsible.

Deborah scanned Mae's face. Her tears were glistening rivers flowing down pasty cheeks, but her jaw was firm, her face resolute. *My God*, she thought to herself, *She's serious. She's really going to do it.*

As if she'd plucked the thought from a page of Deborah's mind, Mae whispered fiercely, "I have no other choice, Deb. Richard robbed me of choice the day he tried to rape his own flesh and blood. My daughter, *our* daughter..." she burst into another wave of sobbing, her breath coming in wretched gasps.

Deborah came around the desk and sat beside her, placing her hands over Mae's trembling fingers. She waited patiently until the heavy sobs slowly ebbed and she was quiet again. Finally, she squeezed Mae's hand. "Mae, if you take Lily away," she began gently, "Rick will be on you so fast...you *know* this man, you know what he can do when he gets his mind in gear. He'll find you. He'll take Lily from you and have you locked away in some prison or mental institution somewhere, any place he can, as long as it's remote and the chances of you walking out are slim—"

Mae snatched her hands from Deborah's grasp as if they were on fire, turning in the chair so she faced her directly. To the doctor, the wide, red-rimmed eyes peeking from a mane of disheveled curls made her look as if she were a hunted animal, desperate to escape one who wished to devour her whole, without mercy. *No, not hunted,* Deborah thought. *Haunted. She looks like she's been walking through a nightmare.*

"I don't think you understand what I'm talking about here," Mae said angrily, her dark brown eyes boring holes into Deborah's. "If I stay, he'll do something terrible to my little girl, and I wouldn't be able to do a damn thing about it. I'd lie next to him every night and wonder about the times he's taken her to the park alone...did he touch her there in secret, within shouting distance of her friends and their parents? Or what about the million times I've gone grocery shopping and he insisted she stay home with him, huh? Did he ask her to play his new 'secret game' as he walked her to school on the mornings after he'd beaten the living crap out of me? Or when he took her up to bed while I was downstairs, only a few feet away yet unable to hear my own daughter praying, hoping, believing I'd protect her from him?"

Mae shot to her feet, her rising voice echoing off the walls of the cavernous space. "I've raised my daughter to recognize the monsters in this world as strangers on the outside, Deb, people who roam the streets long after she's tucked in her bed, warm and safe for the night. When she asks me why people do bad things, I tell her the monsters inside them make them harm others. I tell her those people don't understand why they're doing wrong, that if they did they would *want* to get help, would beg to get the monsters out of their minds..."

She wiped tears away with the back of a trembling hand. "But how do I tell her the monster lives *inside* our home? That he sits across from her at the breakfast table every morning, making jokes and pouring orange juice into her favorite cup, all the while planning to get Momma out of the picture for good so she can take my *place?*"

Mae snatched her purse from the chair, slinging it roughly over her arm. "There are things some women never tell, some secrets we're so ashamed of we keep them close until we fall over exhausted into our graves. I knew Rick was a sick man long before he came after Lily. There were nights I'd have to bite my pillow to keep from screaming because I didn't want her to hear, couldn't bear for her to even have to imagine the inhuman things he was doing..."

She paused again, staring at the carpet as if recalling a distant memory. Her face contorted briefly into a mask of horror and revulsion, the expression clearing almost as soon as it occurred. "...and he *loved* it, Deb," she finished in a bitter whisper, never taking her eyes from the floor. "He loved it most when I wanted to scream..."

"Mae?" Deborah rose from the chair, extending a tentative hand. "Honey, you all right?"

Mae shook her head, eyes still riveted to the floor. She mumbled so Deborah had to strain to catch the words. "No woman on earth should have to endure that kind of pain, that kind of torture. I'll do whatever it takes to keep him from getting to her, even if I have to give myself up trying." She headed for the door to the waiting room.

"Wait!" Deborah called out. Mae reached for the handle, refusing to turn around. Deborah walked up and laid a hand on her shoulder, feeling the trembling even through the thick wool coat she wore.

"Please," she whispered. "Let me help you."

A misty rain drifted from the late afternoon sky as Deborah drove swiftly through the city toward the plush brownstones of upscale Bella Vista District. Grimy streets were transformed into mile-long mirrors, shimmering with the reflected reds, yellows and greens of traffic lights.

Mae leaned her head against the passenger window, listening to the water tapping rhythmically against the glass. She watched as school-children gleefully splashed their way through newly formed puddles on the sidewalks, heading toward home in the old brick buildings lining the street. The windows glowed with lamplight that was as warm as it seemed inviting. She glimpsed a couple waiting for a taxi under a cheap plastic umbrella, their arms locked around each other's waists to keep from shivering. Mae watched the young woman nuzzle her head against the young man's chest, watched the man turn to whisper something in her ear as she laughed, pulling him even closer. Feeling the fatigue she'd been avoiding for the past twelve hours beginning to catch up to her, Mae closed her eyes.

A memory of Richard flashed in her mind. Richard, yes, a Richard four months shy of graduating from the academy, an athletic, attractive man who always knew the right thing to say at the right moment; a man who'd tagged along with his college friends one night to a party given by her sorority…

She met him after she'd fled to the balcony for some fresh air; the alcohol sloshing around in her system was beginning to take effect, and most of her "sisters" were too occupied with fraternity boys to notice her need for assistance.

She managed to stumble outside where the air was cool, cool enough to calm the tidal wave that was her upset stomach. Her eyes were closed as she fought yet another wave of dizziness. Hands flailing about desperately for balance, they gripped only the peeling paint of the balcony railing when he suddenly came up behind her, placing a protective arm around her waist to catch her fall.

"Whoa!" she cried, swaying in his embrace.

"It's okay, I've got you," a voice whispered from behind.

His arms were strong and muscular, yet comforting as they supported her. She straightened, turning to face him. A pair of dark eyes watched her nervously in the dim light. His skin was deep brown, his wavy hair cropped close. He sported a gray Philadelphia Police Academy sweatshirt to fend off the chill.

Concern remaining, his hands remained on her waist as well. "I'm all right, thank you," she mumbled finally, politely brushing his hands away. He dropped his hands to his sides as if they were rendered completely useless. He stared off into the darkness a moment, a rising cloud of confusion distorting his handsome features. Suddenly, he brightened again, smiling as he extended a hand once more. "I'm Rick. Nice to meet you, uh…"

Mae tried to fight the fog settling over her mind as the tidal wave swelled again in her belly, increasing its fury with every passing moment. She swallowed, tasting bile in the back of her throat. Thinking it would help to clear her double vision, she focused all her attention on the floorboards beneath their feet.

Feeling a hand close reassuringly over hers, she glanced up as his lips again formed the words, "I'm Richard, and your name is…"

His voice seemed to come from someplace far away as the sour taste of bile flooded her mouth. Opening it to respond, she bent forward, vomiting on his clothing and the floorboards in one swift motion. "Oh Rick, I'm so, so sorry," she managed in a horrified whisper as the world spun around her and darkened, at last enveloping her in silence.

After exchanging telephone numbers from her hospital bed that very evening, they began to see each other regularly. As a senior in Communications, Mae kept busy with her studies and graduated in June of the following year, just a few months after Richard joined the Philadelphia Police Department as a patrolman. From the very beginning, Mae remembered, he'd dreamt of making detective in Homicide.

"It's the most rewarding position in the department," he'd told her once during a lunch date. "You get to wear the badge, you get to solve the crime, and you get the bad guy in the end. What could be better than that?"

Mae had frowned at the comment. "Honey, don't you think all that death would get into your head eventually? You'd never be able to get away from it when you're off duty, never have peace when it's time to hang your hat up and go home for the night. Imagine being knee deep in sorrow, all day, every day…what kind of person gets off on looking at slashed, smashed bodies all the time, anyway? How could you possibly leave all that at work? It's the stuff of nightmares, if you ask me. And the smell? I'm not too thrilled at the thought of my husband coming home every night stinking of rotting corpses—"

"Hey, I'm not your husband yet," he'd replied with an impish smile, dodging a crumpled napkin she'd hurled across the table.

They did marry eventually, settling into a modest apartment on the northern end of the city. Mae happily accepted a highly coveted position in production at a local TV station, plowing full-speed ahead until Lily was born, just shy of their second anniversary. By then their collective income had expanded enough for them to purchase a large brownstone in a quiet neighborhood.

After Lily came along, Richard began to change. Where he once accepted, even welcomed, Mae's independent nature and her desire to contribute financially, he now wanted her to stay at home full-time with the baby.

"I never saw my mom, Mae. She was always working. Used to have a dried-up old babysitter that liked to spank my ass with a paddle brush right after I got out of the tub. I don't want my kid going through that." She was finally able to get him to agree to merely shortening her hours so she was at the studio only part of the day.

For a woman who'd been a known workaholic and perfectionist since college, settling into an abbreviated work schedule was difficult at first, but soon she began to look forward to leaving the studio at noon to get home and spend time with her daughter. She converted one of the spare bedrooms into an office just off the nursery, often spending most of her afternoons working away while Lily napped in the next room. All was well for a while, but then in December of their third year of marriage, Richard's dream came true: he was promoted to detective in the department's homicide division.

Mae remembered how the trouble started. He began coming home late in the evenings, long after she'd put Lily to bed and settled in for the night. Sometimes she'd feel him slide into bed next to her, but on occasions that increased as time went on, she would hear him unlock the front door, but never come up. She'd go down in the middle of the night and find him slouched in a leather chair facing an empty wall, staring blankly off into space.

One evening as she tiptoed down the stairs in the semidarkness, she heard the unmistakable *clink* of ice swirling in a tumbler of scotch he dangled carelessly from his hand.

"Honey, aren't you coming up?" she'd asked, settling herself on the arm of his chair.

"Go on without me," he muttered, still staring off into space. "I'll be there later." As she approached the stairs, she turned to him once again. "Bad night?" she ventured, waiting a beat before starting up the stairs again when he didn't answer.

"Bad night," she heard him echo when she reached the landing. "Yeah, Mae. Really bad."

He raised the glass and sipped. A low, guttural chuckle issued from his throat then, sliding past the gateway of his lips into the surrounding darkness. The sound of that laugh sent a chill coursing through her, and, without another word, she'd turned and fled to the safety of their bedroom, closing the door firmly behind her.

Shortly after, he began putting his hands on her.

The first time was Christmas Eve of that year at Bow On a Box, a large department store in the area. They were doing last-minute shopping for Lily, who was spending the day upstate with Richard's parents. They browsed the aisles aimlessly, making light conversation when John, a production assistant at the station, startled her from behind.

She'd immediately introduced him to Richard, explaining how the two of them had worked so hard on a local Christmas special airing on their network that evening. The three of them made small talk, then Richard abruptly excused himself on the premise of checking out some digital scanning equipment.

Anxious to finish shopping and get Lily home for the night, she quickly wound the conversation up and headed over to electronics. She found Richard frozen in front of a giant screen television, apparently spellbound by one of the many football games synonymous with late Sunday afternoons. She stepped up beside him and placed her hand in his, affectionately leaning her head on his shoulder.

Suddenly, he came to life beneath her touch, gripping her fingers and squeezing them painfully. Without a word he turned and strode out of the store, pulling her behind him as he would a disobedient child.

"Ow, Rick, you're hurting me!" she yelled as he yanked her toward the parking lot. She fought desperately to release herself, using her free hand to pull frantically at her throbbing fingers, caught helplessly between his own. They passed an elderly couple who said nothing, only offering peculiar stares before hurrying inside the store. The parking lot was packed with cars, and their vehicle was at the far end, near a few potted trees. Shielded by the screen of foliage, he approached their car at full speed and hurled her toward the passenger door. Surprised, she was unable to brace for impact, slamming headlong into the cold steel.

"Ugh," she grunted, gulps of air escaping her lungs. The shock finally beginning to wear off, she spun around to face him. He loomed over her, his face only a few inches from hers. She could smell the familiar yet unpleasant odor of scotch seeping from his breath.

"Rick! What the hell's the matter with you?" she demanded, rubbing her wounded fingers. The knuckle beneath her gold wedding band throbbed in time to the pounding in her skull.

Glancing in either direction, he propped her up against the car door and put his hands in her jacket. "Is this what you like done to you?" he grumbled, rubbing his hands roughly over her breasts. "This is what you do all day at work? Huh? You like it when he puts you on his desk and pounds it into you, don't you?" he whispered harshly in her ear as he pressed himself against her, slipping a hand beneath her blouse.

Mae winced, hating the roughness of his hands and his belt buckle poking and chafing at her most delicate parts. "What the hell are you talking about!" she cried. "John and I work together. He's just an acquaintance, I swear. I hardly even know the guy—"

He began grinding against her, using his free hand to pull her skirt up. He unzipped his fly with shaking fingers, breathing heavily. Mae could feel his breath all around her now, billowing from his mouth in a scotchy cloud that seemed to hang on the frosty air. She clamped her eyes shut, feeling as if she would suffocate in his grasp.

"Yeah I bet you like being his whore, don't you?" he panted, forcing an icy fist between her thighs.

"Rick, what are you doing?" she asked nervously, eyes searching wildly for signs of approaching help. "Honey, come on, don't do this right now. Please, Rick...Rick, no! I said *stop it!*" she screamed as he started to unbutton her blouse, her voice echoing easily over the parking lot. A red Mercedes traveling down their row slowed nearly to a crawl, the occupants gawking at them through the windshield.

Richard loosened his grip as they passed, waving the car on. "Keep going, nothing to see here." They seemed to hesitate a moment longer, then drove out of the parking lot.

She wrenched his hands away, pushing him off her. Without pausing a beat, he cocked his arm back and slapped her hard across the face. Bells went off inside her already pounding head. She grabbed her face and sagged helplessly against the hood, sliding to the pavement on her knees. He grabbed the lapels of her jacket, forcing her to her feet as he yanked the passenger door open.

"If I ever catch another man looking at you that way," he hissed, slamming her against the frame, "I'll kill you right in front of him and gouge his fucking eyes out."

He shoved her inside, casually strolled around to the driver's seat and hopped in, gunning the engine. A grainy, tortured voice screeched the lyrics to a heavy metal tune. He turned the radio up full blast and hummed along.

She pressed her forehead against the glass, hoping the cold would numb the ache in her mind. The vocalist wailed of a pain seeming to match her own. Tears sliding down inflamed cheeks, she closed her eyes and focused all her attention on the chaotic music, listening quietly as Richard sped off into the growing darkness.

The car slowed, startling her. She sat up and saw they'd turned onto her street. The old familiar brownstone waited patiently in the falling rain, just one of many carefully restored buildings at the end of their well-kept block. Deborah pulled the car to a stop at the curb, glancing over at her. "So how much time do we have?"

"He isn't off duty 'til eight, but he usually doesn't come in until well after one...or later." Her swollen face twisted itself into a semblance of a smile. "You know the man never makes it in time for the nightly news."

Deborah nodded vaguely in reply, checking her watch. "Quarter-to-six. We should have all the time we need." She turned back to the steering wheel, putting the car in gear. As she was pulling away from the curb, she braked suddenly.

"What?" Mae asked anxiously, frantically scanning the darkened street for signs of Richard's black truck.

"It's not that," Deborah answered quickly. She placed a reassuring hand on Mae's shoulder, probing her face for signs of trepidation or uncertainty. Mae only held her gaze. She looked frightened, but showed no indication of having second thoughts. "You sure you want to do this tonight? There may be another way..."

Mae shook her head vehemently, curls falling into her eyes. She tucked the errant strands firmly behind her ears, sighing in frustration.

"We've been over and over this, Deb. Now let's go. The sooner we catch that bus out of here, the better."

Deborah nodded grimly, driving off. As they parked in front of the brownstone, Mae glanced in the back seat. Lily slept soundly, curled beneath a thick woolen blanket.

"Should we wake her?" Deborah inquired as she unfastened her seatbelt.

"No. I'll just lie her down on the couch 'til we're ready to go," Mae whispered, wrapping Lily securely in the blanket and lifting her into her arms.

THREE

Mae fumbled around in the dark a moment until her probing fingers happened upon a switch. The living room was bathed in warm light, dispelling menacing shapes lurking in the shadows. Decorated to fit his tastes, most of the rooms were palettes of dark, uninviting color. The walls were papered in a muted hunter green, the somber hue accentuated by portraits of bleak oceanscapes brushed in depressing grays and dismal pale blues.

A huge, gilded mirror hung above the mantle, reflecting heavy mahogany furniture upholstered in a bold, ugly plaid fabric. Richard's well-worn leather chair sat, as it always did, in a corner on the far side of the room. She'd nicknamed it "The Chair of Sorrows" soon after he began spending most of his nights there, untold thoughts of a dark nature echoing in his mind as he nursed glass after glass of scotch.

Mae approached a sofa facing the mantle, laying Lily down on the stiff cushions. She placed a plaid pillow under her head, tucking the blanket tightly around her. "Chilly in here," she whispered to Deborah, lightly running a hand over the child's face.

Lily stirred under her touch. "Mmmm, Momma, we goin' away?" she mumbled, scrunching herself into a tight ball beneath the woolen fabric.

"In a little while, honey," she answered, leaning down to kiss her forehead.

"Is Daddy coming, too?" She looked up at her mother expectantly.

Mae hesitated, gazing down at her as she waited for the right words to come. "No, honey, Daddy isn't coming," she said finally, plopping down next to her with a sigh. "It's just the two of us this time, but Momma has to pick up some of our things before we go, okay?" Mae removed her jacket, draping it over Lily. She was nearly concealed under the covering, her dark eyes and wavy hair barely visible over the collar. She yawned, pulling the jacket tightly around her. Mae stood up. "You can sleep a while longer. I'll be upstairs with Auntie Deb if you need me, okay?"

"'Kay, Momma," she mumbled groggily, eyes drifting shut.

Mae turned and headed for the stairs, where Deborah waited patiently. Deborah unzipped her own jacket and folded it carefully over the banister as Mae approached.

"Momma!" Lily's shrill voice echoed in the expansive room like a host of clanging bells.

Mae hurried to her side. "What is it, honey?"

"Will Daddy come looking for us when he knows we're gone?"

A moment of sheer terror swept over Mae at the thought. She wrestled with that fear even as Lily reached for her, waiting to lock her arms securely around her mother's neck. Mae leaned in close and held the little girl, pressing her lips to her ear. "He may come looking," she murmured, "but I won't let him find us. He's not going to hurt you again, okay?"

Lily nodded, squeezing even tighter. Mae held her until she felt her breathing slow and become regular. When at last she drifted off again, Mae tucked her beneath the blanket and covered her with the jacket once more.

"She looks like an angel, sleeping like that." She glanced up to find Deborah standing over her, gazing lovingly at Lily.

A mournful sigh escaped Deborah's lips before she abruptly turned away, striding purposefully toward the stairs. "Ready?" she called over her shoulder.

"As I'll ever be," Mae replied, rising and following close behind. "Let's get started."

The women walked up the stairs, entering a long hallway painted a bland brown color. Sepia photographs lined the walls. A cluster of people posed stiffly in a larger one hanging next to the bedroom she and Richard shared. Their clothing was clean but worn; their strained faces evidence of the wear and tear their difficult lives had exacted on them.

"Rick's family," Mae replied when Deborah glanced at her inquiringly. "His mother gave them to him on his last birthday and insisted he hang 'em *right here*, this very spot." She frowned, pointing an accusing finger at one of the larger photographs. "Had to take down the watercolors I painted this spring to give him room for *this* thing, or risk finding them in pieces someplace." She opened the door to her bedroom.

"I'll get Lily's things," Deborah said, crossing the hall to the adjacent door. "It'll be faster that way."

"Suitcase is in the closet, top shelf," Mae called over her shoulder as she entered the room, quickly walking over to the mirrored closet doors. While fumbling with the handles, she caught a glimpse of herself in the reflection. Her normally creamy coffee-hued skin looked dry and splotchy, the fresh bruises standing out in stark purple contrast. Her shoulder-length curls had been pulled taut from her swollen face and tied haphazardly in a damp, frizzy bun, loose strands spiraling out in every direction. She donned an oversized navy Notre Dame sweatshirt and pair of old gray sweats that nearly obliterated her shapely figure. Glancing down at her feet, she realized that under her Nike running shoes, she'd neglected to put on any socks.

"Come on, Mae," she muttered to herself, "you used to be better than this." Fighting yet another wave of tears, she ran a quick hand over her hair and yanked the closet doors open. Ignoring the pantsuits and silk skirts she usually wore to work, she grabbed a few pairs of jeans and threw them into a suitcase she'd dragged from under the bed. She rushed to the dresser and opened each drawer, removing socks, underwear, several sweaters and sweatshirts and tossed them in. She went into the bathroom and grabbed a small quilted purse she used for travel, dropping a hairbrush, comb, toothbrush, and other toiletries into it before hurrying back into the bedroom to fling it atop the clothing. Kneeling on the bed, she straddled the large suitcase, pressing all her weight onto it while she struggled with the zipper.

Deborah stood in the doorway, Lily's floppy-eared rabbit dangling from her hand. She slung a small lavender suitcase over her shoulder. "Got it?"

"Yeah," Mae huffed, forcing the suitcase onto its wheels and lugging it behind them into the hall.

"Okay then," Deborah said, heading for the stairs. "We'd better get moving. It's six-thirty. That bus leaves within the next hour—"

"Wait!" Mae cried, halting in front of the door next to Lily's room. She pulled a set of keys from the pocket of her sweats. "Deb, I've gotta get something from the office real quick."

Deborah whirled around in exasperation, lavender suitcase plunking to the floor. "Mae, we've got to get you out of here as soon as possible. Am I not echoing your own words from a half-hour ago? You know as well as I the last thing we need is for Richard to come runnin' up those stairs with smoke blowin' out his ears."

"I know, I know," she replied, unshouldering her burden and stepping over it to the door. "But it's important. It'll only take a second, I swear."

Deborah snatched both suitcases up, using all her strength to drag them toward the stairs. "I'm going down to put these in the car, Mae. I'm coming right back, and you'd better be ready. Tonight you don't have the luxury of time, you need to remember that."

Ten minutes later, she stuffed the last of the large suitcases into the trunk of her convertible, using all her weight to slam the hood down. She sighed, checking her watch. Six forty-one. Would they have enough time to make the bus? The tickets she'd purchased that afternoon said it was scheduled to depart Philadelphia at exactly 7:35 P.M., driving non-stop to New Orleans. They weren't quite five miles away—a little speed and a couple short cuts, and they should make it in plenty of time.

Leaning against the car, she fished in her purse for a cigarette. She lit it, gazing up at the night sky. The rain had all but ceased, and stars were clearly visible through the thin veil of clouds. She drew deeply on the cigarette, breathing coils of puffy white smoke into the damp air. The world smelled of wet earth and tar. The streets were slick, dotted with puddles of iridescence where leaky cars had left patches of oil on the asphalt.

Just what the hell are you getting yourself into, Debbie? she thought bitterly, taking another drag off the cigarette. *What if it doesn't work? There may be too much on the line this time...*

Debbie had known Mae since their days in college; they met when she pledged Mae's sorority at the start of her junior year, pre-med. The two were only passing acquaintances until Mae began dating Richard. At the time she'd been seeing a fraternity brother named Allan Fitch, and the two men were the best of friends. The four of them started hanging out frequently, going to campus theatre and local bars on the weekends she could afford to forsake her studies for a while.

After she and Allan went their separate ways, the two women still made time to hang out, even roomed together for a semester or two at the sorority house. She saw less and less of Mae after they graduated; she'd been accepted to Yale Med, and by then Mae and Richard were nearly inseparable.

Though they were divided by miles and changing circumstances, the two women managed to keep up on the details of each other's lives by frequent correspondence. The summer she carried on an all-too-brief affair with an assistant pharmacology professor, she wrote fervent letters to her friend nearly every week, sharing details of intimate encounters forever engraved on her mind and heart. The time she unfolded a letter and read that Richard had finally proposed, she immediately booked a flight and rushed down for a weekend visit.

Mae was overcome with joy, she remembered. The very next day the three of them drove to Richard's parents' home upstate and spent the day there. That evening, after generous helpings of fried chicken and mashed potatoes, Richard and Mae stood before a small gathering of his family and close friends. He placed a hand on her waist, raised his wineglass and announced their engagement to a speechless room.

Deborah chuckled softly at the memory, crushing her cigarette beneath an expensive boot. She glanced around a final time, searching for signs of an approaching black GMC pickup. Nothing. *Hell, I was there when she was married,* she thought, striding toward the house. *I was there when her little girl was born. I've always been there, and I guess I'll always have to be. Who else is gonna step in and fill those big ol' shoes?*

She jogged up the porch steps and opened the door. Lily was still asleep on the sofa, so she tiptoed up the stairs. She found Mae rifling through a large stack of papers sprayed haphazardly across the blotter covering her desk.

"Mae, it's time. We gotta head out *now*." Using a neatly manicured thumb, she gestured impatiently toward the door.

"I know I know, just need to…" Mae muttered under her breath, shoving part of the stack into a heavy manila envelope. She was fastening the clasp when she paused to pull a yellowed piece of paper out, looking it over carefully.

Deborah sighed, high spirits ebbing away as she felt knots of irritation beginning to form and fester in her gut. She bit the inside of her cheeks to keep from screaming before she spoke. "Mae," she began patiently, "Honey, I need you to stay with me in the here and now. This really isn't the time to start gettin' all nostalgic—"

"I'm sorry about earlier," she interrupted, holding the paper out to Deborah. "But I knew I couldn't leave without this. It's a notarized letter granting me rights to a house in Beau Ciel. My grandmother's house, actually."

Deborah quickly scanned the paper and handed it back. "*Beau Ciel?* So this place I've never heard of and can hardly pronounce is where I'll be able to find you from now on?"

Mae nodded, stuffing the paper into the envelope again and securing the clasp. "I'll call when we get settled, I promise." She sighed, folding the bulky envelope in half and shoving it into the front pouch of her sweatshirt. The women stared at each other across the desk a moment. Blinking back tears, Mae finally walked around it and embraced her friend. "Deb, thank you so much. I swear I couldn't have gotten this far without you. You know that, right?"

Deborah laughed, fighting tears of her own. "I was outside, thinking about the first time you told me you were gonna marry this jerk. You asked me what I thought." She sighed. "If I only knew then…"

Mae pulled away, placing her hands squarely on Deborah's shoulders the way she'd done with Lily that very morning. "You don't understand, he was different before. I used to think he was everything I ever wanted, but the man who's done me like this over and over is a stranger, nothing like the Richard I fell in love with." She reached up and tentatively touched her swollen eye, wincing at the pain. "Sometimes I wonder if the demon Richard was there all along, hiding under the surface of that smile, his laugh." She turned and snatched her keys off the blotter, shaking her head sadly.

As Mae hurriedly shoved the rest of the papers into open desk drawers, something on the blotter caught Deborah's eye.

"What's in that one?" she asked, pointing to another bulky envelope lying near the edge of the desk.

Mae shrugged. "Just some cash I managed to squirrel away over the past year or so. One day after he'd had too much to drink and landed a few too many punches, I started thinking it'd be a good idea in case…well, you know. In case Lily and I ever needed to get away or something. I hid it all in the last place he'd look—in Lily's room, inside her stuffed animals, if you can believe it."

Deborah picked up the envelope, flipping through the sizable stack of bills. "How much?"

"Hmmm…maybe sixty-eight hundred?" she replied, using one of the keys on the ring to lock a file cabinet in the far corner of the room.

"He was always bringing her a new one, so one day I thought, 'why not?' When he left for work, I ripped open the seams on a few of the ones she'd quit playing with, stuffed the money inside. A couple weeks ago, I caught him snooping around in Lily's room and got a little nervous. The very next time he was away from the house, I went right in and took the money out. Shoved it inside a half-empty bottle of gumball vitamins I keep hidden away for Lily in my desk." Mae approached a nearby window. She gripped her keys tightly in her palm, searching the deserted street for signs of trouble.

"Hell, they sure broke the mold when they made you, Mae." Deborah checked her watch again. "Come on, we needed to be on the road five minutes ago. You'll miss the bus if we don't hurry up, and—"

Mae gasped, dropping her keys. They jingled loudly against the polished hardwood floor, shattering the tranquil silence surrounding them into sharp fragments of panic. She yanked on the drapery cord, letting the blinds crash to the windowsill before whirling to face Deborah, the ashen tone of her skin deepening with each passing moment.

"H-he's here, he's—Oh god Deb, I left Lily down there!" She struggled to catch her breath, bent at the knees and clutching her belly as her body was seized by a monstrous wave of cramps.

Deborah rushed to the window. Indeed, Richard's black truck was parked in the driveway. He jumped out the vehicle and laughed loudly, the booming tenor of his voice echoing easily over the quiet street. Moments later, the passenger door swung open and another man got out. The two were dressed in casual work attire: Richard in a black polo shirt and slacks, the younger one donning a pair of khakis and a dark sweater. *Must be the new guy*, Deborah thought as she watched them lean against the truck bed with hands in their pockets, talking and laughing uproariously. She cracked the window and listened.

"Aw *man*," the younger one grinned, punching Richard playfully in the shoulder. "She was wearing *what*? *And* you got to search it and slap those cuffs on? Where the hell was I when nature was callin'?"

"Where the hell else, Pete? In the john, as usual." Richard chuckled. "Now what am I always sayin', rookie? Better be careful. I'm tellin' you you'll miss some of your best days daydreamin' and spankin' it to death in that precinct can."

"Oh, is *that* right?" Pete replied sarcastically, cocking an amused eyebrow. "I certainly didn't hear no complainin' when you were standing right there holdin' it still for me."

"You know, anyone ever tell you ya got a real bad mouth on you there, kid?" he asked soberly, pulling a ring of keys from his pocket.

Pete rubbed his chin in slow circles, appearing to be in deep thought. "Think I heard some old goat say that to me just the other day..."

Deborah closed the window again and frowned. Had Richard simply forgotten something? Had he somehow learned of Mae's hastily scheduled appointment with her this morning? If he actually followed Mae's trail of breadcrumbs to her practice, did her flighty receptionist reveal she'd abruptly cancelled the rest of the day's appointments and left early, a woman in shades and small child in tow? What if he'd rushed here with the sole intention of stopping them?

These thoughts and more raced through Deborah's mind as she peered through the blinds at Richard, trying desperately to ignore the alarm bells going off in her own body. She glanced over at Mae. She was crouched on her knees, still cradling her stomach and wailing softly to herself. "Oh God...he'll kill me, Deb...he'll take her away..."

Deborah had one last look at the men as she slowly backed away from the glass. They were on the walkway, heading for the porch steps. She watched as Richard paused briefly and glanced over at her bright red mustang convertible, parked in plain view on the street. *At least we don't have to worry about the luggage*, she thought with a measure of relief, helping Mae to her feet.

"Mae, listen," she said sternly, shaking her friend's shoulders. "We don't have time for this. You've got to get it together." The hysterical sobs ebbed, and she grew quiet, though the tears continued to stream silently down her face. "Now this time you've gotta help *me* out. Why would Rick come home before his shift is up? You said he normally doesn't get in 'til after one—you have any idea why he's so early tonight? He's got a friend with him too, by the way. *Think* about it. Help me out here. There has to be a logical explanation in this somewhere…"

Mae sniffled, trying to clear her thoughts. Tears stained her Notre Dame sweatshirt in an irregular smattering of tiny dark circles. Suddenly, her fingers clawed at Deborah's arm, recollection written across her face in bold stripes. "Oh my God, Deb. I was supposed to make dinner tonight for Rick's new partner. It's his birthday. They switched shifts with some other guys so he could bring him home for dinner before they go out with a few of his buddies from work. A party, I think. Said there'd be lots of strippers or something…h-he wanted me to make my special meatloaf…"

"Geez," Deborah muttered sourly, coaxing her toward the door. "Picked a hell of a night to go bringing the new guy home, didn't he? Day after he tenderizes his wife's face like a piece of choice mignon? Here's what we're gonna do. You make that meatloaf?"

Mae nodded, suppressing another wave of sobs. "Of *course* I did. Rick…he always wants his food waiting on the table, even if he doesn't actually come home to eat it, you know? Or else I'm paying for it that night *and* the next. I never know when he's gonna storm through the door demanding a hot plate of whatever. When he left for work this morning, I was makin' it up to put in the fridge so he wouldn't think anything's out of line. I'm so sorry Deb, I forgot about everything by the time we got to your office. I just thought we'd be long gone by then…"

Deborah nodded reassuringly. "Don't worry, Mae. We'll get through this just fine, so listen up. You run downstairs and wipe your face. Snatch that meatloaf out the fridge, stick it in the oven on HI and wait for me."

"But how are we gonna get out of here—" Mae began.

"Just let me worry about that. I think I've got it covered." Deborah smoothed Mae's unkempt hair away from her face as she would a young child's. "It's gonna be all right, I promise. You'll protect Lily, and I'll protect you both, but you've got to hurry up and get down to that kitchen if we're gonna have any shot at getting you out of here tonight."

As Deborah followed Mae downstairs, she could still pick up snippets of Richard's conversation as she approached the thick wood door. "Can't believe I'm havin' such a smartass in my house for dinner," she heard him say when she was standing in front of it. *Bastard,* she thought, closing her fingers around the knob. Pete muttered something else and Richard burst into laughter again, inserting his key in the lock. As he was turning the knob, she yanked the door open suddenly, pulling painfully on his arm. He yelped and lurched forward, grabbing onto the doorframe with his free hand to keep from landing flat on his face. Bent at the knees and fighting for balance, he soon focused his attention on what lay just beyond his nose...

A pair of chocolate high-heeled boots stood on the hardwood floor of the entry, one leather-clad foot tapping impatiently. As he straightened, his gaze slowly traveled upward. The boots snaked up slim, well-developed thighs, stopping just short of the split hem of a cream woolen skirt. A matching v-neck sweater rustled gently over a well-defined bosom with every breath. His head snapped up. There was Deborah holding on to the inside knob, tapered fingers drumming lightly on one hip.

"Well hellooo there, Doctor Debbie. Long time no see, huh?" He grinned again, brushing past her. "Mmmm, gettin' more and more beautiful each time. Where's Mae?"

"In the kitchen. It *is* a woman's place, right Rick?" she called over her shoulder, rolling her eyes. She turned back to the doorway. The one called Pete stood there motionless, eyes moving hungrily over her body.

Oh, surely he must have me undressed by now, she thought sarcastically, holding the door open for him as he stepped inside.

"Hello, have we met?" He paused in the entry, extending his hand. "I'm Detective Peter Blake." Emphasis on *detective.* Pasting on the sweetest, most saccharine smile she could muster she accepted it finally, squeezing the palm and fingers as if she were molding a particularly unyielding block of artist's clay.

"We have now. I'm *Doctor* Deborah Barr, which you would have known sooner had your buddy in there introduced us properly. And *you* must be the birthday boy. Heard you're the man with quite a special evening lying ahead of him."

Peter grinned sheepishly and shoved a hand in his pocket, running the other over an extremely bald, perfectly round head. "Somethin' like that. So uh, Deborah…you staying for dinner?"

She fed him another heaping saccharine spoonful. "Only if you'll have me. Your day, your wish, right?" Deborah took his arm, closing the door behind them. As she was escorting him into the living room, he suddenly leaned in close.

"You know," he began in a low murmur, "we've got plenty of room tonight, and I know Spencer wouldn't mind if I invited someone last minute. I'd love it if you'd come along for the ride. You got plans later?"

She was about to offer a vague answer when her eyes locked on Richard, studying him carefully as he bent over his sleeping daughter, smoothing tousled hair away from her face. Deborah felt her own face twist briefly into a grimace at the sight, a potent mixture of revulsion and pent-up rage beginning to churn slowly in the pit of her stomach. She worked to conceal her turbulent emotions. *Come on, Debbie, you can do this,* she thought, leading the tall bald man over to a pair of over-stuffed plaid wing chairs. *Ain't no dress rehearsal here. Tonight's got to be the performance of a lifetime.*

"Go on and have a seat here, Petey," she patted the arm of the nearest one. "Tonight you can be *my* guest." She rummaged around a moment until she found her most seductive smile. When he was sitting comfortably, she quickly made her way over to the sofa, tugging on

Richard's sleeve with poorly masked irritation. "Rick, leave her alone. She wasn't feeling well earlier. Her mom just got her off to sleep." She waved him away, planting herself next to the slumbering child. She tried to appear relaxed, slowly crossing her long legs to tug idly on the zippers of each boot. *Complete...imbeciles* she thought with a smile spreading across her face, watching the men a moment as they brazenly eyed her rising hemline. Finally, she cleared her throat. "Wouldn't the birthday boy like a drink, Rick? Or do I have to do that, too, seeing as tonight I'm also a guest in your home?"

Richard snickered, shrugging out of his jacket and heading for a well-stocked bar in the corner. "All right, all right, Doc. I can take a hint. You cravin' anything special? And what's on your mind, Pete, the usual?"

Deborah glanced over at the bald guy as he gave an affirmative nod, then turned her attention back to Richard. She flashed the saccharine smile a final time, finding it even more difficult to shield her growing anxiety from the men. Slowly, she rose from the couch, smoothing her skirt.

"Just make it a club soda for now, Rick. I've got my car tonight." She walked toward the kitchen. "Okay boys, gotta check in on the wife. Promised her I'd try to learn something about cooking beyond boiling water and nuking potatoes in the microwave. Wish me luck." She turned to Peter, giving him a swift wink before disappearing through the swinging door.

Mae stood next to an immaculate stainless-steel counter, biting what was left of her nails. She froze when the door started to swing open, relaxing visibly only when she saw Deborah had entered the room alone.

Deborah rushed over to her, squeezing her hands reassuringly. Cold. Trembling. *Lord, give her strength to hold it together a little longer,* she prayed silently as she moved her friend away from the door, just out of earshot.

"Deb, what's happening? Does he know?" Mae asked in a harried whisper.

"Oh honey, no," she replied soothingly. "He's too busy knocking shots back with Boy Wonder in there to notice anything broader than the scope of a woman's cleavage. I'm laying on the charm and sweetness pretty thick. Long as I keep playing the part of Easy Bake Hostess, they won't think to start sniffing around—"

"What about Lily? Did she wake up? Is she asking for me?" She was nearly hysterical again, gripping Deborah's hands so tight she feared her fingers would break.

She shook her head. "She's sound asleep, Mae. I'm doing my best to keep him away from her without being too obvious. Pretty tricky stuff considering I'm debuting my act for a couple of trained noses." She pointed to the oven. "HI, right?"

Mae nodded, finally permitting herself to take a deep breath. "So what happens now?"

"Rick I hate to interrupt, but I think you'd better come in here a sec."

The two men had been laughing, sipping liquor from chilled glasses and chatting comfortably in the matching wing chairs.

Richard nodded in her direction. "'Sup, Deb? My wife blow the pilot light out on the stove again or somethin'?" He glanced over at Peter, impish smile spreading across his face. "Sorry, man. Guess you'll be lickin' fish and chips off your plate at the club tonight after all." Peter just sat slumped in his chair, attempting to hide a grin behind his glass and failing miserably.

Deborah folded her arms over her ample breast, the fitted sweater rising and falling rapidly as she fought to control the anger eating away at her gut. "How many of those you guys planning to have? If I'm not mistaken, don't you *gentlemen* have someplace to be?"

"Cool it, Deb," Richard replied, his words slowly beginning to melt together. "Don't get your lil' pannies tied up in a bunch, I'm comin'." He took another swig of scotch from the tumbler. Beads of amber liquid coated his upper lip and trickled into the corners of his mouth as he brandished yet another smile, to her disgust. He'd swiped it all off with the back of one large hand and started to rise from the chair when he heard it. A thick, slimy retching sound coming from the kitchen. He shot up, nearly dropping the heavy glass on his foot.

"What the hell?" He slammed the tumbler on the coffee table. Peter jumped, startled into stony silence. The smirk disappeared from his boyish face almost instantly.

Serves you right, jerk, Deborah thought in triumph, holding the door open for him. "Get *in* here Rick," she continued with mock concern, the hacking sounds growing so loud they drowned out most of her words. "She's not lookin' so hot."

"Stay here, Pete. I'll be back in a minute." Tossing all humor aside, he turned and made a beeline for the kitchen. "Mae, what's going on in—" he stopped abruptly, eyes widening in shock. Mae was doubled over at the sink, a rasping sound escaping her lungs with every breath. She coughed, gagged, coughed some more.

"Some kind of bug," Deborah said from behind him, shaking her head sympathetically. "She says she and Lily have been running from the bed to the bathroom most of the day. I called on my lunch break to say hello, and she sounded horrible—said she had this dinner thing to do tonight but wasn't feeling like much, so I dropped by after work to try and help with some of the cooking. I don't know, Rick. She and Lily stopped for Cantonese on the way to my apartment a couple nights ago when you were out of town on business…I'm thinkin' the Beef Chow Fun monster got 'em down for the count, but I can't be sure." She rested a hand on his shoulder, squeezing it reassuringly. "Sorry, hon. I know how you feel about home cookin', but I think tonight you and your good buddy may actually be better off ordering the blue plate special."

Mae coughed again into the sink, shuddering all over.

"Damn you, Mae!" Richard bellowed and sprung forward, seizing her arm from behind. He spun her around and gripped her shoulders, shaking her furiously. "I *told* you this was important, didn't I tell you this was important? My new partner turns the big three-oh, and instead of the meatloaf and mashed potatoes I promised my *wife* would have waiting for him on my table, he has to eat his birthday dinner off Styrofoam plates in the parking lot of some fuckin' five-dollar whore-house!" He squeezed her arms painfully, the calloused fingers digging deep into her flesh even through the thick sweatshirt. She bit down hard on her lip, suppressing a scream.

Deborah grasped a fold of his shirt and tugged, trying to pull him away. "Okay Rick, she gets the point, let her go…Rick, hey get your hands off…all right Richard, that's *enough*!" Deborah hollered, eyes ablaze. Final traces of self-control slipping away, she cocked her arm back as far as it would go and slapped the back of his head hard with her open palm. "Get off her, you son of a—"

Richard dropped Mae's arms as if they were made of lead, turned and grabbed Deborah in mid-swing, using his large fingers as fleshy handcuffs to lock both wrists behind her back. Mae fled and cowered in a corner of the kitchen, shaking uncontrollably.

"What do you think you're doing, Deb, huh?" He hissed at her, their faces almost touching. "Where the fuck is this commando girl shit comin' from all of a sudden? This is between me and my wife. Stay out of it."

"What, Rick? You don't like it when they fight back?" The pressure on her wrists was becoming excruciating; still she refused to back down. "Stay out of it, my ass. I'm a doctor, and I'm telling you she's sick. She doesn't need to be standing over your food or anyone else's, *if* she could manage to stay on her feet long enough to serve it in the first place." To his complete surprise, her voice softened and she leaned her body into the confining grip. Her eyes locked on his, her whispering lips only inches away. "Rick, look at her. You know as well as I she needs to be in bed somewhere. Let me work it out, okay? Let me take care of everything. I'll get you some coffee and grab you a cab and you and Petey can clear out for a while."

Richard glanced uncertainly at his wife, sobbing quietly on the floor next to the pantry.

"Now look at *me*," Deborah murmured, forcing a smile when he returned his attention to her. "Don't worry about a thing. I'll look after the two of 'em 'til you think you can handle it." She shifted slightly, and moments later he felt the cool leather of her boot rubbing expertly against his calf, sending involuntary chills of excitement racing up the back of his neck. "That way," she continued, gazing into his eyes, "you can go out there and make *new* messes, like always, while I stay here and clean up your old ones." She snatched her hands from his loosened grip, casually stepping around him to approach the Mr. Coffee machine on the counter. "Go on, Rick," she said without turning, spooning dark aromatic crystals into a paper filter, "Go on and see about your guest. I'll be out there in a second."

He glared at his wife a final time, his handsome features blackening with rage. After a moment, he turned and stormed out of the kitchen, a visibly relieved Deborah following close behind.

Over the next twenty minutes she occupied her time politely declining Peter's repeated offers with vague promises of "a better time," calling a cab company to arrange for pick-up, and serving cups of steaming black coffee to a disgruntled Richard, still fuming over the confrontation in the kitchen. As Deborah saw the men out, Richard edged his partner toward the door.

"I'll be out there, man. Gotta talk to the Doc a minute." As Peter climbed into a bright yellow cab idling on the street, Richard spun around so quickly he nearly toppled over. Deborah stood there in the open doorway, meeting his steely gaze with one of her own. Gusts of chilly autumn air slapped against their hair and clothing like the hands of malevolent spirits, before finally drifting past them into the warm house.

"Rick, you mind hurrying this up? I've got sick folks to look after, in case you've forgotten. I bet it'd help somewhat if I could close the door—"

"You listen close, Doc," he began in a coarse whisper, their faces again only inches apart. "Don't you *ever* embarrass me like that in my own house, you hear me? I know Mae's a good friend of yours or whatever, but she's my *wife*, you got that? How I deal with her is my business."

"Oh right, right. I get you," Deborah nodded, folding her arms. "So I guess it isn't supposed to embarrass a woman at all to have to walk around with dark glasses on all day and recite the 'I just fell down the stairs' story to her coworkers and friends every other week because her husband decides he just can't keep his hands to himself?"

They stared each other down a moment longer until he finally looked away, taking a wobbly step off the porch. "You tell Mae I'll be back later," he called over his shoulder. "Tell her we got some things we need to discuss, in *private*." He stumbled down the remaining porch steps and hobbled over to the taxi.

Deborah watched him get into the passenger seat of the cab, watched as it rolled slowly down the street and turned at a far corner. "Oh yeah, Rick, I'll be sure to relay that one," she muttered under her breath, slamming the door. She returned to the kitchen. Mae was at the sink again, wiping her face with a damp towel.

"Are they gone?"

Deborah nodded, leaning against the tiled island in the center. "Just left. You all right?"

Mae offered up a pained smile, her swollen face straining with the effort. "Don't worry. A hot bath, a couple aspirin and I'll be shiny brand spankin' new." She walked over and turned off the oven, using the towel she held to pull out the warm pan containing the half-baked meatloaf. "My little girl, she's—"

"Still asleep, thank heaven." Deborah chuckled. "You know, kids are so strange. They swear they hear Santa comin' from a mile away on Christmas Eve, but can sleep through quake, wind, and fire the rest of the year."

Mae smiled briefly again and shook her head, the soft curve of her upturned mouth quickly flattening into a straight line. "He would have nearly killed me tonight if you hadn't been here, Deb. If only I'd had the balls to stand up to him like you, maybe Lily and I wouldn't have ended up in this mess." She passed a shaky hand over her bruised eye, pressing the towel to the back of her neck a moment before folding it neatly on the counter.

Deborah nodded, checking her watch again. Seven-oh-three and counting. "Let's get you out of it, Mae. We need to hit the road now before our time *and* our luck run out."

"That the last of them?" an older man in uniform asked twenty minutes later. He crouched beside the luggage compartment, positioning Lily's little lavender suitcase next to Mae's larger one.

Deborah turned to him. "That's all of them, sir. Thank you."

He nodded and went on, making room for the next set of luggage. A row of hunter green buses waited at the curb, bright white Liberty Star logos painted along their sides. Black signs had been placed in the front of each windshield, their destinations printed plainly on the front. Around them, passengers streamed from the building and crowded the platform, rushing onto buses marked DALLAS, NEW YORK, SAN FRANCISCO. The two of them stood off to the side of the oncoming traffic, between an Atlanta-bound bus and the one Mae and Lily would take all the way to New Orleans. From there, Mae had informed her in the car, they would catch another bus that would take them directly to the town she'd once called home as a child.

Mae glanced around at the growing crowd, adjusting the shades and ball cap she'd donned for the long trip. She was careful to avoid touching her face, fearing she'd smear the heavy makeup that covered her bruises. "Well I guess this is it, huh?" she asked, propping Lily high on her hip.

Deborah glanced up at the bus. "You know, even after coming all this far, I'm still not ready to say goodbye." She reached for Lily's rabbit and tugged on one of its ears, pretending to take it away from her. "Can I keep this, so I can hug it when I miss you too much?"

Lily held the ears even tighter. She shook her head, grinning up at Deborah. "No way, Auntie Deb! Bunny goes where I go." She paused, thinking hard. "You can come with us, Auntie. You can sit next to me, and I'll let you hold Bunny for a little while. Hurry up and get your clothes! We'll wait for you, huh Momma?" She looked up at her mother. "We can wait for Auntie Deb to get her clothes, can't we?"

"Honey, you don't know how much I wish Auntie Deb could come with us," Mae said to her, tearing up again. "But she has to stay here in Philadelphia. She takes such good care of so many people, they need her to stay here so she can keep on taking care of them." She glanced up at her best friend. "I know she's taken such good care of us."

Most of the passengers had already boarded the bus. The driver closed the luggage compartment and stood up again, heading toward them. "Ladies," he said, making his way up the steps to his seat behind the wheel, "You better find a seat while you can, 'cause your stuff's gonna be leaving here without you in a minute or so."

Deborah turned back to Mae. "Well, you better get going," she said, loud enough for him to hear. She winked. "This guy sounds like he really means business."

Mae laughed, wiping tears from under the sunglasses. "I'll call as soon as I can, I promise." She hesitated, the deep frown on her face causing the pancake makeup mask to crack and flake a little. "What about Richard? He—"

Deborah shook her head firmly, pushing her toward the door. "I said don't worry about that, I'll handle him. You just focus on what's right in front of you now." She glanced down at Lily again. "Be a good girl?"

Lily grinned from ear to ear this time, showing off her missing teeth. "Auntie, I'm always good."

Deborah planted a kiss on the little girl's forehead, then gave Mae a swift hug. "You be safe out there in bayou country, okay? No feeding my little munchkin alligator stew or anything like that."

Mae giggled, getting on the bus. "I'll be sure to keep her alligator-free just for you." The doors folded shut behind them, and she carried Lily down the aisle until she found a set of empty seats toward the back. Lily climbed onto her lap and gazed out the window. Deborah moved up and down the platform, eyes locked on the windows. Mae held up a hand and waved. She spotted them finally, returning the wave.

"Bye Auntie, I love you," Lily said over and over again, dropping her rabbit in the seat next to Mae. She pressed both of her hands against the glass. "Don't forget us, come see us."

The driver started the engine, shifted into gear. Mae waved once more, mouthing a final *thank you* as the bus pulled away from the curb.

Lily curled up on her lap, leaning her head against her chest. Her eyes remained fixed on the window long after they'd traded the view of familiar city streets for the endless stretch of interstate road.

"Will she come and see us, Momma?" she whispered, rubbing her eyes. She started to cry softly, burying her face in the folds of Mae's shirt.

Mae wrapped her up in her arms, rocking her gently. "I hope so, sweetheart," she murmured, stroking her hair. "I sure hope so."

It's dark. He's searching…

The front door opens, slams against the wall. A large hole is visible now, the force of the accelerating doorknob punching through hardened paint and plaster as if it were only rice paper.

"Where the hell are you?" he calls out.

Again and again, rushing toward the kitchen door—nowhere to be found. The half-cooked meatloaf is sitting cold on the island, the ground flesh looking grayish and unappetizing in the dim light filtering through the windowpanes.

So angry. *She can feel the rage boiling up inside of him, can hear the horrible squeaking sound his teeth make when they grind together, the sound of wet sneaks against freshly waxed floors. His heart beats, pounds against his ribs like an untamed creature thrashing back and forth in its cage.*

His broad nose is flaring; his eyes garnet stone as he races through the ground floor rooms, up the stairs, opening all the doors—Slam! Slam! Slam!—until he stands in front of the door to the bedroom, reaching for the knob. Twists it slowly in the palm of his hand, his wrist straining for control. The knob has turned as far as it will go. He presses on the door with his free hand. It gives slightly, but he still can't see anything, so he nudges it with his shoulder, the door opening all the way onto—nothing. Nothing at all. The room is empty; the mirrored closet doors stand wide open, revealing a large gap where clothing should have been.

He storms into the bathroom and looks down. Her red toothbrush is no longer sitting in its familiar place next to the sink; her personal items are missing from the oaken medicine cabinet hanging over the basin. He runs across the hall to Lily's room. Only frescoed walls and stuffed animals wait for him in the silence.

He opens his mouth wide, large hands working at his sides. She can hear the rumbling from within, lava threatening to overflow. A low, feral growl nearly busts his chest wide open, tumbles from his throat and echoes through the empty house.

"Kill you bitch," she hears him muttering to himself as he paces frantically, grinding dried mud into the vanilla carpet.

"Kill you bitch. Killyoukillyoukill—"

FOUR

Startled by the dream, she awoke suddenly, yet willed herself not to move. The pre-dawn gloom brightened slowly to a murky gray swimming beyond her closed eyelids. As her heartbeat returned to normal and her senses slowly came to life, she focused all her attention on trying to remember where she was.

Rick...

A sudden jolt nearly shook her from her seat. Terrified, her eyes flew open and saw only windows. Windows high above rows of seats, bordering a narrow corrugated rubber walkway running down the center. A bus. They were on a bus, headed for home.

She glanced over at Lily lying scrunched beneath a homemade blanket, the vibrant threads crocheted in a multicolor rainbow of hues. During the course of their midnight journey, Lily's hair had tumbled down like a thick curtain, hiding her face in sleep. As she slumbered on, the rising sun cracked the dark marble sky and shattered it to pieces, vivid rays pouring through the window overhead and expertly weaving themselves through the dark tresses. They seemed to turn to flame on the child's head, crowning her in a halo of luminescence.

Like a mighty angel, Mae thought, smoothing the hair away from her eyes. *I'm sorry I let it go so long, baby. Momma's gonna make it up to you somehow...*

Lily stirred slightly under her touch, moving away from the glowing windows and opening her eyes. "Hi, Momma." she said groggily with a lazy smile, stretching her limbs under the blanket. "Are we there yet?"

Mae looked up at the scene drifting by the glass. Waves of lush grasses in varying shades of green flooded the land. Clumps of lavender fairy danced with white irises in meadows hidden among the shadows of ancient oaks, their branches protective arms reaching for one another over the fertile ground. Mae smiled as the morning sun blossomed in the sky, blanketing the earth with translucent sheets of gold. She nodded almost imperceptibly. "Yes, Lily, we're definitely here."

When the chrome Land Runner bus finally pulled into the deserted depot, she and Lily were the first to step off. The depot was located in downtown Beau Ciel, and when gentle winds sent the gathering dust into the crisp blue haze above, Mae saw they were standing in the center of Marigold Square, named for the flowers that grew in profusion around the town. A huge gazebo stood just to their left, the paint still sparkling white though the structure was nearly antique. True to its moniker, marigolds dotted the area where groups of empty wooden chairs waited patiently for townsfolk flocking to hear notes of velvety jazz played late into the sticky summer evenings. *At least one tradition they haven't done away with,* Mae thought as she nodded approval, the faintest trace of a smile on her tired face. She felt a tug on her sleeve and looked down. Lily was staring up at her, eyes muddy brown puddles against the lighter brown of her skin.

"Momma, can we stay?"

Mae took her hand. "I promise you honey, this is where we call home from now on, okay?"

"Good." Lily nodded as Mae had done earlier. "It's pretty. I want to stay forever and ever…" The smile spread slowly across her face, a small dimple near her chin becoming visible.

On impulse, Mae stopped in the middle of the sidewalk and planted a kiss on her nose. "Come on, munchkin. Let's go get a taxi to take us home."

The downtown area was bustling with early Saturday morning traffic. Cars crawled slowly up and down two main roads flanking the gazebo area as passersby moved at an amiable pace from store to store, peering idly at merchandise laid out in tasteful array. A store called The Louisiana Seamstress sold fabrics of every type and hue, crisply starched cotton draped upon voluminous layers of satin and silk to create eye-catching displays. Lily tugged her hand again when they stood in front of a giant dollhouse adorning a toy store window.

"Not yet, honey. We can look around while we're waiting for the taxi." Not sure of where to call for one, they strolled over to the depot again.

A giant clock was embedded into the paneling over the door, the roman numerals large enough for people to read from any point in the square. Ten thirty-five. She pushed the door open, allowing Lily to enter first as she struggled to wheel their suitcases in behind them.

The depot was nearly empty. A few people browsed at a small newspaper stand in the corner or sat gazing out windows overlooking the busy square. At the counter, an elderly gentleman looked up from a sheath of papers he held, the creases on his face deepening when he smiled. Perfect teeth gleamed at her below a graying mustache that nearly concealed his full mouth. *Dentures*, Mae thought for no apparent reason. His chocolate skin glowed. His very presence seemed to illuminate the small, stale room. He lifted a well-worn baseball cap riding atop his head, running the other hand over tufts of thinning hair the color and texture of lamb's wool.

"May I help…" the man's smile slowly faded, then disappeared altogether. He looked Mae up and down, frowning deeply. His pointed stare embarrassed her, making her feel even more self-conscious about her unkempt appearance. She pulled her own ball cap low over her eyes, at the same time pushing the shades higher up the bridge of her nose. Moments floated by, the perfect silence punctuated only by the sound of the giant clock ticking from somewhere above them. She cleared her throat and shifted uncomfortably from one foot to the other, glancing down at Lily.

Shockingly, a look of recognition suddenly crossed his aged features. "Ella Mae? Ella Mae Carpenter? Girl, what the heck you doin' all the way back down here in Beau Ciel?" The smile was back, and he slapped the counter so hard a couple of kids at the magazine rack turned to look. He laughed, the sound low and gravelly from years of smoking cigars. *Cigars*…then it hit her like a ton of bricks.

"Henry!" she called out, reaching for him over the counter.

"Heck, girl!" he began, opening the partition under the counter and stepping into the room. "Nobody thought they'd ever see the likes of you again, since you ran off and got *citified* with them sophisticated college folk up north."

They embraced, the familiar scents of Old Spice and Havana cigars filling her nose as he stepped into her waiting arms. She wept with joy, brushing a hand under the dark lenses to wipe away moisture. Feeling a laser-sharp stare pointed in his direction, Henry pulled away and looked down. Lily smiled up at him.

"Hello," she said shyly, offering a hesitant wave.

He stooped and lifted her into his arms. "This your baby girl, Ella Mae?"

She nodded proudly, adjusting Lily's coat. "Henry, meet Lily."

The man reached out to touch the little girl's hair, glancing over at Mae. His brownish gray eyes watered with emotion. "Lily…like your grandmother." Fixing his gaze on a damp spot on the ceiling, he retreated to the sanctuary of his private thoughts. Finally Mae placed a hand on his shoulder, squeezing it gently. "Hey there. You all right?"

The old man nodded. He planted a kiss on Lily's forehead and set her down, reaching into the back pocket of his jeans to pull out a wrinkled blue handkerchief. He rubbed the threadbare cloth over his worn face, giving her another one of his perfect smiles. "Henry's fine, girl. Jus' right as rain." He shoved the handkerchief in his pocket again. "You know Ella Mae, your grandma Lily was a fine woman. Finest I ever known."

Mae could only nod in response, trying to swallow the lump of emotion rising in her throat. "She was really something, wasn't she? I just wish my Lily could have known her." She watched as her daughter slowly began edging toward the newspaper stand. Lily glanced up at her, question clouding her face.

"Only for a minute or two," Mae said, a stern warning in her voice. The little girl grinned, skipping off to look through a row of coloring books on one of the shelves.

Henry placed his hands on the small of his back and stretched. "So what can I do today for my lil' Junie?"

Mae laughed, recalling the nickname from her childhood. "Well, we need a taxi to get us over to Bella Bloom—we'll be staying there from now on."

Henry chuckled. "Your grandma's old house, huh? She sure loved you, Ella Mae, she really did. Figured she'd a left it to you instead o' that Lynne. Hell, I'd be happy to take you out there m'self, if you still don't mind my drivin'."

Mae shook her head and smiled, recalling a late Sunday afternoon of a spring from her distant past, riding in the backseat of Henry's old Studebaker, the radio broken but music floating through the car anyway, as he and her grandmother sang old tunes from another time. She sighed longingly as the freshly unearthed memory drifted into her consciousness, the sound carrying easily over the nearly empty room. "Don't be silly, Henry. On the way over you can update me on what's gone down here in the past twelve years or so."

"Woman, so much has changed since you went away, I may have to drive the speed limit for once to get the whole thing out." He signaled to a young man sporting intricately braided cornrows to take his post at the counter. "Go on, Eugene. I'll be back 'round in a while."

The young man nodded, fingering his goatee. He scanned the room. Apparently satisfied with the lack of traffic, he busied himself, sifting through the stack of papers Henry had abandoned when she walked in.

"New generation," he said, extending his arm to her in the typical custom of old southern gentlemen. "M' great-nephew. Dependable, but mighty funny lookin' with all that stuff on his head, don't you think?"

She laughed, motioning for Lily. As she ran over, Mae took the proffered arm, allowing Henry to lead her out into the sunshine. An immaculate magenta Cadillac sat parked between a set of crisply painted white lines, the hood ornament sending sparks of brilliant light in every direction. He led her to the passenger door and reached for his keys.

"Henry!" she squealed with delight. "You mean to tell me this is yours?"

He smiled proudly, unlocking the door. He held it open for her. "Yep. This m' Bessie. I got her 'rectly after your grandma passed on, after you went off to school without sayin' a word. I had no need for that old Studebaker anymore—too many memories. I sold her off and bought this shiny new baby from a dealer over in Metairie." He gazed lovingly at the vehicle, gently rubbing his calloused fingers over the freshly waxed hood.

"Oh, she's beautiful." Mae whistled approval, settling herself comfortably on the soft cushions. "Beats an all-night bus ride anytime."

Henry helped Lily into the back seat and headed for the trunk with their bags as Mae worked to lock her into the heavy belt. She was reaching for her own shoulder strap as Henry got in and inserted the key into the ignition.

"Now," he called out with a flourish as the engine roared to life, "you watch my baby work."

From the Square, the ride to Bella Bloom was simply a long stretch of road rambling aimlessly through picturesque Louisiana countryside. As they drove past fragrant fruit groves and old plantation homes locked forever in time behind heavy wrought iron gates, Henry talked of the changes that had found their way to the old town. He spoke of the fight to limit new housing developments catering to commuting families from nearby Metairie and New Orleans. As they passed a busy construction site, he pointed out the new strip mall currently being built where Beau Ciel Junior High used to stand (*That one burned down years ago—damn kids walkin' around with ci-gar lighters, no good mommas and too much time on their hands,* he'd mentioned with a grimace). He chatted in detail about the new Child Development Center that had only recently opened its doors, thanks to funds donated from the estate of an affluent town widow.

"Miss Bell? You remember her, don't you, Junie?"

Mae nodded, faintly recalling the name. Henry went on. "After old man Bell died, she was left alone to care for that young'un with the mental disablement. Autism, I think she said it was. Anyway, he was a bright one from the likes o' what I heard o' him; said he could play a song on a piano through and through after only hearin' it once. Real gifted. Too bad, though. Died at twelve of pneumonia after comin' home from seeing an aunt o' his that lived way distant. His momma never forgave herself for that one. It was his first time bein' away from home without her, and she felt if she'd a kept him here at home in the warm Louisiana air he was used to, he would'a still been 'round.

"So when she passed on a few years back, the town found out she donated all her money specifically to build that development center for kids, I s'pose 'cause she had no other livin' kinfolk to give it to. She always loved the babies, was always kind and generous with 'em, even after her own boy was gone." Henry clucked his tongue, shaking his head sadly. "Poor soul of a lady. Real sweet, too. In the end, though, she wasn't no good without her boy."

Mae nodded solemnly, turning to glance at her daughter. She sat gazing dreamily out the window, absentmindedly tugging the floppy, oversized ears of her toy bunny. Mae once again recalled her days in the old Studebaker, traveling the maze of endless Louisiana back roads without a care in the world. Who knew then of the trouble that would soon blow into her life like a freakish summer storm, shattering the tranquil world of her childhood to pieces? Would she ever be able to knit the broken shards of her life together again, this time for the two of them?

Suddenly drained of the need for conversation, she turned to stare quietly out her own window. "Wouldn't be any good without my girl either, Henry," she whispered, barely audible against the noise of the roaring engine. "No good at all."

Henry eventually slowed at a fork in the road, turning left onto a private access road heading up a small hill. Mae held her breath in anticipation as the old home slowly became visible at its crest, framed perfectly against the crystal backdrop of sky. It had been maybe twelve, thirteen years since she'd spent her final afternoon on the property, had fled down the porch steps in tears, the *clack, clack* of hard leather soles slapping against brick forever echoing in her ears…

Mae shook her head. *No.* This was the new start she'd never dreamed possible, yet had long been waiting for. She planned to turn everything around for her and Lily, even if the effort sapped the very last ounce of her strength. She turned around and tapped Lily's sneaker. "See, honey? This is Bella Bloom—this is home now."

The little girl strained in her seat to catch a glimpse as Henry pulled up to the house and parked next to a low picket fence bordering the property. *White as the freshly painted gazebo in Marigold Square, white as I remember,* Mae thought as she pressed the clasp to release the confining grip of the heavy seatbelt. She was so excited she had to fumble for some moments with Lily's belt, her fingers trembling with the effort.

"Momma, hurry up! I wanna see!" she yelled, kicking her miniature Keds out in frustration. Mae finally managed to disentangle Lily from the restraints. Without hesitation, Lily jumped out and ran into the yard.

"Oh, you don't have to do that, Henry," Mae said as she got out and noticed him struggling with their luggage. "I brought them all this far by myself—"

"Now, now, Junie I won't hear a thing of it. I'm a grown man, was on the rails twenty-five years strong before m'leg blew out. Turned eighty-one in July o' this year, but I'm still hard as nails, still hearty as your grandma's gumbo." Muscles in his neck straining with the effort, he tucked Lily's suitcase under a sinewy arm, managing to grasp the handle of the heavier one and heft it beside him up to the porch.

Mae smiled to herself. *"That man's head's as hard as flint rock,"* she heard her grandmother saying in her head. A memory flickered in her mind of Granna Lily standing on the porch, fanning silvery sweat-dampened hair away from her face with the apron she always wore, the peach ribbon trim fluttering as it rose and fell through the sticky summer air. *"But I love him so. Now you listen to me, girl. Don't you ever let yourself fall for a man like that. Jus' like that woman says in the Lord's Good Book, don't rush it 'till it's time. Love is strong and thick and won't easy let go of you, even if it ain't right. Can send you right on over the edge, it can. You see that man?"*

She pointed to a much younger and more robust Henry as he worked an ancient lawn clipper over the yard, the furious whuck whuck of the chopping blades turning chunks of grass into a thick green haze swirling about him with every step.

"He's real good for me—real good to me, too. But the love he gives is hard, it grips me so that sometimes I can't sleep for it, have to get up in the night and go walkin' or do my sewin'... just forcin' m'self to be away from it for a while, from the warmth of his body so's I can think straight."

Thirteen-year-old Mae had nodded with rapt attention, accustomed to these frank conversations with her beloved grandmother. She wasn't like the other adults in her life who sought to isolate her from the real world with lies and dirty secrets. Her Granna Lily had always believed in speaking exactly what was on her mind, even to the point of rudeness.

However, she'd loved her tremendously, had always listened intently as she brought tales of fairytale romances and swashbuckling pirates off the pages in living color, and even told the occasional ghost story, of which there were many of legendary account in the south. *My life in Philly was one long scary story,* she thought as she followed her grandmother's lifelong lover up the brick path. *But damn it all if I didn't beat the boogeyman anyway.*

She beamed at the thought, pausing on the walk to watch as Lily played in her grandmother's old garden. Bouquets of white and pink azaleas burst from her clenched fists like bits of popcorn and cotton candy as she ran circles around the great oak standing at the edge of the property. Small patches of Bleeding Heart and Heavenly Bamboo wound their way through a gathering of lemony St. Patrick and iridescent Pearl Essence, their delicate leaves shimmering in the screen of mist drifting from a large fountain bubbling in the center.

A path of carefully laid flagstones along the side of the house led to the backyard where an even larger garden lay in full bloom, filled to capacity with flowers of every petal and hue. Mae thought of Louisiana Iris and Nicotiana; their perfume drifting into the still summer night air, filling the screened-in back porch with their heady scent. She recalled spending a particularly balmy summer evening lying out there on an old makeshift cot, feeling the springs of the thin mattress pressing against the length of her body as gentle breezes tickled her through the gauzy satin of her nightgown…

Don't rush it till it's time…won't let go of you, even if it ain't right…

"Momma, look! A swing!"

Mae turned to find Lily sitting atop an old wooden plank suspended from the large oak by two thick cables of rope. Her navy sneakers flailed about in every direction as she fought to build momentum. "Come push so I can go faster!"

Henry plunked the suitcases down on freshly scrubbed porch boards and opened the screen. He fished in his shirt pocket and pulled out a small key, the metal a tarnished gold in the center of his palm.

Mae glanced back at Lily. "Honey, come on. You can play after we get settled."

She turned to see Henry insert the key into the lock with a flick of his wrist. The door opened without so much as a squeak of protest, as if it were used frequently. Inside, sheer drapes still hung from the windows, drawn to keep out harsh light and perhaps the occasional curious onlooker.

Mae grinned at her old friend. "Still got the keys, huh? So *you're* the one I should thank for keeping Granna's house and gardens in immaculate condition all these years. Isn't that hard on you, Henry? Doing all the work by yourself?"

He shook his head firmly in reply, eyes fixed on a distant point in the cerulean sky. "I loved your grandma, Ella Mae. You know that. She was the only one, has always been the only one for me. She always loved it out here, way out o' reach o' them long-necked gossipin' townfolk. Figured after her death if I kept on lookin' after the place, I'd still be lookin' after her somehow. That's the way I see it. Ain't no hardship doin' somethin' out o' love, Junie, 'least that's what I'm told." He winked playfully. "'Sides, I got my nephews to help me when they come visit in the summertime." He hefted the suitcases a final time, placing them just inside the door. "Now you go on in. This is your place now, and I'm mighty pleased. I know your grandma is, too, with her keepin' good watch over you and yours from up above someplace." He gestured to young Lily, watching as she ran happily up the bricks to stand next to her mother. He turned to Mae again, smiling. "She'd be real proud of you, Ella Mae. This girl is her spittin' image when she was young, all full o' life and energy. One o' the reasons I loved her so, you know. Even in the end when she was too sick to move, she was still so *alive*, like she was bein' kissed by them angels up'n heaven she was always talkin' bout."

He walked to the edge of the porch. "I'll be back 'round in a while to light the pilots on the heaters. Still gets pretty cold out here at night. Water works just fine—never bothered to turn it off. 'Lectricity, too. All the light you need is there."

He started down the steps and paused. He turned again toward Mae, looking her full in the face for a long time. When he spoke again, his voice was barely above a whisper, though the next house was nearly a quarter of a mile away. "Think I'll just run on over to the market and pick you up some goods, Junie, how 'bout that? After all, wouldn't want to take the chance of you runnin' into anyone you may not feel up to seein' just now. You got need for supplies?"

Mae moved forward until her face was only a few inches from his, removing the shades and ball cap. "How did you know, Henry?" she asked, tears from a lifetime of buried pain welling in her eyes. "After all the time that's passed…how did you know it was really me under all *this?*" She gestured to her made-up face, holding the disguise up for him to see.

Henry shook his head softly, reaching out to wipe tears from the cheek beneath the bruised eye. "You know, I never really had need for a wife or children as a young man. When I met Lily, I knew from the start she was all I'd been searchin' for, but by then our hair was goin' gray and we'd long since passed the age o' childbearin'. While she was here, you know she claimed you as her own, and you've always been like mine even though you're grown now, with a baby girl to raise. Bein' a momma your-self, Junie, you tell me just what parent worth a dime *wouldn't* know they own child?"

She grabbed his hands, squeezing them gratefully in her own. "Henry…you have no idea how good it feels to hear that just now."

The old man nodded, a hint of sadness crossing his aged features. "I don't know what trouble you gone and gotten yourself into up there, but if you're lookin' for a place to cast your hurt away and be whole—a perfect place to pray, your grandma used to call it—then this is it. And I don't tell what don't need to be told, if you know what I mean."

Mae smiled thankfully, standing on tiptoe and planting a kiss on his cheek. Smooth skin, warm as cocoa, lovely in his old age as her grandmother's had been. "I've been running my whole life, Henry…I'm just tired now. I can't do it anymore. This is *home*. That is what Lily and I are gonna call this place from now on; where I realize I should have been all along."

She took a step toward the front door. "But I *will* take you up on that offer of supplies, if you don't mind." She screwed her face up as if in deep thought, lightly tapping an index finger against her chin. "I'm pretty sure this house is out of everything, so just bring whatever you think will tide us over for a few days 'til I can venture out," she said, fishing in her pocket for a few bills.

Henry started toward the car, waving her off. "Keep your change, Junie. I got it covered. Jus' glad to see you back in this house after so long." After a few steps, he slowed down. He whirled around to face her, suddenly, his tan work boots sending up tiny clouds of dust. "One more thing. I should let you know Merribelle's been snoopin' 'round this place for a while now. Heard she and Lynne was tryin' to get a lawyer to sneak under your grandma's will and take the property as theirs, with you leavin' like you did and bein' out o' touch so long."

Mae's face fell. She pressed her back against the screen door, wrapping her arms around herself protectively. Inside, Lily romped about from one cavernous room to the next, her echoing footsteps a staccato drumbeat in the velvety silence.

After a long moment she spoke in a low voice, crystal clear intentions resonating in the sharp tone. "You keep them as far away as humanly possible for as long as you can if you happen to run into either of them, okay Henry? I haven't the slightest twinge of desire to deal with any of my kinfolk just now."

Henry nodded, understanding etched deep in the lines of his face. "Sorry to have to break the news to you like this, bein' so soon back in town and all. Jus' wanted to let you in on things, 'case they got up to no good 'fore you'd had a chance to settle in just right. I'll be back 'round in a while with those supplies." He politely tipped the bill of his baseball cap in her direction as he carefully folded himself behind the wheel of the Cadillac. The large vehicle disappeared in a cloud of dust as it made its way back to the main road.

Deborah inhaled deeply, the oppressive paper mask she wore crinkling against her nose with the effort. Beads of sweat trickled down her forehead and splashed onto her thick lashes, turning stainless steel cabinets and pasty green walls into a blur. She blinked frantically, shaking her head slightly to clear her vision. A petite Hawaiian woman named Aimee looked up long enough to grab a sterile cloth, gently patting the damp skin before tossing it into a large white container marked BIOHAZARD in bright orange labeling.

Deborah nodded gratefully. "Thank you, nurse." She returned her attention to the problem lying before her on the operating table. *Heather.* Twenty-six weeks gestation at time of delivery—twins so premature they had to be rushed straight to NICU and prepped for emergency surgery at NY Neonatal. *Shit.* And now their mother, Heather, was hemorrhaging, her surgical team fighting like hell to stop the bleeding. *Shit squared.* On the brink for five and a half hours, and finally there was light at the end of the tunnel.

Deborah turned her attention to the far side of the room. "She good, Dr. Braden?"

The anesthesiologist adjusted knobs on machines and scribbled notations on charts, nodding affirmatively.

He chanced a smile in her direction. "Doin' real good, Dr. Barr. Vitals stable and improving by the minute."

The team breathed a collective sigh of relief. Deborah smiled, stepping away from the table as a fourth-year resident began sewing and stapling. Heather would bear a large surgical scar on her body for the rest of her life to remind her of the near-death ordeal, but Deborah prayed with all her heart that she'd also have a healthy set of twins to bring home with her in a few months.

"Close her up good. Wouldn't want to have to walk down this road again if we don't have to."

As she left the room, she pressed the back of her gloved hand against the woman's cool forehead. "You scared the hell out of us for a minute there, Heather. More than you know. Now you get well and get over to New York—your twins need you."

She headed for the scrub room, de-gowning as she went. She was exhausted, contemplated instructing the unit to contact her at home immediately in case of emergency, but decided on remaining at the hospital long enough to see her patient into recovery after updating the family on her condition. As a physician, she was an absolute perfectionist, and Heather a good friend—both would eat away at her conscience so that, in the end, she wouldn't be happy going home to her warm, inviting bed anyway. Instead, she washed up, and, after checking in briefly with Heather's relatives, headed straight for the body bay with cigarettes in hand.

She needed a smoke so badly, she could practically taste it as she ran her tongue along the inside of her mouth. The surgical team she'd hand picked was seasoned, all well accustomed to handling the stresses of working in the midst of ordered chaos. But as the head of the team, she felt responsible for every last one of them, as if she were standing in the operating room completely alone. On the rare occasions she actually made it home from med school for a visit, she remembered sitting in the familiar sunlit kitchen confessing stresses and concerns about fellow students to her mother as they shared pints of cookie dough ice cream. After such heart-to-heart talks, her mother, sweet and simple by nature, would only spoon more of the stuff past her silver caps, smile serenely and say, "Girl, quit tryin' to take care of the world. It's hard enough running your own show."

But look, Mommy, I'm still trying, she thought with a sigh. *Still trying after all these years.*

She edged between two plain white vans used by morticians surreptitiously transporting the dead to their next-to-final destinations. Parking directly in front of two heavy steel doors, the vans came and went in a steady stream of slow-moving traffic as Deborah lit her first cig and dragged deeply, holding the smoke in her lungs until she felt they'd burst, then slowly releasing tendrils of it into the indigo sky. Dawn would be entering the world again. *A new day,* she thought, taking another drag. *Time to make peace with God and start all over again.*

She thought of Mae, waiting for a bus that would take her into familiar, yet unknown territory, joy and a strange sort of anticipation etching itself into her strained, weary face.

What sort of life are you leading now, friend? She flicked ashes into the wind. *What kind of world do you wake up to each day, now that you're finally free?* Deborah took a final drag off the cigarette, nodding to a couple of well-dressed men loading a black plastic body bag into a van, the doors emblazoned L&S Mortuary in modest script. She watched them work a few moments, silently contemplating the wonder of new life and harrowing predicament of the dead.

Where do they really go while their bodies are being chemically altered, caked with beauty products and dressed for burial? Maybe they slap their hands over their eyes and choose not to watch if they know they're going to be burned. Perhaps they've got a special place to hang while waiting for Heaven or Nirvana or wherever the hell you're supposed to go when you're no longer granted access to walk the earth...

She tossed the charred remains of the cigarette butt into the shadows and watched as it landed near a puddle, the glowing embers sending waves of orange rippling over the surface. She was reaching into her pocket for a sequel when the embers suddenly began to shift and change in her peripheral vision, slowly making their way toward her. She snapped her head up, searching the darkness for signs of unwelcome company.

"Hello?"

The embers continued their rhythmic fire dance and moved skyward, burning brightest moments before exploding into tiny showers that fell to the damp gravel below. The shadows gave nothing away at first. Then they too began to shift in irregular patterns, finally melting around a tall human form. She strained to catch a glimpse of whoever was coming, involuntarily taking a step backward in the general direction of safety offered by the fluorescent lights of the loading platform.

"All right. Who's out there? You'd better make yourself known real quick before I call hospital securi—"

"Relax, Doc. It's just me." Richard emerged from the shadows, allowing the light to wash over him in full. His face was a study of anguish in the glow of the unforgiving fluorescents. He ran a shaky hand over his head, rubbing it absently as he managed a semblance of a smile. "I was looking for you earlier. Unit desk had you paged, but I guess you couldn't answer it since they told me you'd just gotten out of surgery. One of the nurses passing by happened to overhear the conversation and mentioned you sometimes come out here for smoke breaks. Of all places, you choose *this* to unwind?" He pointed in the direction of the heavy steel doors, his smoldering cigarette sending ashes in every direction.

"The quiet helps me relax," Deborah replied distractedly, patting the pockets of the scrubs and lab coat she still wore. "Paged? I didn't get any pages…damn. Must have left it in the locker when I went for my cigs," she groaned, slapping her forehead lightly in frustration. "I'd better go check in, Rick. Got a patient up in post-op. Did they mention anyone else looking for me before you came along?"

"Nope. Just pointed me out here after you didn't call or come to the desk." He shuffled restlessly from one foot to the other, his heavy soles scuffing against the hardpan as he appeared to be in deep thought. An unnatural silence drifted up between them, mingling with the smoke of his neglected cigarette.

"Well, Rick," she said finally, taking another step toward the body bay. "Guess I'd better get going. Got to get to that pager and see what's up. Damn's thing my lifeline around this place, and I leave it in the one spot it doesn't belong—out of reach. Give you a call later, okay?" She turned to go, but was stopped abruptly by a vicelike grip on her forearm. She quickly spun around, watching nervously as he stubbed his cigarette under one of his boots, pressed his hands to his face and bent forward in a somewhat melodramatic expression of grief. The anxiety and adrenaline swimming around in Deborah's system shot up a notch as she took note of the swollen knuckles and deep gashes in the flesh. Evidence of the wrathful fallout that must have occurred after coming home to find his wife and child gone without a trace?

The man sighed mournfully and stood up, forcing his hands to his sides. "They've been gone a week already. Seven days. I need to know, Deb. Did she say anything about where she might be going *at all?*"

Deborah shook her head softly, trying her best to look equally distressed. "Honey, we've been over and over this. That night after you and Pete took off in the cab, Mae and Lily laid up on the couches while I played doctor until about ten-thirty, when she announced she was taking Lily up to bed for the night, and I could go on home. Of course I told her it wasn't a problem for me to stay over, or at least until you came in, but she kept insisting they'd be fine.

"Normally, I wouldn't have even considered leaving Mae alone to care for Lily with her being so sick, but earlier I'd given her something for the vomiting, and she'd improved some. Her color came back, and both of them were able to eat a little soup I found in one of the cabinets. So I looked them over one more time and left. She promised she'd call when you got in because she knew I was worried about leaving them like that, and I swear, Rick—that was the only reason I agreed to go. You know I've always been the mother hen when it comes to someone needing some TLC.

"When I didn't hear from her after a while, I decided to call the house anyway, in case you'd come in while she was asleep or something. That was about 11:30 or so. I was leaving a message on the answering machine when you picked up and told me they were gone."

Richard began pacing around in a small circle, fishing frantically in his coat pocket for another cigarette. He fumbled with his lighter in frustration until Deborah steadied the shaky hand bearing the flame, raising it to his lips. She gave his shoulder a reassuring pat as he inhaled deeply. "How 'bout you? Your noses at the station find anything yet?"

He shook his head vigorously, blowing plumes of billowing smoke from his nostrils. Deborah grimaced out of his line of vision, thinking of mythical fire-breathing creatures stalking their prey wildly under cover of darkness.

"Nothing," he answered bitterly, a cloud of vaporous smoke beginning to envelop him. "Clothes were gone from both closets, socks…hell, even their *toothbrushes* disappeared. If she's done something to my kid, Debbie, I swear—"

"Oh come on, Rick. She's her mother," she snapped. "No matter where she's taken Lily, you know she'd never hurt her."

He tossed the cigarette away, moving so close she could smell the scotch heavy on his breath, could see the fine network of burst capillaries in his bloodshot eyes. Small beads of perspiration stood out on his cheeks, giving his skin a waxen look. "How the hell could you not know my wife was planning on leaving me, huh?" he growled, his pointed finger just inches from her own face. "Come on, she's your best friend, Deborah. You think I'm an idiot? You think I don't know how sneaky you women are, how you tell each other everything? One gets a hangnail and the whole sewing circle's in on it before the husband can say Band-Aid. Us men? Hell, we're always the last to know. Now I left my wife and kid in *your* care, Doc," he grumbled as he locked his hands around her wrists in a vice-like grip, forcing her into the shadows. His form was once again a husky silhouette as the darkness closed in around them. Deborah searched frantically for any other sign of life. The men from L&S were long gone; the bay was deserted for the moment.

"The last time I saw Mae, she was puking her guts into my kitchen sink and embarrassing the hell out of me, and you really expect me to believe she managed to make arrangements no one can trace, pack her stuff, and disappear with a six-year-old in a matter of hours without any help?"

On the outer edges of full-scale alarm, Deborah fought desperately to appear calm. She took a slow breath, carefully choosing her next words. "Rick, I swear to you, when I left her she looked too sick to walk to the corner quickie-mart for a gallon of milk, let alone vanish into thin air with a set of clothes and a little girl. Are you saying you actually believe she told *me* anything? She knows without a doubt I'm the first place you'd come looking when she hit the road. If she needed help at all getting out of town, why the hell would she look my way? She's not stupid, Rick, and neither am I.

"I'm a doctor, for crying out loud—I've spent too much money and half my life working for what I've got now. You actually think I'd give my life up, go to jail for kidnapping and lose everything because my *girlfriend's* having problems at home? If I were you, I'd think of letting go now, Rick," she hissed, eyes boring icy holes into his, "or you may end up sorry you came here looking for me in the first place."

They glared at each other another moment before his grip loosened and she was able to snatch her hands away. She resisted the urge to rub her tender wrists in front of him, not wanting to give him the satisfaction of seeing how much his scare tactics had rattled her.

"Sorry if I hurt you, Deb." He sighed, covering his face again. "You know I'd never want to do that. I'm just so worried…I've combed every database at work, I've run every search report I can get my hands on. I've probably interviewed half the cab drivers in Philly by now. Hell, I even checked the morgue…" his voice faltered as he bent over again, this time stifling a wave of genuine tears. "I haven't slept in three days…"

Deborah hesitated at first, then laid a cautious hand on the back of his neck and rubbed gently as she moved closer to the light, preparing to escape if need be. "I'm worried about Mae too, Rick. I pray every day she'll pick up the phone and tell me they're all right. But in the meantime, you've got to get yourself together here. Got to stop all these crazy ideas from running through your head before you really start to slip, end up goin' off the deep end or something—"

"How could she make a fool of me like this?" he yelled, moving from under her touch. The faint silhouette melted away again as he retreated further into the dark. Deborah could hear the splashing sounds he made as he stomped though stagnant rain puddles. "I'm the joke of the whole damn department now, Deb. Spencer's wife takes his kid one night and goes on the lam. No trace, no clues. No ATM or credit card activity, no car rentals…where the hell could she have gone?"

Deborah shook her head sympathetically, though she knew he wouldn't see it. "Wish I knew."

"Her family…when we got married, she said all her relatives were dead. She has no close friends, besides you. How could she betray her husband like that if she's supposed to love and honor him, huh? She sneaked under my nose and stole my fucking kid!"

Feeling the first icy tentacles of panic sliding down her spine, she slowly backed out of the shadows, toward the safety of the body bay. "Rick, I'm sorry. I've gotta head back and check on my patient; she was critical earlier, we almost lost her."

"I understand," he sighed. "Sorry I came at you like that before. Boy, I sure can pick the perfect time to be an ass, can't I?"

Deborah ignored the question. "I'm just sorry I can't give you the answers you're looking for right now, Rick. Believe me, I miss them every bit as much as you do. Try to get some sleep, okay? If you need anything, you know where I am." Without waiting for a reply, she turned away and walked briskly, then jogged toward the steel doors.

She didn't slow until she'd reached the bay, just as another van pulled up. In her haste, she nearly slammed headlong into one of the doors as it opened on two bored-looking hospital orderlies pushing another plastic shrouded gurney onto the platform.

"Pardon me, I'm sorry," she mumbled as she rushed past, feeling stares of mild interest following her down the hall. She hung a left and headed toward a set of frosted glass doors simply marked: MORGUE - Authorized Employees Only. Two bodies waited patiently on steel tables for cold storage while a young man worked diligently on a third, the scalpel he'd placed against the lifeless skin poised to make an opening Y-shaped incision.

"That better be you with good news, Santos," he said without looking up. "Those two need to be on ice like yesterday—"

Deborah ran into his arms, forcing him back against a nearby sink. The man grunted surprise, raising his arms high above his head as he instinctively held the sharp instrument out of reach. "Geez, Deborah, what the hell you tryin' to do? Cut a man open on his own knife?"

"Sweetie, I'm sorry. I'm just so happy to see you're still here. Glad you decided to work late after all." She yanked the surgical mask from his face, pressing her lips against his with all her strength. She pulled away long enough to manage in a lusty whisper, "I'll meet you back here in an hour. *Then* you'll have the rest of the night to finish what I started."

FIVE

Mae stepped off the porch into the fading light, holding a hand above her eyes in her strained efforts to see. High overhead, a brewing storm churned angrily in the heavens, the placid afternoon devoured suddenly by roiling thunderheads of gray and violet.

"I think you'd better come in now, Lily. Looks like we're gonna get some rain."

"Aw, Momma! Can't I just have a few more minutes? Pleeese?" Lily pleaded as she stretched her legs on the swing, gripping the ropes tightly and leaning far back on the wooden plank in her fight to build momentum. "Come on, Momma! This is the first day I been out to swing since we got here. It's still hot anyway. I don't wanna go inside. Can't we just sit out here and read stories 'til God takes the rain away?" These last words were buried in a loud rumble that blotted out all sound. Darts of lighting slashed their way savagely across the beaten sky.

Mae ran over to the tree just as the first warm drops of rain pelted her scalp and shoulders. She grasped the ropes and crouched next to the swing, pointing up at the darkening clouds. "See that? There's a storm coming in!" she yelled over the noise, grabbing Lily's hand. As they made their way back to the porch, a pair of headlights appeared suddenly in the gloom.

"Momma, it's Henry!" Lily cried, trying to wrench free of her mother's grasp.

"No," Mae shook her head firmly. "Go on inside, munchkin. Henry will be coming along shortly. Besides, you don't even have your jacket with you. Go on, hurry up now!"

Lily stormed up the steps and wrenched the screen door open, slamming it against the frame so hard Mae jumped.

"You do that again, young lady," she shouted at the empty doorway, "and you're not gonna see that swing for at least another week. Keep pushing your luck!" She turned and jogged down the path toward the approaching Cadillac, waiting patiently by the picket fence while he parked the car and locked it.

"Henry!" she shouted when he began making his way toward her. "What on earth could have brought you out all this way in such a storm?" She shook her head, waving her own question away. "No matter, you got here just in time. Lily just came inside for dinner. We could definitely use some good company on a day like this." She greeted him with a warm smile as he approached, flipping the latch on the fence and beckoning him into the yard. "Come on in and catch some warmth by the fire with us a while. I imagine this rain's gonna be brutal, and—"

Henry interrupted her, the strain in his voice apparent. "Didn't want to bring more bad news in the door with me, honey, but word is Lynne and Merri finally found a lawyer who'll formally contest your grandma's will. Hear they wantin' to go to court with it real soon." He watched as Mae suddenly grew quiet, standing there before him motionless as a statue in the midst of the downpour.

After a moment, her expression softened. She moved to take his arm in her own, dutifully guiding him up the front walk. "Let's go on inside. Wouldn't want you coming all this way just to catch your death out here because of me." They hurried toward the house, making it up the porch steps just before another blinding flash of lightning transformed the world into blank white canvas.

The front room was nearly empty, furnished only by an old red sofa placed in front of the crackling fireplace. A sweet humming drifted through the room, accompanied by the squeak of crayons dragged across the surface of rustling paper. The humming abruptly stopped, and Lily's head appeared over the back of the sofa. "Look, Henry! I drew you, see?" She brandished a crayon drawing of a stick figure standing next to a green square marked BUS DEEPPO in scrawling black letters. "I can draw you another one if you want. Here!" She thrust the paper in his direction, smiling proudly.

"Honey, Henry's staying for dinner tonight," Mae chimed in after securing the locks on the door. "You can give it to him before he leaves. You wouldn't want it to get all wrinkled up in his pocket, would you?"

Lily ignored her, turning her attention back to Henry. "I'll make another one for you to take home, okay?" She settled back on the cushions again, humming another tune as she fished through her crayon box for another color.

"You want coffee?" Mae asked with a sigh as they headed down a short hallway and into the kitchen. She approached an island in the center of the room, plucking two mugs from a rack hanging above her head. Henry only nodded, removing his hat and slicker and sagging into the breakfast nook. He folded his hands, pressing them to his forehead as if in prayer. "What's wrong with the little 'un this evenin'?"

"Oh," Mae laughed, rinsing the mugs in the sink, "she's a little upset with me right now. I finally let her spend some time outside today. She was having so much fun she didn't want to come in, even with that storm rising. I was rescuing her from the tree swing when you showed up. Wait a sec, before I forget…" She reached beneath the counter. "Let me get her rabbit cup. I'm thinking cocoa and marshmallows might put me back in her good graces." She brought out an old ceramic mug, the cartoon image of a rabbit eating a carrot nearly faded with age on the front. She held it out to him, smiling faintly.

"Remember this? Granna gave it to me when I was Lily's age. I can't believe she kept it so long. I was cleaning the other day and happened upon it, so I passed it on to Lil' Miss in there. She won't drink anything these days unless it's in here." She filled a tarnished teakettle with tap water and set it on the stove, finally making her way over to the table. "All right, the truth," she said, taking a seat across from him. "They know I'm back, don't they?"

Henry raised his head with another sigh, looking her in the face a long time. "Honestly, I don't know how they found out, Junie," he said finally. "You know I promised to keep your secret long as you saw fit, and like I said before, I keep my word. Beau Ciel's always been a quiet town; we keep to ourselves mos' o' the time, but I'm thinkin' maybe them or one o' they high fallutin' friends happened to drive by one night, see a light or two on in the house ain't been there before an' it got 'em to askin' 'round.

"They know you're here anyway, and since Ol' Lady Lynne always felt I was keepin' you in the know 'bout going's on down here, I'm guessin' they think you finally came back to stake your claim in the house war they tryin' to get started. Don't think they know nothin' 'bout how you really come to be here." He chuckled low to himself, eyes drifting away from Mae to rest somewhere beyond the rain soaked window. "Ol' Lady Lynne, wicked as ever. Always tryin' to put herself beyond the common folk, you know. Always a scheme runnin' through that head o' hers so's she can come out on top o' things, no matter who's got to pay the price. These days it's to the point when I see her comin' up the road one way, I do jus' about anythin' I can to make sure I'm headed the other direction, know what I mean?"

"Sounds like my mother," Mae nodded bitterly. "With her, things never change."

Henry's gaze remained fixed on the window. His fingers began drumming the table, an indecipherable, yet rhythmic, beat against the wooden surface. "Always wanted to give your grandma such a hard time, 'specially after Jonas passed. 'Bout lost her mind after that. Some say she spends her days dabblin' in all kinds o' spiritual workin's up in that house, tryin' to rouse him from the dead or some kind o' thing. My opinion, folks don't need to go 'bout raisin' what God Himself puts down in the ground, you see."

At the mention of the name, their eyes met again over the table. Seconds passed. The gentle sound of Lily's humming drifted in from the other room. A clock hanging on a far wall chimed softly. On the stove, the old kettle screamed over the flames, its tarnished mouth forced open wide by blasts of rising steam.

Mae finally blinked, turning away at last. "Better get that," she murmured, getting up from the table. "Would you like cream and sugar?" She was careful to keep her back to him while she spooned coffee and poured boiling water into their cups, setting the rabbit cup filled with cocoa aside for Lily. Henry sat back in his chair and rubbed his chin, watching her with a mixture of curiosity and concern.

Mae turned to him again, a cup in each hand. In the space of only moments, her eyes had glazed over completely; her expression, perfectly blank. Henry took a deep breath and spoke, his formerly musical hands now folded somberly before him on the table. "There's more you need to know, Junie. Your momma's taken real ill during this past year, to the point where she don't go out much no more. Talk 'round town says she's windin' down to the end o' her days."

She didn't even flinch; instead, she carefully set both cups down on the island in front of her. "I...I'm sorry, Henry," she replied distract-edly, her faraway gaze remaining fixed on the rising steam. "Did you say you wanted cream and sugar?"

He raised his eyebrows. "Black's fine, honey," he answered slowly, his voice taking on hushed, gentle tones. "Jus' come on over here and sit down now, will you?"

Mae picked the cups up and carried them to the table, hands shaking so badly drops of steaming liquid spattered her skin and landed on the wood grain beneath.

Simultaneously, he reached for her hand and plucked a handker-chief from his back pocket when she took her seat again, gently dabbing the clean worn cotton over her wounds. "Close call there."

She shook her head slowly in disbelief. "Even when I was a girl, we...we weren't all that close..."

Henry dabbed and nodded. "I know, Junie, I know. Your grandma filled me in on what was what." He folded the soiled handkerchief and tucked it away again. "There we are, right as rain. You better now?"

Mae flexed both hands and nodded, raising them to bind her thick hair with a rubber band she found laying near the table's edge.

Henry smiled proudly as she worked, pointing to the spot above her left eye. "See there? That herbal poultice I put together really did the trick. None o' that's gonna scar, you know, and your bruises look to be all but gone. Just for some swellin', you're good as new." His smile faded, his countenance darkening as quickly as the storm that rolled in to crush an otherwise perfect day. "Course, if I ever run into the son of a bitch'd did that to you, he'll have a real fight on his hands. Let him tango with someone who ain't afraid to beat the plumb out o' him."

Mae reached across the table and gave his gnarled fingers a reassuring squeeze. "Don't worry, Henry. He doesn't know anything about this place. I told him I had no surviving relatives. Just seemed like the best answer to give under the circumstances, and he never cared to ask too many questions...anyway. It was just one of those things, I guess. That's how I knew we could come here and be safe, instead of taking the bigger risk of trying to start over somewhere else."

Henry nodded. "Jus' glad you didn't lose your way out there, Junie. Glad you knew how to come back to your roots when the time was right."

She laced her fingers around her cup and drew it close, gazing at the contents as if they were a reflecting pool, brimming over with the deepest of secrets. "This has always been home for me, Henry, you know that. Granna's last wish was for me to keep this place, and I'm not going to let anyone scare me away from it again. My daughter will grow up safe and protected in this house, even if I have to lay down my life to make it so." In the next instant, she was on her feet. "That's why I can't let it rest any longer, Henry. I've got to settle this tonight." She held out a trembling hand as her eyes met his again, a silent plea emerging from their murky depths. "I'm sorry, but I have to ask if I can borrow your keys."

Henry stared up at her incredulously. "What's this? You mean you set on goin' over there *now*, Junie?" He eyed her carefully a moment longer, finally giving his shoulders a halfhearted shrug. "Well, if you wantin' to go so bad, honey, I'll get m' slicker back on an' drive you over there—"

"No!" she shouted, startling him into silence. Seeing the hurt in his face, she reached for his hand. "Henry," she began again gently. "Thanks for offering, but I need you to stay with Lily. I don't want her

71

in that house. It's…it's just not a good place for her to be." She shook her head sadly, eyes welling with tears. "So many bad memories, so many terrible things I wish I could just forget…seems from north to south the times I've spent in this house make up most of the few *good* memories I've had my entire life."

Tears of gratitude fell from her face as she watched him fish in his pocket and place the keys in her waiting palm without another word.

"I won't forget this, Henry. I owe you, big time."

He nodded, face clouded with concern. "Driving a big boat like that, in this weather…remember, these Louisiana rainstorms can be tricky to get around in. Rain's real warm. Makes the roads twice as slick, twice as dangerous. You be careful out there, now. Here, you go on an' take my coat." He held out the shiny red slicker for her as she quickly shrugged into it and tugged on the zipper.

She flipped the hood over her head and headed for the back door, Henry following close behind. "Tell Lily I'll be back in time for dinner. I'm pretty sure she won't miss me anyway. As Granna would say, tonight *you're* the star in her sky." She gave his hand another squeeze, opened the door and disappeared into the storm.

Though time had passed, Mae still remembered the way as if it were yesterday. She drove down the hill from Bella Bloom until she reached the main road and turned the car west, toward town. The rain continued to fall, tapping softly against the roof of the Cadillac, sliding down the windshield like tears. She didn't bother turning on the radio; the rain-soaked silence was soothing, the storm providing its own natural melody.

As she watched the landscape roll past her, memories slowly emerged from the depths of her mind, floating and bobbing on the surface like a drowned man on water…

An image of her tenth birthday, cake and candles. So happy because she'd finally gotten the big red bike she'd been bugging her parents about. Months and months of pleading, cajoling, and extra chores, and finally it was hers. Crimson, shiny, reflecting late afternoon sunlight, the bike was perfect in every part.

High-pitched, squealing laughter floated through sticky summer air. The laughter of childhood playmates, running across the yard in floral sundresses and pressed blue jeans soiled with dirt, bubble gum, and smears of chocolate birthday cake; running to keep pace with her frantic pedaling, wanting to be the first to catch up, the first to ask for a turn.

How happy she'd been. And her mother, smiling proudly as she sat with the women in the shade of a black walnut tree, fanning herself and telling them how special her little girls were, how smart and talented—Merribelle and her love of the cello, and Ella Mae. So smart, so creative.

"My little Mae's gonna be a famous writer someday, Jolene. Already best in her class. Did I show you the report she wrote on reptiles? A+, as usual. My A+ little girl…"

So she'd called her that night as she brushed her hair before bed.

"My A+ little girl. You're gonna grow up and make this whole family proud, you and Merri. We may live in a little one-street town, but we own the biggest house on that street," she said triumphantly, gesturing around the room with a flourish.

She turned and grabbed Mae by her tiny shoulders, shaking them firmly as she spoke. "Never forget, Ella Mae Carpenter—you can always make yourself better than your circumstances, no matter what kind of hand you're dealt. I grew up poor, washin' clothes and cookin' food for people who lived in houses like this. I knew I was meant for something more, and I didn't give up.

"I read all I could, anything I could get my hands on. Studied everything 'til it was imbedded in my mind. I went to secretary school for a while, was at the top of my class when I quit just after I met your father. I married him when he was still struggling to make a buck, selling stained-glass windows out the back of his beat up Chevy. Now look. He has a store in Metairie and New Orleans, and he's even thinking of opening up

another in Georgia or even in Florida somewhere." She twirled a lock of coal black hair around her index finger and gazed out the bedroom window overlooking the large front yard, a faint smile on her face. After a moment, she started as if awakened from a daydream, picking the brush up and gently threading Mae's curls through it once again.

"Just remember we are the best, *Ella Mae. We are better than this town, and I'll never let either of you forget it." She pressed her cool hands against Mae's cheeks, planting a scarlet kiss square on her forehead. "You get on to sleep now. Momma loves you..."*

Mae gasped and stamped both sneakers on the brake, narrowly avoiding a calico cat racing across the Square. "Stupid cat," she muttered, turning north onto Mulberry. She switched the windshield wipers to HI, spraying a fine mist of water across the glass in rapid arcs. She shifted into low gear, creeping the Caddie down the lonely stretch of road at about 25 miles an hour. *Stupid cat.* Her father had given her a cat like that once, small and mewling and colorful...

She thought of her father's hands. So large they were, the knuckles rough and cracked and the veins visible, pulsing under the taut skin. "Good hardworking hands," her mother had often said...

Late in the summer of her thirteenth year, he'd come out to the gazebo in the back yard where she'd been lounging in saltwater sandals and shorts, idly flipping the pages of a Teen Dream *magazine. He plopped down beside her on the wicker sofa, loosening his tie and rolling one of his shirt-sleeves up, all the while keeping a hand behind his back. "Got someone who'd like to meet you, Ella. Ready?" He held both arms in front of him now, a shivering bundle of fur in the cup of his hands.*

"Oh!" she'd squealed in delight, the magazine complete forgotten. "Daddy, she's just what I wanted!"

"He's a he, Ella. What are you going to name him?"

"His name is David," she beamed, happily taking him in her arms.

"David?" he offered a perplexed smile. "Why David?"

"Granna told me the story, Daddy. David was the smallest boy, and he killed Goliath, the biggest man around, and he saved all the people. David

was small, but special. God loved him a lot, and I love my cat a lot, so…what better name could there be?"

Her father had doubled over with laughter at that, laughed until he could manage only a hoarse whisper. "Such a smart little girl you are," he chuckled finally, wiping tears of amusement from the corners of his eyes. "Beautiful like your momma, talented like your sister, and a funny fart like your old pop here. Come on and give him a hug—that is, if your little figure hasn't swelled too much in the womanly places and you think you're too grown for it now."

And as she'd held the kitten tightly in her arms, held him close to her so he would trust her, would stop shivering, her father had pulled her close to him, pressing her tight against his own chest. As his calloused hands traveled in soft circles up and down her back, into her hair, over her face, she slowly realized the old familiar comfort she'd always felt in his presence had in a moment been replaced by another feeling altogether.

That was the first day she'd ever felt the icy pinprick of fear.

The thick curtain of rain parted as the house became visible in the Caddie's headlights. Mae drew in a deep breath, turning the car into the driveway. Beyond gates of monogrammed wrought iron, the drive ascended a small hill until it reached the house, standing silent and forbidding in the shadows of giant walnut and spruce trees flanking the property. Sterile, imposing, oppressive…all those feelings came flooding back, washing over her in cold black waves as she sat unmoving behind the wheel, listening to the gentle *swish, swish* of wiper against windshield.

"You can do this, Mae," she said aloud, startled by the sound of her own voice. "It's only a house, just a bunch of wood and glass. It can't hurt you anymore…" Yet she felt a heaviness settle around her like fog as she finally turned off the ignition and headed up the hill.

Darkness, nearly complete. The rain soaked her even through the heavy slicker, though Mae was oblivious to the cold water seeping beneath her clothing, drenching her skin. The rubber band had loosened in her wet hair, and most of it now hung in sopping ropes around her face; she brushed at it impatiently as she fought her way through the shadows. She glanced to her left and saw the yard she used to play in as a child, immaculate as it had always been. A swing still hung from the lower branch of one of the larger trees on the property, just a few feet away from the house. Could it be the very same one she'd spent countless hours on as a child? *Whee! Push me harder, Daddy! I want to touch the sky…*

Mae shook her head hard enough to banish the memory, spraying flecks of water in every direction. *Focus Mae, focus. Just get it over with and go home. Yes, home.* Bella Bloom was her home now, hers and Lily's. She shoved her shivering hands into her pockets, staring down at her shoes as she put one resolutely in front of the other. White gravel crunched beneath her feet with every step—had that been there before? *No matter.* She listened to the crushed rock sliding back and forth under her sneakers, slowly making her way out of the shadow of trees into the harsh yellow glare of a porch light set in amber glass.

She stood before the house, taking it all in. Stepped up onto the porch, reached for the brass knocker, let it fall with a dull thud against the scarlet door. The sound made her jump, her shivering hands clenching involuntarily. Nothing. Then shuffling sounds from within. An unfamiliar human shadow finally appeared, peeking around a sheer curtain hanging from one of the small windows framing the door. "Who is it?"

Mae took one last shuddery breath before answering. "My name is Ella Mae Spencer. I've come home to see my mother."

The servant led her into a small parlor just off the entry hall. "Go on an' take a seat, miss. May I get you anythin'?" As Mae paused to take in the dimly lit surroundings, from behind the woman placed a pair of weighty hands on her shoulders, attempting to remove the rain slicker.

Mae turned and quickly shook her off, stepping away from her as if she were emitting flames. "I'm not staying long. I just need to see my mother, so could you please go tell her I'm here?" She went over and perched at the very edge of a sofa patterned in a gaudy floral print, arms folded resolutely across her chest.

The servant, an elderly black woman with hair the texture of spun sugar, seemed to ignore her and instead busied herself around the room, fluffing pillows and straightening armchairs as she went. As she worked, her substantial hips swung back and forth under the starched cotton uniform.

Mae was reminded of her own grandmother and the way she moved about Bella Bloom, swinging her hips and humming in time to a tune only she could hear. She relaxed a little and settled back on the cushions, smiling faintly at the memory.

"Hmmph, Ella Mae. So, *you* de one we been waitin' on," the woman said sourly as she paused in her tidying up, turning to give her a long look. Snatched from her reverie, Mae glanced up to see the woman standing next to an antique chair, arm draped casually over the back. As she spoke, she screwed her face up more and more as if being forced to savor something unpleasant. "Hmmph. Yo' momma say we might be seein' you soon, gave me instruction to let you in the second you showed yo'self up at de door."

The smile slipped from Mae's face. "Just where *is* she, and *who the hell are you?*"

The old woman patted the top of the chair, a smirk playing at the dimpled corners of her mouth. "Now don't you go gettin' yo'self all worried, miss. It'll only be a few. I know you come from a mighty long way to be here. I'm just keepin' you some comp'ny 'til she's ready to receive a visitor." Deep southern drawl. Smirk spreading to a knowing grin. Did she actually *wink* at her?

She took a seat in the chair and got comfortable, crossing her plump legs at the ankles while her hands folded themselves primly in her lap. "Now see here, Miss Ella Mae, I've known yo' folks a long while, long before you an' yo' sis' came along". Her dark eyes narrowed, her booming voice dropping to just above a whisper. "Yep, I'm an *ol'* friend o' this fam'ly. Not so diff'rent from you, either—things got too hot for me an' I had to go a ways from 'dis place a while m'self, but I came back to town after I raised m' chil'ren all up. Started work right here in 'dis house 'rectly after yo' daddy passed." She clucked her tongue, shaking her head wistfully. "T'was a shame, it was. Jonas Carpenter was a good man—"

"I've had enough of this," Mae interrupted. She shot to her feet and glowered down at her, hands clenching into fists. She was shaking all over. "Now you get up from that chair right now and take me to her, or I swear I'll bust this place up looking myself." She could hear the blood rushing in her head as she reached out and grabbed the antique chair's arms, putting herself face to face with the woman. "I don't know what you've been told, but I assure you, you don't know me as well as you think you do," she whispered through clenched teeth, eyes boring into hers. "So I'll just tell you. I've got nothing *but* time. If you don't want me ripping up every floorboard or busting down every door, then I suggest you get moving. Bullshit ain't my game, lady. I don't play it very well."

The woman recoiled from her words as if bitten, her mischievous, almost impish expression turning stony in an instant. As Mae backed away from her, she rose slowly from the chair, taking what seemed an eternity to smooth her skirt and apron.

"Well, well, Miss Ella Mae," she said at last, arching her brows, "Seems we got more in common'n even I knew at 'de first."

Mae planted her fists on her hips. "I hope I made myself perfectly clear—"

"Oh, but you have, you surely have…" Her ice-cold gaze traveled over Mae once more, as if she were contemplating a sinister plan of action. Finally, she turned and walked to the hallway, tossing a dismissive wave over her shoulder. "...though none o' that big city violence you carried wit' you from all dat way is gon' be needed here tonight. You spoke yo' peace an' you gon' get what you really came back for. You jus' gather yo' things n' come on wit' me."

Back into the entry they went, up the winding stairs...how many times had she run up and down them in jumpers and denim shorts? How many days had she and Merribelle sat there playing dolls or jacks, wiling away those endless summer afternoons under the air conditioner when it was too sticky to go out? Those days were long gone, but how she wished that brief interval of happiness had lasted; how she wished now she could simply pluck those moments from her life and re-run them like matinees on a movie screen...

They made it to the landing and started down a long hallway. The floor remained paneled in hardwood, still waxed to perfection. *Wonder if my mother made this crude, shameless woman scrub it on hands and knees just today? Hmm...probably.* She beamed, dragging her muddy sneaks with each step. As they left the weak lighting below and moved higher and deeper into the shadows, a flicker in the corner of her eye caught Mae's attention. She paused in front of an open bedroom door and peered inside, eyes drawn immediately to a night table filled with clusters of burning candles. Her mother's old bedroom. Though the windows appeared to be closed and the shades tightly drawn, a cool breeze swirled continually from within, causing the flames to move rhythmically in every direction.

The shuffling footsteps of her companion faded down the hall. Mae hesitated a moment in the doorway, then finally gathered her courage and stepped over the threshold. The darkness in here was palpable; it seemed to press in on her from every side. The air smelled strange and felt stifling, as if it had the power to crush her lungs if she dared breathe in too deeply. Though she chided herself for entertaining such thoughts, Mae found herself taking shallow breaths anyway as she moved toward the room's single source of light.

She approached the night table, staring down in bewilderment at its contents. The array of flickering candles cast their faint light on what appeared to be some sort of altar or shrine. Ribbons of purple and black were draped carefully across the night table's surface; atop these a Virgin Mary figurine sat, a beautiful silver rosary pooled neatly at her feet. Faded photographs, pungent-smelling incense, and a collection of silver bowls completed the display; most were filled with fruits, nuts, and candy, though three smaller bowls were filled to the brim with unknown substances.

Mae crouched down in front of the makeshift altar. To her own horror, and before she could stop herself, she took her index finger and dipped it in the first of the liquid filled bowls. The substance was golden brown and sticky; she rubbed her fingers together and sniffed. *Honey.* Frowning, she quickly wiped her hand on one of the purple and black ribbons and continued her investigation. The second bowl contained a darker brown substance; she dipped her fingers and raised them once again to her nose. This time they smelled of something containing alcohol, the fragrance bold and spicy. The heady scent of aged rum.

"Not bad," Mae muttered with a note of sarcasm, sniffing her fingers again before wiping them on the ribbon. "I see Mom still likes the good stuff." The third bowl was furthest away from the candlelight. She leaned into the shadows and dipped her finger. Another sticky substance, darkest of them all. As she pulled her hand back to examine it in the light, one of the old photographs grabbed her attention. She was sure the background was of the house she stood in, though the face of the person in the snapshot was hard to make out. The substance on her fingers all but forgotten, she reached down with her free hand and picked the photo up. Within seconds of staring at it, she knew. Henry's words from earlier came back to her in a lightning-like flash. She backed away from the altar in horror, the photo slipping from her trembling hand. With a growing sense of dread churning in her gut, she raised her fingers to her nostrils, then held them up to the light. *Blood.*

A blast of rushing air swirled over the altar, extinguishing every candle and immersing Mae in total darkness.

Fear paralyzed her body to the spot; her blood felt like ice water coursing through her veins. Her feet stubbornly refused to obey any command. Her shallow breathing became labored in the oppressive air; she fought for every breath as she struggled to get her feet moving again. She tried to back away…and suddenly felt hands on the small of her back. *Strong hands.* The old woman must have noticed she'd gone missing and come back up the hall after her.

Fear melting quickly to anger, Mae wrenched away from her touch and whirled around. "Get your hands off me, you…" only the open doorway greeted her. The room was completely empty. The cool air swirled around her ankles. To Mae, they felt like bands of iron.

The hands found the small of her back again. Mae could hear breathing that was not her own. The swirling air pressed up against her ear, called her name…

…and mercifully, her feet were propelling her forward, taking her to the safety of the open doorway.

She hurried down the hall in time to see the old woman stop at the last door, hand on the doorknob. Their eyes met, and she grinned. "Ah, so you meet de ol' Baron an' de Gede, hmm? 'Dey hold de keys to life beyon' death, 'dem two. Like I *say*," she whispered, grin widening, "you gon' get what you really came back here for." She opened the door onto a large well-lit room, the multi-paned windows providing an unblemished view of saturated front lawn and impenetrable blackness beyond.

Her old room. Her mother sat before an open window, knitting quietly from the comfort of an antique wooden rocker. Ornate scrollwork had been etched delicately into the glazed headrest and arms. As Mae slowly crossed the room, she realized with a touch of sadness that the chair was hers, had sat in a corner of this room when it was still a nursery, when she was still small enough to be held, small enough to be rocked on her mother's lap as she was read countless tales of Happily Ever After.

"She's here, missus," the woman said crisply, swaying hips carrying her over to the chair to gather the sweater her mother wore more tightly around her shoulders. A large green canister rested on a portable rack next to the chair, tubes connected to the canister feeding her oxygen through the nose. Despite the open window, the faint odor of sickness still permeated the room. "You want a blanket, missus? It's nippy out 'dere now 'de storm's come all 'de way in."

Her mother shrugged away from her touch as Mae had done earlier. "No, Cina," she said without looking up, "I'm fine. Leave us in private."

Cina walked over to the window, reaching for the clasps. "You'll catch yo' death o' cold like 'dis, Lynne."

Her mother scowled at her back. "Don't fuss over me, Cina. I like it open. The air cleanses my bones. Now leave us, please. I'll call if I need you."

The woman turned, giving Mae a frosty look. She brushed rudely past her on her way to the door, closing it firmly behind her with a twist of her thick wrist.

Absolutely nothing had changed. The room looked as if she'd left it only moments ago, instead of decades. Old pictures of classmates and posters of movie stars remained tacked to peach sherbet wallpaper with clear tape. The cream painted wood furniture rested just where it had when she was fifteen, the mirror over her dresser reflecting a large canopy bed standing near the windows. Mae sat on the quilted coverlet, running her hand gently over faded peach roses. "Mother." It came out hollow, forlorn like the rain falling outside.

"I knew you'd come, Ella Mae. I know *you*." As she spoke she never turned, never once looked up from the complicated, colorful mass of yarn she clutched in her lap.

"How did you know I was here? Who told you?"

She rocked slowly, the old chair squeaking loudly in the otherwise silent room. "I'm your momma, Ella Mae. You mean to tell me you really believed you'd be able to sneak back into town without me knowing anything of it?" She laughed hoarsely, the sound light, papery, floating effortlessly out the window to the earth below.

Mae cleared her throat. "I didn't come all this way to bother you. I came only to tell you I'm home for good, and I'm laying claim to what's mine. That's all I want—for you to stop all this talk about lawyers and property and leave me in peace. You know full well I'm the legal and rightful owner of Bella Bloom. You knew Granna intended to leave it to me well before she passed—"

"Your grandmother was just a feeble minded old bitch, Ella Mae, and I hope she's burnin' in the pit of some godless hell right now," the old woman spat, rocking faster. "She was never good to my Jonas. When he needed his momma the most, she just abandoned him like trash on the side of the road—"

"Stop it!" Mae screamed at the back of the chair. "I'm not gonna let you sit here and tarnish her memory like that. She was a good woman. Once she even came to your daughter's rescue when her own momma could care less…"

"Oh, how the facts become jumbled over the years, Mae," the woman hissed, clicking the needles together furiously as she worked. "You think you know everything. Always did. Well you didn't know my Jonas. He was a beautiful man, good and kind. He took care of me, gave me things I'd only dreamed of having: a beautiful home filled with nice things, the laughter of children running and playing in the yard…for a time, we were so happy…" the rocking slowed, nearly stopped. Rain blew through the window on a light breeze, small droplets of water landing on her mother's hands. So fine, so delicate. Nothing like her father's hands…

"But *you*." The chair started again with a vengeance, the rockers grinding against the polished hardwood so violently Mae wondered if they'd leave permanent grooves in the floor. "*You* took my Jonas. You ruined everything with your lies, the vile filth spewing from your dirty little mouth. How dare you speak of my husband, your own daddy, that way? And then leaving my household in chaos to go run off and live with that bitch of a grandmother. Your whore's lies put him in an early grave—"

Despite the oxygen tank, Mae flew off the bed and gripped the rocker with both hands, shaking it furiously. "You're the liar, you know that! You're nothing but a selfish, heartless…" she drew a sharp breath and bit down hard on her lower lip, trying to stop the dam from breaking, stop the waiting flood of insults and accusations from spilling over into the frigid room. "I didn't come to stir all this up again, Mother," she began again in a whisper, an eerie calm settling over her. "I just came to tell you I am *home*, and you are not going to run me away again. Bella Bloom is mine, and no matter who you try to manipulate or how much money you're willing to pay, there ain't a damn thing you can do to change that. It's in *ink,* Mother, whether you like it or not, so you can take your precious money and your fancy lawyer and go straight to…"

"That house belonged to her son, her only son, and now it rightfully belongs to me!" she screeched in a shrill voice, her arthritic hands reaching up to pry Mae's fingers from the chair. "I was planning to burn the cursed thing to the ground first thing after she died! It was a den of whores, what with her shacking up with that hired man while her husband wasn't even close to cold in the ground. I hope she's sitting on the devil's lap right now, frying like catfish in a skillet where she belongs. It's where all you whores belong! She may have slighted your daddy and me with that will o' hers, but I'm not the kind of woman who just lies there with a pretty smile while someone's rakin' shit in my face." She paused to turn a dial on the canister, adjust the tubes in her nose, and inhale deeply a couple of times before she continued.

"The Good Book teaches us you reap what you sow, Mae. I've lived sixty-seven years by that principle. Taught you and Merribelle that from when you were barely old enough to grab onto my apron strings. Just know yours is comin', though. You can't escape your sins, even in death. That way we all get our justice in the end, don't we?" she laughed her papery laugh again, reaching for another thread. The needles worked quietly again. Humming a cheerful tune under her breath, she continued rocking and knitting as if Mae had simply evaporated into the damp air.

"Mother, look at me," Mae said after a moment as she reached over the back of the rocker, resting a hesitant hand on her frail shoulder. The bone and skin beneath the sweater felt insubstantial under her touch, and Mae was careful not to squeeze for fear she'd simply crumble in her hands and blow away. Tears blurred her vision and landed on her mother's feathery hair, now dusted with gray, small patches of chocolate scalp peeking through. "Please."

The older woman sighed, clearly shaken. She looked up, apparently staring out the window at nothing as mists from the falling rain landed in her lap, turning her knitting into a soggy lump of thread. Mae followed her gaze. One of the panes of glass reflected the women, framed them as if in portrait. Their eyes met. Her mother's still retained their almond shape; light brown beacons in a sea of dull skin. The full mouth had slackened with time, the lips now pinched and bloodless. Hatred had ruined her, shriveled her the way grapes shrivel away in the relentless glare of the sun. Mae slowly realized any lingering hope she carried of reconciliation was lost. Years of turmoil and separation had created a rift so large it could never be repaired.

Mae released her shoulders, swiping tears away roughly with the back of her hand. With a final mournful glance at the glass, she turned and headed for the door.

She was nearly there when her mother spoke again. "You have a daughter." The words were whispered, yet traveled easily over the room and swept over Mae with such force she halted in mid-step. She turned around slowly, watching her mother nervously from across the room. The rocker. It began moving again, the rhythmic squeaking echoing in her ears. It would drive her crazy if she didn't leave soon. "She's almost seven, yes?"

"How did you know about her?"

She laughed again. "You really think there's any place on this earth you can go where I won't find you, Ella Mae? Your sister said you mentioned something about Philadelphia when you left, though she refused to tell me much else. I had some friends of mine that owed me favors digging in that city a good while before they struck gold, and sure enough, there you were. Been keeping a close watch over you and yours ever since." More squeaking, followed by the clicking of needles. "You sure married well. A police detective, no less. Well, Momma must have taught you somethin' about this life after all."

Mae sighed. "I'm going now, Mother."

"I want to see that girl at least once before I—"

"*Absolutely not!*" Mae shot back, a tone of warning in her voice. She chanced a few steps in her direction. "You may have found reason to punish me most of my life, Mother, but there's no way in hell I'm going to let you take it out on my child. She's innocent; she deserves none of this." She walked back to the door and clutched the brass knob, the metal icy to the touch.

"I don't think—is it Richard? Yes, I don't think Richard would appreciate you taking his child so far from home to claim a life he probably knows nothing about, Ella Mae. He and I have common ground, you see. He knows what it's like to have something precious snatched away by someone they made the fool mistake of trusting. Yes Lord up above, I imagine he's plumb out of his mind with worry 'bout now."

The old woman sighed, staring out the window. "When I found out you'd finally dragged your filthy tail back down this way and was set on turning my *rightful* property into a whore's den all over again, I couldn't wait to set to making things straight between you and me, once and for all. I'd been so good, I'd waited such a long time…" she clasped her hands to her breast and shook her head, beaming with delight. "It felt like God Himself plucked you from your little dung heap like a roach and placed you right in the palm of my hands. I had a mind to call those big city men and watch them take you back up there and have you promptly thrown *under* the jail…but I reminded myself that patience is a virtue, that I had much more satisfying ways at my disposal to deal with you…"

Mae thought of the blood on the altar again, trembling. She raised a shaky finger and aimed it squarely at the back of her mother's head.

"You stay the hell out of my business. If I find you've been up to anything, I'm coming back here." She wrenched open the door and stepped into the hall.

"Ella Mae?" the voice was gentle, soothing to her ears as it was once in childhood. Chills slid down her spine. She refused to turn around this time, afraid of what might be waiting.

"The Good Book also says 'an eye for an eye,' you know. I'd been out shopping that day. Called him to come help me with my packages as usual…but he never answered, never came outside. I searched this whole house until I finally found him in your tub, soaking in his own blood. He'd lain there with his wrists filleted open like that for hours.

"I climbed in there with him. I could think of nothin' else. I just wanted to be with him right then, to let him know I still loved him, still believed in him though he'd given up, stopped believing in himself…" her voice quavered. She wiped her face with a handkerchief she produced from her sweater pocket. "As he'd lain there dying, he'd written 'Forgive Me" on the mirror in some of his blood. I wiped it all off with the hem of my dress, the brand new dress he'd brought home to me only the day before, and just held him, sat with him in all that blood 'til they finally pulled me away. They said I was screaming, but I don't really remember that part." The knitting slid off her lap, the forgotten needles clanging loudly against the bare floor. "I don't think I've ever stopped crying, even with the passing of time. Grief and sorrow follow me wherever I go. But I'll tell you something, Ella Mae. I still get on these old weak knees every night and pray for only one thing—that I live to pluck your eye out as you've plucked mine. Then I can rest. Yes, *then* I can sleep through the night again."

Only the sound of falling rain greeted the woman in the silence; Mae had already fled down the hall, swallowing a scream.

"Cina, where are you? I brought you guys some leftover lemon pie from dinner tonight." Merribelle slammed the door against the driving rain, nearly slipping in a small puddle in the entry. "Dammit! *Cina, where the hell are you?*"

She shrugged out of the heavy trench coat, letting it fall at her feet. She kicked off her suede heels impatiently, scowling as she watched them slide across the entry into the parlor. Two-hundred-seventy-five dollars, now waterlogged and completely ruined. Tim had warned her not to wear them out in the rain. He'd trumpet he was right yet again…

She shook her head. Timothy. Handsome, hardworking, and completely self-absorbed, an air of arrogance trailing behind his every step like colorful plumes behind a peacock. A fair husband, a good father, but an excellent businessman. Always traveling, opening new divisions of his parent company all over the world, Tim was usually much better at making money than making love. Or taking vacations with her and the children. Or even getting home before nine on most nights. But today he'd surprised her by taking the afternoon off. How she'd enjoyed their midday tryst, his hands on her body as he pressed her against the kitchen counter, pulling her down to the floor with him. Cold linoleum against warm flesh. More than makes up for the mistake with the flight attendant in Switzerland last winter…

She was making her way into the kitchen when she heard scuffling sounds from upstairs. "Get out of my way! Lady, I don't know who the hell you think you are, but I'm warning you; don't start what you don't want me to finish!"

Setting the pie on a counter, she raced back to the entry and froze. She could see Cina on the landing, struggling in the dim light with a woman wearing a red slicker. Wet hair hanging in her face obscured most of her features, but even from a distance Merribelle saw her eyes come ablaze as she pried the older woman's plump fingers off her arm. "You keep your hands off me!"

"What the hell's goin' on here, Cina?" she shouted from below. "Who let her in here? Must be another one o' them junkies from outside town. I tell you, when will these people ever learn…" she raced into the parlor and snatched the cordless phone from the cradle before jogging back to the stairs. "I'll get the sheriff over here. How's Momma? She didn't hurt her, did she?"

Mae pushed Cina away, stomping down the stairs toward her. "Your momma's just fine, Merribelle. I wouldn't dare touch her. She's hardly worth it anymore."

As she got close, Merribelle looked her full in the face and dropped the phone, eyes widening. "Oh my God...Ella Mae?"

"How could you do this to me, Merri?" Her eyes continued to blaze anger, floods of wrath seeming to devour her where she stood. "You know full well Granna left that house to me. You saw the papers yourself!"

"I...I didn't..." she stammered, taking an awkward step toward her. "Mae, I had nothing to do with this, you gotta believe me!"

Mae waved her off, shaking her head bitterly. "Just get out of the way. I've already said my piece. It's over, I'm done here." She shoved past her sister, heading for the door.

Merribelle reached out for her, grabbing her shoulder as she walked by. "Mae, wait! Don't go just yet, 'least not before we've had a chance to talk." She racked her tired brain for something, anything to get her to stay. "There's lemon pie in the kitchen. I just brought it from home. I baked it myself. Your favorite, remember?"

Mae gawked at her sister, staring up at her in disbelief. "Keep...your pie, Merri," she said finally. "You know, coming here tonight really confirmed it for me, even though I believed I'd washed my hands of you and that witch upstairs a long time ago. But I'm back now and putting down roots, so I strongly suggest both of you stay the hell away from me and my house for good, you got that?" She snatched her arm free of her sister's grasp, yanked the door open and slipped into the darkness without another word.

She thought she was drowning. Sheets of rain poured in her face. Water landed in her open mouth, slid down her throat and choked her with each gasp for air. She could see the Caddie at the bottom of the hill, and she ran even faster, ran even though she felt her muscles weakening, her body breaking under the weight of emotion. *Just get home to Lily,* she thought, panting.

She slipped just as she reached the bottom, sliding on a river of mud and white gravel until she slammed into the chrome grille. She struggled to her feet, numb fingers fumbling in her pocket for the keys. Finally, they brushed against the cold metal, and she tore them from the slicker pocket. She jammed them into the lock, yanking the door open and hurling herself inside.

Safe in the warm interior, she collapsed on the plush seats, covering her face with trembling hands. Fighting the urge to scream again, she sunk her teeth deep into her lower lip, biting down until it bled. Her chest heaved, her heart ached, and her mother's face swelled up to meet her in the darkness of her mind. The face of a corpse, pale and dead except for those eyes, alive and burning with hatred for the daughter that had robbed her of happiness, and something else—hope? Hope she would someday suffer enough, grieve enough, to atone for sins she'd never committed...

"It wasn't my fault! I was just a little girl!" she sobbed, leaning against the steering wheel. The anguish her mother had long prayed for slowly began to coil itself around her like a snake, and she screamed then, twelve years of pent-up sorrow pushing all thoughts of Lily and Bella Bloom out of reach. She beat her fists against the wheel, beat them until welts swelled on the skin and the bones beneath felt as if they would crack.

Finally spent of emotion, she leaned her head against the seat and listened to the rain falling around her. How she wished she'd drowned out there, wished the darkness had simply swallowed her up as if she'd never been...

"No." She sat up, turning the key in the ignition. "Can't do this to yourself, Mae. You've got to get home to Lily."

The engine roared to life, and she shifted into reverse. As she was backing into the street, a pair of hands appeared on the windshield, startling her.

"Stop the car, Mae, please! Let me explain!" Merribelle stood at the window, soaked through and shivering. Her expensive suit and trench coat looked completely ruined in the pouring rain. Mae shook her head vehemently, inching the car toward the road. Merribelle disappeared into the shadows again, and Mae thought she'd returned to the house until the passenger door opened and her sister jumped inside.

Mae brought the car to a halt. "Get out!"

"Not until you let me help you." She reached for her seatbelt, locking herself in place.

"Look, I'm not talking to either of you about this anymore, okay? All the time I'm away there's no problem, but when you find out I'm in the house all of a sudden it's time to drag me to court over it. Now you chase me out here in the dark and jump into a moving car, for what? What the hell are you trying to prove? I would have expected mother to do something shady like this, but you, Merri? We've never had issues growing up, and yet you want to punish me anyway." Mae leaned over her, opening the passenger door. "Get out, Merri. You're ruining the seats."

Merribelle quickly closed the door again. "I didn't have any part in this, Ella Mae, it was all Momma's doing. The whole time she's been doing all these underhanded dealings right under my nose. I didn't even find out about the lawyer myself until this afternoon. I came over tonight to let her know I'd gotten my *own* lawyers on the job, that they were preparing to squash her petition flat before it ever made it to a courtroom. When I saw you coming down those stairs, I was so happy to see you, I just..." She placed a hand gently on the steering wheel, covering her sister's with her own.

"Momma's been ill a while now," she continued. "If worse comes to worse, and she tries to keep this land battle locked up in litigation even after her passing, you know I'd be willing to testify on your behalf. I'd tell them the truth, I'd tell them how Grandma Lily intended for you to be the sole inheritor of Bella Bloom all along, that, even on her deathbed, she took legal action to make sure her wishes were carried out."

Mae pulled away from her touch, reaching for her own seatbelt. Undeterred, she went on. "You need someone on your side right now, Mae. I'm just trying to help in any way I can, if you'll let me. I know you're runnin' from something. I know something's got a hold on you besides this thing with the house, and it's scaring you pretty bad. With Grandma Lily long gone off the scene, you'd never have come back here unless you were in some kind of trouble."

"Trouble?" Mae laughed in spite of herself. "I haven't robbed any banks or shot anyone lately, Merribelle."

"You know what I mean. If you picked up and brought your baby all this way, it can only be because you don't want to be found by someone who's lookin' for you, right? The one you married in Philadelphia, that detective. Momma hired folks and found out where you were. She told me all about him—"

"Keep sniffing around the wrong pile long enough and you usually get your nose rubbed in it, Merri. Stay out of this. It's none of your concern."

Merribelle turned in her seat, stared at her long time. "If you really are running from him," she whispered, "I know people who can help. Women, good women who believe keepin' a secret like this is a matter of life and death. 'Cause if he finds you, Ella Mae, it could be bad."

Mae raised her hands to her throbbing temples. "Please, please don't patronize me. I've had a hell of a day, and ain't a cigarette in sight. I am well aware of what'll go down if my *loving* husband ever finds Lily and me."

"Well then, you also know you can't just stroll boldly around town like this." She tugged on a strand of Mae's hair, plucked at her slicker. "Your picture is probably plastered on the front of every major paper in the country by now. Even in this backwater, people from big places like N'Orleans and Metairie'll spot you soon as you step out the door in proper daylight. If he's looking, he won't stop until he finds you, Mae.

I know people who've been down this road. Men like that never give up. Long as you've got what's his, you'll never be out of his head—"

"She's mine!" Mae blurted, tears welling in her eyes again. "Not his, she never was his. He never really loved us. She's mine, and if it's any of your damn business at all, I'm doing this to protect her from him."

Merribelle laid a hand on her shoulder. "Then if you want half a shot at giving her a normal life, you'd better put this car in gear and drive where I tell you."

"Why on earth should I believe anything that falls out your mouth tonight, Merri?"

She sighed, shifting uncomfortably on the seat. "You've got to be kidding me. I've got wet undies and a brand-new Chanel plastered to my ass, and you think I'm supposed to find all this amusing? Drive."

SIX

"Thanks, Serena, we'll be at your door in ten." Merribelle snapped the cell phone shut and dropped it in the pocket of her trench coat. She glanced over at her younger sister, who was nervously gripping the wheel as she drove. "Ready?"

"Guess I'll have to be," Mae muttered, turning a corner. "We're almost there, right? I'm running out of houses."

"Yeah, it's about a mile down this road. Just keep straight and you'll see it. Big white farmhouse on the right."

They drove on in silence, the heavy downpour fading to a light drizzle though the night was still black, the moon shrouded in a thin veil of cloud.

"So what's she like, your baby girl?" Merribelle asked lightly, a half-hearted attempt to diffuse some of the electric tension building in the confined space. She brushed a strand of dark brown hair out of her eyes. The rest of it lay in a limp mess plastered against her forehead, another seventy-dollar updo down the drain. Her carefully applied makeup was gone, and she continuously rubbed a finger over her bare lips, wishing again and again she'd had the presence of mind to bring her cosmetic bag along in her haste.

"Brilliant, soulful, passionate and full of energy," Mae answered, slowing as the house came into view. "She inherited my looks and intellect, his temper. Oh, if she got anything from him that brings me regret, it's that temper."

She pulled into an oil-stained driveway, small cracks in the cement punctuated by weeds struggling for survival. They got out and headed up a small walkway. As they approached the porch, lamps came on inside. Before they could knock, the door opened and a petite brunette woman in black shorts stood before them. She donned a matching black T-shirt bearing the catchy equation:

GIRL

+ No

- Fear

= POWER

Her frizzy hair was tied back with a crimson bandana. Socks and a pair of black bunny slippers hugged her feet, eyes rolling madly in their sockets with every movement.

"Come in, ladies, please." She ushered them into the dim interior. The room was spacious and open, furnished with sofas and chairs covered in deep shades of burgundy and brown. Tranquil autumn landscapes adorned the walls, and potted plants grew in proliferation in every corner. Smooth jazz drifted up from small speakers on the floor, and cones of incense burned fragrantly on a small ottoman doubling as a coffee table.

Beyond the seating area a group of young women sat together at a kitchen table, chatting amiably. They looked up, offering polite smiles as Mae and Merri entered. Bunny Slippers gestured to them. "These women walked in your shoes once upon a time, Ella Mae. Say hello to Genevieve, Alyssa, April and Karen. Ladies, this is Ella Mae and…well, you all know Merri."

The women nodded at each other. A tall blonde in a No. 14 jersey and pigtails who couldn't have been more than eighteen spoke first. "Oh, Merri, we've missed you!" she said cheerily, leaving the table to throw her arms around her. "Sure been a while since you stopped in to see us." She turned and gave Mae a radiant smile, extending her hand. "It's good to finally meet you, Ella Mae, though we feel we practically know you already. We have local and national papers delivered here daily, and it seems that pretty face o' yours is always on at least one of 'em. You know, that police detective husband o' yours just put a big reward out on you and your little girl—"

"Maybe you can tell her about it another time, Genny," Bunny Slippers interrupted gently, clearing her throat. "How was group tonight?"

The girl's face lit up, and she nodded eagerly, pigtails bouncing as if they were attached to springs. "Gee, Serena, it was wonderful. It went really well."

"The ladies are downstairs watching a flick in the rec room." This came from a pretty Asian woman dressed in a lavender plaid shirt and jeans. A pair of wire-rimmed spectacles rested on her head, holding her short dark hair out of her eyes. Mae glanced at her ID badge. Karen Nakagawa, Peer Counselor I.

She also stood and held her hand out. "Good to see you again, Merri. Ella Mae, we'd formally like to welcome you to Victory House. Please make yourself comfortable, and don't worry—confidentiality is gospel here. Without it, the lives of the women seeking refuge under this roof are at greater risk than if they decided to go it alone."

Mae stared at them. "You're all counselors? So I'm standing in the middle of some kind of shelter or halfway house—"

"We're a little of both, Ella Mae," Alyssa interjected, getting up to head for an industrial-sized refrigerator in a corner of the room. A beautiful Latina in sweats and a lemon-colored tank top, her long copper-colored hair sat knotted in a tight bun at the nape of her neck. "We take women in who've had the courage to flee abusive and threatening relationships, give them new identities. Our goal is to try to bring a sense of healing to an otherwise broken existence, make sure they're capable of adapting to a life apart from cruelty in order to live healthy again, much as you've already done." She held the fridge door open wide, peering inside. "Like something to drink? These thunderstorms can sure wipe all the energy out of you."

Mae shook her head, glancing at her sister uncertainly. "No thanks, I'm fine."

An older lady at the table glanced up from a page of handwritten notes she'd been pouring over. "Then I guess it's time we get started." Obviously the leader of the group, she was elegantly dressed in a plain white sweater and navy slacks, her salt and pepper hair artfully arranged around a pretty oval face. "Judging by the unusual circumstances, Ella Mae, it appears we've definitely got our work cut out for us. After all, making the wife of a law enforcement official disappear for good certainly isn't the easiest task we've undertaken. While we waited on you and Merri to arrive, I went on and gathered what info I could, just a few basics." She consulted her notepad. "Originally resided in Philadelphia PA, employment lists producer at a local TV network, hitched eight years to homicide detective Richard Spencer..." she flipped a page. "Minor is daughter Lily Spencer, aged six..." she glanced up at Mae, frowning. "And just where *is* Lily at the moment?"

"She's with a friend of mine, a good friend."

"You trust this 'good friend?'" she asked pointedly, leaning forward.

Mae met her gaze over the table. "With our lives."

April smiled briefly and fell back in the chair, visibly relaxing. She looked around at the group of women, clapping her hands together loudly. "All right, ladies, let's do what we do best."

Serena led the way down a flight of stairs to a locked basement area in the rear of the house. When she opened the door and flipped the lights, Mae was amazed to see several computers, printers and scanners on a large desk lining one wall; a photocopier, laminate machine and two tripod cameras aimed at blue background screens lined the other. Genny and Karen immediately sat down at two of the consoles and began to type furiously while Serena adjusted the cameras. April picked up a ream of printouts and settled in to read.

"So what's the deal with that one," Mae whispered to her sister as they passed the older woman.

"April?" Merribelle shrugged. "An old friend of mine. Real intense, I know, but she's definitely got reason for it. Lost her niece to some psycho boyfriend after a really bad scuffle. She tried to leave in the heat of the moment, but he sliced her throat, and then hung himself. She was expecting their first child at the time."

"How horrible." Mae grimaced, glancing at the woman calmly sipping coffee across the room, methodically examining one page of data after another.

Merribelle nodded. "Took out a second mortgage on her home to get Victory off the ground. Serena and the rest came along when she was still running the place single-handedly as a temporary shelter. After they spent some time getting themselves together, they returned and joined her staff as peer counselors. April saw the need for victim re-identification from afar, so she specifically selected and trained each of them according to their individual talents."

Alyssa gestured for the women to follow her into an adjoining room. A large barber chair stood in the center, a mirror and washbasin resembling the kind in hair salons mounted behind it. Bottles and bottles of hair products lined an overhead shelf. Alyssa patted the chair. "No need to worry, Ella Mae. I used to own a salon in Albuquerque until my husband came in one day and beat the living hell out of me in front of my customers. Said it was because his best friend *Ramon* saw me flirting with one of my patrons. Unbelievable. I never even looked at another man in the ten years we were together—I was too afraid he'd kill us both."

Mae shrugged off the red slicker and handed it to Merribelle, taking a seat in the chair. Alyssa pulled the rubber band out of her damp hair, letting her hair fall freely at her shoulders. She ran her hands through it. "*Muy bueno. Tal pelo encantador, Ella Mae!* Such lovely hair, flowing down in thick curls. What would you have me do with it?"

"Cut it all off," she replied without hesitation.

"What!" the women cried in unison.

"Mae, don't be silly…" Merribelle began.

"Ella Mae, you have beautiful hair," Alyssa said gently as their eyes met, hers reflecting a touch of concern. "I would hate to cut it all off, only to have you cry later in regret. We can try trimming it a little, change the color, the style. No matter what we do with the hair, you will still resemble the picture in the papers. After all, it is your own face the camera has photographed. Even a major haircut will never be as good as plastic surgery—"

Mae slapped her leg in frustration. "Look guys, if I'm truly on page one of every major paper in the country right now, I have to do something to live without constant fear of recognition weighing me down. You've gotta understand, I've come all this way…I picked up one day and abandoned a life I'd struggled for years to build—my home, gone. My career, over. My friends, my interests…but don't you see? I don't mind losing all that, as long as he can't hurt Lily again. You said it yourself, Merri. That kind of man won't stop looking for us, ever. Because he didn't really believe I'd have the balls to do it, or maybe just because we got away. I'm a fugitive as we speak, and good as dead if he catches up to us, so please don't question my judgment when it comes to my daughter's safety." She laid a gentle hand on the Latina's arm. "Make life a little easier on us, Alyssa. Pick up the scissors and cut."

Alyssa nodded and tilted her head into the basin, reaching for a bottle of shampoo. "All right, Ella Mae. The call is yours. Now you just close your eyes and relax a minute while I wash the rain out…"

For the next hour, Merribelle watched as Alyssa skillfully clipped her sister's curls, watched them fall like black rain to the floor in a feathery pile. Halfway through, she excused herself. "Be back in a minute, Mae. I've got to talk to Serena about something." Twenty minutes later, when Alyssa had combed, cut and dyed to her satisfaction, she stepped back in triumph, eyeing Mae carefully.

Merribelle walked back into the room and gasped, covering her mouth with her hands. Mae sat ramrod-straight in the chair, shades of apprehension clouding her features. She reached up, gently feeling the back of her head. "What's wrong, Merri? What do I look like?"

Merribelle shook her head slowly, hands still covering her mouth. "Merri!" she cried in exasperation. "Don't just stand there! How does it look?"

Merribelle smiled and grabbed a small hand mirror off the shelf, holding it in front of her face. "See for yourself."

Alyssa walked over and opened a drawer, pulling out a small box. She held it under her arm while she walked back to the barber chair, setting it atop Mae's lap. Opening the lid, she reached for a pair of silver wire rims not unlike the kind Karen wore and handed them to her. "But before you put those on…" she said, rifling through the box until she found what she'd been looking for, a tiny white plastic container. "Put *these* in." Mae opened the box and stared down at a pair of colored contact lenses.

Alyssa folded her arms over the stretchy lemon fabric covering her bosom, giving her a playful wink. "Don't worry, they aren't prescription. The glasses aren't, either. They just help the illusion along."

Mae turned to face a small rectangular mirror mounted on a wall next to her, carefully balancing the container on one leg as she worked to insert the delicate lens onto her eye.

"All righty everybody! *La transformacíon es completa! Mire sobre mi obra maestra!*" Alyssa trumpeted loudly when she re-entered the main room. "Feast your eyes upon my masterpiece!"

She gestured dramatically toward the door as Mae emerged. The wire rims fit snugly, illuminating the hazel contacts she wore. The dark curls hanging past her shoulders had been cut into chestnut waves framing her face in a short bob, the hair just long enough to tickle her earlobes. Mae draped the rain slicker over her arm, looking around the room nervously. "Well?"

Serena grinned, grabbing her hand and leading her toward the tripods. "You're a new woman, Ella Mae. I tell ya, Alyssa's just a magician when it comes to color and clippers. A snip here, a dollop there…" she positioned her in the center of the blue background and focused the camera. "Now don't move. This'll only take a second." She snapped a couple of photos, then removed the camera from the tripod. She walked over and handed it to Karen, still busily typing away at the console. "Have a seat, ladies," she said, gesturing to a couple of folding chairs on the far side of the room. The two of them followed her over and sat down. She grabbed a third chair from an empty console and sat facing them.

"We have ourselves a bit of problem here, Ella Mae. According to Merri, the FBI has already been in Beau Ciel looking for you. She tells me they've paid a visit to her house, and your mother's as well."

"They *what?*" Mae glared at her sister. "Why on earth would you fail to tell me something like that? Do you *want* to see me go down in flames? Is that what this whole thing has been about all along?" She rose from the chair, turning to leave.

Merribelle grabbed her arm. "It's not even like that, Mae. I knew you were on the edge about Momma and this whole house thing already. I didn't want you to get scared off by her *or* them and run away from me again, 'least not before I had a chance to get you some help."

Mae pulled away from her. "How can I ever trust you, Merri, if you think it's okay to give me the whole truth only when it suits you? Why should I even bother?"

Serena held up her hands. "Ladies, please. We don't have time to argue about this." She turned to Mae. "I know you're upset, Ella Mae, but I truly think it's in your best interest to lay the matter aside for now. Your sister is a caring, warm-hearted person who's helped a lot of women in your situation over the years. By the way she talks about you, I know she loves you dearly. If you can't trust her, you can trust *me* when I say she is only after your good."

Mae stared at the women a moment, then sat down again. "Now, the important thing is getting this situation under control as soon as possible," Serena continued. "Merribelle told me about the problems you and your mother have been having. To be frank, her knowing both your exact location and the fact that the FBI is actively investigating your disappearance can't be good. I'm afraid we're going to have to figure out a solution to this one pretty quick, or you won't be getting very far at all in this, Ella Mae. Your new identity would mean nothing; with just a few words in the right people's ears, she'd manage to destroy everything you've worked so hard to build."

"I can talk to her," Merribelle said. Mae and Serena glanced at her uncertainly. "Don't worry about it," she assured them. "I know Momma can be strong and stubborn as an oak tree when she sets her mind on something, but I've got my ways of making her bend."

"Then you'd better talk to her soon," Serena replied. "Honestly, I can't impress that upon you enough. We're walking dangerous ground here the longer she remains a threat to Mae's cover." She turned to Mae again. "April and I went over your situation in greater detail while you were getting made over, Ella Mae. We just wanted to verify a few things in case an even bigger problem pops up down the line."

"I'll tell you whatever I know," Mae said.

"You left town with only your daughter, and though the authorities suspect you acted alone, you in truth had an accomplice. I assume you've made no contact with this person recently?"

Mae thought of Deborah, shaking her head.

"Good," she continued. "Now because of this, law enforcement officials believe you're holed up somewhere alone with Lily. They're instructing the general public to keep their eyes open for a woman and young girl fitting your descriptions, so naturally any female new to a small town locale automatically becomes suspect, especially if she's traveling light with a little girl.

"Even in a town as tiny as Beau Ciel, the chances of you two being recognized are great. This is problematic, at the very least. If worse comes to worse and the ruse fails to fool anyone, you'll likely be extradited to Philadelphia to face federal kidnapping charges, and your husband can and will immediately take Lily into custody. He'll be free to take her anywhere after that, even out of the country without your consent. That means if you're ever convicted and the child fell into his hands, you'd probably never see her again, and there'd be no law to protect your interest in the matter—"

"Yes, Serena, I understand," Mae nodded emphatically, holding her hands up. "I'm aware of all this. What can be done to fix it? We're here now. My hands are tied; packing up and going elsewhere is just too risky."

Serena rocked the chair back on its heels, letting one black bunny slipper dangle aimlessly above the floor. "Well, we've worked out a little plan to try to keep you as far below radar as possible, but it may not be exactly what you want to hear just now. All we ask is that you at least consider the idea."

Mae sighed. "Okay, run it by me then. I'm all ears."

Serena lowered her chair to the floor. "In the best interest of keeping Lily safe, we think it's best she not be seen with you for a while. It'll make it a little less obvious for folks around here to make the connection if you two aren't together on a consistent basis."

"What do you mean?" Mae glanced over at her sister, fear rising in her voice. "Don't be silly, Serena. Of course she'll be seen with me, she's my daughter. She goes where I go."

"Which is exactly why the authorities would be tipped off that much faster, Ella Mae. You come to a backwater like this, do your daily business in plain view, and it's a given someone somewhere'll take one good look at the two of you and call up the law. That's all it'd take to completely blow your cover, if your mother doesn't get to it first. Worst-case scenario has you opening the door to feds with guns coming to take Lily away, straight to her father. You wouldn't even have the chance to get her someplace safe."

She gestured to the women working diligently in the room. "Is all this for nothing? When you left Philadelphia with Lily, you abandoned your life. In a few minutes, Ella Mae Spencer will no longer exist. Your identity will be gone, totally erased. You have nothing to go back to now except a lengthy prison sentence, which would be the least of your worries, considering what will happen to Lily if she goes back to her father."

"Then what exactly are you suggesting, Serena? If you say I brought my little girl all this way just to be separated from her, where the hell is she supposed to go? Who's gonna care for her if I can't even go near my own child?"

Serena nodded at Merribelle, smiling gently. "Who better than your own blood, Ella Mae?"

"Hand me one of those, Merri. I think I've earned it under the circumstances."

Merribelle nodded, fishing another cigarette out of the pack. She held a gold plated lighter up as Mae lit it and inhaled deeply, tiny flames dancing in the wire-rimmed reflection.

"It'd only be for a little while, Mae. Relax."

Mae blew the smoke out in a vaporous cloud. "You're telling me to relax while I go home and tell my kid she won't be seeing momma for just a *little while?* Come on, Merri. I don't know about your kids, but mine has never been away from my side longer than a few hours since the day she was born. *I* look out for her, *I* decide what she eats, what she wears, how her hair is done…that's what moms do, and I'm a damn good one. How am I supposed to get through this without her?" She paced the length of the porch as she spoke, sucking on the cigarette and flicking ashes as she went.

"Mae, you heard Serena. Keep Lily with you, and you risk losing everything, your daughter, your freedom…" Merribelle gazed out at the vast backyard, watching the trees sway gently on the autumn breeze. "You're in it so deep right now, right up to your damn eyeballs. We don't have time to sit on our thumbs and spin. You can bring Lily over to the house this weekend. I'll prepare the bedroom across from Kyra's. They're so close in age, and she'd love the company. She constantly complains about being the only girl, what with Ben and Isaiah always giving her trouble…" Merribelle chuckled, pausing to drag deeply on her own cigarette. "She's asked Tim and I for a little sister the past three Christmases in a row. I tell you, that girl is something else."

"Can we please not discuss this now, Merri? I've had enough for one day." Mae tossed her cigarette into the damp grass, watching the embers fade and disappear.

Merribelle took a couple of steps closer to her sister. "What happened at the house tonight, Mae?" she asked, voice suddenly low. "Why were you so upset with Momma?"

"Please, Merri…" Mae hesitated, rubbing her eyes with the back of her hand. In the dim light streaming through the windows, Merribelle saw she'd been crying a while; her eyes were puffy and blinked furiously as they struggled to adjust to the contacts. "If you really care anything for me at all, you won't ask me about that…about *her*."

She laid a tentative hand on her sister's back. "Mae, tell me. What's going on between the two of you? I ask her all the time, but she just keeps saying it's bad blood, no need for me to worry about it. I've always wondered what happened—why you moved in with Grandma Lily after you turned fifteen, why Momma wouldn't even allow me to speak your name around her after you left…I was in the dark, even then."

"Merri, don't do this now—"

"I know there's only three years between us, but I guess at that age three years can feel like a lifetime. You never came to the house; I always had to sneak and visit you at Grandma's, then lie to Momma about it so she wouldn't fly off the handle. I was a grown woman by then, it just seemed so strange. And Daddy just acted like everything was peachy cream, though I knew it bothered him deep down…" Suddenly, the shoulder beneath her hand tightened. "Mae? What is it? Is it Daddy? Oh, honey, I know his suicide was hell on us all, especially Momma. She was a wreck afterwards—don't think she ever recovered, really. And then losing Grandma Lily…" her words trailed into silence as she took a final drag off the cigarette, crushing it underfoot.

"Actually, that was doubly shocking. I remember I had another year to go in college, and you'd just turned eighteen. When Grandma passed, I rushed home for the funeral, and was bowled over when you told me you were heading to Philadelphia for college a quarter early. The day of the funeral, your suitcases were already waiting by Grandma's front door. I just assumed you'd be staying on with Momma, since she had that big house all to herself…I could tell she was going a lil' bonkers by then, and she could have used the company."

"Look, Merribelle," Mae whispered, shrugging away from her touch. She stood shivering at the foot of the porch, clutching the red slicker around her as if fending off a sudden chill. "That was a long time ago. They offered me the chance to start school in the summer. I wanted to get a jump on my studies, what was the harm in that? You yourself chose to attend college on the *West Coast* after all. Didn't see anything wrong with leaving the homestead then, did you?"

"Come on, Mae, you know that's not what I meant." Merribelle was next to her again. "I didn't mean to put the burden on your shoulders, really. This town was nothing more than a watering hole back then. Leaving for school was the only way I knew to finally part with those childhood demons, you know what I mean."

Mae snorted, digging her heel into the floorboard. "You don't know the half of it, Merri."

"Then tell me."

"No! Just leave it be!" Mae tore away from her grasp. "What's done is done, Merribelle. No use dragging up the past. It belongs with the dead, and the dead are always best left undisturbed. I know coming back into your life so suddenly must have been disturbing enough, and I'm thankful for your willingness to take my child into your home. But if I agree to this arrangement, it's gonna be on my terms, okay?"

Merribelle shrugged. "Of course. I know we've got a lot left to discuss. You'll remember I have to go home and tell my own children that a cousin they've never even met is coming to live with us. But if we follow the plan to the letter, I believe everything'll work out just fine. I'll tell anyone who asks that Lily's my newest foster child. Tim and I have done this kind of thing before, and the kids have always referred to their foster brothers and sisters as 'cousins,' so they'll adjust to the change quickly. All in all, it wouldn't arouse suspicion around town for us to suddenly have another child living in our home. She'll go to school in town with the kids at Sacred Shield—"

"Huh-unh," Mae interrupted, shaking her head. "Sounds way out of my price range. I can't afford to send Lily to private school right now. We don't even have furniture yet. We're sleeping on an old fold-out couch in the main room and sitting on mismatched dining room chairs. I've only got enough funds to keep us afloat 'til I find a steady job. Aren't there any decent public schools around here?"

"Don't worry about it, Mae. We'll pay Lily's tuition, and provide anything else she needs while she's with us. She's my niece, for goodness sake; I'd never let her go lacking. And as for your job search…the school administrator and my husband have a regular Wednesday tee-time. Word around is he's looking to hire a new receptionist."

"Did you not hear the part about me being broke, Merribelle? I have to support myself and a six-year-old in a big old house that could use some help, and you think a receptionist's salary's gonna do it?"

"I should interject and add that staff at Sacred Shield are very well compensated. They're a small school, but they're funded by big money. Besides, pay is only part of the package, Mae. Think about it. You'd see Lily all the time. Of course you'll have to keep up pretenses, but it's better than nothing. You're not Ella Mae Spencer anymore, remember? Your college degree, your career accolades…everything from your life before is null and void here. This is your clean slate, Mae, a real second chance…and more than ever, your daughter needs you. It's important for her to know you're still near, even if you can't be with her as much as you'd both like."

Mae nodded, running her hands through her short hair. "Okay. Okay, we can do this. But only on one condition."

"Name it."

"Lily's not to be around our mother at any time. She won't be taken to that house or anywhere near her, you hear me? That woman is poison. I'm surprised all that venom running through her veins hasn't gone on and killed her by now."

"Mae!"

Mae shook her head. "I'll do anything it takes to protect my little girl, Merri. I'm even willing to give her up for a time, let her live with you until things die down, but under no circumstances will that woman have access to my child. If I find you've gone against me, I'll take Lily and bolt. You'll never see either of us again, I can promise you that."

"What on earth has she *done* to you, Ella Mae?" Merribelle cried in exasperation. "For God's sake, please tell me—"

"Hey hey ladies, we can hear you all the way down here." Serena stood in the doorway, smiling warmly as she held the screen open for them. "You two care to put those heated words on ice and come in now? We've got you all squared away, Ella Mae Spencer. Or should I say...Anne Marie Croft?"

"I'll bring her up on Saturday around nine. That good for you?"

Merribelle nodded. They sat parked in front of their mother's home, at the bottom of the drive. The house was silent in the distance, the rooms dark beyond thick shades drawn tightly for the night. Merribelle scribbled directions on a crumpled paper napkin and jumped out of the car. She jogged toward a silver sedan waiting near the top of the hill, throwing a half-hearted wave over her shoulder as she pulled her keys from her pocket. When Mae pulled out of the driveway and into the street, she turned and walked up the steps to the front door. "Time to bend the oak tree," she murmured, sliding a key into the lock.

She closed the door behind her moments later, expecting Cina to suddenly pop out of the parlor or the kitchen, a million questions on her lips. As her eyes began to adjust, they searched the darkness for signs of the heavyset woman. When it was clear no one was waiting to ambush her, she removed her heels for the second time that night and made her way upstairs. She crept past the door to her old bedroom, now the guest room Cina sometimes used when her mother was having one of her "bad spells," those nights when she was too sick to be left alone. Merribelle hesitated in the hallway and leaned in close, listening. A low grumbling sound was coming from behind the closed door, the sound of thick, heavy snoring. Apparently, tonight had turned into a "bad spell" kind of night after all. She moved down the hall to the next door and opened it.

The room was as dark as the rest of the house, save for the few candles burning on the night table. Her mother lay in bed, the silhouette of her sleeping form easily glimpsed in the shifting shadows.

Merribelle closed the door behind her again. Her mother stirred, turned over. "Wh-who's there?" she called feebly, switching the bedside lamp on.

Merribelle glanced at the altar in disgust and immediately looked away, walking over to the bed. "Momma, we need to talk."

Lynne tried to sit up in the bed. "What's the matter, Merribelle? Something wrong with the children?"

Merribelle shook her head. She approached the altar, steeling herself. The sickening smell of honey, rum, and blood filled her nostrils with each step she took closer to the morbid display. She picked up one of the faded photographs. "The children are fine, Momma. I came here to talk about Mae."

The old woman's expression soured, the papery skin around her mouth appearing to fold in on itself. "You mean to tell me you came all this way and disturbed my sleep, all because of that mangy-tailed whore?" She frowned up at her. "What on earth's gotten into you, girl?"

"I also came to tell you my lawyers are drawing up a petition to knock yours in right into the trash, Momma, which is just where it belongs."

"Ah, so *this* is the heart of the matter," she said, sinking back on the pillows. "Would this happen to be about those lovely FBI men showin' up at my door as well?" She smiled contentedly, palsied hands reaching for a bottle of pain medication. "You shouldn't go snooping your nose around things that don't concern you, Merribelle. Thought I taught you better than that."

Merribelle turned away from the altar, walked right up to her again. "Momma," she whispered. She leaned on the bed, planting both hands on either side of the ailing woman. "It's both in your best interest to leave the FBI out of this *and* consider withdrawing that petition right away. As the trustee of your estate, I'd hate to have to take 'adverse action' on your behalf. You may find you're not so pleased with the results."

The old woman peered up at her. "Are you actually *threatening* me?" She barked laughter, fumbling with the top of the prescription bottle. "Why, you're dealing with a master of them! After all the enemies I've conquered to attain my desires, after all I've given and taken freely in this life, what on earth makes you think for a second I'd be concerned about *your* piteous attempts to frighten me?" She shook her head, popped a pill in her mouth. "Shame on you, girl. Shame on you. Go home and get some rest. I know you'll regret this conversation in the morning. You'll come back and apologize, and we'll take our breakfast out in the gazebo, just like always."

"All right, Momma." Merribelle stood up. "We'll do it my way, then, since you're so determined to make things harder on yourself." She flashed her the picture of Jonas she'd been holding and ripped it to pieces, tossing the remnants on the bed like confetti. "This is going to be your whole world from now on, by the time I get through with it."

The old woman's hands flew to her mouth, nearly knocking the oxygen tubes loose from her nose. "Merribelle!" she cried, an expression of pure horror washing over her face. "What are you doing? That's your *father*, for goodness sake! How dare you desecrate his memory like this!" She pointed a trembling finger at the Virgin Mary figurine and the silver rosary. "Go," she breathed. "You pick that up and kneel down before her, you pray for forgiveness right now! I won't tolerate this grievous sin in my house!"

Merribelle left the bed, casually walking up to the altar again. "As trustee of your estate, Momma, you've given me legal power to handle your affairs as I see fit." She picked up another photograph, this one of her father down at the Square, standing proudly in front of his first stained glass shop. "I have the power to place you in an institution, the power to sell this house and your belongings, one by one…" she took the photograph in both hands, preparing to rip it in two. "The power to crush and destroy everything dear to you, even in this very room, if you don't lay off my sister. She walked out of my life twelve years ago, and it nearly killed me. I don't care what happened to cause all this bad blood between you two, I will not stand by and let you take her from me again."

"Please," her mother begged, reaching for the faded photo. "Please don't tear it. I can't, I can't…" she faltered, her hand fluttering to her chest. "I can't live without him…"

Merribelle stood there, fighting back tears. Finally, she sat down on the bed next to her, handed her the photograph. Her mother clasped it to her breast, looking up at her gratefully.

Merribelle reached out, smoothing thinning hair away from her harried face. She took her hand. "Momma, I love you, I'd never want to hurt you. If you keep your place and keep quiet, then I won't have to."

Mae drove up to Bella Bloom, pulling into her own driveway at last. The porch light flicked on immediately, swathing the front lawn with intense white light. She jumped out and slammed the door, hurrying up the front walk as Henry stood there in the doorway, holding the screen open for her. She met his stunned expression with a brief smile, squeezing his hand as she walked past him into the living room. Lily lay sprawled on the red sofa, arms wrapped tightly around her stuffed rabbit. A ribbon of saliva dribbled down her chin as she snored softly.

Mae reached for her daughter, pulling her into her arms. Lily squirmed in her sleep, fussing and fidgeting until her head finally came to rest on her mother's thighs.

"Mmmn, Momma…" she mumbled, drifting off again. Mae ran her hands through the child's thick waves, over her small back and arms, across her tiny hands. Six years, and never a full day apart. The day's strain washed over her, leaving her hopeless and gasping for air through thick ragged sobs. She clutched her child protectively with one hand, holding her heart with the other.

"I…I just don't think I can do this, Henry," she moaned softly as he laid a gentle hand on her arm.

"Hey, hey! Since when has the TV become more riveting than I am?"

Dr. Malcolm Williams sat up quickly, lifting the woman off his hips and tossing her onto the mattress. He grabbed the remote from the nightstand and pressed POWER. The screen flashed and went blank.

"Mac, I was watching that!" Deborah yelled as she climbed over him, straining for the device as he tossed it playfully from hand to hand. They wrestled beneath the sheets until she finally managed to perch herself atop his chest and wrench it away from his grasp. He slowly caressed her thighs, chuckling to himself. "Don't I at least get a kiss before heading to work anymore?"

She slapped his hands away impatiently. "Shhh, this is important!"

The TV came on again in a flurry of sound. This time, the screen showed a group of men standing in front of the police department, some in well-pressed suits and others in jeans and jackets marked FBI. Richard stood in the center answering questions posed by a mob of reporters, microphones bearing various television insignia pushed eagerly in his direction.

"Do you have any leads as to your wife's whereabouts, Detective Spencer?" This came from a young black woman, her raven tresses swept stylishly away from her pretty face.

Richard cleared his throat, looking directly into one of the many news cameras blanketing the area. "As we've pointed out before, the case on my wife is far from cold. We are vigorously pursuing leads as to where she may be keeping our child. Current photos and vitals have been relayed to the public via papers as well as local and national networks, and I believe we are fast approaching a breakthrough.

"This woman poses a danger to herself as well as our child, and yet in the midst of my grief, I cast none too little blame upon myself. I'm her husband, and I would have picked up on signs of her instability sooner had I simply paid more attention." He paused to blink back invisible tears. "I don't believe my wife is a bad person, but I do believe she is in desperate need of help. She needs to be in the care of professionals who can give her the treatment she needs, and my family and I desperately want my daughter back home with us, safe from harm.

"Please America, help if you can. Once again, if you see this woman, please don't hesitate to call local law enforcement or the FBI. Remember, you can remain anonymous…" Pictures of Mae and Lily remained on the screen as he closed up and stepped away from the mics before a Suit & Tie approached to address the group.

Deborah turned off the TV. She was alone in the bed now. Steam drifting from the bathroom told her Malcolm was already showering for work. They were both on duty today, and she crossed her fingers in hopes they'd be off at a reasonable hour. She'd been praying Mae would call every day for the past two months, but so far hadn't heard a thing. She even checked her P.O. box during her lunch breaks, but the box had always been empty, save for the usual junk mail and utility bills. She had to find a way to contact her, see if she was okay…

Malcolm entered the bedroom, humming the final chords of the opera they'd attended the night before. Deborah got on her knees again and crawled seductively to the edge of the bed, grabbing the towel he'd tied carelessly around his waist.

"Hey, girl! Too cold for all that, now. I've got goosebumps where there should *be* no goosebumps, if you know what I mean." He winked playfully, reaching for the towel. "Now hand it over to Daddy…"

"You know, I've always wondered how you do that," she replied, holding the towel behind her back.

"Do what?" he leaned forward, grabbing for it again as she slid across the bed.

"You know…just pick up music in your mind like that. I think you dozed during most of the final act, yet you hum the entire opera today as if you'd been sitting wide awake in the front row the whole time." She pressed the towel between her thighs, sliding her fingers over the buttons of the cornflower blue dress shirt she wore.

"Oh *now* look at you. Five minutes ago I was no better than the furniture, but now you can't wait to get out of my shirt. Well forget it, woman. I'm all clean and smelling good now. 'Sides," his hand flew to his brow as he leaned back in a dramatic pose, his deep voice rising a couple of octaves, "I think I feel a headache comin' on. You'll just have to wait 'till I'm in the mood again."

Deborah fell over on her side, laughing. "Well, if you're as cold as you claim to be," she giggled, "you'll come for this towel. It might be the last clean one we've got left." She pouted her lips as she undid one of the buttons. "Honey, don't make me wait that long. You always smell like a mad scientist just out the lab when you get home." She squeezed her thighs together, enjoying the thrilling sensation traveling through her groin.

Malcolm licked his lips, a sneaky smile crossing his face. Suddenly, he leapt onto the bed, grabbing the towel in his teeth and yanking furiously.

"Stop it! You are so bad, Mac, I swear." She released the towel, laughing hysterically.

Malcolm winked at her, draping the towel over his broad shoulders. "See, what do I always tell you? Don't mess with Daddy." He walked over to the dresser and pulled out a pair of boxers and gray scrubs. "Don't wait up for me, I might be home pretty late. We're backlogged like crazy, not to mention the fact we got a couple of bad burn vics in last night, just as I was coming off my shift." He unfolded the boxers, a bright red pair with tiny white hearts dotting nearly every square inch of the fabric. "So what was the deal with the news bulletin earlier? They finally find Mae and Lily or something?"

Deborah stopped laughing, propping an elbow under her head as she watched him dress. "No, they're still missing…" she paused. "Can you keep a secret, Mac?"

"Shoot." He picked up a paddle brush and slid it over his closely shaven head, watching her carefully in the mirror's reflection.

"I know where they are."

The brush froze in midair. "You *what*? Deborah, you told me when this whole thing started you weren't involved in this! I said you could trust me. I asked you not to lie to me, just don't *lie*. And I'll be damned if you didn't do it anyway." He slammed the brush on the dresser. "You're gonna call the cops then, that's why you fessed up, right? That detective…come on, you're friends with his *wife*. You owe him at least that much."

"I don't owe him a damn thing for what he's done to her!" Deborah yelled. She leapt off the bed, storming toward the bathroom.

"Wait a minute, Deborah! What the hell's gotten into you? What do you mean, 'what he's done to her?' That man's worried sick about his kid while you sit on this like a goose on a golden egg, and I'm supposed to be okay with that? *Hell* no." He marched over to the nightstand, snatching the phone from its cradle. "I'm calling him right now. He's in homicide, right?"

"No!" Deborah rushed across the room, yanking the phone away from him. "Mac, I can't let you do that. I promised to help her, and I stand by my promises."

Malcolm snickered, pulling his cell phone from his pocket. He flipped it open, holding it away from her. "Yet you'll lie straight to my face without blinking an eyelash. All right, I see where we stand now. But my mama raised me to do the right thing, and I'll be damned if anything you've got to say's gonna keep me from that. Give me one good reason why I shouldn't dial PD and clue this cat in, tell him his wife's best friend's known all along where she's been keeping his kid."

Deborah glared at him. "Because I know for a fact he beat the living hell out of her for years, and then tried to rape the little girl he's supposedly so damn concerned about. *Now* call 'em, if your self-righteousness is still compellin' you to do your civic duty."

Malcolm sighed, massaging his temple with his free hand. "If you knew this all along, why the hell didn't you call the police yourself?"

"It's complicated, Malcolm. I don't expect you to understand." She sat down on the bed, hastily unbuttoning the shirt. "Here, you can have your damn shirt back." She brushed hot tears away from her face as her fingers worked, avoiding his gaze. Moments later, she heard the telltale snap of the tiny phone sliding shut. She looked up as Malcolm sat down beside her.

"Then I guess you've got a lot to explain, don't you?" he said, pulling her hand away from the shirt and placing it in his own. "You should get dressed. I've got a feeling it's gonna be a long ride in to the hospital."

"Paging Dr. Barr. Dr. Deborah Barr, please report to the nurses station."

Deborah groaned as she heard her name repeated over the PA system for the next minute or so. When it was over, she took a final glance at her patient's chart, flipped it closed and hung it on the footboard. Fourteen-year-old Lauren Andover. Ectopic pregnancy, D&C, minimal scarring, full recovery expected.

"Okay, Lauren. You're pretty lucky, looks like you'll be out of here really soon. I'll stop in and check up on you before I head out for the night." She smiled warmly at the young girl.

Lauren nodded vaguely in her direction, scratching at one of the many freckles sprayed across her nose. She yawned, reaching for a scrunchee on the bedside table and pulling her strawberry-blonde hair into a tight bun. Settling herself on the pillows, she picked up the remote and turned on the TV. Garish talk-show guests yelled back and forth for a captive audience as Deborah closed the door behind her.

A damn shame, she thought to herself as she heard the page ring out over the system a second time. *What the hell is a fourteen-year-old doing pregnant in the first place? The world's going to hell in a hand basket...*

She rounded a corner and approached the nurses' station. A small Filipino woman glanced up from the console she was typing at furiously. "Dr. Barr," she called out in her thick accent. "You have a call waiting on line two."

"A patient?" Deborah queried as she leaned over the desk, reaching for the phone.

"No, doctor, it's no patient. They did say it's urgent, though. Here, let me get them for you." She pressed a blinking orange button and handed the receiver to her.

"This is Dr. Barr."

"How secure is this line?" A hushed voice, so familiar.

Deborah inhaled sharply. "Could you hold just one moment please?" She cupped the phone and asked the nurse to transfer the call to the break room, then ran down the hall. She reached the door and peeked inside. Empty for the moment. Deborah locked the door behind her, rushing over to a bank of phones reserved for staff and snatching up one of the receivers, pressing another blinking button.

"This is Dr. Barr again. Are you there?"

"Deb," Mae breathed a sigh of relief. "How are you?"

Deborah let out a shuddery laugh, wiping tears from the corners of her eyes. "Are you kidding me? How am I? Girl, I'm worried sick, that's what I am. I thought I'd never hear from you again."

Mae chuckled. "You should know by now I always land on my feet."

"How's my munchkin?"

There was a slight pause. "She'll be with my sister awhile, at least until things quiet down a bit. The FBI is definitely on their job—

they've already been down here, already dropped by Merri's place looking for me, even before we had a chance to work out an arrangement for Lily. It's just a blessing she managed to send them off without so much as a hint of suspicion, but she'll still have to be extra careful with Lily out in public. As for me, I had to cut all my hair off, and even change my name. But we've been blessed so far. No double takes, no close calls…" her voice wavered on the edge of tears.

"Honey, I'm so sorry."

"No no, don't be." Mae's voice came stronger over the line. "I don't regret anything I've done so far down here. Sure it's difficult and more than a little inconvenient, but this arrangement works for us. She's with her aunt, uncle and cousins through the week, and Merri sneaks her over on the weekends so the two of us can spend a little time together. I get to see her every day at school though, at least for a few minutes anyway. I'm the admin secretary here, can you believe it? Some uppity crust deal I swore I'd never make her go to. But she's thriving now, I'm glad to say. For a while the sudden change was a bit overwhelming for her; she was withdrawn, temperamental. She seems to finally be coming out of her blue funk though, so just keep us in your prayers, okay?"

"Definitely. You've been watching the news, haven't you?"

"I have friends here keeping a good eye out. They keep me abreast of new developments."

"Then you know your ex is apparently showing no signs of letting up. He's posted quite a big bounty on your head, my friend."

Mae sighed. "Doesn't surprise me. Sounds as if he hasn't changed a bit."

"Oh, I don't know about that. He's drinking more, sleeping less. He surprised me here one night right after you took off. Scared the hell out of me, actually. He's furious, regardless of the grieving husband/father act he's putting on for the cameras."

Mae was silent a few moments. "We're really never gonna be completely free of him, Deb, are we?" A barely audible whisper. So forlorn, so helpless.

Deborah leaned against the wall, phone pressed tightly against her ear. She could feel her friend's despair coming through the line in waves, and for a moment it threatened to overwhelm her. She was suddenly filled with a rage so virulent it blackened her vision. She pressed her head against the cold plaster, forcing the thrumming in her brain to cease.

"Hey, you still there?" came Mae's concerned voice on the other end.

"I won't let him find you," Deborah whispered into the phone with conviction. "I owe you that."

"What do you mean? Listen, Deb, you've done more than enough. You put your neck on the line for us. Who else would be willing to sacrifice themselves like that? I couldn't ask for a better friend. If anyone is in debt here, it's me." A muffled pause as Mae held the phone away from her ear. She came back on the line seconds later. "Look, I've gotta go. I'm on my lunch, and I usually spend part of the hour in the solarium, watching Lily romp on the playground. I take a book so anyone crossing my path just assumes I need a quiet place to gather my thoughts."

"Good idea."

"Yeah, it's working so far. If any of these jokers get snoopy, I guess I'll have to come up with something else. Take care."

"Wait!" Deborah cried, panic entering her voice. "Please keep in touch, okay?"

"Sure I will, when it's safe. I'll be writing you now and then, in case I can't get a call in 'cause my ex is still nosing around your turf. Still got that PO box?"

"Same number."

"Good. When you open your box, take a little friendly advice: some of the best junk mail is delivered in the A.M., okay?"

Deborah frowned uncertainly. "Yeah, I guess. I'll be sure to keep that in mind. Kiss the munchkin for me."

"Will do. Love you." The phone clicked several times; finally a dial tone droned on endlessly in her ear.

"Love you, too," Deborah whispered into the empty line, gently placing the receiver back in its cradle and slumping into a nearby plastic chair.

Won't let him find you...

"I owe so much more than that, Mae," Deborah said aloud to the empty room. "More than you'll ever know." She pulled her pager from her scrub pocket and punched in a brief text message:

Mac -

We need to talk. Very important. Be right down.

- Deb

She left the lounge and headed for the body bay.

SEVEN

Mae placed the receiver in the cradle with a sigh. She scanned her desk calendar again, running her finger down the list of penciled-in notations. When she arrived at the office this morning, she'd found a note taped to her computer and had scribbled *W. Thibodeaux* in the slot marked 11:00. Thibodeaux hadn't made it in, and she'd received no phone call from him to reschedule. She slid her finger down to the 11:45 slot and tapped the name printed neatly under it: *Dr. David Jasper.*

She glanced up at the clock and frowned. Ten after twelve. Her eyes traveled over the waiting area, noting the empty chairs sitting across from her desk. She got up and walked to the door, checking the administrative hallway for men who appeared to be running late. No sign of anyone. "Geez, where *are* these people?" she muttered, returning to the desk. She glanced up at the clock again. 12:15. She drew a line through both names, wrote *No Show* in the margin and opened one of her desk drawers, producing a sack lunch and a well-worn copy of D.H. Lawrence's *Lady Chatterley's Lover.* She'd stumbled across her grandmother's old book collection one day while rummaging around in an attic on the third floor. She plunked the items on her desk and crouched down, reaching for her purse.

"Pardon me, miss, is the director still in his office by any chance?"

Startled, Mae jerked at the sound of the voice, nearly hitting her head on the sharp corner when she stood up.

A tall gentleman was there, dressed in a pair of black slacks and an olive button-down shirt. Though his tie was still immaculate, his shirt-sleeves were rolled casually up to his elbows. The trail of light brown hair on his well-defined arms glinted golden in the early afternoon sun.

He smiled down at her. The same light brown hair covered his head in close-shaven curls, trailing into his sideburns and goatee, which he fingered curiously as he watched her. He cocked his head to one side, tapping an index finger on full sensuous lips.

"I'm almost ashamed to explain why I'm so late," he began with a chuckle, casually sliding his hands in his pockets. "See, I was down at Marigold Square for lunch as usual, parked on my favorite white bench, just watching the world pass me by…I like doing that, you know. Anyway. Guess the world was passin' a little slow today, cause I knocked right out on that bench. Slept a good half-hour before anyone thought to wake me. Lil' old lady finally did, but I don't even think she was meaning to, what with her steppin' on my shoe as she was walking past. Normally, that type of thing don't stir me at all you know, but you gotta believe this lady was a bit more…ahem," he cleared his throat, "…more *endowed* than most lil' old ladies I've seen since I been here. Yep, she was one of them real buxom southern women, kind of like my momma's folk—"

"Excuse me," Mae interrupted, holding up her hands. "Sir, it's not a problem, really. If you'll just give me your name, I can buzz the director and let him know you're here. Wouldn't want to be any later than you are now, right?" She glanced anxiously at the clock again. Her spirits fell. *Five minutes left. Will Lily still be out on the playground? If only this big-shot mouth would can it…*

"Well if you ask me, late is late, Anne Marie."

Mae turned her attention to him again. He pointed at the name plaque on her desk. "Anne Marie Croft. Pretty, real pretty. Fits you like a glove."

Mae fiddled with the paper sack in front of her, smiling politely in an attempt to mask her growing irritation.

He eagerly returned the smile as he continued. "But if it would make you feel better, sure. Buzz ol' Stan and tell him David Jasper has finally slunk in with his head hung low—late, and very apologetic, I might add." He gestured to one of the chairs in the waiting area where a bottle of apricot brandy sat, the slim neck adorned with a fancy green bow. "Don't care too much for it myself, but you know Stan lives for the stuff."

Mae nodded, this time suppressing a genuine smile. On more than one occasion while in her boss' office, she'd reached into the bottom drawer for correspondence and found smaller bottles of the same, wrapped in dark tissue paper to conceal the label.

She reached for the intercom. "Okay sir, I'll just buzz the director and tell him Dr. David Jasper is here—"

"Call me Jasper, please," the man interrupted. "Everybody else does." He extended an arm and shook her hand gently, caressing the fingers lightly with his own.

The pleasant sensation sent chills coursing up Mae's spine. She cleared her own throat and snatched her hand away, reaching for the intercom again. "I'm sorry. Jasper it is, then. I'll buzz the director right away."

Stan appeared in the doorway moments later, arms outstretched. His striped tie hung loose around his flabby neck. His navy blazer was unbuttoned, allowing his generous middle to spill over wrinkled tan trousers. *Maybe he should have brought gourmet coffee instead*—strong *gourmet coffee* Mae thought, smiling to herself.

"Well isn't it young Doc Jasper! I've got a bone to pick with you, son—you know how I hate late!" He planted his pudgy hands on wide hips for emphasis, jowls moving up and down as he chuckled.

Jasper grinned at Mae again, waving him off. "Yeah, yeah, old man, I've heard it a thousand times before. Just back in town limits this afternoon, and already you're tryin' to whup me. Can't I be spared this tired old lecture 'til Monday?" He walked over to the chair to retrieve the apricot brandy.

The older man's grin widened when his eyes fell on the bottle. He patted his belly in anticipation. "Well why didn't you say you'd brought company, Doc? Hell, son, we got a meetin' to conduct. Bring yourself on in here." He turned to Mae. "You heard anything more from that rascal Thibodeaux?"

She shook her head. "I'm afraid not, sir. I scheduled him for 11a.m. like you requested, but he never showed."

The smiled faded, replaced quickly by a scowl. "Well, when and *if* he gets the nerve to call here again, you be sure to tell him your lil' appointment book there is all full up. Got no time in my schedule for someone who ain't man enough to see to their business bein' handled correctly." He glanced down at the bottle again, then back at her. "Go on and clear my schedule for the rest of the day then," he continued, anger dissolving as quickly as it had appeared. "Hell, I'm in such a fine mood, you can take the afternoon off yourself. It's the weekend, after all, and I know a good lookin' lady like yourself has got lots of plans and plenty of places she needs to be."

"Thanks," Mae mumbled, coloring slightly. She straightened her spectacles, glancing over at Jasper. He was fingering his goatee again, staring at her intently. The full lips spread in a languorous smile.

"You have a good one, Anne Marie. We'll be seeing you." Jasper crossed the room and approached the inner office, hesitating at the doorway. He turned around slowly, again fixing her in his gaze. "Oh, and uh…" he pointed to the paperback. "That's a really good one, by the way. Happy ending, just like it should always be. Perused it from cover to cover a few times myself." He flashed another brilliant smile and winked, closing the door behind him.

"All right, Stan, fess up. Just who is that fine woman out there? I can most assuredly say I've never laid eyes on her before."

The bulky man waddled over to his desk, pulling two small shot glasses out of the bottom drawer. He heaved himself, the glasses and the brandy bottle into a leather recliner in the sitting area, gesturing to an equally comfortable chair across from him. "Oh come on, Jasper, you? Why, you wouldn't remember a woman you'd seen just five minutes after she rolled out o' your bed, you make your way 'round with so many."

"No way." Jasper shook his head emphatically, walking over to a large window overlooking the playground. "No way I'd forget a woman like that crossing my path. She been here long?"

"Hired her a couple months ago, just after you called it quits with that Kerri Jordan over in K-3 and ran off to Europe for a break."

Jasper stiffened at the mention of the name. He turned to watch his old friend admire the bottle's gold label. "How is she these days?"

Stan shrugged. "Seems fine, to my idea. Still looks good as ever, though I'd advise you to keep my staff out o' your private boudoir repertoire in the future, Doc." He gestured around the cluttered office. "Like to pride myself on the fact I run a tight ship 'round these parts." He fiddled with the green bow, contemplating his options. "How was Italy, anyhow?"

Jasper turned back to the window. "The vistas were breathtaking, the food was delectable…"

"And the women?" the old man inquired eagerly, beginning to salivate as he finally ripped the ribbon off the brandy bottle.

Jasper sighed, watching children march single file into their classrooms. Lunch had officially ended for the day. "The women were gorgeous, ripe and plentiful as summer fruit…"

"That's my, Jasper. Good for ya!" Stan crooned, slapping his portly thighs with meaty palms. "We gon' have to get you a studded leash pretty soon, boy. Woof!" He sloshed a generous portion of amber liquor into his glass. "Have a drink with your old pal to celebrate."

"You know I don't touch the cheap stuff, old man."

"What? Those sexy I-talian women get you into that shi-shi $80 a glass stuff?"

Jasper moved away from the window, taking the proffered seat across from his friend. "Not that it's any particular business of yours, but I didn't invite anyone into my bed while I was there, Stan." He sat back in the chair and stretched. "Don't get me wrong. I was tempted, mighty tempted, believe me, but for the first time…" he shook his head slowly, staring down at the plush burgundy carpet. "I don't know. I just wanted *somethin'* for once that'd amount to more than a continental breakfast and a quick kiss goodbye."

Stan took another sip of the brandy and let out a loud belch, indicating his approval. "Aw hell, Jasper. Must be the jetlag talkin'. You've had every available woman in and around town since you blew in from N'Orleans two years ago, and you tellin' me your cock all of a sudden wants to develop a *conscience?* You better sell that bridge to someone who's buyin'. Now get your mind in gear, son, we got business to handle…"

Mae switched the monitor off, smiling to herself. At last, the week had come to an end. Merri would be pulling into her driveway with Lily around four, so that gave her some extra time to relax before getting dinner started. She locked up her desk and headed for the door, plans for their weekend together already running through her mind. Perhaps she'd take her Lily to the zoo in Metairie. With a couple of ball caps, they could easily lose themselves in the busy Saturday morning crowd…

She drove home as fast as the speed limit would allow in the nondescript compact she'd bought from the Metairie classifieds the month before. The vehicle registration, as well as all her other official documents, were under her alias—Ms. Anne Marie Croft of Beau Ciel, Louisiana. To the world, Ella Mae Spencer was a mystery; she'd simply walked out of her home one evening and vanished, and Anne Marie Croft wished to keep it that way.

She locked up the car and ran into the house. Despite the purchase of such a large ticket item, she'd managed to save enough money to buy decent furniture from estate sales and quaint little thrift stores in the area; the new pieces, coupled with her grandmother's remaining furniture, made a beautiful space. The sheer drapes danced along the hardwood floor as warm breezes drifted through the living room windows. The plush red sofa still sat in front of the fireplace, but it had been joined by wing chairs re-upholstered in creamy fabrics. A matching beige area rug had been placed under the furniture, and overstuffed crimson pillows tossed about completed the room.

Mae smiled as she passed through on her way upstairs, thinking of Lily's excitement as they'd chosen the palette for one of their favorite rooms. She enjoyed reading stories to Lily by the fire as they curled up on the sofa or lay sprawled out on the area rug, big red pillows resting comfortably under their heads. She longed for the day when she would bring Lily home for good, but for now she kept herself occupied with the house itself, spending hours painting and clearing the vast space. When she'd lived here before, the second floor housed four bedrooms and a large open bath overlooking the garden. As a young girl, she remembered spending summer afternoons going from room to room, pulling her grandmother's beaded gowns and hats out of heavy wooden wardrobes to parade in front of mirrors placed in nearly every room...

"Look, Granna! I'm gonna be a dancer, just like you!" Mae crooned, *spinning elaborate circles around her grandmother, hands on her hat and hips to keep the oversized gown from falling to her knees. She balanced carefully on the balls of her feet, arching her back in a feeble attempt to fill the voluptuous gown with her budding fifteen-year-old figure. She tossed her head to one side and posed, winking seductively. "Ha! You take that, lady!"*

Lily laughed, her generous bosom heaving with the effort. She sat in one of the spare bedrooms that had been converted to a sewing room, threading folds of colorful fabric through her ancient Singer. "Well, lady, I'm mighty impressed. You fill out that gown better than I ever did in my dancin' days."

"What was it like, Granna, being up on stage in front of all those people?" Mae asked, plopping down in a nearby chair. *"Were you nervous?"*

Her grandmother smiled as she re-pinned the onionskin pattern to the cloth. "I think I was so young then...I wanted to dance my whole life you know, and when I finally got the chance...well, I guess I was just too excited to be nervous. I was happy just to be doin' what I liked, and gettin' paid for it at the same time."

Mae got up and walked over to the windowsill, fingering a faded photograph of her grandmother in an elegant silver frame. "You were so beautiful then."

"Well," Lily chuckled, lightly patting her hair, "I'd like to think I kept at least some of my girlish looks in my old age."

"Oh, stop it, Granna," Mae scolded, embracing her from behind. "You know you're still as beautiful now as you were then. You'll always be beautiful."

"Now who told you to say that?"

"Henry said it just the other day, when I was out helping him plant tomatoes in the garden." She kissed her grandmother's cheek, loving the scent and feel of her smooth, unlined skin. She turned to pose in the mirror, fiddling with the beads on the gown.

Lily put down her sewing. She turned the machine off before removing her glasses, gently massaging the nape of her neck. She smiled at Mae, carefully studying her face as she spoke. "So when you gon' tell me about what happened over there with your momma and daddy?" The question was spoken gently, the words seeming to hang on the air a moment before floating away on light summer breezes blowing through an open window.

Mae folded her arms around herself, looking away from her reflection. "No, Granna. I'm not gonna talk about that. It's over now. I live here with you and Henry now, and I'm happy. Aren't you happy having me here all the time?"

"Honey, of course I am," she replied, taking a seat next to her. "I love havin' you here with me. I fell head over heels for you the day you were born, and Henry—well, Henry thinks of you as his own kin, girl. He worships the ground you walk on.

"You make this big ol' house come to life," she continued, taking Mae's fidgety hands in her own. "We watch you dancin' round this place with all that spunk and energy, and it reminds us of how we were when we could move that fast."

She smiled at her granddaughter, reaching up to tug on one of her curls. As quickly as it appeared the smile faded. "That day me and Henry came to get you, your momma was in such a heat, and Jonas was nowhere to be found. Now I love your daddy, Mae. He's my son, and I raised him up all by myself on the lil' income I got from dancin'. Turned out real fine, too, he did. Made some money with that stained glass business, got that fancy new house built in all them trees. He even built the house we're standing in. Handed me the keys on a Mother's Day way distant, just before you were born. I'm real proud of him, but if he's gone and done somethin' wrong to you, Mae, I gotta know. I gotta know so I can protect you. If that silly momma of yours won't do it, then someone has to…"

Mae smiled briefly at the bittersweet memory. Granna and Henry, always trying to keep an eye out for her…

She jogged down a second floor hallway, passing the sewing room and her old bedroom on the right. She planned to convert them into a playroom for Lily and small library for the two of them to share. Her grandmother had been an avid reader, and she was glad her nose had been forced between so many hard covers while she'd lived here. After Granna's death, most of her furniture and books had been stored away in the attic on the third floor. One evening this week she would lug the books downstairs and begin redecorating. *Screw your brown walls and plaid couches, Richard,* she thought, picturing the drab brownstone she'd abandoned in Philadelphia. *So much better off without you…*

Mae rushed into her bedroom, hurrying out of her floral print sundress and into a pair of jeans and khaki T-shirt. She pulled her short chestnut waves away from her face with a scarlet bandana and plodded down to the kitchen with bare feet.

Two hours later, she held a dripping spoon suspended above a mixing bowl as she read the hands of the clock on the far wall: 3:40. Lily would be leaving Merri's by now, probably after a busy afternoon spent running around the yard with her cousins and their new cocker spaniel, George. She smiled at the thought, spooning rainbow swirled cake batter into pans dusted with flour. As she set them in the oven side by side, she glanced up at the clock again. Won't be long now before her little girl will walk through the door, surprised by her favorite dessert hot and fresh from the oven. Mae pulled a tub of rainbow chip icing from the refrigerator, setting it aside on the counter to warm to room temperature. She rummaged around in the utensil drawer until she found two old spreaders, placing them next to the icing. Back in Philadelphia, Lily would love to sit with her in their efficient little kitchen and help her ice cakes she'd baked in attempts to appease Richard's volatile temper, licking frosting from the extra butter knives Mae always provided. She glanced up at the clock a third time, wiping her hands on a dishtowel. Won't be long now...

A half hour later she was back in the kitchen, removing the steaming cake pans from the oven. She set them on top next to a lasagna she'd cooked earlier and turned it off, checking her watch. 4:15. "That's funny," Mae muttered, going to one of the kitchen windows and peering out at the empty driveway. "Not like Merri to be late on a Friday..." she glanced at the clock on the far wall again, checking it against the tiny hands spinning slowly around her wristwatch. The sun was well on its way toward the western horizon; daylight was starting to fade, and the breeze blowing through the open windows was turning cool. Her bare feet felt cold against the hardwood. She left the kitchen again with a sigh, heading upstairs to grab a pair of sneakers and a light sweater.

Ten minutes later she was back downstairs with cordless phone in hand, staring out the living room windows with growing worry. She'd dialed Merri's house four times, her cell phone she'd dialed twice. No one was answering at home, and each time she dialed the cell...

She forced herself to look away from the empty driveway and down at the cordless, punching her number into the keypad a third time. Once again, the rings led straight to her sister's voicemail. "Hi, you've reached Merri. I'm unable to take your call right now, please leave a brief message..." She hung up the phone, checking her watch for what seemed like the hundredth time. "Where could they be?" she mumbled over and over, beginning to pace the floors. "Why wouldn't she have called if they were gonna be late?" Perhaps she'd spent one too many lunch breaks in the solarium watching the children play, or perhaps a teacher or one of the janitorial staff had noticed her paying a little too much attention to one child in particular...

What if her daily habits had inadvertently given them away, causing someone to unearth their true identity? What if the Sheriff's Office had taken Lily into protective custody on a tip, sure to hand her over to Richard as soon as he arrived in Beau Ciel? What if he was on his way to Bella Bloom this very moment, intent on getting to her even before the authorities could?

She froze in the middle of her third trip between the sofa and the front door, eyes fixed on a set of keys hanging from a peg in the entry. "Don't panic," she whispered aloud, beginning to tremble anyway. She dropped the phone in one of the wing chairs and snatched her purse up from the sofa. "Just drive over to Merri's, find out what's going on..."

She'd just stepped into the entry for the keys when the familiar sound of an approaching motor filled the room. Dropping the purse and keys at her feet, she ran out on the porch, down the steps and over to Merribelle's silver sedan. Merribelle parked the car, opened the driver's side door and got out. "Mae..."

Mae hardly took notice of her, racing straight around to the other side of the car. As she approached the passenger side she froze again in her tracks, realizing the seat was empty through the windshield. Her blood ran ice cold. "Where's Lily?" she demanded as she stormed back around the car, getting right up in her sister's face. "Is she okay? What happened, did someone at school get suspicious? Were you able to get her someplace safe? Why couldn't I get through on your cell? You knew I'd be worried sick—"

"Mae," Merribelle interrupted, taking her arm. "Lily's fine, and no one's on your tail. I'll explain everything in a sec, but first, let's go inside."

Mae pulled away, glaring at her. "I'm not going anywhere, but you sure as hell are—back to wherever you just came from to get my little girl, damn this agreement."

"Mae, will you listen for a minute?" Merribelle smacked her leg in frustration. "She's not at my house. She fell and hurt herself—"

"Oh my God," Mae cried, running around to the passenger side again. "Did she hit her head? Is she conscious, is she bleeding?" She flung the door open wide, started to get in. "Well what are you waiting for, Merri?" she yelled when her sister didn't budge. She pointed at the steering wheel. "Get your butt behind that thing and drive me over to the hospital so I can be with her. Hurry up, she's probably wondering where I am by now!"

"Mae, pay attention to what I'm saying," Merribelle replied gently, resting her hands on the hood. "She's not hurt bad, she just tripped and bruised her wrist. It's not a serious enough injury to even require hospitalization."

"Drive me to the school then," Mae continued, not missing a beat. "You can run into the nurse's office and get her right quick, and we can take her to the children's clinic for a more thorough exam. I'll wait for you in the car, let's go."

Her sister shook her head. "She's not there either, Mae."

Mae slammed the hood with her fists. "Stop this cat and mouse crap, Merri! Where *is* she?" Her frustration gave way to hot, angry tears. "Do you really think," she began as they spilled down her cheeks, "Do you really think I'd be cruel enough to do this to you, if you were standing here in my shoes?" She lowered her face in her hands, beginning to sob quietly.

Merribelle sighed. "Mae, she's at the Child Development Center over on the edge of town. She's there because..." she faltered, stared at the hood a moment. "She's there because she was selected to participate in a study they're conducting. I should have told you sooner, but I thought—"

"You *what?*" Mae looked up at her, wiping tears away. "You dropped her in the middle of an experiment like some sort of lab rat and didn't even have the audacity to tell me?" She beat her fists harder against the hood this time, leaving a dent in the flawless finish. "I'm her MOTHER!" she bellowed. "Who the *hell* do you think you are!"

"I, I didn't…" Merribelle faltered again, searching for the right words. She drew a deep breath. "I didn't think it would be that big of a deal, Mae. Honestly, I didn't. Her teacher thought it would be good for her, so did I. They just called a few minutes ago, I'm on my way to pick her up now. I'll bring her back here right away—"

"You've done enough," Mae said coldly. "She's *my* child, *I'm* her mother, *I'll* go get her." She turned away, started back toward the house. "I'm going to lock up. I expect you to be gone by the time I get back."

Merribelle ignored her sister's words, choosing to follow her up the porch steps instead. "Mae, you can't, it's too dangerous. She's in a secure facility—"

Mae turned on her so suddenly she nearly fell backwards off the porch. "The hell I can't," she said, glowering down at her. "Give me your access code, special key, secret password, whatever it is you use to get through the front door of that crazy house."

"I can't do that," Merribelle replied, looking braver than she felt. "Just let me get her. You'll arouse suspicion."

"We wouldn't even be in this situation if it weren't for you, Merribelle," she sneered, her arm shooting out. Her sister moved away from her, nervously backing down one of the porch steps. "Oh, don't worry," she continued, smiling without humor. "I'm angry enough, but I haven't got the time. Give it to me, now."

Merribelle bit down on her lip, shaking her head firmly. "I can't let you take my key, I'd be sued for breach of contract. They see you walking in there, and we're all screwed. Come on, Mae," she pleaded, stepping onto the porch again. "You know this would never work, they'd never let you get past the lobby without me. You'd be arrested on attempted kidnapping charges, and *then* what would happen to Lily?" When Mae didn't respond, she plunged on. "Serena said it herself. She'd go straight back to Richard, and there'd be nothing anyone could do to stop him from hurting her this time." She saw fear creep into in her sister's eyes at the mention of her husband's name. "Just let me get her, okay?" she said gently, taking her arm again. "We can drive over there together, we can even take her by the clinic to see Dr. Weston, just like you said."

Mae didn't pull away this time, but her pained expression unnerved Merribelle all the same. "You'd better not screw this up, Merri," she said without blinking. "If anything happens to my little girl, I will never forgive you."

Merribelle's sleek sedan rolled through the lush countryside toward a stretch of privately owned land along the town border, just a few miles away from Metairie. Henry had mentioned once that the CDC had been built on the funds of some rich widow, a woman who'd loved, and then lost her only child. Mae could only imagine the anguish she must have felt after realizing she had go to on, though the light had vanished from her world forever. *How could Merri be so irresponsible?* she thought, staring out the window. Why hadn't she simply asked her permission to send Lily to this CDC place? No warning, no clue her daughter was spending hours with some of the very people that wouldn't hesitate to take the light from her own world by destroying her attempts at giving Lily a normal life, if given the opportunity…

She brushed more tears from her cheeks, rolling the window down to allow cool evening breezes to float over her face. Merribelle fiddled with the dials on the radio, trying to get the local blues station but only coming across country music, talk radio and endless static. Finally she switched the radio off, sighing in frustration. "So much for the fancy amenities in this thing. I told Tim we should have splurged on a satellite radio."

"Why didn't you answer your phone?" Mae asked without turning, watching the landscape drift past. "Earlier, when I called. I tried you three times, and it just kept going to voicemail."

Merribelle sighed again. "When you called, I was already on my way over. They phoned me at the house just as I was leaving to pick

Lily up. I came straight over to your place because if I drove halfway out of town to get her first, you'd be out of your mind with worry by the time we arrived. I didn't answer because I knew you wouldn't take the news so well over the phone." She reached across the seat and covered her sister's hand with her own, giving it a reassuring squeeze. "As a mother, I know I'd want to hear something like that in person."

Mae pulled her hand away, balling it into a fist on her lap. The sun slipped behind a row of distant mountains, blanketing the sky with shades of orange and purple. "How did you get my little girl mixed up in this mess anyhow?"

Merribelle put her hand back on the wheel. "Her teacher, Ms. Valçon—I remember you telling me you bumped into her once down at the Square—anyway, last week she called me in for a conference. I was worried, considering how Lily's still having some trouble adjusting to the new living situation. I went in there thinking she'd been acting out or maybe falling behind in her studies, but I was surprised when Ms. Valçon reported that Lily was doing exceptionally well in her schoolwork. In fact, Mae, she's one of the brightest kids in her class."

"Tell me, Merri, please," Mae replied, rolling her eyes. "What does all this have to do with her being at the CDC right now with a sprained wrist?"

Merribelle was silent a moment, biting the inside of her cheek to keep her anger in check. She turned onto a desolate stretch of road before she continued. "At the end of the conference, Ms. Valçon tells me about this pilot program the academy has going on in conjunction with the CDC. The psychologists there have dubbed it the 'Immersion Project'—they're researching the possibility that integrating the autistic child with the average child can increase their ability to communicate with the outside world. Every Friday, a group of selected children from the academy are bussed there for supervised play sessions with autistic children. It's a unique opportunity, and Ms. Valçon recommended Lily for the program. She believes Lily has a lot to offer to the project. Tim's company built this place from the ground up last year, and because I'm on the board that approved the CDC proposal, we both know a little about how the place works. They're doing good things over there, Mae, they really are."

Mae turned away from the window at last, leveling a steely gaze in her direction. "Just like I thought—this *was* one of your bright ideas, like that high priced lawyer who was workin' so hard to take my house from me."

"Damn it Mae, can't you see I'm not the enemy here!" Merribelle yelled, slamming the steering wheel with her palm. "I thought I made myself clear before, I had nothing to do with Momma's plan. Why can't you just trust me?"

Mae glared at her. "Trust you? Oh, I don't believe…" she turned back to the window again, eyes welling with fresh tears. "After everything I've sacrificed to keep Lily safe, you do *this?* You keep saying 'I'm your sister, trust me,' then go right behind my back and feed us to the wolves anyhow. I'm just sitting here kicking myself, wondering how I could have been stupid enough to trust you in the first place!"

"What the hell are you talking about, Mae?" Merribelle asked, bewildered.

She grabbed her arm, turning her around until they faced each other once more. "I don't see how Lily playing with special needs kids a couple hours a week affects her safety. Don't you think you're being just a little melodramatic?"

"Psychologists, Merri," Mae breathed through clenched teeth. "Child psychologists, everywhere. People trained to hone in on that one kid who doesn't quite fit in."

Merribelle shook her head. "No Mae, it's not like that. Don't you see? Lily fits in just fine. If I'd been the least worried about the possibility of exposing her to any kind of danger, I would never have agreed to it in the first place. You have to know that."

"Then why wait till today to tell me?" Mae shouted, the sound of her voice nearly deafening in the cramped confines of the car. "You're living so high and comfy up in that house on the hill you don't even realize, do you? Lily knows we have to live in secrecy to survive. She knows her momma had to change her name and appearance just to be able to make it. She knows she stays with you because it's too dangerous for her to be at home with me, where she belongs. She's only six, and the most important lesson I've managed to teach her so far is that lying can protect you; it can be the difference between life and death.

"Don't you think that's a bit much for someone her size to swallow? She's just a little girl who's been forced to look adult problems straight in the face because of me. Maybe if I'd left Richard sooner, she wouldn't have had to know about this life at all. She could play tag and run around like other kids and never worry that one day her momma might not be home when she gets there, that someone may take her back to her father, let him do all the things he'd planned to do to her in the first place…"

Mae rubbed her swollen eyes in frustration. "Don't you understand, Merri? She's keeping all that inside, and thanks to you, every week she's surrounded by people who read her up and down like one of their stupid textbooks. It'd only take a hint from one of them, a slight nudge in the right direction before she'd be spilling the truth about everything." Mae looked away again. "She's so tired of lying, I wouldn't blame her at all if she did it just to be free of her burden."

Twilight had fallen, sending tall trees and high grasses into deep shadow. Just up ahead, a massive building came into view. "Mae, I'm so sorry," Merribelle said quietly, pulling into the parking lot. "I didn't think I was doing anything wrong. I was only trying to help, honest."

The building that served as the Child Development Center was indeed elaborate. Mirrored glass covered every inch of the five-story structure, even the large automatic doors that served as the entrance. Immaculate shrubbery bordered the immense property, their simple elegance punctuated by colorful perennials dotting the landscape. Beyond, there was nothing but fields of wildflower and stately evergreens in each direction. *Beautiful, and completely isolated,* Mae thought. Just what kind of "research" would afford such a lavish display in the middle of nowhere?

Merribelle parked the car and released her seat belt. "Wait here, I'll be back in a minute."

Mae pushed the release button on her own seat belt. "You can forget about it, Merri. I'm going in to get my child, I don't care what you say."

Merribelle laid her head against the headrest and closed her eyes. "I'm not going to sit here and argue with you, Mae. There's only one access card between the two of us, and I have it. That means if you insist on coming in, you follow my lead and just nod in the right places, okay? No hysterics and no funny business, I mean it."

"Fine." Mae started to open her door. "Let's go."

Merribelle frowned. "Mae, I'm serious. There are guards posted on every floor, and believe me, these people don't play. They won't hesitate to haul your butt right down to the Sheriff if you give them any reason to whatsoever. I won't be able to get you out of that one, you hear me?"

"I understand." Mae's fingers clenched on the door handle. "Time's not passing any slower Merri. Let's *go.*"

Mae followed her sister up to the entrance. As she approached the glass doors, she quickly checked her appearance, smoothing the wrinkles from her t-shirt and sweater. She removed the scarlet bandana and brushed loose strands of hair away from her face, straightening her glasses. The change in eye color still took her by surprise, and she blinked a few times at her reflection. *Ella Mae is still in there somewhere,* she thought as she watched Merribelle remove the access pass from her coat pocket and slide it across the magnetic pad. Though her sister had reassured her that everything was fine, Mae found herself holding her breath until the red ADMIT light blinked green and she heard the lock click. The doors slid open with a *whoosh* of air, and the women stepped into a well-furnished lobby.

Mae glanced to her left, toward an empty seating area decorated in cool shades of mauve and gray. Her gaze traveled around the space until it fell on a bank of elevators, a color-coded map resting on the wall above the glowing buttons.

She started off in that direction, but was stopped by the sound of a pleasant and insistent voice: "Miss? Miss, may I help you?"

She turned to her right to find Merribelle standing next to a pretty young receptionist watching her uncertainly from behind a large desk. Her straight dark hair hung down her back in a thick braid. Eyes the color of ocean storms glanced over her curiously as the woman rose from her seat, straightening the light gray suit she wore. Mae noticed a tiny headset around her neck. If she aroused suspicion, how long would it take for this pretty young thing to radio security? *Just play the game,* Mae thought, taking a deep breath. *Play it just right, and you could have Lily out of here long before anyone starts asking the wrong questions...*

She walked up the desk and stood next to her sister, giving the receptionist her most disarming smile. The young woman glanced at Merribelle and sat down again, visibly relaxing.

"Now Anne Marie, just where did you think you were heading off to?" Merribelle chuckled, giving Mae a pointed look before turning back to the receptionist. "Please excuse my cousin. She's new to town and just started working for the administrator over at Sacred Shield, who happens to be a good friend of mine and my husband's. I've told her so much about this place she thinks she practically knows her way around the building."

The receptionist smiled. "It's okay, ma'am. How can I help you today?" Mae read the name off the light blue tag pinned to her lapel. As she did, she noticed TRAINEE written in smaller print below it.

"I'm here to pick Lily Tidwell up," Merribelle answered, glancing around the empty lobby. "She's one of the student volunteers in the Immersion play study."

The receptionist turned her attention to a computer sitting in front of her. "Just a minute, ma'am. We have the strictest of security around here..." she punched the EXECUTE button on the keyboard, scanning the screen. Mae's heart quickened, realizing it may be harder to get to Lily than she'd originally thought. *What the hell is a place like this doing in a backwater like Beau Ciel anyway?*

"Oh! Here we are." The young receptionists' eyes slowly traveled from the screen to Merribelle's face, as if checking it against some highly classified information she had in front of her. Apparently satisfied that everything was accurate, she stuck out her hand. "Mrs. Tidwell? Pleasure to meet you, ma'am. I've heard all about you and your husband. I was told Mr. Tidwell's victory with the zoning board was a big contributor to finally getting CDC off the ground and running. I haven't been here very long, but I'm already excited about all the stuff they're doing for special needs kids these days."

Merribelle shook her hand, glancing at the woman's tag as well. "Ms. Aiken, is it?"

The woman nodded. "Yes, ma'am."

"Why, you must be brand new. Tell me Suzanne isn't leaving us?"

Ms. Aiken shook her head. "Oh no, she's just training me to handle the desk while she's out on maternity leave. She's expecting a baby girl this winter, you know."

Merribelle tapped her chin thoughtfully. "Now that you mention it, I remember her saying something about taking an extended leave to welcome that little bundle of joy into the world." She gave the woman a warm smile. "Well, it's awfully nice to know she's got such a great replacement, even for the short term. You planning on remaining here full time after she comes back?"

Ms. Aiken nodded eagerly. "I'm in my third year of undergrad, majoring in Early Childhood Education. When I finish my credentials, I'd love to work up in Elementary Education Research on the third floor." She reached for a phone nearby. "Well, I've chewed on your ear enough, Mrs. Tidwell. Let me get Lily for you. She's an adorable one, she is. Met her just today as I was on my way in. I'll just ring up on five, have 'em send her down—"

"Oh no, that won't be necessary," Merribelle interrupted, edging Mae toward the elevators. "Think I'll just go on up and introduce Anne Marie to everyone. My good friend Stan wanted her to meet the

Immersion staff so she'll be better prepared to run errands for him over here in the future. Thanks a bunch."

"Just a second," Ms. Aiken called after them. She reached into a drawer and pulled out a light green badge with the CDC logo and the word VISITOR clearly written on the front. "Your cousin will need this to get on the fifth floor."

They walked back over to the desk. Ms. Aiken smiled and handed Mae the badge. "Just make sure this is visible on you somewhere, and you should have no problem with the guards." As Mae pinned it to her sweater, the receptionist produced a clipboard. "The entire fifth floor is a Restricted Access Area. You won't get too far up there without a Visitor's Pass, even with Mrs. Tidwell vouching for you. All I need is a photo ID and a signature, and you're good to go. We make a copy of all ID's and enter the information into the system, so if any of the guards stop you, they can just call down here for verification."

Mae unzipped her purse and pulled out her wallet. She glanced at her sister, then back at the woman. "You run fingerprints in here, too?"

Ms. Aiken laughed. "You're pretty funny, Miss Anne Marie."

"That's what they tell me," Mae sighed, handing her the forged ID.

Ms. Aiken disappeared into a small room off to the side, then returned a minute later. "Here you go," she said, handing it back, "and you guys have a good one, okay?"

"We sure will," Merribelle smiled. Mae waved goodbye over her shoulder, starting off toward the elevators again. When she arrived she quickly scanned the map, then pressed the 5 button several times. Nothing happened. Mae was about to press the button again when she noticed another magnetic access pad, like the one by the doors, at the entrance. *Now, this is just ridiculous,* Mae thought as she crossed her arms, tapping her foot in frustration. *I bet the White House doesn't even have it this good.*

"It was a pleasure to meet you, Ms. Aiken," her sister continued, stepping away from the desk. "I look forward to seeing you up in Research sometime in the near future. The world needs more folks who are as passionate about kids as you are."

Ms. Aiken grinned from ear to ear. "That means so much, Mrs. Tidwell, thanks." Noticing Mae standing impatiently by the elevators, she pressed a button on a hidden console, apparently unlocking it for use. "By the way, Mrs. Tidwell, you can call me Annie. Annie's just fine."

"You have a good one too, Annie. Don't work too hard." Merribelle joined Mae at the elevators and pressed the 5 button. One of the sets of doors opened instantly, and she stepped inside. Mae rushed in behind her.

"Could you be more slow?" she asked sarcastically, leaning her head against the mirrored panel lining the elevator's interior.

Merribelle rolled her eyes. "Could you be more rude? Geez, Mae, haven't you heard? You can always catch more flies with honey than you can with vinegar."

Mae scowled at her sister. She was about to respond when the doors at the lobby's entrance suddenly opened again. She clamped her mouth shut, pressing the DOOR CLOSE button just as a couple of men in white smocks entered the building.

The elevator opened again on a long carpeted hallway. The women emerged and quickly walked past several rooms, the walls facing the hall completely encased in thick soundproof glass. Mae glimpsed children of varying ages playing with toys and scribbling furiously on sketchpads while other white-smocked therapists carefully observed the scene, making notations in notebooks of their own.

They passed a couple of classrooms and even a small lab, all the standard scientific equipment scaled down to fit tiny hands. She watched as instructors led a group of children in plastic aprons and safety goggles through an experiment centering around a bisected orange with electrodes attached to it. She marveled at the intensity of the children, noting their tiny brows furrowed in concentration.

Though she'd slowed her stride to get a better look, most were too absorbed in the experiment to notice. *Child prodigies? Perhaps.*

One glassed-in room remained at the end of the hallway. A smaller group of children were engrossed in painting each other here, their miniature easels set back-to-back as they worked in pairs. Lily sat near the window, her curls piled high on her head and fastened tight with a red ribbon. Her tiny wrist had been wrapped with a cloth bandage and secured with metal clasps. Mae let out an involuntary cry, walking up to the door marked IMMERSION – RESTRICTED ACCESS and grabbing the handle. Locked. She glanced down and almost burst into tears. Yet another magnetic key pad.

Merribelle pulled Mae aside, out of sight of the classroom. "You have to wait out here, Mae. It's restricted even for you beyond this point. Just play it cool if one of the guards comes around. Your badge should keep you in the clear if you say as little as possible."

Mae nodded miserably. "I got it, Merri. Just hurry, please."

Merribelle squeezed her hand. "Don't worry, it's going to be fine. I'll be in and out in a few minutes, I promise."

Mae paced the hall in front of the elevators, checking her watch for the twelfth time. Merribelle had gone into the restricted access classroom to retrieve Lily nearly a half hour ago, and she'd heard nothing from her since. No movement in the hall bordering the glassed-in rooms whatsoever. She'd moved her pacing closer to the elevators after a couple of white-smocked staff began casting funny glances her way each time she passed their room.

A set of restrooms stood at the end of this hallway, their universal blue MEN and WOMEN plaques visible even from a distance. Directly across from them at the corner of the building was an additional glassed-in room marked STAFF LOUNGE. Yet another magnetic pad was affixed to the door just below the knob, marking the only means of access to this room as well.

Mae glanced at the blinking red ADMIT light as she walked past. "Can't even get a cup of coffee around this place without having it approved first," she muttered, shaking her head. She turned around and walked back toward the elevators again, her eyes falling on another door at the other end of the hall. This one was simply marked STAIRS. She was about to make another circuit of the hallway when the door opened and a pair of uniformed guards stepped through. One of them glanced at her badge and nodded politely; the other unclipped a radio from his belt and spoke rapidly into it. "Copy, Front Desk. Yeah, we're gonna need a verification up here on five."

Mae froze in her tracks, giving both men a nervous smile. *Your badge should keep you in the clear if you say as little as possible,* she heard Merribelle repeat in her mind. Her sister's words continued to play over and over again, even as her heart sped up and her palms grew clammy. What if the friendly Ms. Aiken had discovered her ID was really a fake after all? What if she'd sent these men to arrest her and take her into custody, as Merribelle had mentioned earlier? *These people don't play. They won't hesitate to haul your butt right down to the Sheriff if you give them any reason to whatsoever...*

From somewhere behind her, she thought she heard the elevator doors open and close again. More guards? She could hear her heart pounding away in her ears, could feel the blood rushing to her temples. Adrenaline surged through her system, the sense of panic nearly overwhelming now. She turned to make a mad dash down the hall to Lily...and for the second time that day, came face to face with Dr. David Jasper.

"Anne Marie!" he called as he approached, smiling warmly. "How on earth did you get..." when he noticed the distress on her face and the approaching guards, he faltered a moment. "So we meet again," he said louder when the men were within earshot. "Thought I'd lost you on the way up here."

The friendlier of the two men spoke first when they arrived. "This is your visitor, Dr. Jasper?"

Jasper pointed to her badge and nodded. "Indeed, gentlemen. This lady works over at Sacred Shield and has pressing business to take care of in the building; I'm afraid we got separated at the elevators down in the lobby. A parent was waiting for me at the front desk when we came in, so instead of making her wait on my account, I used my key to unlock the elevators and sent her on up here."

The other man clipped his radio to his belt again. "You know the policy on visitors, Dr. Jasper. They have to be accompanied by you at all times or they have to remain in the lobby."

Jasper shrugged, smiled. "I sincerely apologize, it won't happen again. Now, if you'll excuse us gentlemen, Ms. Anne Marie and I have some matters we need to attend to." He turned to Mae and placed an arm around her shoulders, startling her. "You up for a cup of coffee in the lounge before we get started?"

Mae glanced up at him, then back down the hall where the classrooms were. Still no sign of Merribelle or Lily. Finally, she nodded weakly. "Whatever you say, Dr. Jasper. Sounds good."

They walked to the lounge together in silence. Mae watched Jasper slide his key across the magnetic pad. When the lock clicked, he held the door open for her. "Ladies first."

She stepped inside, wheeling around to face him. He said nothing as he closed the soundproof door and leaned his body against it. They stared at each other a long time until he spoke first. "You want to tell me what you're really doing here *now*, or would you prefer to discuss it over that cup of coffee I mentioned?"

"I thought you said you were a doctor," Mae replied, checking the hallway again over his shoulder.

He tapped the ID badge he'd re-clipped to the front of his lab coat. "Ph.D. Child psychologist, I'm afraid. Guilty as charged?" He crossed the room to a counter lined with restaurant-sized canisters of freshly brewed coffee. "What's your pleasure, Anne Marie?" he asked, reaching for two Styrofoam cups. He strolled the length of the counter, scanning each of the labels. "Let's see, today we have Irish Cream, French Vanilla, Double Chocolate Espresso…"

"I'm fine, thanks. I won't be staying long." She folded her arms, glancing around the room. A group of comfortable looking chairs resembling those she'd observed in the lobby were tastefully arranged around a small coffee table. Large potted palms sat in each corner, and drapes hung from picture windows overlooking the property and the growing darkness. If she closed her eyes a moment, she believed she could have been standing in the middle of a cozy living room instead of a sterile lounge in a high security building.

"Kinda hard to get in this place without some help," Jasper commented, turning to her with the steaming cups in his hands. "Here, you look like a French Vanilla kind of girl." He handed one of them to her and selected a chair near the glass wall, gesturing to another one directly across from him. "You know, I really enjoyed our first meeting, and I consider it sheer good luck just to be running into you again so soon." He sipped his coffee. "Right now, though, I'm afraid I'm mostly interested in how you came to be here in the first place. You may have guessed by now we have strict policies concerning visitors at the CDC."

"You said it yourself, Dr. Jasper," Mae replied, eyes on the empty hallway again. "I've got pressing business to attend to, that's exactly why I'm here."

"Jasper'll do just fine," he said, motioning to the chair again. "I'm only Doc when I'm hard at work." He watched her for a second, then nodded at the glass. "I guarantee whoever it is you keep checking for out in that hallway will see you clearly then as I see you now."

Mae stormed over to the chair. "And you'll see them too, won't you? Isn't that why you really lied to those guards and brought me in here? Because you hoped I'd be so grateful I'd just spill my guts and give up the person who used their key to get me in the building?" She plopped down in front of him. Their eyes locked on each other for some moments as she sipped the coffee he'd given her.

Finally, Jasper chuckled, looking away. "Wow, you sure have a wild imagination, Anne Marie. Anyone ever tell you that?" He stared deep into his cup as if musing over the contents. "Actually, the whole thing wasn't a lie. I did run into a parent in the lobby." When she didn't respond, he continued. "Look, I wouldn't have to go to such extremes to learn the truth. I could just escort you down to the front desk right now myself and find out from that cute little Ms. Aiken the what's what. I've done it before."

"Then what's stopping you from doing it again tonight, *Doctor* Jasper?" Mae asked pointedly, crossing her arms again.

Jasper looked up at her, stared at her a long time. "Don't know," he said finally. "Just thought I'd give you the chance to set the record straight before I got others involved, I guess."

She glanced down the hall again in time to see Merribelle finally emerge from the classroom with Lily in her arms.

Jasper followed her gaze. "Oh, that's just Mrs. Tidwell. Her foster child was selected as a participant—"

"Lily," Mae whispered, rising from the chair. She slammed the coffee down on the table so hard the cup overturned. Steaming liquid splashed across the surface, dripping into the carpet.

"You know Lily?" Jasper asked, bewildered. Understanding suddenly dawned on his face. "Wait a minute, you mean to tell me *Mrs. Tidwell* let you in? What's really going on here, Anne Marie?"

Mae was already at the door. She flung it open wide, racing down the hall to meet them.

Merribelle smiled as her sister approached. "Sorry it took so long, I had to sign some forms before they'd release her…" when she noticed Jasper striding up the hallway toward them, the smile fell from her face. "What happened?" she whispered, turning to Mae. "One of the guards gave you a hard time and decided to turn you over to the top dog for an interrogation?"

"What are you talking about?" Mae took Lily in her arms. "That guy came into Stan's office today trying to charm my pants off. He's part of that pack of nosy, smart-mouthed psychologists running around this place. Just tell him something quick, and let's go."

Merribelle shook her head. "I'm afraid it's not gonna be that easy. He's not just some random psychologist, Mae, he's the head of the Immersion Project."

Mae held Lily close to her chest. "Then you have to do something, Merri. Don't let him take my little girl away, please."

"You just worry about Lily, I'll handle everything." Merribelle turned to greet Jasper when he joined them. "Hello Dr. Jasper!" she said brightly. "Good seeing you again. I was looking for you in there, but one of your staff told me you were probably off handling business elsewhere. We've been missing you a while now. Sure hope that long getaway proved to be a restful one, as well."

He nodded, gesturing to both women. "I see the two of you know each other quite well after all." He glanced at Mae holding onto Lily for dear life, tugged on one of the little girl's sneakers before turning his attention again to Merribelle. "Mrs. Tidwell," he began, stroking his chin. "My, my. Seems the two of you got a whole lot of explaining ahead of you this evening."

He turned to Mae. "What do you say, Anne Marie? You up for givin' that cup of coffee another try?"

Mae sat with Lily at her easel, watching her paint with her good wrist. They'd been alone together in the classroom for some time now; the CDC had closed over an hour ago, and most of the staff had already left for the day. On the other side of the room, next to a dry erase board, was an office door that had been closed for a while; on the other side of it, she was certain Merribelle and Jasper were locked in a heated discussion.

"Look, Momma," Lily said cheerily, climbing onto her lap with her finished picture. Mae stared at a watercolor scrawl of a boy with blonde hair and bright green eyes, his lips and plump cheeks painted a candied pink.

"Who's he?" Mae asked, pointing to the picture. "Is he one of kids you got to play with today?

Lily nodded. "He painted me, too. He doesn't talk all that much, but he's real nice. His momma's real nice, too. She brought cupcakes for us." She waved the paper back and forth through the air, trying to dry it. "I hope he comes again next week. Maybe he'll talk more if he keeps coming."

Mae wrapped her arms around her, planting a kiss on her forehead. "Maybe he will, sweetie, maybe he will."

The door to the office opened, and Merribelle and Jasper entered the room.

"Dr. Jasper, look!" Lily jumped off Mae's lap and ran over to him, showing him the picture. "I drew Logan today. Is he coming back?"

Jasper kneeled in front of her. "I don't see any reason why he won't. Are you interested in becoming his new buddy?"

Lily nodded eagerly. "He's nice. I can't wait 'till he talks more."

Jasper grinned. "You and me both, Lily. From your lips to God's ears."

Merribelle reached for her hand. "Come on, honey, say goodbye to Dr. Jasper. Let's go out in the hall and try to get that thing dry so you can take it with you in the car."

Lily tried using her bandaged wrist to wave goodbye. "It still hurts a little."

"No more running next time, right?" he asked, patting her shoulder.

Lily shook her head and smiled. "No more running, I promise."

Merribelle looked over at Mae. "We'll be right outside."

Mae offered a half-hearted salute. "Be there in a minute."

When they left, she turned back to Jasper. "So, was the explanation to your satisfaction, Doctor?"

Jasper sighed. "She told me the truth about your little situation, of course. How you're actually her cousin and Lily's real mother. That after struggling for so long to provide a stable home while you were making a go of it in New York, you signed over full custody of Lily and sent her down here. Then you pop up on her doorstep a couple of months ago, ready to settle in and be a part of the girl's life again."

Mae bent down and picked up the plastic watercolor container, avoiding his eyes. "She said it about right."

Jasper went on. "She told me all about you running into some legal troubles up there, how you thought it best to get Lily as far away as possible before the roof caved in on you both." He crossed the room, stood with her by the window. "Knowing what I do of the Tidwells, when you found yourself up to your neck in it and reached out for help, they were more than willing to make that beautiful child a part of their family. I trust a petition for permanent transfer of parental rights is currently making its way through the courts?"

Mae nodded numbly, still fiddling with the lid of the container.

"Just to let you know," he continued, "I did some checking while I was in with Mrs. Tidwell. Your contact with Lily is permitted under Louisiana law, provided you have Mrs. Tidwell's permission and don't do something crazy like try to take her back to New York or anything. In all fairness, I'm letting you know ahead of time I'll be closely monitoring this visitation agreement you two have going. Normally I wouldn't think to become involved in such a complicated family situation, but as an advocate of children, I'm obligated to make sure Lily's best interests always remain at the heart of the matter." He laid a hand on her arm. "I'm afraid I'm also obligated to remind you that because of your decision to surrender your parental rights, the final word on keeping Lily in the Immersion program ultimately lies with Mrs. Tidwell."

She looked up from the plastic container. "I understand," she whispered, handing it over to him. "Everything's perfectly clear."

Jasper took it from her. "Lily's extremely creative, and has a natural aptitude for communicating ideas well to others, you know. She has such a way with the kids here. I'd prefer having her back here next week with your consent rather than without it. I suggest you at least talk it over with Mrs. Tidwell before the final decision is made."

"I'll give it a lot of thought, thank you." She turned to leave.

Jasper set the container back on the easel. "Wait a sec, I'll see you out."

They walked down the hallway together. Merribelle and Lily were at the elevators. "I really enjoyed meeting you, Anne Marie," Jasper said, waving to Lily again. "I really did."

"You already said that." Mae smiled in spite of herself. "Twice in one day isn't enough for you?"

Jasper returned the smile, stroking his chin again. "I'll have to answer that one the next time we meet...perhaps over lunch sometime."

"You seem awfully sure of yourself, Dr. Jasper."

He shrugged. "I'm of the belief that everything happens for a reason." He stopped and turned to her, holding up a finger. "Once..."

Lily starting running up the hallway toward them.

Two fingers. "Twice..."

"Lily!" Merribelle called after her. "Dr. Jasper told you to stop running! You'll fall again and hurt yourself!"

He grinned and held up the last finger. "Three times a charm."

Lily slammed into Mae at full speed, wrapping her arms tight around her legs. "Ouch," she said, pulling her bruised wrist back to stare at it. She held it up for her to see. "Momma, this really hurts."

Mae lifted her into her arms. "We'd better go, now. Thanks again."

"Good luck, Anne Marie," he replied as Merribelle pressed the 1 button on the console and the doors opened. "Hope you get your troubles ironed out in the future, if not for your sake, then at least for the little one." He shoved his hands in his pockets, the faintest trace of a smile touching the corners of his mouth. "I'll be seein' you around."

Mae carried Lily into the elevator. As the doors closed, their eyes met one last time. His were black as onyx and seemed to be searching for something deep within her, passing easily through the barrier of lies and deception to her very core. Mae shuddered as a chill crept up her spine. She breathed deeply, trying to slow her palpitating heart. How on earth could she feel such excitement for a man who had the power to destroy her life with a single phone call?

EIGHT

"I think it moved."

"And I think you're a crazy woman," Malcolm replied, turning the radio up. Smooth jazz floated from the speakers, filling the van with a liquid rhythm. Deborah released the clasp on her seatbelt, turning in her seat to get a better look. A large gurney sat in back, the frame attached to the rear door handles with strips of colorful bungee cord. Deborah shivered, thinking the cords resembled snakes with their fluorescent diamonds gleaming at her in the dark.

Slowly, carefully, her eyes moved over the black plastic shroud. She shuddered, thinking of what lay beneath. Victims caught in an abandoned house fire on the outskirts of the city, a mother and her five-year-old daughter. Burned beyond recognition, no identifying information available. No family to claim their remains. They were assumed to be transient, frequently shifting from one hollowed-out shell to another until their luck finally ran out. What luck that Malcolm had been preparing to discharge them to the county crematorium when she'd burst into cold storage with this incredulous, insane idea fresh in her mind.

Deborah faced forward again, locking her seatbelt a second time. She leaned her head against the window, watching the bright city lights of Philadelphia slowly fade to blankets of onyx. She remembered how upset he'd been at first. They slept in separate rooms for days before he would even speak to her, but somehow she'd been able to convince him there was no other way...

She gazed at Malcolm, watching him expertly maneuver the large white van toward their destination. She placed a hand on his leg, giving it a playful shove. He winked at her. "Well, Deb, they haven't gotten up yet. Think we're finally safe?"

"I think you're not very funny right now, Malcolm Williams."

"Hey!" he laughed, shoving her back. "What's life without humor? You do what I do all day, and you learn to take a joke where you can get one." He glanced in the rearview mirror. "They're not rolling around back there, are they?"

She shook her head. "Nope. The bungee cords really helped." Her hand floated over to him again, gently caressing his cheek with the backs of her fingers. "Thanks, Mac. I don't know what on earth I'd do if you weren't with me now. I don't think I've ever been so frightened in my life."

"That'd be both of us, Deb. The both of us." He angled the vehicle to the far right, heading for a turnoff. Deborah sat up to read the writing on the mint green sign: Elysium State Park –20 mi.

"You bring everything?"

Deborah nodded, tapping a small knapsack lying at her feet. "I went over to the house when I was sure Rick would be on duty. Used Mae's spare key—I can't believe she still keeps it in such a lame place—birdhouse on the porch, under some seed. Anyway, I grabbed a couple of things he wouldn't miss. I even managed to find this." She reached inside her jacket pocket, pulling out a tiny gold locket. "Lily's," she explained as she held it up for him to see. "I gave it to her on her last birthday. She loved this thing, even though her mother hardly ever let her wear it. She was always afraid she'd break it, or lose it on the play-ground somewhere. Hell, Lily's such a sweet girl she'd trade with the devil if he asked nicely, so I could see some punk kid running down the street with it around their neck, my picture hanging out for all the world to see."

She chuckled softly, carefully folding the locket into her palm and pressing it to her chest. She leaned against the window again, staring out at the darkness. "Tell me it's gonna work, Mac. I know you had your objections in the beginning. To be honest, I had my own doubts. All those years he beat on her like that…I knew it the whole time, and didn't say a word. If I'd just listened to my gut in the first place, maybe things wouldn't have gotten this bad. All those times I swore to keep her secret, I actually failed her. Now I just want to make it right..."

Malcolm maneuvered the van onto the turnoff, reaching for her hand. "All I can say is we'll do our best. I mean, body snatching ain't exactly how I like to get my kicks, but if you say you need help, I'm gonna be there for you. No doubt about it." He brushed the hair away from her face, cupping her chin in his palm. "You believe me, right?"

"I believe you're the best thing that's ever happened to me," she whispered, cradling his hand in her lap. "Where were you all those years I was kissin' frogs?"

Malcolm laughed. "Don't know. Probably with the wrong kind of girl, doin' all the wrong kinds of things for all the right reasons."

She shoved his hand away. "Am I supposed to be offended by that comment?"

He gave her thigh a reassuring squeeze. "I'm joking, try to get some sleep. We've still got a ways to go."

Deborah curled into a ball on the seat, pulling her jacket to her chin. "Okay Mac." She yawned. "Wake me when we get there." Moments later she was breathing deeply.

Malcolm turned the radio down to a murmur, settling in for the long drive. He fished in his own pocket a moment, producing a tiny box of strike matches and tossing them on the dashboard. Reaching behind his seat, his fingers brushed the top of a large paper bag containing a small mallet he'd purchased that afternoon from a hardware store, as well as several bottles of cheap liquor.

"When this is over, Deborah," he whispered to the quiet interior, "I think I we should seriously do some talkin' about making things permanent."

"So exactly what kind o' legal woes would bring a person all the way down here to Beau Ciel?" Jasper asked as he brought his glass to his lips, tiny pieces of crushed ice sliding effortlessly onto his tongue. "Don't you think it defeats the purpose of adoption to go on working and living right near the child you gave up, always running straight to her doorstep?"

"Well you certainly come to the point, don't you, Jasper?" Mae replied, stabbing a segment of tomato with her fork. She bit into the ripened fruit, savoring the taste. The two were dining at Beau Ciel Grill in Marigold Square. Mae watched as passersby roamed past the store-fronts or rested on benches as they ate lunch or read the afternoon paper.

Jasper eyed her carefully as he took another sip of water. "No offense intended, just curious. Lily's a wonderful girl, very special. Guess what I do *is* what I am after all. An old friend told me that once." He smiled at her over the checked tablecloth. "Didn't step on any toes, did I?"

"After a couple of months of knowing you, Jasper, I think I might actually be growing accustomed to the particularly bold flavor of your scrutiny." She offered a smile of her own, pointing across the table. "Pass me the rolls?"

He held the basket of bread out. As she reached for it their hands met, his fingers lingering on hers a moment. Mae moved away from his touch finally, placing the basket within her reach. "Thank you," she mumbled, avoiding his gaze.

"You know," he began, watching her carefully select a roll and smother it in margarine, "I'm mighty glad you started having lunch with me. After a month of asking, I was starting to give up hope."

Mae took a bite of her roll, swallowing quickly. "You and I have an arrangement of our own, it seems. I uphold my end of the custodial agreement with Merribelle, and you hang around making sure it goes down that way. Or else, right?"

Jasper sat back in his chair, staring out the window. Bright noonday sun beat down on the country square, filtering onto their table. "I've been around you long enough to know, A.M: you're a good mom who fell into some bad circumstances, and you want the best for

Lily as much as anyone. 'Course I was suspicious of the situation at first. Could you blame me? How many moms give their kid up for adoption, then turn around and break their neck tryin' to keep a part in their lives? The emotional and psychological impact alone could be dangerous for a child put in that situation…"

"I understand," she nodded, dabbing the corners of her mouth with a napkin. "I do now anyway, so stop worrying about me being offended by your direct line of questioning. All that really matters is Lily's happy, well cared for, and apparently thriving in this 'Immersion' project of yours. Her grades are incredible. Merri tells me her teacher's thinking of advancing her to the second grade."

"Wow," Jasper whistled appreciatively, folding his hands in his lap. "*Now* you see what we do out there at the CDC. Do it damn well, if I don't mind saying so myself."

He chuckled softly, eyeing her across the table. A shaft of sunlight turned his handsome features to a stark profile of light and shadow. "You should come by after hours sometime, A.M. I'd love to show you around the whole place. Fewer distractions."

"Oh, I don't know," she began, removing her napkin from her lap and tossing it on the table. "I'm usually so busy around the house when Lily's away. I live for the times I can bring her home to sleep in her own bed. I just miss her so much, every day…" She looked away, watching as patrons paid their checks and left, filtering onto the sidewalk in small clusters.

Jasper gestured to the crowd. "Probably got the right idea. It's about that time…drop you back at work?"

"Thanks." She was getting up when a shrill chirping sounded from her purse under the table. Mae reached for it, holding a finger in midair. "Just a sec, Jasper. It's my phone."

"Phone?" He chuckled, opening his wallet and tossing a couple of bills on the table. "Since when did you get one of those?"

"When I realized I needed to be accessible to my daughter at all times," she replied, pressing the SEND button. "Hello?"

"Mae, are you watching TV? You won't believe this. The police think you're dead, both of you."

"What!" she recognized Merri's panicked voice on the other end. "I don't understand. What are you talking about?"

"Where the hell are you? It's all over the news. They broke in with a special report this morning—they say they found two bodies up at an Elysium Park, someplace up above the city. They're burned beyond recognition, and they're saying it's you and Lily."

It just can't be.

Detective Richard Spencer sat behind a squat metal desk, shaking his head. In one hand he held an unfurled paper clip; in the other, a black and white photo taken of the Elysium scene early that morning.

How the hell did they end up there? he wondered, fiddling with the paper clip. The photo was of an old hunting shack, left desolate long before tree huggers upstate decided the wild stretch of forest along Interstate 9 should be fenced in and renamed a state park. The shack had existed until about late last night, when one of the rangers on patrol spotted a column of smoke rising in the hills. Fire crews were dispatched, under the impression teenaged vandals had somehow made their way in and torched the shack out of sheer boredom. The grue-some discovery came when one of the firefighters was sifting though a remote corner of the structure. Looking for small pockets of smol-dering flame, his axe uncovered the remains of a skeletal hand…

He glanced up to see Peter standing silent before him. His partner moved around the desk and patted his shoulder, gesturing toward the station's front doors. "Go on home, man. I'll drive up and check it out, let you know what I come across."

Richard shook his head, slamming the photo and broken paperclip on the table. "I got it, man. I can handle it." He placed a shaky hand over his face, rubbing the bridge of his nose furiously. Peter remained silent, shifting uncomfortably from one foot to the other as the moments ticked by.

"She took her," he said finally, rising to his feet. "I'm her father and she took her from me. I gotta check this out for myself, see if she's really out there in that mess with my own eyes. I'll go crazy doing nothin', just sitting in that empty house waitin' for the final word." He grabbed his keys, getting to his feet. "You coming?"

Peter nodded. "Yeah, I'll ride out with you, man. You sure about this?"

Richard only turned away in answer, carefully picking his way through the mob of officers and suspects as he made his way toward the doors.

Early morning sun drifted through the trees as the men drove through the gates of the park. A uniformed officer handed them a map, the trail to the shack outlined in thick red ink that bled through the pages. As Peter read the map and pointed out directions, Richard maneuvered the large truck deeper and deeper into the forest, climbing steadily upward until they reached a plateau about three miles above the forest floor. They parked in a small clearing and got out. Perimeter tape wrapped about heavy tree trunks cordoned off the area, blowing in the breeze like yellow ribbon.

The men walked over to one of the waiting detectives. He stood next to another unmarked vehicle, scribbling furiously in a small notepad. Peter spoke first. "Detective Hollis?"

The man looked up, pencil in mid-stroke. He squinted into the sun, looking them over carefully. "You got 'im," he said finally. "Who the hell's asking?" He closed the cover of the notebook with an impatient flick of his wrist and ran his fingers through his thinning blonde hair, absently rubbing a small spot of pink scalp showing through. He wore a rumpled gray trench coat over an equally rumpled navy suit. His striped red tie hung loose under thick jowls. "Well?"

"Detective Blake," Peter answered, extending his hand, "and this is Detective Spencer—"

The rumpled man straightened instantly, holding out his hand toward Richard. "Detective Spencer? Man, so sorry. It's either real early or real late, depending on my clock, and I'm on my last legs. Got the call for this one as I was heading in for the night. You sure you want to—"

"What you got so far?" Richard interrupted, ignoring the proffered hand as he stepped around the men. He eyed the scene, watching as a few tendrils of smoke from the wreckage swirled lazily into the crisp sky. He zipped the down jacket he wore over a dark shirt and jeans; the air was turning icy with the approach of winter.

"Not much. Two bodies, one adult, one child. Just skeletal remains after the fire. We called it in to you guys because of certain evidence recovered from the scene. Techs found this." He held up a small plastic bag to the sun.

The men strained to get a better look. Richard froze when his eyes fell on the bag's contents, eyes widening in their sockets. Inside, burned and twisted on the remaining links of its chain, lay Lily's gold locket. Now it made sense. She'd been wearing it in the picture he'd distributed to the press, a fancy portrait Mae had given him as a Christmas gift the year before. Virtually everyone in his unit was familiar with the little girl and the locket; he kept this same picture on the corner of his desk, glanced over at it every evening as he came in for duty.

Detective Hollis stepped up to the edge of the yellow tape. "The scene's still a bit unstable because of the heat. Firemen are on standby in case of rekindling. Bodies are still on site; we're waiting for the coroner to get his butt on up here. They were found over there." He pointed to a bundle of blackened wood.

" 'Course it's hard to tell at this stage, but we believe they were probably already dead at the time of the fire. Must have been hard up here alone at night, especially with winter on the way. We found bits of scorched cotton fiber nearby—you know, the kind they put in sleeping bags? Anyway. Hard to determine exact cause of death, with the bodies being burned so badly and everything…"

He paused as Richard dropped his head, pads of his meaty fingers digging deep into his brow. Peter reached out and put a tentative hand on his partner's shoulder. Richard shook him off, edging as close as he dared to the spot where the bodies lay. The lingering smoke, coupled with the strong odor of burnt debris, nearly knocked him off his feet. He swayed, pressing both hands to his temples. The thrum of voices slowly ebbed as other officers on the scene turned to glance in his direction.

A hush fell over the forest as the men gave their fellow detective a moment for reflection. In the midst of their respectful silence, Richard's voice echoed loudly, scaring a family of nesting birds into flight. "Hollis! *What the hell happened to the bodies?*"

The two men rushed over, careful not to disturb the debris at the edge of the area.

"Wha…" Peter whispered to himself, peering at two sets of shattered bones partially buried in a heap of charred wood. "Now *that* doesn't make—"

"Sure it does, Detective Blake," Hollis interrupted. "We're in a forest. There's plenty of wildlife up here, scrounging around for food. They were probably deceased only a short while before scavengers came along. Bears, a couple of wolves maybe. Pretty savage, but most large predatory animals can easily rip an average-sized human apart—"

"How long?" Richard swallowed, eyes trained on the desiccated corpses.

Hollis shrugged. "Like I said, it's hard to tell. But if I had to give an estimate…summer season ended a couple of months back, rangers were up here a couple of weeks ago and didn't report anything unusual, so a few days, a week at most? Maybe they holed out somewhere else for a while, Mom started getting' jumpy 'cause of all the TV exposure, decided to sneak up here after things got quiet and met up with some bad luck.

"We think there's a strong possibility hypothermia may have been a factor. She probably couldn't carry much with the kid along, hardly enough to survive up here in the middle of nowhere with winter coming. In all likelihood, they crawled into a couple of sleeping bags one night and snuggled as best they could, went to sleep and never woke up. Some stupid punks probably came along after the animals did their thing and lit the place up like a Christmas tree for the hell of it, never bothering to check what, or who, was inside."

The men turned as a black van marked CORONER pulled into the clearing. The scene resumed its normal volume as officers returned to business as usual. Detective Hollis started toward the van. "Got to get him in and out of here before those damn reporters come snoopin' around." He slowed, glancing at the men over his shoulder. "You're welcome to hang around if you like, but I've got hours of reports to file before I can even think of getting some shuteye."

He started to go but turned around one last time. "Oh, and Detective Spencer. Just want to say once more how sorry I am for your loss, but there's really not too much you can do here now. We haven't classified this as a homicide, so maybe you should give some thought to going home and getting some rest, huh? Any family or friends in particular you maybe want to call or be with right now?"

Richard started to reply when his cell phone chirped, startling him. He nodded goodbye to Hollis, pressing the SEND button as he watched the rumpled detective approach the coroner.

"Spencer."

"Rick! Call the TV station right now! Those bastards on the news, they said…they said…it's not true, is it? TELL ME IT'S NOT TRUE, RICK!"

"Just hold on, Deb, I'm coming," he replied, ripping his keys from his pocket as he sprinted toward his truck.

Mae closed her eyes, seeing the light of the flickering candles beyond her closed eyelids.

Breathe. She inhaled and exhaled slowly as she held her hands in front of her, letting them float through empty space until her fingers gently brushed against the canvas.

Again, breathe. Mae inhaled even more deeply, this time taking the scent of vanilla into her lungs. She pictured the ivy plant hanging near the window, a stick of incense planted firmly in the soil as tendrils of its heady scent wafted over the room. She allowed her hands to drift over the blank canvas, feeling the grainy texture sliding effortlessly beneath her fingers. Her ears perked up as the opera hit its climax; she listened attentively to the lilting voices coming from the stereo as she strained to see it in the darkness of her mind. For a while there was nothing. She was about to give up and have another sip of wine when the vision finally came: a surging waterfall, crashing violently against parched earth the color of bone, crystalline water flowing to a tranquil pond in the middle of…

Mae opened her eyes immediately, choosing a medium–sized brush and soaking the bristles in plum paint. She had only covered the canvas with a few strokes before the doorbell sounded from below.

You gotta be kidding me, she sighed irritably, slamming the brush down on the easel tray.

"Thought dead women stopped having visitors," she muttered as she trudged down the stairs, wishing the person would just give up and go home. For most of the week she'd kept an even lower profile than usual; it was almost too good to be true to believe Philly PD would find two burned bodies in a deserted state park and simply assume she'd be stupid enough to take Lily into the hills and die of exposure, end of tale. What if the story of their apparent death was just an elaborate ruse to flush them out? Erring on the side of caution, she'd been frequenting the solarium less at work, instead forcing herself to occupy her lunch hour reading in the faculty lounge or taking long walks. She'd even returned to the Square with Jasper a few times for a quick bite and some window-shopping.

Mae smiled, thinking of the silly stories he'd shared as they bought fruit at the market or peered at storefront displays. He continued to hold his tongue in approval of the unusual "arrangement" between her and Merribelle; he was good at his job, and a good influence for Lily, so why did she fail to consider him a true friend after all this time?

As she reached the foot of the stairs, the doorbell sounded again. Mae walked to the door, standing on tiptoe as she strained to see the waiting figure though the peephole. Definitely a man, tall and broad-shouldered. Perhaps Henry, stopping by for one of his regular visits. She reached for the knob. Or…*Richard?*

"Henry? That you?" she called out shakily, checking the locks on the door instead. "Henry?"

Silence. Mae called out again, the fear in her voice palpable within the confines of the small entry. "R-Rick…"

"Rick? Who's *he* supposed to be?" an all-too familiar voice sounded from the other side of the door. "Well, I see you were expecting *select* company tonight, so I guess I'll try stoppin' in another time—"

Mae flipped the locks, yanking the door open. "Jasper! What the hell are you doing here? It's after eight!"

He stood smiling on the porch in jeans and a black sweater, a bag of popcorn gripped tightly in one hand. In the other, he held an iced bottle of Chardonnay, drops of condensation slipping from the chilled surface to land on the tops of his boots. "Who, me? Oh, I was just passin' through and thought I'd drop by to keep away some lonelies."

Mae covered her mouth with her hands, stifling a laugh. Jasper grinned. "So what's the deal, lady? You gon' let a gentleman in the door, or you gonna scrape him all frozen of your porch boards in the morning? It's *cold* out here."

Mae brought two ceramic mugs into the living room, handing one to Jasper before settling herself on the big red sofa. She was barefoot, in a well-worn pair of denims and gray cotton tee, her waves pulled away from her face with a clear plastic barrette. "Sorry I don't keep wine glasses around. I drink mine out of plain old coffee cups, just like everything else."

Jasper laughed as he stood by the mantle, stoking the fire with an iron poker. "No problem here. Wine's good out of a fast food cup, long as it's the right year." He sat on a couch across from Mae, folding his long legs under him easily.

Mae shrugged. "Tastes the same to me no matter what year, Jasper."

He smiled again, taking a sip from the #1MOM coffee cup. "Then you've never had good wine. You keep hanging with good ol' Jasper, and you'll know your wines in no time." His dark eyes sparkled as he watched her.

Mae felt a blush of embarrassment rising to her cheeks and looked away, focusing all her attention on the flickering fire. In the dimness, the flames seemed to be thousands of tiny tongues, licking provocatively at her from across the room. She shivered, rubbing her arms lightly.

"Cold?"

She nodded. "A little. Left my sweater in the library upstairs."

"You have a library?" he asked eagerly, setting his mug down on the coffee table.

"My grandmother had a lot of hardcover classics I wanted to display, so I converted one of the spare bedrooms into our library. Lily loves it..." she faltered, staring at the floor.

Jasper fingered his goatee in the silence. "I know it gets hard sometimes. I don't have children of my own, but I find myself getting attached to a lot of my CDC kids. They sure feel like mine, least for a couple hours or so." He reached for the popcorn bowl, offering it to Mae before tossing a handful of caramel kernels in his mouth.

She fought an ill-concealed smile. "So who on earth gave you the idea popcorn and wine go together like peanut butter and jelly?"

He gazed into the fire, chewing thoughtfully. "An old friend, A.M. A very old friend."

Mae stared at him, firelight casting shifting shadows across her skin. "You probably learned a lot from her then, Jasper. Looks like she made you."

"Me?" he chuckled, setting the bowl back on the table. "Oh, now how come you women always thinkin' you gotta pick us up and put us back together right? Us men handle our own pretty well."

"Trust me," she answered, draining her cup. "Experience is the best teacher, and I can tell you for sure the best men alive are those who've loved great women. We show you what it is to be compassionate, considerate…" she nibbled the inside of her cheek, deep in thought. "Okay, okay. I take it back. A woman doesn't *make* a man—"

"Now *that's* what I was waitin' to hear," he trumpeted, broad grin spreading across his face.

She returned the smile, folding her arms across her chest. "A woman just makes a man *better*."

The two stared at each other a moment from their opposite couches, tendrils of flame licking the air between them.

"Well it's obvious you've loved before, A.M.," Jasper began, pouring more Chardonnay into their empty mugs. "Obvious it comes natural for you. So what man on earth could've been dumb enough to let you get away?"

Mae shifted uncomfortably, smile fading as she gazed into the fire again. Jasper corked the bottle and glanced up at her, a somber expression erasing the beautiful smile. "Uh-oh, I screwed up, didn't I? I've gone and offended you yet again…"

She silenced him with a firm shake of her head. "Like I said before, don't worry about offending me, Jasper. We both know our friendship has gone way beyond the crisp politeness of strangers by now." She brought the cup of wine to her lips, their gazes locking over the rim.

A slow smile spread on Jasper's face again as his dark eyes held hers. Mae was, suddenly, aware of shadows enveloping them as night approached, with only the soft ivory glow of a voluptuous moon to light their way…

"So how about showin' a guy like me what a lady does to keep herself occupied Wednesday nights?" he whispered, grinning.

"Wow," he whistled appreciatively. "You mean to tell me you do all this kind of paintin' for ol' lady Smith down at the Square? No wonder Lily's a natural." He slowly circled the room, pausing every couple of steps to admire canvases leaning against walls or hanging over rows of books. "How many have you sold?"

"About twenty," Mae replied as she closed a window near the ivy, sliding the latch into place. She grabbed her sweater off the back of a chair in the corner, wrapping herself in the fuzzy fabric.

"This is beautiful work," he marveled, stooping to pick one of the canvases up. "She actually sat still long enough for this one?" He held out a painting of her daughter sitting on the swing in the front yard, smiling gaily as she held a pink rose.

Mae laughed, reaching for the canvas. "Must have been one of her good days."

"She's a great kid, A.M. One of the best. You and the Tidwells have done well with that one." Jasper glanced around the room a final time and turned to her, smiling his mischievous smile. "So *this* is how a woman like you fills up a night alone?"

"Besides waiting for my kid to get home?" She gave a decisive nod. "Yep, this is how I keep sane Monday through Thursday, week in and week out."

He shrugged. "Well there's nothing wrong with it to my eyes." He watched her replace the canvas and walk around, slowly blowing out a cluster of candles illuminating the space. As she held up the candle nearest him he touched her arm, chuckling as she looked up at him questioningly, her lips puckered as if in a kiss.

"What?"

"Don't blow it out just yet." He took the candle, placing it on the small lamp table she'd taken it from.

So close...

He came as close as he dared, holding her in his gaze. Mae watched him silently, willing her body to move, though she knew her bare feet were rooted to the spot. She thought of the flames then, licking at her from downstairs...

"Come into the city with me next weekend," he murmured, moving ever closer. "We could find a good eatin' joint, dance to the blues 'til your feet get sore and you beg me to carry you home..."

"Come on, Jasper," she laughed nervously, backing away from him as if awakening from a spell. "I just finished telling you how important the weekends are to me. That's the only time I have with Lily. I'm not willing to give a moment of it up for anyone."

"I'm sure we can come with something more agreeable to your schedule, then." His hand floated up to her face, brushing a strand of hair from her cheek.

Like tongues of flame...

"We can drive up Thursday afternoon instead," he continued, taking her in his arms with surprising ease. "Enjoy some music, see the sights...it'd be fun, you know that. We always have fun together, don't we?"

Mae thought the flames had somehow followed her upstairs, tasting the path she'd traced on the hardwood floor in her bare feet. They seemed to insinuate themselves between her thighs, bathing her in warmth.

"Oh sure, you bet," she replied sarcastically, "'cause we're either stuffing our faces or discussing my child's stellar extra-curricular progress. I hardly think that's reason enough to take things to another level." Despite her words, she sighed in the comfort of his arms, feeling him move her expertly around the canvases until they leaned against a wall. "You know me well enough by now, Jasper," she whispered, his lips only inches away. "You know anything having to do with Lily perks my ears up, unless…" she pushed him away, taking a step toward the door. "Unless you're just using Lily to get me to—"

Jasper held up his hands to silence her, disappointment written in his dark eyes. "Don't even take it there, Anne Marie. I was hoping you at least thought a little better of me than that." He stepped around her into the hall. "Guess it's about time for me to be heading on home. I get the feeling if I stay here any longer, I'll be in real danger of wearing out my welcome in this house."

He started for the stairs as Mae blew out the remaining candles and closed the door. They walked down to the first floor in silence, Jasper pausing briefly in the entry as she saw him out. "So can I give you a call sometime?"

Mae opened her mouth to respond, her words silenced by the shrill ringing of the telephone. She placed a hand on his shoulder. "Could you hold on just a sec? That might be Lily."

He nodded, crossing his arms over his chest and leaning against the door. She ran back into the living room, snatching the receiver up on the fourth ring. "Hello?"

"Mae, it's so bad…" Merribelle's voice, thickened as if she'd been crying.

Mae felt the earth giving way beneath her feet. She gripped the arm of a nearby chair, trying to steady herself. "Oh God," she cried, sinking into the chair. "Lily…"

"No!" her sister yelled into the phone. "Not Lily, Mae. She's fine. She's just fine. It's Momma. She's come down real ill, even worse than before. Doctor thinks she may be going tonight."

Mae looked up as Jasper walked into the room. He instantly read the anguish on her face and took her hand. Their eyes met, and Mae shook her head: *Not Lily.*

He nodded understanding, rubbing her back lightly with the other hand. Mae continued to shake her head as she listened to her sister. Finally, she placed the phone back in its cradle and lowered her head, wiping the tears sliding from beneath her wire rims.

Jasper squeezed her hand. "I'm here for you, A.M. Tell me what you need."

Mae looked up at him wearily, deep sorrow etching itself into the lines of her face. She took a shuddery breath. "I need…I need to go to my mother."

NINE

Mae wanted to cover hear ears. The screaming was killing her. High, piercing, earth shattering, her mother cried and screamed like a banshee as she lay in bed clinging desperately to life.

Lung cancer.

So the old woman's poison devoured her in the end after all, Mae thought as she stared out the window. The doctor hadn't had much to say when she and Merribelle arrived, just to keep her comfortable and supported on the mound of pillows Cina had gathered from other parts of the house. She was drowning in her own bodily fluids, coughing up viscous sprays of blood and thick brown phlegm with every breath. Even the oxygen tank did little good.

Merribelle lay on the bed beside the old woman, singing softly to her as she held a damp washcloth against her cracked, fevered skin. After another wave of fitful coughing, Lynne turned to her daughter, tugging on her shirtsleeve with all her strength.

Merribelle leaned as close to her mother as she could, her ear nearly pressed against the woman's mouth. "What is it, Momma?" she whispered anxiously.

"Why…is *she* here?" the old woman rasped loudly, startling them both. Mae turned from the window in time to see her sister wince and jerk away, nearly falling off the edge of the bed.

They both watched as Lynne pointed a gnarled finger at Mae, her entire body trembling with the effort. "She's not welcome in this house. If her father knew, he'd turn right over in his grave—"

"Hush, Momma," Merribelle scolded. "She's your baby girl. She's your own, just like I am."

"My own?" the old woman cackled. "My *own*? A murderer's what she is, and she's going straight to hell right with that grandmother o' hers!"

"Momma, I'm warning you," Merribelle said sternly. "I'll walk out that door if I hear one more foul word against my sister. Just so you know, she's only here 'cause of me—*I'm* the one who asked her to come. I was hoping you could at least try to put this thing between you to rest for good. Especially now..." she paused, plucking a tissue from a box on the nightstand and blowing her nose. "Especially now the doctor has given us such bad news."

"She ruined my life, that one," Lynne whispered, pointing again. "She took my Jonas."

"Momma! Daddy hurt himself because *he wasn't well.* That wasn't Mae's fault, she was just a girl."

"A curse from the devil's what she was! She broke up my family and brought this misery on me!" Another wave of coughing racked her frail body mercilessly.

Mae turned back to the window, staring up at the clouds ringing the moon. How many times had she lain in her bed as a child and wished she could be up there, so far from this house and her life in it even the memory of her would have eventually blown away like dust?

"I truly believe the Good Lord will avenge all wrongdoings heaped upon His saints," she continued. "I may be leaving this life soon, Ella Mae, but as the Almighty is my witness, I'll see you pay for your sins in the next!" This last sentence broke off into more watery hacking.

Mae sighed, pressing her face against the glass. The cool slick surface was soothing to her aching forehead.

"All right, I've had enough," Merribelle said, getting to her feet. "I think we should give you time to rest some." She grabbed the bedcovers, yanking them fiercely up to her neck before placing a heavy hand on her brow. "Feverish, but cold to the touch. Here." She grabbed a brown prescription bottle from the night table, shaking two small white tablets into her palm.

Mae was relieved to see the macabre display of bowls, and the altar, gone. Since leaving the house that night, she'd never spoken to anyone about the frightening shadows that could touch with real hands and call out her name…

She massaged her forehead and watched as Merribelle placed the tablets in their mother's waiting mouth and held a water glass to her lips while she struggled to drink. At last she set the glass down with a sigh. "You rest, Momma. Mae and I will be right down the hall if you need anything." She turned down the lamp as they left the room.

The two women walked along the upstairs hall in silence, listening to the lonely sound of their footsteps echoing through the empty house. As they reached the landing, Merribelle's fingers locked onto her sister's arm, forcing her to cry out in surprise.

"What the hell's your problem, Merri!" Mae yelled, wrenching her arm away. "What the hell is *my* problem?" Merribelle cocked her hand on her hip. "Damn it, Mae, Momma's dying up there, and I still don't have answers. You tell me right now why she can't stand the sight of you anymore, why she can hardly bear to speak your name without following it up with a slough of curses, why she paid good money to have you tracked by bloodhounds but didn't care to contact you all those years after you left…" she turned away, wiping tears. "What the hell is *wrong* with this family? I thought we were happy. I thought we had a good life growing up. Why does it feel now like everything I ever believed about us was a lie?"

Mae plopped down on the top stair with a sigh. "Because it was, Merri. Everything was."

Merribelle sat down beside her, carefully folding her legs under her beige cotton skirt. She was quiet a moment before she turned to her finally, looking her straight in the eye. "It was Daddy, wasn't it? What did he do, Mae? Please. He was my daddy, too. If he did something terrible, then I gotta know. I have a right to know."

Mae drew her own legs to her chest, resting her chin on her knees as she'd done so often in childhood. "It's too late to change anything that's happened, Merri. Granna wanted to change things, but everything, *everything* was rotten by then, everything was dead long before anyone ever knew."

Merribelle reached out, gently stroking her sister's hair. "Sometimes I find myself wishing you'd let me hug you again. After Granna passed, it was like you never wanted to be touched, like you purposed to shut yourself off from everything and everyone you ever loved from that day forward…" she continued to caress her head as her words floated into the still air. "You were always so beautiful, Ella Mae. You've grown into such an amazing person. I was always in trouble at school for fighting the boys 'cause of you, remember that? Remember when Momma used to take me up to her room and pop me on the bottom with those hard house shoes of hers? Well I never once told her why I hit those boys, Ella Mae. I never told her I beat 'em up because I was protecting you.

"I was proud to be your big sister, even then. I was proud of your smarts and your beauty, though I'll admit I was a little jealous sometimes when I couldn't quite fill my dresses up the way you could." She offered a faint smile. "But you were everything to me, and you have to know leaving you here was one of the hardest things I've ever had to do.

"I remember hugging you that day before Daddy took me to the airport, how you clung to me like you were drowning…I remember the look in your eyes, how terrified you were, but I kept thinking 'she'll be fine—she's just jittery about the distance'. I thought you'd be all right without me 'cause I just *knew* I'd done more than my share of protecting when we were young…but I was wrong, wasn't I?" She drew her hand away, pressed her fingers to her temple. "I wasn't there to protect you when you needed me most; I knew you were scared of something that day and still I walked out of this house, just relieved 'cause, for once, I'd only have to look after myself…" she clamped a hand over her mouth, tears trickling between her trembling fingers. "I'm so sorry I let you down, Mae," she sobbed. "I don't know how you can forgive me…"

"Don't do this to yourself, Merri. You weren't the cause of what happened." She reached for her sister's hand, taking it in her own. "Don't blame yourself for what's dead and gone. *He's* dead and gone, that's all that matters to me now. So we're not the carefree little girls we once were. I've got Lily now, and you've got Tim and the babies…life has changed so much. Let's keep moving forward, for their sake. They deserve all the love we have to give now, at least that's how I like to think of it." She returned the smile at last, giving her sister's hand a reassuring squeeze.

Merribelle sniffled and nodded, bending down to wipe her face with the hem of her skirt. She glanced at her watch as she sat up, then jumped to her feet. "Oh my gosh, I've gotta get back to the house. Tim's out of town for the night, and the kids are home alone."

"Who's gonna stay with *her?*" Mae frowned, using the banister to pull herself up.

Merribelle hesitated. "I'm afraid you're it, kiddo. There's no one else to look after Momma on such short notice."

"Well, why can't I just spend the night with the kids while *you* stay with her?" Mae whispered anxiously, rubbing her arms as a chill crept over her. "She can't stand being in the same room with me, Merri! How could you even consider leaving me alone with her?"

"Because, like I said, there's no one else," Merribelle replied over her shoulder, heading downstairs. "Come on, it's only a few hours. Cina sometimes stays overnight when Momma has her bad spells, but she's got family in town for the week and has to tend to them. She's usually here before eight though, sometimes sooner. With Momma being so ill, she might just be in well before the sun is up. She likes to rub on sweet oils and pray these weird prayers over her and stuff." Merribelle reached the ground floor and walked to the coat closet in the entry. "Besides, I don't think it's wise to risk much more than necessary when it comes to you. We still can't be 100 percent sure that story leaking from up north is legit…well, you know what I mean. If it's just some big hoax to flush you and Lily out in the open, we could end up in deep trouble here. Better to keep up pretenses and play it safe a little longer, don't you think?"

"I think," Mae began as she watched her sister shrug into her jacket, "I think this is a terrible mistake."

"I gave her a strong sedative for the pain. It should keep her out most of the night. You can take one of the spare bedrooms and check up on her every couple hours or so, watch her close to see if she takes a turn for the worse." She propped the front door open with the toe of her shoe, rummaging through her purse for her keys. "Tim should be home around seven, and I'll be over right after to relieve you." She started out the door, but turned and wrapped her arms around her sister anyhow, giving her a big hug. "You call if you need anything, anything at all. I keep the phone next to my bed, so don't worry about waking the kids. Hell, I doubt I'll be doing much sleeping tonight anyway." She stepped out onto the porch, shutting the door behind her with a soft click.

Mae stood alone in the entry, beginning to tremble as the house slowly enveloped her in a shroud of silence.

Mae folded a corner of the page she'd been reading, resting the book on her lap as she glanced over at her mother. She hadn't screamed once since Merribelle left hours before; her craggy features, so prominent when awake, were smooth and unlined in deep repose as she slept on quietly, the thick quilt she lay under rising only a fraction of an inch with each labored breath.

Mae sighed, taking a glimpse at the bedside clock. 2:30 A.M. and counting. At least four more hours until she could even hope to be relieved of her duty. She'd almost prefer Cina's crude remarks and brusque behavior to the eerie silence of the house. It was as if it knew death was coming to claim its remaining occupant; the house seemed to be waiting with baited breath for the slightest creak of a door or rattle of a window signaling entry…

She sighed and turned her attention back to her current literary pastime: a book of Vodoun practices titled *Crossing the Horizon*. She'd discovered it amidst a stack of books on the subject while wandering around downstairs. *The divide between the world of the living and of the dead is but a fine line indeed; this is a bridge that must be considered carefully before it is to be crossed. The* Baron Samedi *is the keeper of this bridge; in his hand rest all the secrets of the dead, and the living who hunger after this knowledge eat willingly from it. While the* Baron *stands at the doorway to the world beyond, the* Gede *provide communication and even transport between the two realms; they are tricksters of a sort who are not above taking on the form and likeness of humans who have previously crossed over. These spirits are reported to possess great strength and often make their home among the shadows…*

Mae paused, a memory of her last visit to this house fresh in her mind. The thick, nearly impenetrable darkness of this very room. The grotesque altar. Cina standing in the hallway, grinning. *"So you meet de ol' Baron an' de Gede, hmm? 'Dey hold de keys to life beyon' death, 'dem two…"*

Mae jumped, the hardcover sliding off her lap and smacking the wood floor with a loud thud. She glanced again at her mother, still sleeping soundly.

"Hello?" she called out, grabbing the book and heading for the hall. She thought she'd heard a sound downstairs. Perhaps Cina hadn't been able to stay away after all with her beloved employer so ill? If she was lucky, Mae could get out of here much sooner than she'd dared hope…

She crept down the hall toward the stairs, looking over the railing as she went. Lamps burned in the front entry and parlor; from where she stood at the top of the stairs, the rooms looked empty and undisturbed.

She came down and walked over to one of the windows flanking the front door. Only her tiny compact sat in the driveway. So she was still alone in the house after all. *Just great,* Mae thought sarcastically as she plopped down on the floral sofa in the parlor, curling herself up on the stiff cushions. She grabbed a small throw off the back and spread it over herself, opening the book to the dog-eared page as she settled in again to read…

This love…this love is a strange love…

Mae sat bolt upright on the sofa, searching frantically in every direction. Nothing but shadows cast by low lamplight in the room. Must have dozed off a minute there, *she thought to herself, shivering. She draped the throw over her shoulders, reading the grandfather clock by the door: 3:15. She'd go upstairs and check in on her mother soon, but first…*

Mae swung her legs onto the floor, reaching for her sneakers. Cold, *Mae thought.* Too cold. Now where was that thermostat again?

As she bent to tie her laces, she detected a flash of movement out of the corner of her eye. Her head snapped up, once again searching the dimness. There in the hallway, the shadows began to shift, slowly taking on form…

"Daddy?" she whispered hoarsely. The saliva in her mouth suddenly dried up; the book tumbled off the edge of the sofa, crashing to the floor again. To Mae, the sound was hollow, muffled like steel hammers landing on beds of cotton.

The shadowy figure seemed elated at the thought of being recognized. He flapped his arms and tapped his feet jovially as he turned about, finally posing in a ta-da gesture. At last he stepped forward, letting the light of the parlor wash over him in full. The cuffs of his starched navy dress shirt were rolled to the elbows, a pair of black dress slacks held on his sturdy frame with scarlet suspenders.

He shoved his right hand in his pocket as he leaned casually against the doorframe, holding the left one in front of his nose. Watching her closely with his dark eyes, he slowly curled the fingers until only the index remained visible. He smiled, puckering his lips in a shhh gesture. "Hey there, Ella. Has my little girl been good today?"

"Yes, Daddy," Mae answered hollowly, cringing as far back against the cushions as she could manage. This was their familiar routine she remembered, acted out dozens of times in childhood.

"You know that momma o' yours won't be home from shoppin' for at least a couple hours. How 'bout you keep daddy some comp'ny, hmmn?"

Mae suddenly realized the room looked strange. The furniture hadn't moved an inch, but...

She looked out the windows. They were thrown wide open. Light of a late afternoon sun streamed into the room, drenching her skin with warmth. Springtime, *Mae thought. But spring was months away...*

Jonas Carpenter beckoned to his daughter, waiting patiently as she slowly got up from the couch, letting the throw slide to a puddle at her feet. "Come on, darlin'," he said, taking her hand. "You can tell Daddy how your day went." As they passed the front entry, she chanced another glance out one of the narrow windows. Night had fled completely, along with her vehicle; her father's late-model Buick sat alone in the gravel drive, shined to perfection, as always. Please, *Mae thought miserably when they reached the stairs.* Please, Momma. Hurry up and come home...

"I'm real glad you're here to keep me comp'ny," Jonas began, carefully placing a polished loafer on each step. "Daddy comes home real stressed most every day, but when I see you in that parlor, boppin' your head to that record player or lookin' at one of them cowboy flicks, it makes all my ails go right out the door." He released her hand, the fingers trailing slowly up her arm until they rested on the small of her back, moving there in soft circles. A sensual touch, inappropriate for a father to give, yet almost normal, it happened so often...

Mae suddenly realized she'd been in error; this was no memory from childhood. Her father had always wanted her to 'keep him comp'ny' late at night, long after her mother had gone to bed. The two of them had always been night owls, and he'd often join her in the parlor as she watched Technicolored westerns or listened to late night radio. He would make cocoa for the two of them, attempting to engage her in light-hearted chatter until she'd finally get the courage to excuse herself, telling him she was tired, needed to rest. At that point, he'd always insist on "tucking my girl in snug," escorting her up the stairs to her bedroom at the end of the hall, far from the safety of her mother's sleeping form.

He would massage her back as he helped her undress, singing softly to her when she began to cry. She always cried at that time, knowing what was coming...but he never cared, laying her back on her coverlet of peach roses while he worked to unfasten his belt, breathing heavily. She could always smell his favorite scotch on his breath long before she was forced to taste it on his lips, and when she focused on the moon high above, counting the bands of color in the rainbow circling the luminescent orb, she would hear him hum "This love...this love is a strange love..." as he stretched the length of his sweaty body atop hers, grinding against her as his twitching fingers clenched in her curls...

If this is no memory, *Mae thought fearfully as they entered the upstairs hallway,* then what the hell *is* this?

Hand in hand, they walked slowly down the hall toward her old bedroom. Mae glanced in her mother's room as they passed. The bed was completely empty, the covers crisply tucked and folded neatly in place. A shaft of light lay across the immaculate coverlet. A solitary orchid in a crystal vase decorated a small lamp table before the open window, the delicate petals yielding to the weight of intermittent spring breezes.

As they stood before the door to her old bedroom, she froze, planting her sneakers firmly on the polished hardwood. "Daddy, I don't want to go in there anymore."

Jonas offered a bewildered smile. "Well of course you do, darlin'. It's your room. Why on earth wouldn't you want to go in your own room?"

"Because it isn't *my room anymore, Daddy. I'm not fifteen anymore, you can't make me go in there with you again—"*

Jonas placed a gentle hand under her chin, lifting her face until their eyes met. She flinched away from his touch, stunned at the sorrow she read in his countenance.

"Just one more time, darlin'. Please. Do it just once more for your daddy."

Mae covered her face with her hands, weeping softly. To the house, the sounds were those of a frightened child. "Daddy, please don't make me, please..."

"Shhh now," his ice-cold hand fluttered across her cheek. *"It'll be okay this time, I promise you. Daddy's gonna make everything okay again, just trust me."*

Mae heard him circle behind her, felt his hands press on her shoulders as he led her into the room. If I just stay here in the dark, *she thought, fear quickly giving way to hysteria,* if I just keep my eyes closed and think of the moon, he'll go away, he'll leave me alone, it'll be over soon...

He guided her toward the bed. Mae felt the pressure of his hands on her shoulders increase when he forced her to sit. She let out a sharp cry, feeling the coils of the old mattress pressing against the backs of her thighs. Lord, how long would this go on...

"Ella, please look at me."

"Daddy, I can't," she whimpered in response, still shielding her face with her hands. Surely the darkness would comfort her as it had Lily when Richard came to her...

Mae jumped when she felt her father's hands on her wrists, gently pulling them apart.

"Look at me."

She forced herself to look up at him, watched as he slowly loosened his tie. He stared silently at her a moment, his misery so profound it seemed to distort his features. Finally, he reached for her hand again, closing his heavy fingers around hers. "Come on, darlin'. It's time Daddy made everything right. You'll see. Daddy's gonna make everything like it was before."

Slowly, Mae allowed herself be pulled to her feet and led to the adjoining bathroom she'd once shared with her older sister. Twisting the brass knob, he swung the door open wide to allow room for Mae to enter. She shuffled into the tiny room, slumping on the toilet as her father walked in behind her. Without a word of protest, she watched him turn on the rusty faucet, sending a spray of warm water into the dusty porcelain tub. She stared dully ahead as he removed his dress shirt and undershirt, unfastened his belt and shimmied out of the dark slacks.

He removed his underwear, stepping into the warm bathwater. Mae shuddered convulsively, staring out the tiny bathroom window at nothing in particular. So cold in here...

"Hand me that razor, darlin'. Over there, the one in Daddy's shaving kit."

Mae looked around her for the familiar bulky leather pouch. She finally spotted it next to the sink, nearly hidden under her father's clothing. Shaving kit? But Daddy never shaved in our bathroom, *she thought, flailing it in his direction before turning back to the window. She heard him unzip the pouch; imagined him opening it and reaching inside for his tools. Long before he started "tucking her in" at night, she used to love to sit on the toilet in her parent's bathroom while he bathed, listening raptly as he told tall tales and whispered raunchy jokes her mother would never allow him to tell at the dinner table. The view beyond the bathroom window began to blur; Mae blinked away hot tears, hating the way they felt against her icy skin.*

The sound of her father's voice startled her. Was he crying?

"I always loved your momma, Ella. Knew I was gonna marry her the first day I saw her, and when you and Merribelle came along, I felt like my whole world was complete. I had a healthy business, a big house, a family…I just knew I was the luckiest man on earth, that God had smiled down on me the day He'd given me all this."

Mae slowly turned away from the window. And screamed.

"But I messed everything up," her father wept, scraping the shaving razor across his skin. Trails of dark blood snaked across his arms and trickled into the clear water, turning it a pink color. He smeared bloody handprints around the edges of the tub as he fought to keep himself upright. "I took everything God gave me and threw it right back in His face. I destroyed my life and sealed my place in hell the night I took my own daughter to bed, my own flesh and blood…"

The blade had turned completely scarlet, the bathwater now a river of blood as Jonas Carpenter slashed diligently at his flesh. "I let those unnatural desires control me, and I broke your heart, Ella. I broke your trust. You can't imagine how much it hurt me seein' you so frightened day after day, can't know how it made me feel to see hatred in your eyes whenever you looked at me…"

"Daddy, stop!" Mae screeched. "I don't hate you! I don't hate you!" She fell to her knees before the tub as if in prayer. "Please, Daddy, don't do this," she wailed. "Look what you'll do to Momma. You're all she's got left; it'll kill her to find you like this. You don't understand. It'll drive her crazy…please, Daddy, get out of the tub so I can help you…"

His head fell back against the rim of the tub, the hollow thud of skull against porcelain deafening in the small room. The sorrow that had so tightly wound itself around his features began to fade, gradually replaced by an expression of peace Mae had never before seen in all the days she'd known him. Her hysterical screams fell to a whimper as she watched her father slipping away.

"There's no place for me in heaven anymore, Ella Mae," he gasped, eyes beginning to flutter in the back of his head. "I know that now. All I need is to know you'll find a way to forgive me someday for what I've done to you. I wanted to make amends; I wanted you to see your daddy could make things right again…"

"Shhh," Mae whispered, holding a shaky finger to his lips. "It'll be okay now, Daddy, I promise. Go on to sleep. Go on and rest…" she pressed a trembling hand to his cheek as his eyes closed for the last time. Curling into a fetal position on the cold tiles, she wept in a puddle of her father's blood as grief washed over her in black waves. An uneasy sleep had almost claimed her when her mother let out a piercing scream.

Even as she fought her way to consciousness, she could hear her mother screaming.

Mae opened her eyes. She was on the sofa in the parlor again, exactly where she'd been when she first noticed her father's shadow standing in the hall a lifetime ago.

Thank God, just an awful dream…

She jumped to her feet when she heard the scream a second time. "I'm coming!" she shouted as she sprinted into the hall, taking the stairs two at a time.

She stumbled into her mother's room and froze, realizing she was surrounded by darkness again. As her eyes struggled to adjust, Mae could vaguely distinguish her mother's slight form from the other shadows in the room. She approached the bed slowly, wanting to slap her hands over her ears to shut out the gurgling sounds the old woman made as she struggled to get air into her decaying lungs. She could feel her mother's piercing stare even as she bent to switch on the bedside lamp.

Her mother's face was twisted into a vicious snarl, the rheumy eyes bulging from their sockets. Mae recoiled, realizing her mother was trying to smile at her.

"What?" she whispered, backing up a step.

"He has come home tonight, Mae. My Jonas." The snarl widened as she continued. "Tonight is the last I will spend in this house, here among my precious memories, my beautiful things…" she hacked a thick clot of brown phlegm into a soiled handkerchief she held in her gnarled hands. In the low light, the old woman resembled a skeletal corpse lying under the blankets; Mae blinked to clear her vision as she took another step toward the door.

"Tonight is my last on the earth, and I'm a happy woman 'cause my daughter has finally seen with her own eyes the horror I witnessed that day. Oh yes, there was so much blood, wasn't there? Blood everywhere, and I laid there with him in his blood for hours, wept in his blood, kissed away his bloody tears…" the woman sighed, her entire body rocking with the effort. "I've paid my dues, Ella Mae. I lived all these years in misery, worrying this day would never come. But God answers the prayers of His saints, and His ways are just. Tonight He's made the ultimate barter with the devil; He's given me peace in exchange for your pain. Now you'll suffer as I have, reliving that day every day as I've relived it for years. Now *your* eye will be plucked and dashed on the earth…and you must know, nothing has brought me greater joy in this life, Ella Mae. Nothing." The old woman's eyes slid shut and her head drooped on her chest, the soiled handkerchief tumbling to the floor in a crumpled ball.

Though light from the lamp illuminated the room, Mae felt herself sinking back into that unpleasant, yet familiar, darkness, the stress of the night eating away at her sanity like the cancer had eaten away her mother's insides. She managed to snatch the phone from the bedside table and dial as she slumped against the wall, eyes locked on her mother's lifeless form.

Her sister picked up on the first ring. "Hello…Mae, is that you?"

The world swam in slow motion around her, the colors in the room fading to dull shades of gray and brown. Mae bit down hard on her lip to keep herself alert, wincing at the coppery taste of blood filling her mouth. "Come get me, Merri. It's over."

"Momma? Momma's *gone?* Hold on, Mae, I'll be right there." There was an audible click as Merribelle hung up.

"Come get me Merri," she repeated again and again into the empty line. "Get me out this house before it eats me alive."

TEN

Deborah held up the last blood-red rose, pressing the velvety petals against her lips. She twirled the long stem between her fingers, tracing an aimless path along the ebony casket lid before placing it reverently atop the others. She stepped back under the shelter of Richard's black umbrella, unfurled and held high to protect them from the downpour.

Rain fell mercilessly from the sky, pelting the mourners as they stood clustered around the burial site, heads bent in silent contemplation. The minister murmured a final benediction, grabbing a handful of moist earth and tossing it onto the casket. Deborah's rose tumbled off the side of the lid, landing in the mud six feet below. She looked up at Richard, watching his face crumple in misery. He held his head in his hands, weeping silently.

She put her arm around his trembling shoulders, pulling him close. He collapsed in her embrace, and the two stood there, swaying in the rain as the minister and mourners began to retreat to the warmth of their waiting vehicles.

He gripped her waist, pulling her even closer. "Deborah, I can't…"

"It's okay," she whispered, wishing desperately that Malcolm were there beside her instead of working a double shift at the hospital. "It's gonna be all right, honey. We'll get though this, I promise."

"My God…Lily," he wailed, falling to his knees before the casket. Deborah looked around, searching for assistance. Most of the mourners had driven away. The rest stood near their cars, chatting and smoking a final cigarette before making the long drive upstate to his parents' home. They'd insisted on hosting the gathering, understanding their son would need more of their love and support than ever before…

Deborah dropped to her knees beside him, cradling his hand in both of hers. She sat with him on the muddy ground in silence, feeling the cold rain seep through her clothing to her skin. She shivered involuntarily, gripping his hand even tighter. When his sobs quieted, she stood to her feet, pulling him up with her. "Come on, Rick. We'll be the last ones to show at your parents' place."

"Take me home, Deb. I just want to go home."

"But they're expecting us—"

He turned away, snatching his hand free of her grasp. "Go on without me, then. Give everyone my regrets, tell my folks I'll call 'em in a couple of days, whatever." He started for his truck.

Deborah watched him a moment before running to catch up. "Rick, wait! I can follow you home, at least, before I head up there. I'd feel better being able to tell them I made sure you settled in for the night."

Richard stared blankly at her, then shrugged noncommittally. "I'll wait while you get your car."

Richard stepped into the entry, letting the wet trench coat and umbrella fall to the floor beside him. Deborah followed him into the dim living room, at once overwhelmed by the oppressive silence. He stood in the center of the room, his back to her. She slowly walked up behind him, pressing a comforting hand between his shoulder blades. "Rick. If you need to be alone, I can go…"

"Deb," he heaved as sobs again wracked his body, "I…I don't know…how am I gonna make it through this alone?" He collapsed in her arms and they held each other again, sliding to the floor together in an awkward heap. "She was supposed to come home to me, Deb. This was her home. All her clothes are upstairs, all her stuff…what am I gonna do with 'em now?"

Deborah opened her mouth to answer but paused, feeling a sudden buzzing sensation against her thigh. She felt around in her trench coat pocket, at last pulling her pager out to read the blinking text message:

Thinking of you. Call me when you can.
Love, M.

She stared at the flashing letters for one indecisive moment, then dropped the pager to the floor beside her as she placed Richard's head in her lap.

"I can't, I can't…" he muttered over and over, barely coherent.

Deborah rubbed his head, gently rocking him in her arms. "Shhh, Rick, it's gonna be okay. I'll stay with you. You won't go through this alone, I promise…"

"Hey, stranger! You don't answer your phone anymore?"

Mae jumped, watching helplessly as the cantaloupe she'd been holding slipped from her fingers.

Jasper quickly kneeled down, catching the melon just before it could crack open on the worn linoleum. "Whoa, lady. Close call. Here, let me get that for you." He placed the melon in her basket, giving her a playful wink. "Must have somethin' particular on that mind of yours, A.M. Care to share some of those woes over a glass of red? I promised to teach you about good wine, and I never forget a promise."

Mae started the basket up the aisle again. "Don't you think it's a little early in the day to be celebrating?"

He shrugged. "I always want to celebrate whenever I'm with you. Thought you'd figured that one out by now." They rounded a corner and stood before several brands of bread.

"Oh, you're pretty good," Mae chuckled, grabbing a loaf from the bottom shelf. She moved to toss it in the basket but paused as Jasper clucked his tongue, shaking his head slowly. "What?"

"Bargain bread never makes for a good meal." He cleared his throat dramatically. "If I may." He held his hand out for the bread, and after a moment's hesitation, she handed it to him.

"I'm hoping this isn't gonna too take long, Jasper. I'd like to leave the store sometime today." She planted her hands on her hips, fighting a smile. She watched as he shoved the bread back in its place, carefully selecting a name brand from one of the upper shelves.

"Take a good look at this one."

Mae shrugged noncommittally. "Looks wonderful, same as it did a few minutes ago when I passed it up, on my way to the cheap stuff." She bent down, reaching for the loaf she'd chosen earlier.

"Now hold on just a sec, A.M.," he said, placing a hand over hers before she could grasp it. "Close your eyes."

"Jasper, I really don't have time for this…"

"Humor me, all right? Close your eyes a second. Won't hurt a bit." He crossed his thumbs. "Eagle's honor."

Mae sighed in frustration, closing her eyes. In the darkness, she felt him take her hand in his. He placed it on top of the bread, caressing the fingers lightly while sliding them back and forth over the clear wrapping. Mae drew in a sharp breath and giggled, unnerved at the excitement she suddenly felt. She leaned her head against the store shelf and grinned, praying they weren't being watched. "Jasper," she whispered into the dark, "Just what exactly do you call yourself doing?"

"Getting you in touch with your senses. Keep your eyes closed." Still holding her hand to the bread, he gently pressed down on the loaf, squeezing it between their interlocked fingers. "Feel anything?"

Mae giggled again. "Ohhhh, yes. I'm feelin' real bad for the person who ends up buying this loaf of bread we're molesting with our sweaty hands."

"I swear girl, you got no imagination." He released her hand with a chuckle and she opened her eyes. "What'd you think?"

"Soft," Mae observed, thoughtfully stroking her chin. "Very soft…but still too rich for my budget."

"Tell you what," he said, leaning in close. She could smell the spicy scent of his aftershave, mingled with the wintergreen mints he chewed almost constantly. "I'll buy this sweaty loaf for you, IF you promise you'll share some of it with me this evening."

"Is that your quacked method of asking me to dinner?" Mae inquired, heading for the canned goods on the next aisle.

"Only if this is your roundabout way of accepting," he replied, falling in step beside her. He bumped her shoulder playfully. "Come on, it'll be good for you to finally get out of that big ol' house. You been shut up in there since…" he trailed off, walking along in silence.

Mae nodded understanding, plucking an industrial sized can of peaches from the shelf and tossing it into the basket. "It's been rough lately."

"Well why don't you come up to my place tonight, then, say 'round six-thirty or so. Kick back, relax, let me cook you up something real special. I know you can't forget your troubles forever, but you can at least let me help you put 'em out your mind a few hours, if that's what you really want."

They strolled toward a teenaged cashier sporting an EFFIN' GODDESS tee and a bored expression. Mae thought it over as Jasper bagged her groceries for her, laying a large bill on the counter for all her items. As he grabbed the bags and started for the door, she laid a tentative hand on his arm. He glanced at her questioningly. "Think you can make it?"

"You cook Cajun?" she asked coyly, arching a brow.

"Catfish Courtbouillon and red sauce work for you?" he shot back, grinning broadly as they stepped into the parking lot.

"Mmmn…" Mae nodded, returning the smile. "Now *that's* the Cajun I remember. I'll be there a little before seven."

"With our bread, right?"

"Huh-uh," she laughed, opening her trunk so he could place the groceries inside. She reached in one of the bags and pulled out the loaf, pressing it gently between her fingers with fluttering eyelids. "No, sir. This bread and I have gotten pretty close in the last half hour, thanks to you. So close in fact," she said as she arched her back, tossing a melodramatic hand to her brow, "the idea of paahtin' with it now just *pains* me…"

"Don't matter," she heard him say as he slammed down the trunk lid. Moments later she felt his hands close firmly over hers. Startled, she opened her eyes, staring deep into his own.

"You're the only thing I want to see tonight, lady," he whispered mischievously. "The *only* thing. See you at seven." He backed away swiftly and began wading through the sea of vehicles, heading toward a hunter green SUV parked a few lanes down.

"Hey, wait a minute!" she called after him. "Where the heck are your groceries?"

"Already been to the store this week," he answered, turning around. "You know, you should really try doing some of your shopping on Saturday mornings in the future, A.M. It's so calm and peaceful around then." He smiled, reaching into his back pocket. "Happened to be driving through the Square when I thought I noticed your car pulling into the lot. Took a chance and drove in behind you, hoping for more luck…" he pulled his hand from his pocket, holding up an unopened pack of wintergreen mints for her to see. "…and of course, I wasn't disappointed." He ripped off the cellophane wrapping, popping one of them into his mouth. "See you tonight."

Mae smiled as she watched him jog to his car, shaking her head softly.

Hours later she sat on the deck of Jasper's lakeside home, sipping Merlot from a crystal goblet as she watched him clear the table. "Sure you don't need any help with that?"

He looked up, cradling their dinner plates expertly in the crook of one arm. He was casually dressed in jeans and sneakers, the navy polo he wore fitting comfortably on his wiry frame. A soft breeze tousled his hair as he smiled. "Guess you don't hear very well, do you?" He sighed, rolling his eyes theatrically. "Women. Look, all I'm asking you to do tonight is forget about your troubles and relax." He gave a swift wink, heading for a sliding glass door. "Be right back. Have a look around if you're feelin' inclined."

Mae watched him step through the door and enter the kitchen. She took another sip from the goblet, savoring the deep flavor of wine flowing over her lips and tongue. She got up and walked to the edge of the deck, glimpsing her reflection when she passed the sliding glass door. She herself was dressed in a red cotton sundress and white sweater, her feet clad in a pair of matching white sneakers. Her waves hung loosely about her face, tickling her cheeks with each lingering breeze.

Taking another sip from the goblet, she gazed out over the sprawling expanse of back yard. Beyond the immaculate lawn and vegetable gardens, Mae noticed a small footpath leading into the surrounding wood. Curious, she headed down the deck stairs. When she reached the path she turned, searching for Jasper. He was still wrestling dishes inside, so she continued to follow the path as it wound through the trees before opening up on a small meadow.

She stepped off the path into a field of wildflowers, casting her eyes toward the setting sun. The sky was an artist's palette of pinks and blues, spun together expertly like celestial cotton candy. Mae folded her arms, watching reverently as day turned to night. She closed her eyes, listening to the wind blowing through the trees overhead and the crickets chirping from their shelter in the high grasses.

"Figured I'd find you back here."

Mae spun around, nearly losing her balance. "Geez, Jasper, I see why they call you the heartbreaker. Keep scaring me like that and my heart'll surely be broken soon—"

"Who said that?" he interrupted, walking past her toward the middle of the field. He held the bottle of Merlot they'd begun at dinner in one hand, a heavy flannel blanket and antique oil lamp in the other. He spread the blanket out before them, seating himself and filling his goblet with more of the crimson liquor. "Join me?"

Mae walked over and sat down, folding her legs under her comfortably. He refilled her glass and re-corked the bottle, staring placidly up at the sky. They watched as the sun burned its dying impression into the heavens before finally disappearing behind a line of distant trees.

Jasper was the first to break the silence. "So who says I'm a heartbreaker, A.M.? Man has a right to know who's calling him out his name so he can at least defend himself."

Mae shrugged. "Just something I overheard one day at work. I was finishing up lunch in the solarium when a couple of the kindergarten teachers sat down on the bench next to mine. Ms. Jordan and Ms. Willows? I'm sure you know them. They're young, beautiful…the only single women working there, besides myself. Anyway, I was about to get up when I heard Ms. Willows mention your name. The redhead, Ms. Jordan…" she paused, waiting for him to show the slightest sign of recognition. When he didn't say anything, she plunged on. "She bursts into tears, mumbling something about you and a broken engagement. She was real upset, Jas; she couldn't be comforted. I felt so sorry for her…" her words trailed off again as she searched his face for emotion. In the shadow of semidarkness, his features were nearly unreadable. She could tell he was troubled, however; she waited patiently for him to respond.

After a few moments, he finally cleared his throat. "Well I guess this town's not much for keeping secrets, now is it?" he chuckled, shifting uncomfortably on the blanket. "We talked about it a while, getting married. At first it seemed like a good idea. She thought she was ready, hell, I know I was. It just became clearer and clearer as the day got close that we just weren't ready for *each other,* know what I mean?" He looked up at her, eyes pained and pleading for understanding.

Mae looked away, nodding vaguely. She sipped the Merlot, once again attuning her ears to the cricket serenade. "Do you still love her?" she whispered finally, picking a stray piece of grass off her dress.

Jasper sighed. "Enough to know I couldn't give her what she wanted, couldn't be the man she needed me to be."

"And just what does that really say about *you,* Jasper?" she demanded, suddenly turning on him. "She seems so sweet, what was the problem?"

"I, I don't understand what you're getting at—" Jasper stammered.

"Just what *is* it with you men?" she put the glass down, starting to get to her feet. "All you know how to do is use a woman and toss her aside like trash when the excitement's gone, when all of a sudden she isn't doing it for you anymore. What was it like for her the day she searched your eyes and saw that the look of desire, the look of appreciation and respect you'd given her for so long had simply faded away? How many times did she try to turn herself inside out for you, to make you happy just so you'd stick around? I've been where that woman's been, I know how it feels to be forgotten." She closed her eyes briefly as an image of Richard flashed through her mind. "No woman deserves to be treated like that, I don't care who she is. Tell me, Jasper. What was it she wanted and needed so badly that you couldn't—or *wouldn't* give her?"

"It wasn't even about give or take, A.M.," he began as he placed a hand on her wrist, pulling her back down on the blanket. "She needed an ideal man who fit into her ideal world. She wanted a Ken doll, and I'm definitely no Ken. I broke it off with her gently as I could, took off to Europe for a while to clear my head. I'd just come back in town the day I met you." He ran his fingers through his wiry curls, pushing them wildly out of place. "What can I say, Anne Marie? I thought I loved her, even came home with the notion I'd made a mistake in calling it off. I was prepared to go back to her, to try and make it work anyway, until…"

"What?" Mae prompted when he paused, brow furrowing in confusion. "What changed your mind?"

Jasper opened his mouth to speak and clamped it shut, only shaking his head in answer. He glanced up at the sky again, noting the fading light. Smiling hesitantly, he reached for the oil lamp. "I'm glad you headed down this way. This is my favorite place to hang when life gets too crazy. Here, I want to show you something."

He turned a small knob at the bottom of the lamp, watching as the tiny flame burst to life, held in check only by the thick glass cover. Mae was suddenly aware that twilight was quickly dissolving around them. She was grateful he'd thought to bring the blanket and lamp along.

"Right about now, something special always happens out here…now, just be real quiet and watch." He turned the knob again, diminishing the lamplight to a dim glow.

Mae looked around her anxiously, becoming nervous in darkness that was nearly complete. "Maybe I should be heading on home…"

"Shhh." He took her hand. "Just a moment longer, I promise. They're almost here."

"They? Who's th—"

Jasper silenced her again with a finger to his lips. Mae bit the inside of her cheek, suppressing another surge of anger. In a few more seconds, she would get up and walk back to the house alone to retrieve her car. She was just getting to her feet again when she saw them. Tiny points of light dancing in delirious circles all around them. She froze, watching in wonder as the lights seemed to multiply, hovering above the edge of the meadow like fallen stars.

She sat down again, careful not to disturb the spectacle. Jasper gently pulled her into his embrace. "Fireflies," he breathed softly against her ear.

Mae shivered slightly when his goatee tickled her skin, enjoying the sensation. She leaned her head against his shoulder as he closed his arms around her protectively. "They're beautiful," she whispered, watching the lights dance over the meadow.

"I knew you'd like 'em." He grabbed her hands, lacing the fingers with his own. "You know, after all my time living here I think they're actually startin' to get kind o' fond of me."

Mae closed her eyes, breathing in his spicy aftershave. "Or maybe they put up with you because you come with the territory? You know what they always say. Take the bitter with the sweet."

Jasper tapped her thigh playfully. "Now you know that's not funny."

"Ah," she chuckled, turning to face him. "Can dish it out, but can't take it, huh?"

Jasper gazed down at her, brushing her hair away from her fore-head. "You wanted to know what changed my mind, about Kerri…"

Mae nodded, waiting patiently for the answer. She glanced at the fireflies again, fascinated by their movement. The stars had finally come out, twinkling high in the night sky like jewels against ebony cloth.

"It was you," Jasper whispered, turning her face to him again. "I don't know what happened when you came to this town, Anne Marie, but ever since I saw you that day in Stan's office I haven't been the same. It's vexin' me even now, 'cause try as I might, I can't make good sense of it."

"Jasper, we don't have to talk about it—"

He shook his head. "I tell you, I think about you all the damn time now. It's driving me crazy, wanting you so much it keeps me awake some nights." He leaned in close, brushing her lips with his own.

Mae pulled away from his touch, moving toward the edge of the blanket. "Jasper, we probably shouldn't do this. You know I have Lily to think about. I have to stay focused on my priorities, and her well being is priority number one in my life, always. That doesn't give me time for much else, especially…"

"You don't think I understand how difficult the separation is from your daughter?" He sighed, running his hands through his hair again in frustration. "Lily's the most wonderful kid I've ever met, A.M. She's so smart, so talented. She's got everyone at that damn Center practically wrapped around her little finger, and I love her for that. She's amazing, and I'd never want her to question her place in your life 'cause of me. It's my job to heal kids, A.M., not destroy 'em. Please…" he moved to close the distance between them, cupping her face in his hands. "You told me what Lily needs, but you haven't said a thing about how you're feeling."

"That's because I don't know *what* I feel right now, Jasper. I need time to think things over…" she placed her hands on his shoulders, not knowing if she wanted to push him away or pull him close. He leaned forward in answer, still cupping her face gently in his hands.

Mae could feel the excitement coming off him in waves. As he pressed his lips against hers a second time, she too became excited, instantly aware of the fire burning urgently in her loins. Jasper covered her mouth with his own as she ran her fingers through his tousled hair.

"Mmmm…*Chéri*" he mumbled, his fingers trailing over the red hem of her dress. Mae gasped when she felt them slip between her thighs, stroking her there over the plain cotton underwear. *My bright whites…how sexy,* she thought, bursting into nervous laughter. She covered her hands with her face, bits of night sky peeking through her trembling fingers.

"What's wrong, sugar?" Jasper asked, gazing down at her. The smooth skin of his forehead wrinkled when he frowned, confusion and concern evident on his face. The hands between her thighs ceased their movement.

"Jasper…" she began as he moved her hands away from her face. "I'm not…you know, very experienced with this kind of thing. I've only ever had…you know, just the one."

"Lily's father, I get it." Jasper nodded understanding in the darkness. "It's okay," he whispered as he kissed her again, the hands beneath her skirt beginning to move again in slow, tantalizing circles.

"Wait," Mae said, pulling away again. "You don't understand. It wasn't…it wasn't the greatest relationship. When we were together, it wasn't…I didn't…"

Jasper moved until he lay beside her again, placing a hand under her head. "If I've overstepped my bounds you can tell me, A.M."

"I…I just don't want it to *be* like that anymore," she wailed, tears welling in her eyes. She tried to wipe them away with the sleeve of her sweater, watching the stars swirl a slow pattern across the night sky. She searched the onyx mirrors of his eyes, desperately wishing she could read what lay beyond them.

He gazed silently at her, moving forward again until his lips brushed hers once more. They lingered there only a moment before drifting across her skin to taste the tears spilling down her cheeks. Mae closed her eyes, the erratic pounding in her chest easing as her body began to relax. She lay there unmoving, feeling Jasper's lips tickle her forehead, her cheeks, her chin. The warmth building in the center of her seemed to radiate outward, and it was as if her entire being were on fire now, demanding satiation.

She reached for him in the gloom. When his lips found hers again she pressed her hands firmly against the back of his head, tasting him deeply.

His mouth. The raw, earthy, natural taste of his mouth, wine from his tongue spilling onto hers as he returned the kiss with fervor, moving between her thighs until he pressed himself against her, his arousal apparent. "If it's too soon," he panted when their lips parted, "I'll stop. Just say the word and I'll stop…"

Mae reached for him again, the warmth of her body beckoning to his delirious senses as she silenced him with more kisses. They tangled themselves in the blanket, the silken grasses of the meadow tickling the backs of Mae's thighs as she moved under him, yearning to be ever closer. He paused, light from the oil lamp illuminating him as he gripped her hips and slowly moved downward, planting a trail of kisses as he went. Mae closed her eyes again, the evening breeze sending wildflowers swaying in her direction. They caressed her face and hair as she felt Jasper's fingers slip into the waistband of her panties, felt them slide down her thighs with the underwear until they grazed the tops of her sneakers, the sensation vanishing almost as soon as it occurred.

Mae lay there listening to the crickets, imagining fireflies dancing at the edge of the meadow beyond her closed lids. The breeze tickled her inner thighs sensuously and she parted them, relishing the feeling. She breathed deeply, exhaling late autumn air when she gasped, the warmth of Jasper's mouth startling her from her reverie. His lips moved over her thighs, his tongue tracing lazy designs of his own creation on her clitoris, sucking at her gently, rhythmically until she cried out, rushing air from her lungs sending wildflowers blowing every which way.

She found herself reaching for him yet again, pulling at the collar of his shirt until he lay beside her. Her fumbling hands found the zipper of his jeans, tugging it as she stared up at him, intent clearly written in her eyes. He placed a hand under her head once more, kissing her passionately. He used the other to unbutton his jeans, setting his erection free.

"Please," she whispered, covering his neck with kisses. He pressed himself between her thighs again, skin to skin and nothing in between. When her trembling hands found him, gently guided him to the source of her immense warmth he groaned aloud with pleasure, forcing himself to pull away at the last second.

"What?" she asked uncertainly, trying to catch her breath. "What is it, Jasper? Did I do something wrong?"

"Not here," he panted. "Not like this." A sheen of perspiration covered their bodies in the humid air. She reached up, running her fingers though his damp hair.

He brought her palm to his lips, kissing it affectionately. "I want this to be right for you, A.M. I think you're owed that after so long of…whatever it is you went through with Lily's dad. I want to give that to you, sugar. I think we both need it to be that way."

He sat up, reaching for his zipper. Mae pushed herself up on her elbows, watching him as he dressed. Without a word, she planted a hand behind his neck and pulled him to her again, giving him another lingering kiss.

"I'm going to make love to you, Anne Marie," he whispered as he pulled away, smiling gently. "Just not tonight…not tonight. I want you to be ready for me."

"Ouch!" Deborah cried, jerking her thumb away from the box reflexively. A dime-sized spot of blood welled to the surface of the cut, which Deborah sucked diligently as she stuck her thumb in her mouth.

Richard laughed, carrying a bottle and two glasses over to the coffee table. "I didn't know docs were closet thumb suckers."

"Funny." She wiped her hand on her sweats, walking over to the couch and grabbing one of the iced tumblers. She sniffed the amber liquor, carefully swirling it in around in the glass.

Richard watched her amusedly, a smile playing at the corners of his mouth. "Old habits die hard, I see."

"Mmmn?" Deborah replied, distracted.

He pointed to her drink. "Always a sniff, a swirl, a sip and then it all goes down."

She offered a wan smile. "You taught me well, I guess. Besides, the routine's etched in my mind by now. How long have you been making me drink this crap?"

"Hey, I don't have to bring a $100 bottle home to get a good buzz," he chuckled, downing his drink in one swallow. He slammed the tumbler on the table, sliding the back of his hand across his mouth.

Deborah plopped down on the couch and crossed her legs, bouncing a tennis shoe against the edge of the table as they stared each other down. "You belch once, and I'm outta here."

"Oh no missus, I wouldn't dare," he replied in a shrill voice, folding his hands primly in his lap. "Momma always said never do it in front of the ladies."

Deborah smiled, glancing around the cluttered living room. The space was piled high with boxes and bags, filled to the brim with Mae and Lily's belongings. She examined her injury, a small gash she received from the masking tape she'd been using to secure the last of the boxes. Ironically, they were to be donated to a local battered women's shelter per Richard's request.

"So Petey's supposed to drive this stuff over tomorrow, huh?"

He shrugged. "Guess so. Said he was going to when I talked to him last. Anyway, the stuff's all ready for 'em."

"Uh-uh. We performing our moral and civic duties at last?" Deborah asked sarcastically, crunching a sliver of ice between her teeth.

He reached for the bottle on the table, pouring himself another generous shot. "Nah, just figured it'd be easier to get rid of the stuff that way. The type of broad who'd leave a house and a man takin' good care of 'em to go lay up under another broad in some shelter is always in need of clothes, right?"

"Suppose so, Rick," Deborah muttered, gazing out the front windows. They sipped their drinks in silence, watching neighborhood children play on the street. Since the funeral, Richard had begun calling more, leaving frequent messages for her at home and at the office, even at the hospital when he couldn't reach her anywhere else. He even showed up at her job on several occasions for impromptu lunch dates with expensive bouquets of "friendship roses," as he referred to them whenever she'd attempt to politely refuse his overtures.

He'd been demanding even more of her time lately, asking her over nearly every Saturday to watch a movie or have a drink, using his newfound loneliness as an excuse every chance he got. Unfortunately, she'd been forced to honor his unreasonable requests for one reason: fear. The fear he'd discover he's been duped, that Mae was actually out there somewhere with Lily was palpable, so palpable it has kept her awake many a long night.

Saturday, she thought, as she took another sip, brow furrowed in concentration. *What the heck's so important about* this *Saturday?*

"Oh!" Deborah exclaimed, getting to her feet. "I almost forgot, Rick. Here, let me get it for you." She walked over to the pile of boxes nearest the door, plucking a large white one off the top. She went over and sat next to him, watching his expression carefully. "I was going through Mae's personal things earlier today when I found these."

He pulled the lid off and looked inside, eyes widening. "Oh, I haven't seen this in years," he whispered, pulling out a book covered in pale lavender cloth. "Lily's baby book, right?"

Deborah nodded, tugging the lavender ribbon so the pages fell open in his hands. "Have a look. They're all the pictures taken of your little girl since the day she was born."

As he flipped through the laminated photographs, Deborah reached inside the box again. "Now I *know* you'll remember this," she said, holding a large blue album up for him to see.

Richard grinned, grabbing the book. "The College Years. Yeah, I remember. Mae saved everything. She was always trying to keep track of the important stuff."

Deborah leaned over his shoulder as he slowly turned one page after another. Lost faces of people they hadn't seen in years stared back at them, along with medals and certificates engraved in his wife's name. Several photographs depicted the three of them in various wacky poses at college rallies, theme parks and neighborhood fast food haunts.

"We were so nutty then," Deborah remarked as she gazed at a photo of their graduation. Richard stood in the center with an arm around both women, smiling proudly in his favorite Police Academy sweatshirt. "Remember? We thought we were gonna take over the world." She laughed. "At the time, I really thought we would."

Richard sighed, closing the book and carefully placing it back in the box. "So did I, Deb. I thought we were magic back then, man. Like we had just enough voodoo flowing in our veins to have anything we wanted, make everything go our way. " He gave another mournful sigh, running a hand over his head distractedly. "How things change."

Deborah squeezed his shoulder. "Yep, life's one big gamble. But your luck of the draw was pretty good, Rick. Nice job, good benefits, a pretty house, and most of all…" she tapped the albums. "You had the chance to love two wonderful women who would have done anything for your happiness. Hurts, doesn't it? Knowing how much someone means to you after they've already left your life. Most guys would have killed just to have even a small piece of what you've been given."

Richard nodded, tears welling in his eyes. "It's all gone now, Deb. Everything's gone." He lay his head on her shoulder, crying softly into the fabric of her sweatshirt.

Deborah held him as she'd done so often since the day of the funeral, comforting him as a mother would comfort a heartbroken child. "Rick, I can't promise you everything's gonna get better overnight—in fact, grief probably gets a hell of a lot worse before it can even begin to get better. But we try, honey, we try. We just have to keep working at it every day, no matter what."

"I...I can't even get out of bed half the time anymore," he sobbed, burying his face in her chest. "I th-think God's punishing me 'cause I let it all get out of hand...I let my family get away, and now I'm payin' the price..."

Deborah held him a while longer, rocking him in her arms until his sobs quieted, and he was breathing deeply. She closed her eyes, resting her head on the back of the couch.

"We could have tried harder back then, you and me," Richard whispered against her bosom. "Maybe if we hadn't given up so soon, things would have been different..."

"Rick," Deborah said impatiently. "It's probably not a good idea for us to talk about this. Just rest a while, okay? We're completely exhausted, we've had a long day. Right now, you're a little more than drunk, and I'm in desperate need of a nap. Just lie still and dream..."

"I *do* dream," he replied, moving up on the couch until he lay facing her. "I dream all the time, Deb. I've never stopped. I swear I've never stopped. *You* did this, cast this spell on me, and I can't seem to break it." He caressed her face, the tips of his fingers sliding over her lips. "I guess you do have some voodoo left in you. It's kept me loving you all these years..."

"Don't." Deborah sat up abruptly, pushing his hands away. She got up and headed for the entry, grabbing her jacket out of the closet. "It's getting dark. I'd better be on my way."

"Debbie, wait!" he called, following her to the door. "Wait," he repeated as he grabbed her arm. "I'm sorry, guess I am pretty tired. Let me make it up to you over dinner tonight. We can order takeout from that Italian place you like so much..."

She shook her head. "It's just not a good idea right now, Rick. Why don't you call Pete and grab a movie, huh? It's the weekend. Who knows? Maybe a night on the town is just what you need to get your mind off things."

"Deb, I said I was sorry—"

"I'll call you tomorrow, promise." She planted a perfunctory kiss on his cheek as she left, closing the door softly behind her.

Richard watched helplessly as she jumped in her car and started the engine. Deborah shifted into gear and pulled away from the curb, the rumble of the tiny convertible echoing on the street long after she'd left the brownstone behind in her rearview mirror.

"I made reservations for seven," Malcolm began when she stood there in the open doorway.

He sat on the couch in a dress shirt and slacks, suit coat draped carelessly over the back. He checked his watch, shrugging nonchalantly. "Guess I was wrong to do that, wasn't I? I was wrong to think my woman would want to celebrate our first year together…"

Deborah's mouth dropped open as she stepped into the apartment, glancing at the calendar hanging on the wall in the kitchen. Even from this distance she could see the date circled in red, ANNIVERSARY – DINNER AT 7 – DON'T FORGET ?! scrawled in block letters beneath.

Deborah let her purse fall to the floor, pressing her hands to her mouth. "Mac, I'm so sorry. I was with Richard…"

"You were with Richard," he echoed hollowly, eyes burning smoking holes into hers.

"Yes, honey," she began, crossing the room to take a seat facing him on the coffee table. She planted her hands on his knees, rubbing them in soft circles. "I went over to help him go though their things. He said he couldn't handle it alone, so he asked me to come by. I left a text message on your pager this morning after you went to work. Didn't you get it?"

"Sure, sure, I got it all right. *Ten hours ago.*" He pushed her hands away, rising and walking over to the giant window overlooking the busy avenue. He watched the evening traffic far below, the cars resembling toys with their flashing brake lights. "You been with him all day, Deborah. All *week,* in fact. Every time I look around now, you're always running off with this cat, having lunch here and eating dinner there, doing this and that for him…" he turned to her, his body a lean silhouette against the evening sky. "Is there something I should know here? What the hell's going on?"

Deborah joined him at the window, taking his hand. He pulled away from her, roughly shoving both hands in his pockets. "Malcolm, I swear there's nothing between us. He's grieving. He needs someone right now—"

"Deborah, are you listening to yourself? You were with me when I drove those bodies up to the state park and dumped them in that cabin."

"Mac, I know…"

"I did it for you, dammit!" he yelled, slapping her hands away when she reached for him again. "Everything I did that night was for you!"

"And I'm indebted to you, you know that." She slipped her arms around his waist, gripping folds of his shirt in her fingers so he wouldn't pull away again. "You put yourself on the line for them, and I'll never forget it. Mae will never forget it. You saved her, honey. Her and her little girl, you saved their lives." She caressed his cheek, cupping his face in her hands. "I love you, Malcolm. There's no one else, I swear. You and me, this is forever, right? You don't feel that?"

Malcolm gazed at her a moment. Slowly, gently, he pulled her hands away from his face and walked over to the couch. She watched him pick up his suit coat, reach in one of the pockets and pull out a small black velvet box. He walked back to the window and stood there, opening her hand and placing the tiny box in her palm. "I made reservations for seven…" he began, eyes welling with tears. He cleared his throat as he continued. "I made them because tonight I was finally ready to ask my woman to be my wife, my life companion."

Deborah gripped his arm, sensing what was coming. "No," she cried, tears spilling down her cheeks. "Please, please don't do this…"

Malcolm planted a light kiss on her lips. "I love you, Deborah, I always will. You keep this ring 'til you're ready for the same commitment, 'til you're ready for me. I want to believe there's nothing more to the situation, but I can't. Something inside keeps tellin' me it's not all out in the open yet." He grabbed her other hand, closing the fingers over the top of the box before walking away.

Deborah watched her tears trickle through her fingers onto the box, soaking the dark fabric. "Don't go, Malcolm. I need you," she whispered as he opened the door.

He paused in the doorway, looking at her one last time. "When you're ready, Deb, you know where to find me." He stepped into the hall, closing the door behind him.

"I need you here," Deborah sobbed to an empty room. *"How am I supposed to get through this without you?"*

ELEVEN

Mae stepped over the threshold and handed her jacket to Jasper, planting a brazen kiss on his full lips.

"Mmm, you sure taste good," he murmured when she pulled away. "How's Lily?"

"Better, thankfully." She stepped down into the sunken living room, pushing pink sweater sleeves above her elbows as she shoved her hands in the back pockets of her jeans. "This is the first Friday night we've spent apart since I got here. She begged to go skating with Merri's kids. Who's Momma to say no, right?"

Jasper tossed the jacket in the hall closet, followed her into the living room and took her in his arms. "Lily's the kind of girl who shows no fear when it comes to what she wants." His lips trailed down the side of her neck. "I'm hopin' she learned that one from her momma, too."

"That supposed to be some kind of hint, Doctor?" she giggled, tangling her fingers in his curls.

"Take it any way you like, I'm open," he whispered lustily. He grabbed her hand, leading her toward the kitchen. "Come on, I've got goodies in here waitin' on you."

"More catfish?" she inquired innocently, taking a seat at the table.

"Nope," he shook his head. "Tonight my famous Jambalaya's on the menu. You know your Jambalaya, don't you?"

"Of course," she said, toying with a cloth napkin. "Grew up on it. My grandmother used to make it all the time."

Jasper picked up a wooden spoon and stirred the pot on the stove, tasting the steaming broth before he turned the fire off. "Needs to cool some. Hope you don't mind the wait."

"Not at all." She patted the table lightly. "Come sit down, talk with me for a spell. It's been a crazy week, and I..." she stared out the windows at the deck, fighting a smile. "I guess I missed you a bit, Jasper. You have a way of growing on people, you know."

"Good to hear," Jasper said, grinning. He wiped his hands on a cloth towel. "Be right back. Got something I think you should see." He left the room, returning moments later with a manila envelope in one hand. Sitting across from her at the table, he opened the clasp and shook out two pieces of white paper. He smoothed the creases, sliding them across the table so she could pick them up. "They're Lily's. She drew 'em earlier this week."

Mae stared at the drawings, beginning to tremble violently. Lily's tiny hand had drawn three stick figures on the separate pages. On the first page a woman cowered in a corner, shielding herself from a tall man standing over her as if ready to strike, a carton of ice cream in one hand. The woman was sitting in a pool of blood; red crayon streamed from a gash on her scalp to the floor beneath. The figures had been labeled MOMMA and DADDY in a six-year-old's shaky script.

On the second page Lily had created a self-portrait. Mae gasped when she saw it, covering her mouth in horror. The drawing was well done for someone so young; Lily's naturally wavy hair flowed over her shoulders as she stood in her favorite pair of overalls and pink shirt, but...

"Her eyes," Mae whispered. "Jasper, she has no eyes..."

He nodded, watching her carefully. "When one of the interns brought this to me, I was as blown away as you are now. I called Lily into my office right away and asked her about 'em."

"What did she say?" Mae forced herself to meet his gaze.

Jasper sighed, folding his arms as he sat back in the chair. "Nothing. Absolutely nothing at all. She refused to admit she'd even drawn the pictures, just sat there the rest of the time goin' on about a red bike she saw down at the Square."

"Oh, she's just dying to have that thing." She forced a smile. "You know kids. Won't leave me alone about it until it's hers."

"Anne Marie," Jasper began, reaching across the table for her hand. "I think we should talk about this."

Mae recoiled from his touch, pressing the drawings against her bosom. "There's nothing we need to discuss here."

"Oh come on, A.M., you saw the pictures—"

"I *said* there's nothing to discuss," she repeated, rising from the table.

"*Now* where are you going?" Jasper called after her, following her back into the living room. "How can you brush something like this off your shoulders like it's nothin'? Your six-year-old's drawing pictures of you gettin' beat over the head with ice cream and you think everything's fine. Do I look like I got 'idiot' written across my forehead? What the hell's *wrong* with you?" he yelled, grabbing her arm as she was shrugging into her jacket.

"Get your hands off me!" She pushed him away, holding a trembling finger in his face as she spoke. "Don't *ever* put your hands on me like that again Jasper, or I swear—"

Jasper reached in his pocket, a folded newspaper clipping emerging between two of his fingers. He grabbed her hand and shoved it roughly in the palm. "What the hell you been tryin' to pull, Anne Marie?" he hollered. "I want to know, right here and now. I'm not letting you leave before I get some answers." He glared at her, folding his arms over his chest again.

Mae's eyes traveled to the crumpled scrap of paper. Lily's face stared up at her once again, this time from beneath SEARCH FOR MISSING GIRL COMES TO TRAGIC END typed in bold ink.

"Is that right?" Mae scoffed. "Who the hell are you to think you can stop me?"

"Oh, I'm just the one man who can blow this whole damn thing out the water for you with a two-minute phone call." He snatched his cell phone off the coffee table. "And I seem to recall how nervous you get around telephones."

Mae made a desperate grab for the phone, Jasper easily holding it out of her reach. "You're bluffing," she whispered finally when she gave up, tears of defeat sliding down her cheeks. "You wouldn't do that to Lily."

"Really? You must have forgotten our 'agreement' then. You keep Lily's best interests at heart, and I make sure you keep up your end of the deal, remember?" He pressed the ON button on the phone's keypad, poised to dial. "I said I wouldn't look too deeply into this arrangement you and Merri have going on here, long as Lily's needs came first. But after what I've seen in those pictures, and with no straight answers coming from your way, I got no choice but to get involved.

"This is what I do for a living A.M., what I've built my life around. I take care of kids 'cause I'm damn good at it, and if you know anything about me by now, you understand I can't look the other way if Lily's in trouble, even if I have to overlook the fact her mother's startin' to mean a whole hell of a lot to me." He took a step toward her, letting the phone rest at his side. "I may lose your trust forever if I make this call tonight, but it's a chance I'm obligated to take. Please…" he moved until his face was only inches from hers. "Please help me understand. I can't help either of you unless you're completely honest with me."

Mae sunk to the floor in a crumpled heap. "You don't know what we've been through," she wailed, pressing her hands to her face.

Jasper took her in his arms. "I know. I just want to understand," he whispered, kissing her forehead. "Just help me understand."

"I can't tell you everything," Mae began, staring into the fire. Outside, pouring rain came down in sheets, playing chaotic melodies on wind chimes spinning wildly out on the deck.

"There's just too much pain to relate in words, things I vowed I'd never share…but I'll tell you one thing, that little girl has seen more in six years than most women see their entire lives."

"I believe you," Jasper replied, sipping hot chocolate from a steaming mug. They sat crossed-legged in front of the living room fireplace, watching the flames crackle and hiss as they devoured the log he'd placed in there not long before. The crayon drawings lay open on the floor between them. Jasper picked one up, pointing to the tall man standing over her. "Let me guess…this 'mourning' detective from Philadelphia I've been hearing about lately…*he's* Lily's father?"

Mae nodded, turning her head away. She stared into her mug, feeling the warmth touch her cheeks. "Don't, please. That day brings back so many unpleasant memories."

Jasper folded the drawings along their crease, sliding them back into the manila envelope. "How long did it go on?"

"Almost ten years," Mae sighed. "The day I walked out that door was the last day I ever considered myself his…anything. I had to divorce my entire life to divorce one man, I guess." She sipped the cocoa, deep in thought. "Leaving everything behind was closure for me."

"So what was the final straw, sugar? What made you decide you'd had enough?"

Mae shut her eyes, the memory of Lily crying on her lap returning as if it had been yesterday. The memory was quickly replaced by a nightmare image of her father, lying in his own blood as he begged forgiveness…

"I…wouldn't let him have her," she whispered finally. She gazed into the fire, overcome with grief. "Do the things he wanted to…I wouldn't let them h-hurt her like they hurt me…" she buried her face in her hands, gasping for breath through ragged sobs.

"What is it?" Jasper asked, attempting to pull her to him. "Who's they, sugar? You said—"

Mae pushed him away, folding her arms around herself protectively. "I don't want you touching me right now. It's hard sometimes even letting Lily get close…when she climbs on my lap and gives me hugs, I get this sick feeling in the pit of my stomach, like she'll get dirty by touching me, like what's wrong with me'll be wrong with her someday…" she shook her head, wiping her face with the heel of her hand. "I just want to keep her clean, but when she touches my hair or kisses my cheek, sometimes I can't *stand* it. In the shower, I stand under the hottest water I can take and try and try to wash the dirt off, but the feeling never leaves. It's always there…my burden to carry with me forever, and it wasn't even my fault…"

"There are folks like me in this world who actually want to help you, sugar. Why don't you let me schedule you an appointment with a good friend of mine. Therapy could give you some more of the closure you're needing—"

Mae interrupted, shaking her head vehemently. "I'm afraid that's not possible, Jasper."

"Oh, so you think it's perfectly acceptable behavior for six-year-olds to draw pictures of themselves minus a pair of eyes?"

"No, doctor," Mae replied, a hint of sarcasm in her voice. "I don't think my daughter's art is normal by any stretch of the imagination. Don't you think I know I'll always be the blame for that? She drew those horrible things because she saw them for so long…" she paused, pressing a hand to her chest. "And I let it happen, Jasper. I'm her momma, and I let that man beat on me because I convinced myself if I took it, he would leave her alone.

"For years I thought I was doing the right thing; he never bothered her, never touched her. But one day my little girl came and told me he'd tried to get her to *do things…*" she took a deep breath, meeting his eyes. "It was like a light came on all of a sudden. Something inside my heart snapped, and I knew I'd finally had enough." She covered her mouth with trembling fingers. "But I was too late, wasn't I? I couldn't protect her from him after all. Now every time I hold her in my arms, every time I brush her hair or read her favorite bedtime stories, I'm reminded of my failure as a mother…"

Jasper attempted once more to pull her to him. She shook him off again, getting to her feet. "I should go. I need time to think over some things."

"It's storming out there somethin' serious," he replied, heading for the windows. "Why don't you wait 'til the rain lets up somewhat. Promise, I won't bite," he added as he surveyed the drenched landscape, turning to offer her one of his most disarming smiles.

Mae shook her head softly. "I'm really sorry. There's just too much on my mind right now that needs sorting through." She shrugged apologetically. "Take a rain check on dinner?"

"You know I will," he sighed dejectedly. "However, as a gentleman, I can at least walk you out to your car, in case I'm the last to see you standing before you get swept down the road in that little foreign piece of machinery you drive."

"You're not funny," Mae said, giving him a wan smile. "Grab your slicker if you're coming along, at least. I don't want my guardian angel catching his death while he's on the job."

"Oooh, it's nice to see she's got a sense of humor." Jasper chuckled. "Lead the way, woman."

The couple ran out to Mae's compact sedan parked in the sloping driveway. Jasper attempted to shield her with the rain slicker as she fumbled with the lock. Finally, she managed to get the door open, looking up at him gratefully. "I'm really sorry I couldn't stay, Jas. Tonight was supposed to be special…"

"You don't have to explain," he yelled over the noise of the storm, twirling a rain-soaked strand of her hair through his fingers. "Just make sure you're not a stranger around here in the future. I plan to cash that rain check you wrote."

Mae reached up to caress his face. "You're good for me. Thank you for keeping our secrets. You don't know how much it means to both Lily and I."

Jasper gazed at her in wonder, pushing her hair away from her face. He tried to lift the glasses off her nose. Mae smiled, slapping his hand away playfully.

"What do you *really* look like under all this, A.M.?" he whispered, kissing her lightly.

"Someday, Jasper," Mae began as she climbed in the driver's seat, "Someday you'll know all you need to. For now…" She shrugged, inserting her key in the ignition. She was about to start the engine when she felt his hand in her hair again. She glanced up at him in surprise as he pressed his lips against hers once more. Though the cold water was seeping through her clothing and she was chilled to the bone, she felt the warm familiar stirrings of her body slowly responding to his touch.

"Don't go," Jasper whispered when he pulled away, caressing the back of her neck. Mae let her head fall against the headrest, closing her eyes and relishing the sensation of his lips on her cheeks, her neck, the cleft between her breasts. She raised her arms over her head, gripping the seats as she fought for control. "Jasper, we can't do this…"

Jasper kneeled in the gravel before her. "I don't know the men who've hurt you before," he said, arms circling her waist. He rested his head on her bosom. "But I hope you realize I'm not like any of 'em."

Mae slid her fingers beneath his chin, lifting his face. When their eyes met, hers were filled with sadness. "So sweet, so wonderful…but you don't understand, do you? I'll never be clean…"

"I don't care *what* went down before, you'd never be dirty to me. Only lovely…and broken." He took the top button of her sweater in his mouth, tugging on it lightly with his teeth.

"Jasper…" his name was a sigh on her lips. She held him to her, tears slipping from beneath her closed eyelids.

"I don't want you to feel that way anymore, like you're less of a woman 'cause of what they done to you. I can't promise to make it all go away, but I want you to feel good with me, even if it's for the first and last time."

He stood and pulled her from the driver's seat. She went to him willingly. Together they fell against the car, holding each other tight. "Don't go, Anne Marie," he repeated. "Stay here tonight…" he kissed her deeply, drops of cold rain filling their open mouths.

Mae returned his kisses with fervor, pressing herself against him as water pelted them from the heavens. "What am I doing," she mumbled over and over as he kissed her breasts through the wet fabric. She gasped, tendrils of excitement coursing through her. "Don't know why I'm doing this…"

Jasper pulled away, gazing down at her lovingly. "You trust me anyway, don't you?"

Mae nodded silently as he closed the car door, taking her hand and leading her back to the house.

Mae sat on the bed smiling to herself, listening to the sounds of rain tapping softly against the glass.

"Those eyes still closed?" Jasper's voice came from a far corner of the room.

She nodded, bursting into giggles. "Why on earth are you making me do this?"

"Because this is special, sugar. Just be patient a while longer, okay?" She jumped, feeling his lips touch her forehead an instant before they lost form, evaporating into the darkness surrounding her. "Be right back."

She heard him moving around the bedroom, shuffling this and that on his way out. She forced herself to concentrate on the rain again, aware of the heat growing in her bones. Beyond her closed lids, she could make out a faint glow that hadn't been there before.

"Jasper?" she whispered uncertainly. Moments later, she felt his hands close over hers, pulling her to her feet.

"Open up."

Mae opened her eyes and smiled. Wild roses lay strewn about the bed and floor, and dozens of candles burned brightly around the room, their flickering light casting soft shadows on the walls.

"What do you think?" Jasper asked as he stood behind her, arms around her waist.

"Never seen a thing like it...except in the movies and TV, of course." She turned to him, enfolding herself in his embrace. She lay her head against his chest and laughed again, the sound echoing easily over the hushed space.

"What's so funny, woman?" he asked, suppressing a smile.

"The thought of you tiptoeing around me, throwing roses everywhere and hauling at least ten of those candles in here at a time. What did you do, carry them in a basket? Or perhaps you just loaded them up under your arms, and—"

"Shhh..." he interrupted, silencing her with another kiss. He pulled back, looking down at her.

"What?" she whispered, smile fading.

"I want to make you happy, Anne Marie," he answered. "Names don't matter a bit. I just know I've never wanted a thing so much in my life."

He kissed her again, laying her back on the coverlet. Mae closed her eyes and felt him caress her face, his fingertips trailing softly over her lips. She kissed them lightly, pulling him down to her. He took the buttons of her sweater in his fingers and slid the fabric away, lingering to kiss each spot where they'd lain against her skin. Smiling, he tossed it to the floor, cupping her breasts in his hands. He ran his tongue experimentally over the ebony lace covering them, reaching around to unclasp her bra.

Mae shifted her body to give him more room, leaning on her elbows as she gazed down at him. "You're really beautiful, you know that?"

Jasper paused in the act of unbuttoning her jeans, glancing up at her questioningly. "Think so, huh?" he grinned.

She nodded. "Thought so the first day I met you. My mind was on so many things, yet I couldn't take my eyes off this talkative man with the Cajun accent…"

Jasper chuckled, kissing her navel. "Well, you'll be happy to know I felt the same way. Now lie back," he murmured. "Let me look at you…" He slipped her jeans over her hips, sliding them to the floor. They lay there in a puddle at the foot of the bed as he removed her underwear, planting kisses down her thighs as he went.

Suddenly self-conscious, Mae covered herself with a corner of the coverlet as he stood before her, removing his own clothing. As if noticing her trepidation, he turned and spun slowly in a circle, hips moving provocatively as he pulled the soaked shirt over his head. He tossed it to her, grinning broadly.

Mae giggled and pushed it to the floor, pulling the coverlet tighter around her. "You gon' do a dance for me, doctor?"

The rest of his clothing fell forgotten at his feet as he climbed onto the bed and lay beside her. He gazed at her a moment, smoothing her hair away from her face. "I'll do anything you want me to, Anne Marie," he whispered finally, taking her in his arms. "Anything."

Mae watched the shadows move slowly across the walls and gasped, biting her lip so she wouldn't cry out. Jasper took her breasts in his mouth again, flicking his tongue sensuously over her nipples. Mae groaned softly, tangling her fingers in his hair. She rocked her hips against his in perfect rhythm, each wave of pleasure rocketing her ever closer to ecstasy.

"Mmmm…so *warm*," he grunted as he moved deep within her, his body straining for control. He buried his face in the side of her neck. "Like fire inside you…"

Mae dug her nails into the muscles of his back, giving voice to her euphoria as the final wave claimed the last of her will. He reached under her, pressing her body against his, and she felt him flood into her, rivers of liquid warmth flowing and overflowing between them.

Jasper lovingly kissed the length of her body as she rolled over, pressing her face into the pillows with a contented sigh. He moved his mouth over the backs of her thighs, the curve of her buttocks, the gentle slope of her lower back. Suddenly he paused, concern crossing his handsome features. "Oh, sugar, what happened? What did he *do* to you?" His fingers trailed over two clumsily drawn letters burned deep into her flesh. "This some kind of tattoo?"

Mae shook her head, turning to him. "He called it a mark of ownership, sort of like a—"

"Brand," Jasper finished for her, grimacing. "A brand, like the kind ranchers use to mark their cattle."

Mae nodded, eyes watering. "One night he came home late, grabbed a bottle of the scotch he always drank and turned on the TV. Some old western was playing, I remember that…" she slid the heel of her hand down her face, wiping away tears. "Anyway, I must have coughed too loud or sneezed too many times, hell, maybe I blinked wrong…when he was in one of those moods it was hard to tell, even breathing seemed wrong.

"So I'm walking past him, and he grabs me by the wrist and pulls me onto his lap, like he always did when he wanted to 'make love,' if that's what you'd call it. I said no—Lily had caught some virus and I'd been up with her half the night before. I was on my way to the stairs when he got me."

Mae stared out the glass patio doors, watching the rain pound the damp earth outside. "He dragged me over to the fireplace, threw me down. I hit my head on the floor and lay there, hoping he'd rant awhile and walk away when he got tired. Then I felt it, that searing pain. He'd taken his pocketknife and held it to the fire before slashing me up with it. I remember screaming until I passed out, yet none of the neighbors came to the door to see what was happening, or even called 911, for that matter. Next morning I woke up under some throw blanket he'd tossed over me in a halfhearted act of sympathy, I guess.

"He'd already left for work by then, so I went up to our bedroom and looked over the spot where he'd cut me. It was a mess. It's a wonder there was no infection. Anyway, it hurt like hell. After I cleaned the wound I could see it, plain as day…"

"R.S.," Jasper muttered, running his fingers over the scar. "His name. So anyone else who got close enough to get a look would know—"

"That I belonged to him," Mae finished, closing her eyes. "That I'd always belong to him, no matter what. He was always accusing me of cheating, whether it was with the postman or the butcher or even the man who smiled in the car next to ours, it didn't matter. In his mind, I was with everyone I could get my hands on the moment he stepped out the door."

"That's horrible," he whispered, closing a hand over hers.

"It was my life." Mae lay down on the pillows again, lost in her own thoughts. Finally she spoke. "The truth, Jasper. Do you think it's ugly?"

Jasper considered it a moment. "I think it's a permanent, nasty reminder of what you had to go through with this guy. Nothing I ever do can erase all that's happened before, sugar…but I *can* touch you where it hurts most, if and when you need me to. I can kiss your scars."

He leaned forward, gently pressing his lips against the letters as Mae began to cry softly.

Newly planted Dwarf palms danced just outside the open window on mild afternoon breezes, the light hissing sound like ocean waves to Mae's fifteen-year-old ears. Her mother stood at the kitchen island holding a corn-flower blue bowl in the crook of one arm, a look of intense concentration on her face as she worked to stir the thick yellow substance inside. Mae slowly entered the kitchen, dragging her scuffed Mary Janes across the freshly

mopped linoleum. She paused just inside the doorway and sniffed, the familiar aroma of lemon cake mix filling her nostrils.

Lynne glanced up at her daughter, wiping her hands on a gingham apron the color of roses as she sat the substance on the tiled countertop. "Your favorite, birthday girl."

Mae didn't respond. Lynne put her hands on her hips, eyeing her curiously. "Well, don't just stand there like a cigar store Indian, Mae. Come on in if you're gonna help your momma out." She smiled brightly, waving her over to the island.

Mae approached with hesitation, taking a seat on a wooden stool across from her mother as she began to work with the cake mix again.

"I'll make sure to save the bowl for you, Mae, just like always."

Mae shook her head softy. "It's okay, Momma. You don't have to worry about that this time."

Lynne laughed, stirring the cake mix even harder. The clanging of metal spoon against porcelain bowl was maddening. "What are you talking about, girl? You always like me to save the bowl. I've been doing it long as I can remember. Why on earth would you want a change now?"

She paused in her stirring once again, looking her daughter square in the face. Their eyes met for a moment over the colorful floral tiles of the island, then Mae looked away. She gazed out the window, watching the palms as they seemed to beckon to her beyond the partially raised glass.

"All right," her mother said, sighing. "I'll just toss the bowl in the sink and give it a good wash, then. It's not a big deal, but I figure turning fifteen doesn't necessarily mean you have to start givin' up all the stuff you used to do when you were little—"

"Momma it's not that, I swear." Mae shifted uncomfortably on the hard wooden stool, watching her index finger trace a scarlet rose painted on one of the tiles. "Momma, I've got something to tell you, now that Daddy's out of the house."

"If it's about changing our plans to go to the ocean this weekend for your birthday, then forget about it. Your daddy's been looking forward to this for weeks—"

"Momma! Will you please listen to me?" she reached for the arm holding the metal spoon and grabbed it, moving it away from the bowl. *"I...I just need you to listen for once, Momma. I mean really listen."*

Lynne leaned against the kitchen sink behind her, folding her arms over the gingham apron. *"All right, Ella Mae, you've got my full attention. Now what's got you so bent out of shape? Must be bad if you can't even enjoy the fuss people are makin' over you 'cause of your birthday."*

Mae dropped her head, folding her hands in her lap. Taking in a shuddery breath, she whispered, *"It's Daddy, Momma. I have to tell you something about Daddy—"*

"What about your daddy?" Lynne rushed to the island again, resting her trembling hands on the tiles. *"Is something wrong with him? I just saw him a couple hours ago. He went out shopping for your present. It was supposed to be a surprise..."* Hands fluttering to her bosom, she whispered, *"I haven't heard the phone ring all day. Did someone call with bad news, Ella Mae? I'm always telling him to drive safe in that new truck of his..."*

"The phone didn't ring, Momma. Daddy's fine, for all I know."

"Then what the hell are you doing, scaring your momma like that? What is it with you today, girl?" She leaned against the sink again, a look of slight irritation settling on her face. *"Get on with it, Mae. You know I hate hysterics. 'Sides, I've got a lot to do before the party this evening—you know who's comin' tonight? The* mayor *of all people, and* his *new wife. Making a connection like that? It's the chance your daddy and I have been waiting for..."*

The rest was lost in a swirl of muffled sound. Mae felt herself becoming ill, her stomach heaving as if it were ready to simply turn over and empty its contents onto the immaculate floor. She shook her head furiously, balling her fists and raising them to her ears. Suddenly, she slammed them down on the tiles, causing the bowl to shift ominously toward the edge of the island.

Lynne paused in mid sentence, eyes widening. *"What the hell's gotten into you—"*

"Daddy hurt me!" Mae screamed, the sound echoing through the empty house. "He h-h-hurt me, hurt me…" she sobbed, burying her face in her hands.

"What?" Lynne whispered, taking a step toward her daughter. "Ella Mae—"

"Hurt me, hurt me, for years," she continued, looking up at her mother. "For years. Almost every night, after you and Merri were in bed. I wanted to scream, scream so loud someone would have to hear, would come help me, would make him stop…but I couldn't, Momma. He wanted me to be quiet. He kept singing…"

"Ella Mae, this isn't funny," Lynne barked as she faced her daughter with hands balled on her hips, the tiled island serving as a multicolored barrier between the two women.

"Singing that fucking song!" Mae screeched, slamming her fist down hard on the tiles again. The flesh was red and throbbed furiously, though she was nearly oblivious to the pain. "Every night, every time, 'This love is a strange love…'"

"I said it isn't funny, dammit!" Lynne screamed back at her, banging her own fists on the island in frustration.

"And if you don't stop him now, Momma," Mae continued, "tonight after you kiss the mayor and his new wife and all your other important guests goodnight, he'll wait 'til you're asleep, come into my room and do the very same thing—"

"You little bitch, I said STOP IT!" Lynne picked the bowl up and hurled it at the wall behind Mae, splattering half of the kitchen with cake batter and shards of blue porcelain.

"M-momma, what are you doing?" Mae stammered, sliding off the barstool.

"No," Lynne hissed as she came around the island, grabbing her daughter by the shoulders and shaking her viciously. Mae cried out, her mother's acrylic nails digging deep into her flesh.

"What the hell you think you're doing, huh? You think this is funny, Ella Mae? Huh? Do you see me laughing?" The nails dug even deeper into Mae's flesh as she pushed her toward the hallway.

"Momma, why are you doing this? I'm telling you the truth, I swear. I'd never lie about something like this. I never told anyone, not even Merri. I'm just so scared now that's she's gone away to school. I'm all alone here now, I can't find a place to hide anymore. He's everywhere, all over me, all the time. I can't stand it anymore, Momma. I need your help, please…"

The women were standing in the hall now, the telephone table by the staircase only a few steps away.

"You think I don't know what's going on here?" Lynne growled as she held her daughter tightly in her grip. "I'm not stupid. I know what you've been doing since you started getting older and your body started changin'. You think I don't see the short shorts and tight shirts you prance around in every evening, your daddy sittin' there in plain sight? You think I don't notice the flimsy little nightgowns you wear to bed? You think I don't know what my own daughter's tryin' to do to me?"

Mae's mouth hung agape as she surrendered to the wave of shock threatening to overcome her. She ceased her struggling, pushing her mother's hands away with ease as she backed toward the staircase. "Oh, Momma…no, no," she sobbed. "Tell me you don't think I…"

"Jonas is the love of my life. Been with him since I was about your age. In our time together, I've had to fight many a woman off him…and I'll do the same with you, Ella Mae. I'll do the very same. I'm not about to lose him to some silly mess like this—"

"He raped me, Momma! Your Jonas took off my clothes, climbed in my bed and raped me every night for the past two years! And all you do is stand there defending him? I'm your daughter, Momma! Your flesh and blood! I'm supposed to matter to you! You're supposed to protect me! What kind of a mother do you call yourself—"

Lynne reached out and struck Mae hard across the face with the back of her hand. Mae tumbled to the floor, smacking against the wood with a dull thud. She curled into a ball, all coherent thought swallowed up by the sound of piercing screams pounding mercilessly against her eardrums. There was so much noise in the room she could no longer tell which belonged to her own vocal chords.

"*After all I've done for you! After all we've sacrificed for you and your sister, you have the nerve to be ungrateful like this! How* dare *you!*" *Lynne lunged for her daughter, but was stopped in mid-step as Mae suddenly raised her knees, an unearthly howl escaping her fifteen-year-old lungs. Instinctively, she kicked out with both feet, sending her Mary Janes straight into her mother's abdomen. The woman fell against the staircase, knocking the telephone table on its side. "Ooof," she managed to utter as she fought for breath.*

"*Momma…" Mae began, pulling herself into a sitting position. "I'm so sorry…I just…you didn't…"*

Lynne reached out again, startling Mae as she grabbed her by the ankles and began dragging her across the floor. "I'll show you, you ungrateful whore!"

"*Momma…PLEASE!" Mae screamed until she thought her throat would burst like an overripe melon, screamed and fought and kicked even as the door opened in the entry and her father stepped inside.*

Jonas immediately dropped the large gift box he held at his feet and ran over to her mother, restraining her easily with an arm around her waist as he pulled her away from the screaming girl. "Lynne, what the hell's goin' on here?"

Her mother disentangled herself from his grasp. Mae lay on the floor shaking uncontrollably, hands over her face as if expecting another blow. Lynne picked the phone up off the floor and hurled it at her daughter, striking her on the thigh with the hard plastic cover. "You get your grandmother on the line," Lynne said, straightening her apron and patting her hair back in place. "Tell her I want you out of this house before my guests arrive."

Jonas grabbed his wife by the arm. "Lynne, you'd better start talkin' right now. Why the hell you whoopin' on that girl like she's grown? Now this is my *house. Ain't no party gonna happen here 'til I get some answers."*

"*Well you tell your 'girl' to get her stuff packed and wait on the porch 'til Lily or her manwhore Henry gets here. I don't want to have to kill her." Wiping her mouth on the sleeve of her silken blouse, she wrenched her arm away from her husband, walking back into the kitchen as if nothing had happened.*

Pushing her father's hands away as he tried to help her up, she dialed her grandmother's number. Lily picked up on the first ring.

"Mae? Honey, what's wrong?"

"Please," she sobbed into the phone. "Please, Granna, please come get me, I need you...no, come right away. Hurry, she says she wants to kill me, please..."

Please...Please...

"Please," Mae moaned softly, fighting her way to consciousness.

Dawn illuminated the world beyond the glass patio doors, sending rays of milky light spilling onto the bed she and Jasper shared. Outside, the trees shook off the rest of last night's rain in gentle winds, drops of dew falling to the damp earth as flocks of tiny birds searched the area for food. Tears she'd cried during the night lay in a pool of dampness on her pillow. She buried her face in it, tasting their saltiness as she stifled more of her cries.

Jasper stirred as he lay next to her, arm draped over her protectively. "Mmmm, sugar," he mumbled, pulling her close. She watched him a few moments, running her fingers through his light brown curls as he slept. Trying not to disturb him, she slowly slid from under his arm to the carpet.

She stood at the foot of the bed, listening intently. His breathing remained rhythmic; his bare chest rose and fell regularly as if he were walking in the midst of the most peaceful dream.

Mae leaned over and kissed his forehead. "So sweet, so wonderful. Sleep on, beautiful one."

Barefoot, she crept across the carpet toward the patio doors, pulling a flannel shirt from his closet and shrugging into it as she went. She stepped onto the damp wooden planks of the patio, heading for a set of stairs leading to the lower deck. From there she made her way into the backyard and the trail leading into the woods, careful not to step on any sharp rocks or twigs lying in her path.

The sun had barely reached the tips of the trees as she stood shivering on the shore of the lake, Jasper's oversized flannel shirt billowing around her. The surface was so calm it resembled glass, mirroring the tranquil landscape above. Mae sighed and closed her eyes, the memory of the dream washing over her in full. She remembered that day clearly. How her mother had cleaned up the cake batter and continued the preparations for her party, ignoring Mae lugging her suitcases down the stairs, out to the front porch so Henry could heft them into the trunk of his car.

To her, I was just a whore, Mae thought, watching the still water. A feeling of despair welled up from deep within.

"So *dirty*," Mae sobbed, opening the flannel jacket. "Just...just want to be clean..." She pushed the heavy fabric off her shoulders, letting it slide to her feet as she stepped forward. The thin nightgown she wore brushed against her hips and thighs as she walked, reminding her of the harsh words her mother spoke on that fateful day. The hard packed dirt gave way to cool mud that squelched between her bare toes as she approached the water's edge, shivering without the protection of the warm jacket. Before her, the lake seemed to stretch infinitely in every direction. She gasped as she stepped in, the water so icy her feet throbbed with pain.

Teeth clattering hopelessly against each other, Mae sucked in a few breaths to calm her shocked system as she waded deeper into the water. Before she could change her mind, Mae dived beneath the crystalline surface, using all her energy to propel herself into the depths. Away from the rising sun of the world above, down, down, down into murky darkness before pushing herself toward the surface again at last. As she swam, the water around her grew brighter and brighter until she suddenly burst into morning air again, gasping for breath.

The surface of the lake began to shimmer, becoming molten gold in the light of the sun breaking through the trees. Mae treaded water a while, relishing the feeling of the sun bathing her in warm luminescence. She closed her eyes and tilted her head back, dipping it into the water again as if in baptism.

Baptism, Mae thought as she floated carelessly along. *Like Granna's story about John the Baptist and Jesus.*

Mae envisioned the scene as her grandmother had described it so long ago. The Savior of the world standing in the midst of the Jordan as God's spirit descended upon him, filling up the river and the land with His incredible golden light.

You have been cleansed, daughter, a tiny voice whispered in the stillness.

Startled, Mae turned this way and that in the water, searching for one who could have been out at the lake so early in the morning. No one in either direction as far as she could see. Mae thought of her grandmother again…

"But Granna, how do we know when God's talking to us? Does He have a voice like thunder? Does lightning come when He cries angry tears? How do we know when it's really Him?"

"Oh, honey," Lily replied as she'd sat a bewildered young Mae on her lap. "You'll always know the Lord's voice. Sure, He can make all that noise whenever He gets ready, but I'd like to think He don't get too much fun out o' scarin' us like that. No, Mae, I reckon God speaks to His children in a still, small voice; the quietest, kindest voice you ever heard. Sometimes that voice is so still I'm afraid I'll have trouble hearin' the words, but don't you worry 'bout that at all, little 'un. That voice may be small, but it travels all through your bones, all through your soul. Oh, you'll know God's voice. It's the sweetest, clearest, most beautiful thing you'll ever know."

The sun disappeared behind a thickening veil of clouds as Mae continued to tread water. Suddenly, they burst open, spilling more rain in tiny droplets. To Mae, it looked as if an enormous strand of heavenly pearls had broken and fallen to the earth, the beads sparkling on the large body of water moments before disappearing beneath the surface.

Mae laughed, and then cried silent tears of joy as she swam toward shore, running through the mud to snatch the thick flannel jacket up before it could be completely drenched in the downpour. She started toward the trail leading back to the footpath and Jasper's home, but decided to take shelter under a thick canopy of cypress when the rain began to fall so hard it was nearly impossible to find her way.

Fumbling around in one of Jasper's pockets, she found a small notebook and pencil.

"Why not?" Mae whispered, twirling the pencil between her fingers. Settling herself against the trunk of a nearby tree, she flipped open the notebook and began to write.

TWELVE

The elevator doors slid open, flooding the quiet chamber with evening noise. Deborah stepped onto the sidewalk in front of the Women's Allied Health Building, heading for the parking garage across the street. She was about to cross when a black truck approached quickly, stopping short just a few feet away. She held a hand above her eyes, trying to see the driver through the windshield's glare.

"*Richard?*" she cried incredulously. "What the hell?" She marched over and leaned in the open passenger window. "What's going on, Rick?"

"Get in," he grinned. "We'll be late for our reservation in another twenty minutes."

"Reservation?" Deborah frowned. "We don't have plans tonight."

"Are you gonna stand there in that skirt bent at the waist so the world can see your goods or are you gonna get in the car?" He patted the seat next to him, smile widening. Deborah sighed, opening the passenger door and climbing in.

"Good." His fingers closed around the gearshift. "Now let's get us back in traffic—"

"Wait a minute." She grabbed his hand, shaking her head firmly. "I'm not going anywhere with you. I'm soaking my weary bones at *home* tonight. The office was swamped today, and I…" Deborah faltered, thinking of her newly emptied apartment. "I need the rest, Rick. It's been a long week."

Richard dropped his hand in his lap, sighing in frustration. They sat there a moment in silence. "I haven't seen you at all this week," he whispered finally, staring out the window.

"I'm sorry, I've been busy lately. Between rounds at the hospital and my practice, it's a wonder I get any time for myself." She looked over at him, resting an empathetic hand on his shoulder. "Why don't you call Petey or one of your other boys up, treat 'em to dinner. I'm sure you could find someone to tag along. Cops love the expensive stuff, especially if it's free, right?"

Richard reached for her hand, plucking it from his shoulder and gently caressing the fingers. "Remember the last time we had dinner?"

"Of course," Deborah replied, frown deepening. "We ate at that little Greek place you like so much a couple days after the funeral—"

"No." He turned to her. "I mean *before*."

Deborah sighed again, slowly pulling her hand out of his grasp. She gazed out her own window, watching the crowds as they made their way home after a busy workday. Home to their families, loved ones...

An image of Malcolm flashed vividly across her mind, standing in the doorway of her apartment for the last time. A twisting feeling took hold of her then, tying her stomach up in knots. "I thought you heard me the first time, Rick. I don't want to discuss this. It was the past. So much has changed since then..."

"What about all the time we've spent together these past couple weeks, Deb?" He moved closer, searching her eyes for traces of hope. "You telling me that doesn't mean anything to you?"

"Richard!" Deborah cried, slamming her hand on the dashboard. "What are you talking about? I thought I was doing the right thing by comforting a friend who'd just lost his family."

Richard's jaw worked furiously. "So now were just friends, huh?"

"Yes!" she yelled in exasperation. "What more could we be for each other now? I felt you needed me to help you get through the loss of your wife and daughter. I needed a friend, too. I thought we were on the same page here." She shook her head apologetically. "I'm truly sorry if I've misled you." She moved to get out of the car.

Richard reached out like a bolt of lightning, grabbing her arms and holding her down on the seat. He leaned over her menacingly. Deborah could feel his hot breath on her face, was forced to take huge gulps of it in each time she opened her mouth in a desperate search for air.

"Richard!" she screamed, giving in to a surge of panic. "Let go of me!"

"Stop…struggling with me, Deborah. It won't help." His grip on her arms tightened, and she thought of Mae in that instant, of all she'd endured for so long. She forced herself to be still, closing her eyes and turning her face away.

"I don't want this to be over, Deb. We were good, so good for a time, and I know we can be good again if you just give it another chance. You broke my fuckin' heart, Doc. You fucked my brains out and shit all over me when you felt you'd had enough."

He jerked his arms up, pulling on her shoulders painfully. "Don't think I don't know about the others. I know about all of 'em. I bet you like doing that to men, don't you? I bet it's just one big fucking power trip for you. Women's Lib and all that. They teach you to fuck as you please, fuck as many men as you can and dump 'em off the side of the road to make a fucking social *point*? You bitches don't need men, sure, men are expendable pieces of shit, but you keep 'em around for a good fuck when you're tired of fucking yourselves and your dike bitch friends—"

"You're a pathetic drunk, Richard," she spat, her struggles beginning again in earnest. "Do the world a favor, go home and drown yourself in a bottle of scotch." She wrenched away from him, scrambling for the door handle. God, couldn't anyone see this lunatic in the car with her?

Richard's arm snaked out again, grabbing a handful of her hair and pulling her back to him. "Sit *down*. We're not even close to done talking yet."

Deborah dug her nails into his hand and snatched it away, her pent-up rage finally releasing itself in a malevolent cloud. "You think I'd want to spend the rest of my life with someone like you? Are you out of your *mind*? I knew it was a mistake getting involved with you right after things got started between us. And you were right, asshole. It *was* just a fling—just one fuck between others, and not even close to the best."

Richard raised his arm as if to strike. Deborah didn't flinch, instead angling her chin toward the upraised fist. "You just remember, Rick. I know all your dirty little secrets, all of them. I could ruin your entire life with just one well-placed call, I've got so much shit on you. So go on, motherfucker, if you're so brave. Go on and hit me like you hit your wife. Ooh, what's the matter?" she mocked, voice softening. "Is poor Detective Spencer afraid he might be seen slapping on a woman in broad daylight? A *doctor*, at that? Yeah, you wouldn't be anyone's hero then, would you?"

He lowered his hand slowly, seeming to shrink away from the venomous words. "You know I'd never hurt you, Deb. I love you too much."

Deborah snorted. "You've got to be kidding me. How can you say you love one woman and put your fists on another like she's your personal punching bag? That ain't love, Rick. If you couldn't love your own wife, what the hell makes you think you could ever love me?" She inched as close to the door as he would allow, ready to flee again at the first opportunity. "We had fun for a while, I'll admit that. But the whole thing was wrong, Rick. Mae was my *best friend*. I would have done anything for her, yet I found myself sleeping with her husband under her nose, in her own bed. I could hardly look myself in the mirror for months after it was over, I hated myself so much."

"But you called me up and just ended it like that. Over the phone, no warning. Just 'we can't do this anymore'—"

"Of course we couldn't do it anymore," Deborah interrupted, rubbing her aching arms. "Mae was eight months pregnant by then. Lily was coming, and she'd just asked me to be her godmother. How could I be an example for her little girl when I was more fucked up than ever? We'd had our fun by then. It was time for it to be over, and I really wish you felt the same way."

"How the hell could you say something like that to me after killing our kid, huh?" He started to reach for her again, but appeared to think better of it, apparently trying to keep his roiling emotions in check. "You went and did it under my nose, Deb. You didn't even ask me how

I felt about it. I wanted to start a life with you, I was ready to tell her and you wouldn't even let me—"

"Rick, I couldn't. She was about to give birth to a child you'd created long before our 'accident.' I thought about keeping the baby, I thought about it a lot, but every time we went out to do things for Lily, I would look in her eyes, see how happy she was…and I realized I couldn't hurt her that way. I couldn't force her to raise a baby alone in this world, and I wouldn't let any child of mine come here knowing I couldn't give it the father it deserved. It was just too painful.

"So I scheduled the appointment, and I went through it alone because I knew if I'd told you beforehand, you would have tried to talk me out of it. You would have convinced me it was perfectly okay to break a friend's heart in order to preserve my own happiness."

Richard stared solemnly at her, eyes filling with tears. "I wanted you so much, Deb. I wanted that baby. It was my child, too. It should have been *our* decision, not just you calling all the shots—"

"I thought I was doing the right thing for everyone," Deborah said, reaching for her purse. "I'm sorry you're still so hurt about this. Hell, not one day goes by I don't think of what I've done. But I can't go back, and neither can you. All I can do is ask you to forgive me and move on, make a new life for yourself as best you can. What's done is done, we both have our mistakes to live with."

"Deborah," he whispered gently, reaching for her hand again. "We could try again. There's nothing stopping us now."

Deborah opened her mouth to reply just as another image of Malcolm flashed in her mind. She was assaulted by the engagement ring in its black velvet case; his crestfallen expression as he'd placed it in her hands etched indelibly in memory. She snatched her hand away from Richard's grasp as if it were on fire, finding strength enough to wrench the door open.

"Deb, please," he begged as she got out. He grabbed at her purse as she slung it over her shoulder. "Don't you see how this is killing me? You're fucking killing me! You and your fucking voodoo!"

Deborah froze, refusing to turn around. "Richard, I've lost so much because of you. To be honest, if I never see you again, it'll be too soon. Get the hell on with your life and stop following me around." She yanked the purse over her shoulder once more, slamming the door in his face.

"Deborah!" he called out the window. "We're not over here. We'll never be over! This is *it*, baby. Fucking forever, this is it!"

Deborah raced across the street toward the parking garage without a single backward glance.

"Shit," Richard whispered to himself, slamming his hands against the steering wheel repeatedly. He sat there fuming a moment, willing his tears to stop. Finally, he put the truck in gear, pulling back into traffic as he headed for the brownstone. He drove on, slowing to a stop as the light in the intersection turned red.

He turned the radio on, muttering to himself as rock music flowed from the speakers and filled the cab. "Thinks she can shit all over me. Fuck her. I'll get back at her. I'll catch up to—" he paused in mid-sentence, glancing on the floor of the passenger seat. A small peach colored envelope lay on the carpet. He reached over and picked it up, reading the return address. "A.M. Croft in Louisiana? Must be another long lost fuck trying to get back in good with the bitch."

He opened the envelope, shaking a piece of folded stationery into his hands. He unfolded the paper, settling on the seat as he began to read.

Deb,

I know it's been a quite a while since I last made contact, but I've been trying to play it safe in light of all that's happened. Now upon hearing news of my tragic "death," I felt it finally safe enough to chance a quick letter to my very best friend—if being married to a paranoid cop for almost a decade taught me anything, it's that no phone line is ever truly secure.

So how are things on your end, my love? And how's that sexy Dr. Malcolm? Be good to that one, girl—he definitely seems like a keeper. If any nuptials are to be exchanged, I insist on being the very first to know.

L's doing well enough. She's laughing more, playing more, though I sometimes worry she may not be dealing with things as well as I'd hoped. Jasper showed me some pictures she drew recently, which were very frightening. Oh, Deb, she's seen and heard so much…much more than any little girl should ever have to. I was telling him that I don't know how I'll ever be able to forgive myself for allowing things to get so out of hand…if it weren't for you and my little one around to snap me out of my haze, I know Rick would have killed me eventually.

I'm sure he's entertained many fantasies about it, which is why I'm absolutely elated to know he won't come looking for us anymore—to him and the rest of the world, our voices have been forever silenced, and I sleep better at night because of that knowledge. When I heard about the bodies found up at Elysium, I told myself right then I wouldn't ask too many questions; it's probably best I know as little as possible about how those poor souls really ended up there in that lonely cabin.

I lost my mother a short while ago. Lung cancer. I won't go into the ugly details around that situation. What's dead should stay just that way. L. and I know that better than most—dwelling among the dead has saved our lives, and I can't thank you enough, dear friend, for what you've done for us. God in his mercy and kindness must have known I'd need as good a friend as you someday, and he must have sent you from Heaven to care for me and mine. I love you, Deb. You are truly the best.

You may be wondering by now just who is this Jasper I speak so fondly of. He's a child psychologist who works for an agency devoted to studying exceptional children. Our friendship began as a chance meeting at work, but it seems the friendship has evolved of late into something deeper…anyway, he's a good guy, and he just adores your little munchkin. Now now, don't go raising those carefully sculpted eyebrows of yours. Whatever's going down between us is definitely on a day-to-day basis. I've only got time enough in my life for one special little girl; everyone else takes a number, including this southern sweetheart. I'll admit I'm happy he's a part of my life, and that L. has the chance to interact with him regularly. I don't want her to grow up having a biased opinion of men, Deb. I want her to know there are good ones in the world as well as bad, and she can't judge all simply by the actions of one.

Got to run now. I've been painting again lately, and with all this Louisiana color and splendor outside my door, there's never a lack of inspiration. I just love being home again, and my only regret is that I didn't come back here sooner. I could have spared L. and I so much pain...

You and Malcolm come down and see us sometime, y'hear? Yes, not all of my southern tongue left me while I was away. I'm hoping to regain everything I've lost...in due time.

Love You,

Anne Marie Croft

The intersection light turned green on the busy street, and tired commuters honked angrily at Richard. He read the letter a second time before folding it again, carefully placing it back inside the envelope. He placed his hands on the steering wheel, gripping it so hard the knuckles became pale irregular knobs under his skin. His mouth worked furiously as he mumbled silently to himself. Angry drivers sped around him into the intersection, cursing and making obscene gestures as they passed. He paid them no mind, staring blankly through the windshield at the light as it turned from yellow to red. His handsome face suddenly cracked a large smile that seemed to split the smooth surface of his face in half, the mouth open so wide a passerby could have glimpsed his back teeth.

He chuckled to himself, shifting the car into gear. "Oooh, baby," he whispered. "You've been a naughty girl. But that's okay, I'm coming down to put you back in line. Oh baby...my *baby*." He gunned the engine, speeding recklessly into the red intersection.

He picked up his cell phone as he went, dialing information, then the number of Globe Trekker Airlines. "Yes," he began pleasantly as he sped around slower cars, nearly crashing into a station wagon as he drove through another red intersection. "I'd like to get a flight out of

International bound for New Orleans? When? Oh, soon as possible, sweetie—*soon as you can get me seated.*"

Deborah tossed one last pair of underwear on top of her clothing, folded and stacked neatly in a large suitcase on the couch. *Can never have enough of those,* she thought, tugging the zipper closed.

She picked up her glass of white wine and walked over to the living room window in her sweats, gazing up at the night sky. "Full moon," she whispered to herself. "Glad I'm not on tonight at the hospital. Probably a madhouse by now."

She was ecstatic when she'd opened her PO Box this morning to find a letter from Beau Ciel, addressed to her in Mae's elegant script. It wasn't until she'd read the letter in its entirety that she discovered the true meaning of "A.M."— it was her old friend's new identity, part of a new existence she'd carved out for herself in her childhood home. Deborah smiled at the thought of Mae and Lily's long awaited happiness, and she couldn't wait to get to that small town in Louisiana and wrap her arms around them. How she missed Mae's girlish laugh and Lily's beautiful smile, minus the couple of baby teeth she'd have lost by now, of course.

Deborah shook her head, crossing the room to her purse on the kitchen counter. The trip would do her some good. After Malcolm's abrupt departure the apartment seemed twice its size, and incredibly lonely. She'd worked even longer hours than normal right after he left just so she wouldn't have to come home and sit in the cavernous silence.

She sat down next to her luggage, purse in her hands. "Now what gate am I supposed to go to?" she mumbled as she rummaged though the contents, searching for her ticket. *That's odd*, she thought when she pulled the ticket out, *I know I put Mae's letter in here somewhere…*

She searched through the purse again, even turning it over and shaking everything out onto the cushions. Nothing but the usual fell out: lotion, makeup, hairbrush, wallet and keys…but no letter.

"It's got to be here somewhere, I just picked it up this morning." Deborah frowned, heading into the next room to continue her search.

For close to an hour she ransacked her home, opening drawers, searching closets, even lifting the furniture in hopes the envelope had somehow landed in an obscure corner of the apartment, to no avail. Finally, she plunked down on the couch, running her hands frantically through her hair.

"Think, Deborah, think," she muttered. "Went in to the office, picked the mail up at lunch…put the rest in the car, but I kept the letter in my purse because I wanted to have it with me on the flight. So it should be here, but…" she made another cursory search before she suddenly dropped the purse to the floor beside her, completely forgotten.

"Oh my God," she whispered, eyes widening as she covered her mouth. "Rick! Oh no, he grabbed my purse as I was trying to get out of the car…" in her mind's eye she saw herself struggling with him, snatching her purse from his vice-like grip as she'd fled across the street, anyplace to get as far away from him as possible…

"Oh God," she repeated. "What have I done?"

She raced to the bedroom for her shoes, grabbing her cell phone from the counter as she went. "Yes, this is Dr. Deborah Barr. I have a 9 A.M. flight scheduled tomorrow for New Orleans? Yes, well I need you to get me on an earlier flight. As soon as possible, I'm ready to leave now. Cost? Yes, I'll pay the extra cost. I'm sure I'll be paying a lot more than that before this is all over…"

THIRTEEN

Detective Richard Spencer glanced up at the giant clock before swinging the heavy glass door open and hurrying inside. He adjusted his shades and scanned the empty interior, spotting a fan in the corner next to a cluster of magazine racks. He walked over and stood in front of the whirring blades, sighing relief. He plucked his sticky shirt away from his skin, using the hem of it to wipe more sweat from his brow.

A voice from behind nearly startled him. "Why don't you come on over here. You blockin' all the circulatin' air from comin' in the room."

He turned to see an old man watching him mildly from the counter. "Where am I?" he asked, wiping more sweat. "Is it always this humid here so late in the year?"

"Down in the Square's the muggiest part o' town." He beckoned to him. "If you're ailin', let me get a soda to refresh you…"

Richard approached the counter, shaking his head. "No thanks, I'm fine."

"You sure, now?" Henry leaned his elbows on the counter, looking him over carefully. "You ain't gone pass right on my floor or nothin' I hope—"

"I'm fine," he repeated, giving the man a smile. He reached into his back pocket, pulling out a pale blue memo pad and pen. "I was hoping you could help me, though. I'm an agent with Stratford Insurance. We're national, I'm sure you've heard of us." He smiled, snapping his fingers. "We get you back into your life," he sang, "Stratford keeps you happy." When the old man didn't respond, Richard dropped his head, clearing his throat. "Well, anyway. I'm looking for some information."

"Oh?" Henry arched his brow. "Well, son, if you're here for anythin' else 'sides a bus ticket or a cab call, I'm gonna have to ask you to remove your sunglasses."

"Pardon me?" Richard frowned. "You're saying you want me to remove my shades, for—"

"I don't have many rules in this place, son," Henry interrupted, folding his arms across his chest. "But I do have one: I won't give or take an answer from a man who's eyes I can't look into." He shrugged. "I've lived a long time on this earth. Life, she brought me to some strange places and strange faces. Taught me the hard way 'bout how people really work."

Richard reached up, touched the lenses…then faltered, shaking his head sadly. "Sorry, mister, I can't. These are prescription, doctor's orders. They told me the other day I may be starting to develop some photosensitivity."

Henry arched his brow again. "Is *that* right?" He clucked sympathetically. "Sorry to hear. Hope it all turns out well for you."

"Thanks," he nodded, clicking the pen a couple of times. "So would you happen to know the exact address of a place called 'Bella Bloom?' I have business with a new client there, someone by the name of Anne Marie Croft? I'm afraid I'm already late, and I know she's been expecting me."

Henry paused as if deep thought, then shook his head. "'Fraid I don't know an 'Anne Marie,' son. Beau Ciel's a small town; if anyone new came through these parts, I'd a gotten wind of it." He felt in his shirt pocket and pulled out a toothpick, laying it carefully on his tongue. "Never heard of her."

Richard eyed Henry suspiciously. "You sure about that? According to our records, Anne Marie Croft applied for flood insurance on a property called 'Bella Bloom' from this locale just two weeks ago. The company sent me out here to assess the house and surrounding area for fair value. "

Henry twirled the toothpick. "Sorry, son, wish I could help you." He stared at him a moment longer. "Hey, hey wait a minute," he said excitedly, snatching the toothpick from his mouth, "Don't I know you? Weren't you on TV or somethin'?"

"I don't watch TV," Richard replied coldly, scanning the room again.

"Well I watch a whole lot of TV, son. M' nephew Gene jus' surprised me with a brand spankin' new satellite TV, right out o' the blue." He pushed his ball cap up, scratching the top of his head. "You sure do look familiar. Jus' give me a minute, I'll figure it out."

Richard pointed over his right shoulder. "Those magazine racks over there by the fan…they got maps, too?"

"Sure, sure," Henry said distractedly, still scratching his head.

Richard reached for his wallet, pulled a few bills out and tossed them on the counter. "Thanks for your time. Keep the change." A moment later he was out the door again, a stack of maps in his hands.

"But I know I've seen your face somewhere," he heard the old man mumble as the door swung shut behind him.

Richard sat behind the wheel of his rental car an hour later, fingering the letter in his hands as he stared up at the large house on the hill. He pulled the car into a small clearing just off the main road, only a short distance from the private access road leading to Bella Bloom. When he'd lain eyes on the house for the very first time, his palms grew sweaty at the vision of his wife's hair in his grip, her throat stretched taut as he slashed it wide open, spraying her picturesque country hideaway in her own blood.

He'd driven slowly past the access road a few times, tempted to drive right up to the house and take care of business. In the end, he'd decided to wait. "Slow and steady wins the race," he whispered, crumpling the letter in his hands. "Oh, baby, I can't wait to get reacquainted. It'll be just like old times…hell, maybe *better* than old times."

He removed his police issue .38 and the leather holster he carried it in, shoving both inside the glove compartment. *Won't be needing it tonight.* He knew with all the forensics in the world today, the bullets he sprayed into his wife's body down here could be traced straight back to him in Philadelphia, even with a concrete alibi. He strained in his seat to get a better look, wincing as a bulky steel object in the front pocket of his parka pressed painfully against his thigh. "Come on, baby. Come on outside so I can get a look at you…"

Mae checked her reflection in the hall mirror a final time before stepping out into the blinding sun. She paused, gazing up at a perfect azure sky.

"Not a cloud for miles," she said admiringly, shielding her eyes. "Rain'll roll in before the day is over, though. Always happens that way." She glanced over at the garden, thinking of Lily's disappointment at not being able to spend the evening pulling weeds and digging the ground in preparation for the tomato garden Henry would plant later on the property. Oh well. They'll just have to find something else to do until the coming storm moves over the town…

This is good, Mae thought, locking the door behind her. *This is what good is supposed to feel like.* She took one last look at the sky as she walked over to her car.

She'd always loved Fridays, and thoughts of spending the weekend with her little girl only added to her excitement. She could hardly wait to hear her daughter's footsteps racing up the porch, her laughter echoing through the house even before she's stepped inside.

Won't be much longer 'til we can be together all the time, honey, she thought as she started the engine and headed down the access road. *We've been waiting too long for happiness. Thank God it finally found us.* She reached the end of the access road, pausing to look carefully both ways before turning onto the main road, toward town. Realizing she had the road entirely to herself for once, she turned up the radio full blast, bobbing her head to recordings of a spicy jazz band Jasper had given her, hoping she'd someday consent to an evening with him on St. Charles Avenue.

"*Honey it's true, I don't have to tell a tale…you ain't on my heart any more,*" she sang at the top of her lungs, loving the feel of the cool wind gusting through the open windows, blowing her hair every which way. She reached town and drove toward the academy, paying no mind to the dark gray sedan that had appeared from nowhere and been trailing behind her for some time. She parked her tiny compact in a small lot on the edge of the property, rushing inside with only minutes to spare.

Richard pulled up to the curb across the street from the school, parking near an empty, burned out field. Out of habit, he wrote down the license plate number on Mae's vehicle, scanning the school grounds as he did so.

He froze, eyes riveted to a small playground on the far side of the property. Small children in red and white uniforms played tag and climbed a large jungle gym in the center of the area, the structure a multicolored riot of primary hues. One little girl in particular caught his attention. Dressed in a red sweater and plaid skirt, she was playing a game of hopscotch with another girl, her dark waves billowing out behind her as she jumped from square to square.

Lily.

Richard reached for the door handle, jumping out to get a better look. It *was* his Lily, all dressed up in her pretty red school outfit. Tonight he would tell her how much he loved seeing her in red; yes, tonight would be the reunion he'd been hoping and praying about for months.

"Daddy's waited so long to see you again, pretty girl," he whispered, reluctantly climbing back in the car when he noticed a teacher staring pointedly in his direction. "But he won't have to wait much longer. Your momma was naughty—yes, *real* naughty, when she took you from me like that. But Daddy's gonna fix things; Daddy's gonna make everything right, don't you worry.

"Tonight I'm taking you home to your grandma and grandpa and everyone else who loves you. Auntie Deb's gonna be your new momma and, well…" Richard paused, a slow grin spreading over his face. "Daddy has to punish your old momma first for doing this to us, for hurting so many people that love you. It'll be okay, though, I promise. Daddy's gonna make it all go away…"

Richard checked his watch. Just after eight. *The bitch probably won't be off until evening, so…*

He pulled away from the curb, heading toward an anonymous dusty motel room waiting for him in Metairie. He knew where they were now. He could relax, come to them when darkness had settled upon the earth. Yes, he would visit his family when the timing was perfect.

"I just *love* reunions," he said as he turned the corner, whistling a catchy tune.

Deborah pulled into Marigold Square, driving her rental straight up to the bus depot. She emerged from the vehicle in a passing cloud of dust, hacking and sneezing violently as she stumbled over to the front door.

"Geez, is it always this humid here?" she muttered, entering the dim interior. She was making a beeline for a shelf of maps in the corner when a voice halted her in her tracks.

"Matter of fact, ma'am, it's mighty humid mos' of the year here in Beau Ciel. Welcome, by the way. How can I be of service to you this fine afternoon?"

Deborah turned to see an old man standing behind the counter, a worn baseball cap riding atop his gray curls. He smiled, beckoning to her. She walked over to the counter, instantly at ease with the aged gentleman.

"Hi." She returned the smile, glancing over her shoulder at the shelf. "I was just checking out your maps over there, sir. You wouldn't happen to have any local ones by chance, would you?"

He rubbed his chin thoughtfully. "Now where you tryin' to go in town, if I may ask? Mos' of those maps are pretty outdated, you see. We don't get visitors in too often. We're jus' a one horse town that's become a playground for all the kiddies drivin' back an' forth to Metairie and N'Orleans. Damn city folk gonna destroy this town someday."

"I'm actually trying to get to a place called Bella Bloom," she interrupted, nervously drumming the counter with her nails.

The old man's kindly expression faded, instantly replaced by an unguarded look of suspicion. He took a step away from the counter. "Now what business you got that far out of town, miss? Out that way is mos'ly private property. People livin' there like to keep to themselves, and don't take too well to bein' bothered. Who exactly you lookin' for?"

"Oh, I'm…" Deborah stammered, searching for the words. "I'm in town visiting a friend. She told me I could find her there, but I'm afraid I was lost the moment I drove into town. Wonder I found you at all, sir." She chuckled lightly, shifting uncomfortably from one heel to the other. "Beautiful place you got here, by the way," she added, hoping the old guy would thaw. She glanced at the nametag pinned to the front pocket of his shirt. HENRY – HAPPY 2 SERVE U.

Henry stared her down a moment longer. He stepped hesitantly toward the counter again, folding his arms. "So who's the friend you lookin' for, honey?"

"Uh…" Deborah began uncertainly, then it came: "Anne Marie Croft, sir." She crossed her fingers, praying time hadn't run out on her.

Henry unfolded his arms at last, sliding them into his trouser pockets. He was the picture of nonchalance again. "So you know Anne Marie, huh? Great girl, that one."

Deborah nodded, relief flooding her face. "One of the best, sir. One of the best."

Henry came around the counter, taking her arm gently as he walked her to the door. "Come on outside here, then. I'll show you."

They stepped into the muggy air again, walking to the edge of the sidewalk. "See that main road leadin' out o' town?" He pointed to the eastern end of the Square. "You follow that straight out a couple miles, make a left at the first access road, and you've found her."

"Thank you," she breathed, grabbing his hand and shaking it vigorously. "Thank you so much."

"Not a problem. Now I know you're tired after drivin' so long a way, so you best be gettin' on up there. I'm sure Anne Marie would be mighty glad to see a friend."

He scrutinized her a moment longer, finally nodding his head in approval. "Yep, better get on before the storm hits. Weatherman says it's comin' up on us real fast. I'm headed home 'bout now m'self."

Deborah ran over to the car and climbed in. She passed Henry as she maneuvered the vehicle toward the street. He waved amiably. "You tell Anne Marie Henry said hello, y'hear?"

"Yes, sir," Deborah called, turning onto the main road. "I'll be sure to do that, sir. You take care."

Henry watched the car speed away until it was out of sight. "Hope she's truly a friend to you, Junie," he whispered, though he was alone on the street. "For your sake, I truly hope so."

"Whew! Looks like it's gonna come down real hard, A.M."

Mae glanced up at the darkening sky as she crossed the school parking lot, Jasper at her side. He'd popped into the office for a meeting with Stan late this afternoon, and had decided to hang around until she got off work. Massive clouds the color of fresh bruises covered the heavens, blotting out the setting sun.

"See, Jas," she began, shaking her head, "I came out of the house this morning, looked up at that picture-perfect sky, and just knew it wouldn't last."

"Now why on earth would you say something pessimistic like that?" He removed his jacket, placing it around her shoulders.

"Because nothing that perfect ever lasts for long," she mumbled, reaching in her purse for her keys.

Jasper smiled, watching her slide the key in the lock. "Sugar, if you keep hanging around with good ol' Jasper, you're gonna have to get used to happiness, too, as a constant visitor in your life these days."

Mae opened the door, propping her elbows on it as she gazed up at him. "I think I'm trying real hard to get used to being happy, Jasper. I look forward to waking up every morning, and beyond Lily, I don't think I've ever felt that way before. I feel safe for the first time in my life; that has to make all the difference. And my girl's doing so much better since we got here. Her face glows brighter every day…"

"Speaking of the little one, guess what she forgot to take home last week?" He opened his briefcase and rummaged around inside, producing another manila envelope.

Mae froze, staring at him as he opened the clasp, shaking the contents into his hand. "It's okay," he said, handing the piece of paper to her. "Trust me. It would mean a lot for her to have, I just know it."

Mae unfolded the single sheet of paper, staring down at the image. For a moment she said nothing, then burst into peals of laughter. "Jasper, how sweet. Of course she'd love it. Who's the artist?"

"One of her favorites in the group," he replied, looking over her shoulder at the picture. "Name's Logan. He seemed to warm to her more than any of the others, even the first day he walked in there. We were doing peer portraits last week, but Lily had to leave early for a doctor's appointment or something. He finished the entire thing from memory."

Mae nodded, looked at the picture again. Lily was dressed in a purple sweatshirt and jeans, her hair tied back with purple and white ribbon. She was posed in front of the window, a large grin putting her missing teeth on display.

"She's…" Mae began.

"Beautiful, I know," Jasper finished for her, caressing her face. "Like momma, like…"

"Just stop right there." She laughed. "You know that's way too corny for my taste." She folded the sheet of paper and slipped it in the pocket of his jacket. "I've decided I want to bring her home for good."

"You sure you ready for that now?" Jasper asked, twirling a strand of her hair in his fingers.

Mae nodded emphatically. "Of course. I was ready the day she walked out the door. I've always known this living situation wouldn't be a permanent one. I knew it'd only be a matter of time before she'd be back at home with me, right where she belongs…" she frowned, looking up at him questioningly. "What? Aren't you happy for us?"

Jasper took her in his arms, kissing her gently. "I *told* you, I want you to get used to happiness being a part of your life. You know I support you in everything you do for that girl. She's lucky to have someone like you fighting for her all the time. If only all kids were that lucky…"

Mae smiled, pulling his face closer to hers. She kissed him deeply, wrapping her arms around his neck. They held each other for some moments, swaying together in the breezes of the approaching storm. He nuzzled her neck, pressing his lips against the soft skin. "Okay, woman," he whispered. "You better clear outta here quick before I decide to kidnap you or somethin'."

Mae giggled, pushing him away. "I'll call you later. I've got to get home and burn anyway. It's Spaghetti Night, Lily's favorite."

"You mean you ain't feeding that girl Cajun yet?"

Mae laughed again, climbing into the car. "What can I say? She's six. Kids're so picky these days. If it's not cheesy or covered with peanut butter and marshmallows, she's not interested." She moved to shut the door but stopped, shrugging his jacket off her shoulders. "Wait a sec, Jas. I almost forgot."

He waved her off. "Keep it, sugar. I'll get it when I catch up to you next week."

"Uh-unh, you see that sky?" She pointed up at the thickening cloud cover, handing the jacket to him. "Take it. You're farther out than I am. I'll be home in ten minutes."

Jasper reached for the jacket, lips brushing lightly across hers. "You win. Outta here, before you get soaked."

Mae started the car, backing toward the street. Jasper waved as she passed.

"I'll call you," she mouthed through the windshield, flashing a quick wave before turning the corner.

Mae drove the main road as fast as she dared. It was just after five, and the storm seemed to be right on her heels. The light breezes she'd felt while in Jasper's arms had increased, wild grasses on either side of the road blowing about fiercely as heavy winds set in.

She turned onto the private access road moments later, speeding up the low grade as the house came in sight. As she approached the driveway she braked suddenly, planting her hands on the dashboard to steady herself. A navy car sat in the driveway, its occupant still inside. On the verge of panic, she considered making a run for it until she realized the driver was a woman, dark brown hair resting on her shoulders. Mae put her foot on the gas again, driving slowly up the rest of the hill until her bumper was inches from the other vehicle's. The woman in the car opened the door as she approached, her long legs in full view. She watched the woman climb out of the car and stand next to it.

"Deb!" A squeal of delight erupted from her throat. She wrenched her own door open and hopped out.

The women ran to meet each other, embracing as they jumped up and down excitedly.

"You scared the hell out of me, girl!" Mae cried when they parted. "I didn't know who was sitting up in my driveway when I got home. Such a pleasant surprise!"

Deborah offered her a wan smile. "I missed you so much that when I got the letter, I just knew I had to come see you." She glanced around the front yard, taking in the blooming gardens and tree swing. "Wow, Mae, this place is perfect. Of course I'm envious. You know a yard this large'll cost a pretty penny back home."

Mae nodded. "Well *this* is my home now, Deb. For the first time in years, I'm finally where I belong."

"Where's the munchkin?" Deborah asked as Mae took her arm, leading her over to the porch.

"She'll be here soon. Her aunt took her shopping for skates so she could roll right along with her cousins." They glanced up as the heaviest of the storm clouds cracked open wide, pouring showers on the earth.

"Come on inside, I'm making spaghetti. We'll call it an official girl's night *in*—looks like this rain's gonna keep up a while. Want to get your bags before it really starts to come down?"

"Nah, it's fine." Deborah waved her off. "I'll worry about it later."

"All right, lady, you know best." Mae held the front door open as Deborah stepped inside, squeezing her arm gently as she passed. Deborah glanced at her questioningly.

"Just happy to see you, old friend. You're more welcome in this house than you'll ever know. My place is your place. You make yourself comfortable here."

Deborah swallowed the lump rising in her throat, tears in the corners her eyes. "I think I really needed to hear you to say that, Mae," she said. "More now than ever."

The two women embraced again as Mae closed the door on the arriving storm.

FOURTEEN

"Lily's growing by leaps and bounds every day. Do you know she's sprouted nearly an inch in the past six weeks?"

Deborah only smiled in answer, taking a seat at the breakfast nook. She watched Mae prepare the meal, chopping vegetables and stirring ground beef for the sauce. "You've always been good at this kind of thing, Mae."

Mae glanced up from her cooking, pushing her steamed over spectacles high on her head. "What's that?"

"You know," Deborah said, gesturing around the room. "Everything. Your home is immaculate, you've got a garden growing outside your door, you work all day while single handedly raising a six year old. You put women like me to shame…"

"Wait a minute, honey," Mae chuckled, holding her hands up. "You've got me livin' in June Cleaver's world or something. Nothing you see around you has come without the sacrifices of a lot of people. Henry, the guy you met at the bus depot in town? He's my grandmother's old lover. He helped her raise me after…well, that's not important now. Anyway, he's the one who maintains most of the property, including that beautiful garden you see growing outside my window. As for Lily, you know the situation there. We're together only a couple of days a week. The rest of the time I have to wait to see her at school.

"Let's not forget my sister," she continued, dabbing perspiration from her face with a dishtowel. "She's got a family of her own, yet she's sacrificing the most to help raise my child. If it weren't for her kindness, I don't know where we'd be. So don't get the wrong idea." She laughed, reaching into the cupboard for a bottle of seasoning. "There's definitely some deep collaboration going on here."

Deborah nodded, turning to stare out the window.

"So where's Malcolm?" Mae asked cheerily, turning her attention back to the sauce. She held up a finger. "Let me guess, pulling overtime again."

"Mae," Deborah began gently, turning away from the window.

"I swear, he's one of the hardest working men I've ever met. That one's a keeper, I've already told you that. Bet he's saving up for some gorgeous rock he's gonna weigh that finger down with…"

Deborah buried her face in her hands, stifling a sob. She turned to the window again, searching for a lingering moment of solace in the raging storm.

Mae paused, dripping spoon in mid-air. "Sweetie, what's eating you? I hit a sore spot or something? You guys aren't on the outs, are you?" She lowered the spoon in her direction, offering a sympathetic smile. "You're working yourself into knots over nothing, honey. Lover's spats are common, especially when things get serious. You guys are just working out the kinks, that's all. Give it a few days. You two'll be right as rain in no—"

"He said he wanted to marry me," she sobbed. "He even bought a ring…"

Mae turned the flame down on the sauce, taking the seat across from her. "I don't understand, then. Why are you so upset?"

"We had a fight," she answered, wiping tears with a napkin Mae handed her. "We split before he could even get to the proposal."

Mae sat back in her seat, shaking her head in bewilderment. "That doesn't make any sense, Deb. Malcolm loves you. I felt it every time he looked your way. How could one fight put an end to everything? Unless it was over something terrible…"

Deborah turned to her. "Mae…Malcolm broke it off because he thought I was in love with someone else."

"What?" Mae whispered. "You didn't cheat on him, did you? You were faithful this time, right?"

"Mae, of course I was!" she cried, slapping her leg in frustration. "I begged him to see reason, but in the end he thought it best we go our separate ways. I was devastated. I couldn't sleep in that damn apartment with all those memories floating around, so I thought I'd come down to see you…"

"Absolutely," Mae said reassuringly. "Honey, I'm so sorry. I didn't know." She reached across the table, trying to take her hand. Deborah pulled away, folding both of them primly in her lap. "I have to tell you something, Mae. Something very important. I should have told you right after it happened, but I was so scared I'd lose you…"

"Why on earth would you think something like that, Deb? You know you can tell me anything, anything at all. You're the best friend a girl could have—"

Deborah held up a hand to silence her. "Wait, Mae. If I don't say this now, I'm afraid I'll never have the courage to do it."

Mae sighed, crossing her arms. "Go ahead, I'm listening…" she smiled. "But I promise you it can't be *that* bad."

Deborah took a deep breath. "Malcolm left me because he thought Rick and I were sleeping together."

Mae chortled loudly, smacking the table hard with her palm. "Goodness, Debbie, you had me worried a minute there. Why didn't you just set him straight right then? You and I both know you couldn't do something like that, not after everything we've been through together."

"No," Deborah mumbled, shaking her head. "No I couldn't, at least that's what I thought in the beginning…"

The smile slipped from Mae's face by degrees. "I…must not have heard correctly." She chuckled without mirth. "You said—"

Deborah sighed, watching the storm blast against the window-panes as she spoke. "One night about a year or so after you were married, you went out of town on a business trip. I'd just broken up with some loser I was dating at the time. Anyway, I came over to the brownstone to return some self-help book you'd loaned me in your kindness, *How to Love You,* or something.

"I'd only planned to drop it on your porch with a cute note, but it turns out Rick was home that night. He invited me in, offered me a couple drinks, and well…it just happened. And it kept on happening, right up until you were about to deliver Lily…"

"My God," Mae said, staring at her in shock. "I'm not hearing this. I swear I'm not hearing this…"

"I messed up, Mae. I got pregnant." She held her trembling hands to her face again, whimpering. "A month before Lily was born. You were so happy. We spent practically all our time together shopping for baby things…I'd pick up a tiny hat or run my fingers along the edge of a bassinet and think, 'This would be great for my baby' or 'My baby would love this,' but whenever I'd look over at you, so radiant at the thought of starting a family, reality would slap me in the face. I couldn't have that baby. I couldn't hurt you that way, I would have died myself. You were so full of joy, so at peace with your life…"

Mae glared at her. "You're saying you walked alongside me all that time, Deborah, carrying my husband's child while I carried my *own* baby? You sick…"

Deborah sniffled, wiping her face roughly with the back of her hand. "Rick. I told him about the pregnancy. He was ecstatic. He wanted to…he wanted to…" she buried her face in her arms, her voice lost as she succumbed to waves of sorrow held in check for so long.

"Leave," Mae finished for her, tears spilling down her cheeks. "He wanted to leave us, so he could go to you, right?"

Deborah raised her head and looked at her, misery distorting her features. The expensive makeup she'd carefully applied early that morning ran down her face in gummy rivers of violet and black. "I told him it would never happen. He already had a family, a wife and a little baby that needed him. I ended it. Called him up and told him it was over. I did it for you, Mae, I swear. I sacrificed my happiness for yours."

"What happened to the baby?" Mae asked coldly, staring straight ahead.

"The only thing that could happen. I terminated the pregnancy. I had to."

"He was supposed to be on duty the day Lily was born," she mumbled, lips hardly moving. "Said he tried like hell to get there, but she came so fast…"

Deborah shook her head. "Oh no, Mae, don't think that. It wasn't like that—"

"Then *what!*" she screamed, turning on her. Her eyes blazed fury beneath the hazel contacts. "You tell *me*, Deborah! Did he go along with you to your little procedure? Was he holding your hand, watching you give birth to death when he should have been holding the one that was giving him life!"

"No!" Deborah shook her head emphatically. "No. I didn't tell him until it was all over. He was furious; he was inconsolable. He wanted to tell you about us anyway, but I forbid him to say anything. I told him if we just went on as if the whole thing had never happened, everything would be fine.

"I thought he'd be all right Mae, that he'd just get over it, move on. But right after Lily came, he…he changed. That's when he started hitting the bottle hard." She balled her fists, pressing them against her throbbing temples. "That's when he started…"

"Giving me lessons," Mae whispered, clutching her stomach. She felt the room closing in on her, her breath coming in gasps as she struggled to her feet.

"Mae, please," Deborah wailed, reaching for her.

"Don't touch me. I'm going to be sick." She stumbled from the kitchen to the living room, standing before the fireplace in silence. Deborah followed close behind, stopping short in the doorway.

"All those years," Mae began, watching the fire consume the kindling. "So many things he's done, some I'll never speak of…the torture he inflicted on me for so long…" she turned to face her, thinking of Pralines and Cream and the crude R.S. emblazoned in her flesh. "It was all because of you, because he couldn't have you." She took a step in her direction, shaking her head. "He didn't want me and Lily, he never did. He hated us, mistreated us for six years because we were reminders—the only thing standing between him and happiness, between him and *you*."

"Mae, please listen," she begged. "There's more—"

"Why did you do this to us? Why didn't you just tell him to go away, tell him to let go!" she reached behind her, closing her hand on a heavy object. In the light of the fire Deborah saw it was a crystal vase, the shadow of a single tulip etched onto the polished surface.

"I gave that man nine years, Deborah, *nine years* of my life, and he kicked and beat me like a dog on the street because you hurt his precious *feelings?*" She cocked her arm back and hurled it through the air. Deborah ducked and barely missed it, the vase shattering just to her left. Fine sprays of glass pricked her skin as the remnants flew in every direction.

"Mae!" she bellowed, shrinking to the floor. "You don't understand. We argued in front of my office. The letter, he—" she dodged another flying object, scuttling across the floor to take refuge behind a chair in the corner of the room. "I'm sorry!" she wailed. "I'm so sorry. I know you can't forgive me, but you need to hear what I'm saying! I lost the letter, you might be in danger…"

Blinded by rage, Mae searched the mantle for another object to throw. Her feverish eyes darted this way and that until they happened on an iron poker, resting on a rack near the fireplace. "I think you've worked real hard to earn a piece of what I've been gettin' all these years, don't you agree?" she snatched it up and marched across the room, eyes boring into hers. "Momma always used to say 'An eye for an eye.' Know what that means?" she asked, swinging at the chair with all her might.

Deborah screamed, crawling into a fetal position as she held onto the legs for dear life. Mae swung at the chair again and again with the poker, her glasses flying high off her head and landing somewhere across the room. In her growing frustration, she stopped swinging and kicked at the chair with savage strength. The chair spun off to the side of the room, collided with a wall and flipped over, leaving Deborah completely exposed.

Deborah held her hands over her head, whimpering. "Don't hurt me, Mae. Please, don't…"

"You know, Deborah, I'm really tired of listening to your whining." She stabbed the poker into a crack between the polished wooden planks, planting a fist on her hip. "Whine whine whine, that's all you do. Some guy leaves you high and dry, poor me. Fall right into bed with another, and it's the same thing all over again. I think I've probably heard enough yap from your mouth for a lifetime." She reached for the poker and raised it high over her head again, the sharp iron turning scarlet in the light of the flickering fire.

Deborah screamed until she was nearly hoarse. "I know I've done you wrong! I'm a horrible friend, but I pay for my sins every day! Maybe I can't earn a place in heaven after all this, but I'm *trying*, Mae, I'm trying. I came all the way here to make it right. Please, just let me make it right!"

Mae thought of her father and the razor in his twitching hand, dying a sinner's death in the bloody bathtub of her nightmares as he supernaturally begged for her pardon…

"Oh God," Mae shrieked, dropping the poker. The metal slammed against the hardwood, leaving a jagged scar on the wood where it lay. She backed away from Deborah slowly. "Please leave," she whispered. "Please go." She crumpled to the floor, sobbing uncontrollably.

"I lost the letter," Deborah whispered again, climbing to her knees. "We struggled in the car, he might have found it. I can't be sure, but it's why I'm here. I've always looked out for you, always protected you…" Deborah slowly got to her feet and went to her. "It'll be okay," she said, extending her hand. "I'll stay. I'll be here with you, in case he comes…"

"Not if I change my mind," Mae countered as she crawled away from her, collapsing on one of the sofas. "I can't let you stay here. I'm too afraid of what might happen if I change my mind and pick that poker up again. I want you out of this house, Deborah. You're no longer welcome here."

Deborah nodded silently, limping to the door. "I'm still paying for my sins, Ella Mae," she said over her shoulder. "I pay dearly for mine every day. I'll have to die paying for them, though, I see that now." She turned to glance at her friend once more before disappearing into the blinding rain. She ran to her vehicle and climbed inside. *I was there when she was married*, she thought, backing it around Mae's car and down the drive to the main road. *I was there when her little girl was born. I've always been there, and I guess I'll always have to be. Who else is gonna step in and fill those big ol' shoes?*

Richard moved stealthily under cloak of darkness, making his way to the top of the slope. In the driving rain he could make out the vague shape of Bella Bloom, a lighter shadow against a sky black as ink. Had there been anyone around to shine a light on the husky shadow slinking through the wood, they would have cringed, appalled at the malevolent hatred written on his face.

He scanned the back of the property through a thin screen of foliage. He could see vague shapes moving in the firelight, glowing behind gauzy drapes in the living room. The two figures seemed to be involved in a heated discussion. He watched them for a moment, fascinated.

"Not long, baby," he whispered with a malevolent grin, rubbing his hands together. "Not long at all 'til we're reunited. Hope you missed me as much as I missed—" he paused when he saw the figures move away from the windows. "Dammit," he muttered, searching for them in vain. He crouched there in the darkness for what seemed like hours. To keep himself alert, he envisioned Lily on the playground, her hair blowing wildly around her as she played hopscotch. *Daddy missed you more than anything, pretty girl. He's gonna make your old momma pay for everything. Yep, your old momma's gonna pay the price for all.*

He closed his eyes briefly, beginning to feel drowsy though the cold rain pelted him mercilessly through the black parka he wore. His eyes flicked open. He stared at the house again, wondering what had drawn his attention. For a moment there was nothing, then he saw it: one shadow, a solitary feminine form pacing the room.

Not just a shadow. His wife.

He slowly got to his feet again, aware of every nerve in his body coming alive as if touched by electricity. He brazenly left the cover of the trees, jogging bent over across the lawn, past the garden and tool shed. He paused, glancing inside one of the shed windows. A shovel, backhoe, and a pair of well-oiled garden shears hung neatly on the far wall. He tried the doorknob, praying for a miracle. It swung open easily, and he stepped inside. Minutes later, he jogged right up to the rear of the house, borrowed equipment in hand. He quickly crouched down again, inching his way along the wall until he was directly under one of the living room windows.

Only to wait now. Only to wait. Just a little longer before reunion time…

Richard grinned again in the darkness.

Mae lay sprawled on the sofa, staring listlessly at the fire. "How could she *do* this," she whispered over and over. "How could she let him put us through…" she sat up suddenly, wiping tears with the sleeve of her sweater. She glanced over at the grandfather clock on the far wall. 7:15.

Pull yourself together, dammit. She slammed a balled fist against her thigh repeatedly. *You've been through worse. You've also got a kid coming home in forty-five minutes. You can't let her to see you like this…*

"No," Mae said aloud with conviction, getting to her feet. "Gotta keep it together, for both of us…" she shuffled around the room, straightening furniture and picking up shards of broken glass. She cried softly to herself as she finished her spaghetti dinner, thinking of Deborah's warning as she set the dining room table for two with trembling hands. What if Richard had actually found her letter after their supposed scuffle? What if Deborah had been lying about losing it all along to gain sympathy when she realized the guilt of coming clean would be too difficult for her to bear? Mae shook her head, determined to talk it over with Merribelle later when she arrived with Lily. She was carrying a basket of French bread to the table twenty minutes later when she heard a bumping noise coming from the far end of the living room, near the windows.

She set the bread down and walked back up the hallway, taking a hesitant step into the room. Everything was in its proper place; the fire blazed brightly as it devoured more of the kindling she'd tossed in earlier. Mae stood in the center of the room and cocked her head, listening. Finally, she rolled her eyes and sighed, hearing nothing but the ticking grandfather clock and the crackling flames. "Geez, Mae," she mumbled to herself. "Having visions of your dead father, waving fire pokers at people and hearing strange noises…what next?"

She approached the nearest window, staring out at the falling rain. "Rain rain, go away," she chanted, recalling the familiar chorus from childhood. She pressed a hand against the window, loving the cool feel of the glass under her fingers and closed her eyes a moment, thinking of her grandmother. "Granna, what happened?" she whispered to the still air. "Where did I go wrong?" She opened her eyes…and screamed.

She was able to glimpse Richard's face looming threateningly on the other side of the glass an instant before the window exploded in on her.

Jasper tossed the last report into his briefcase, rubbing his eyes. "All work and no play makes Jasper a dull boy," he muttered, sipping the last of his beer. He stretched out on the sofa, tucking one of the throw pillows behind his head as he closed his eyes. Mae's face flashed vividly across his mind, smiling up at him as they embraced that afternoon, her petite form nearly swallowed up in his oversized jacket…

"Jacket," he repeated, sitting up. He smacked his forehead loudly. "Oh, sugar." He laughed, getting up and going to the hall closet. "You forgot Lily's portrait." He dug in each pocket until he found the folded piece of paper. He unfolded it again and shook his head, grin spreading across his face. "Grown folks get caught in the heat of the moment, and they'll forget anything, I guess."

He went to pick up the phone, dialing half the number before replacing the receiver in its cradle. "Hell, I'll just stop in for a minute, drop it off right quick. Sure hope they like surprises." He grabbed the jacket and his keys, whistling as he headed out the door.

One second there was nothing, the next he was simply there, swinging a shovel at her face on the other side of the window. It was as if the falling rain had simply turned to glass. It showered upon her endlessly, tearing and slashing at her wherever it fell against her skin. Mae fell backward and shielded her face with her arms, biting down on her screams for fear the glass would slide down her throat, cutting her insides wide open with its sharp edges. Richard dropped the shovel, leapt through the window and pounced on her with what seemed to be super-human strength.

Oh, the pain. The pain was everywhere. She climbed onto her belly, attempting to crawl through the sea of glass. She made it only a few inches before his hand tangled itself roughly in her hair, the nails scraping against her scalp.

Richard snatched her head back, twirling his wrist to get a better grip as he straddled her from behind. Mae cried out, feeling a searing pain slide up her neck. She could see his knees on either side of her, the black denim torn and revealing lacerated skin beneath.

"Oh God," she gasped, flailing hopelessly in his grasp. "What did you…h-how did you—"

"No no, baby, don't talk. Shhhhh…" he reached in his pocket with his free hand, pulling a flash of steel from his parka. Mae gasped when she saw the blade of the knife, a frantic scream dying on her lips.

"You've been real naughty, Mae. What have I taught you about disobeying me, huh? All my lessons, and what have you learned?" He pressed the blade against her throat, praying for restraint. The muscles in his arm jerked and twitched with the effort. "Nothing. Absolutely nothing."

"Rick please, we can talk about this," Mae whispered, hot tears sliding down her cheeks.

"No no no, Mae." He yanked hard on her hair, puppeting her head from side to side as he spoke. "*My* turn to talk. Now where was I?" The knife pricked her below the chin, droplets of blood congealing on the tip. "Oh yes. I was just telling you how bad it makes me feel when you don't listen. You wouldn't let me teach you when we were in our home, the beautiful home I worked so hard to provide for you, no, of course not. You were *stubborn*, and *willful*…" He dug his fingers deeper into her scalp with each accusation. "Always had to have your way, no matter who paid the price. You took my pretty girl away. *You killed her in my mind.*"

Mae cried out again as he jerked the hair he held firm in his grip, snapping her head violently backward. He leaned over her, his mouth only inches from her ear. "I buried her in the cemetery, Mae. I buried you together in a black casket in the pouring rain. I cried for you. Everyone cried. But did you care? No. You had your perfect life here, lying and fucking and lying some more. It's cool, though. After all this time apart, the scent of your tail was still hot in my nostrils; I sniffed it all the way to your little whorehouse in the woods so I could teach you one last lesson."

"Rick, stop it! Let go!" Mae moved her head as far as he would allow, trying to steal a glance at the grandfather clock from her awkward position. Not long before Lily would be walking through the front door…

"Let's go somewhere and talk about this, okay? I'll go wherever you want me to, do whatever you want, I promise…"

"You know, I think you should seriously consider taking some time to think on what you've done before we begin." He snatched his hand out of her hair, grabbed a leg of her jeans and twisted it, flipping her over on her back. She lay there motionless, terror clearly written in her eyes though she'd long ceased to struggle. He planted both meaty hands on either side of her head, hovering over her again. "In the meantime, where is she?"

Love you, Lily…

"…isn't…here," Mae whispered hoarsely. "It's too late, and …" she mumbled the rest incoherently so he had to lean in even closer to hear. As he moved his ear to her mouth, she bit down hard on the lobe, sending a lightning-like bolt of pain through his head. Richard jerked away, a wounded howl escaping his lips. "YOU CAME TO THE WRONG PLACE, YOU SON OF A BITCH!!" she bellowed at the top of her lungs. "YOU'RE NOT GOING TO HURT HER AGAIN AS LONG AS I'M ALIVE!!"

"Tsk, Tsk, Tsk…" the grandfather clocked ticked in time to Richard's shaking head. He winced, touched his ear and pulled his hand away, showing her the blood on the fingers. "Looks like we're in for another long lesson." He offered a sympathetic smile as more of her tears splashed to the floor, mingling with the blood and glass. "Oh, don't worry. I'm feeling fresh and new and got *plenty* of lesson left in me. Been saving up a lifetime of lesson, it seems…."

"Richard, no!" she shrieked, his shadow looming over her. "*Oh God, somebody help me!*"

Her frantic screams were swallowed up by the raging storm.

FIFTEEN

Mae opened her eyes sometime later. Pain shot through her head, and she tried to cover it with her hands, suppressing a scream. Her eyes were nearly swollen shut; she touched the back of her head and brought her hand to her face, not surprised to see blood on the palm, trickling down her arm to the floor. She strained to catch another glimpse of the clock; no more than twenty minutes had passed.

She groaned long and loud, rolling onto her side. Richard sat on one of the couches, rummaging through her purse. "Lucky," he muttered, kicking the purse into the fire. Odds and ends flew everywhere. Her cell phone slid under the couch. "Lucky I didn't kill you yet, bitch." He got up and crossed the room. "Tell me where she is," he growled, dropping to his knees next to her. He took another fistful of her hair in one of his hands and twirled his wrist, gripping even tighter than before. With the other, he brandished the knife again. "I'll cut you up, Mae, I swear I'll cut you to pieces. You-know-I-know-how," he yelled angrily, smacking the back of her head against the wood with every word for emphasis. "And-you-know-I-can-get-away-with-it."

By now Mae was swimming in and out of consciousness. "Richard," she said thickly when she came to again, tasting blood in her mouth. "I'm sorry, I'm so sorry I didn't listen. I've learned my lesson this time, I promise. I can take you right to her if you help me." He continued glowering down on her, as if silently contemplating his options. She felt herself growing bolder in the silence, her plan becoming clearer in her mind with each passing second. Finally, she pounced on his indecision. "I know I was bad, Rick. Very, very bad. But if you let me take you to her I'll make it up to you, I promise. I'll let you do whatever you want."

When he heard these last words, Richard broke into a grin. Mae's blood ran ice cold. "What-*ever* I want?" He stroked her cheek with the blade of the knife. "'Cause you know, I'm a man of many ideas…"

Mae fought back tears. "I'm yours," she answered, trying to keep the trembling from her voice. "All yours, I promise. Just let me take you to our daughter first."

"You excited about showing Momma your new skates?" Merribelle asked cheerily, glancing over her shoulder.

Lily sat in the back seat, idly spinning the tiny pink wheels on her feet. She nodded eagerly. "Auntie Merri?"

"What is it, sweetie?"

Lily chewed her thoughts a moment. "You think Momma might want to go get skates, too?"

Merribelle chuckled, spinning one of the little girl's wheels. "You know, I think we've got a pretty good shot at gettin' your momma into a pair of skates. She used to wear 'em everywhere when we were kids."

Lily smiled. "She needs to have more fun. Maybe then she won't cry as much."

Merribelle glanced over at her husband in the driver's seat. He reached out and took her hand in his, squeezing it gently. She turned again to the back seat. "Momma's only sad because she misses you, honey. She can't wait to have you back home with her again."

Lily stretched and yawned, crossing her legs at the ankles. The skates clicked loudly against each other.

Merribelle pointed at them. "Want me to put those back in the box for you?"

Lily shook her head drowsily. "Huh-unh. I want to wear them 'til I can go skating…" Her eyelids fluttered closed as she drifted off to sleep.

Merribelle watched her a moment longer. "She's the most beautiful thing, Tim. Looks dead-on Mae."

"Uh-oh," he said, winking. "Sounds like someone wants to have another little 'un running around the house."

"You're gettin' funnier in your old age, Tidwell." She laughed. "You should think about takin' that act on the road sometime."

He gave her thigh a quick squeeze before returning it to the wheel. Merribelle leaned her head against the headrest as her cell phone chirped to life. She pulled it from her purse, expecting to receive a call. Instead, a single text message waited:

HE FOUND US. DON'T BRING HER HERE. TELL LILY I LOVE HER.

The phone went dead in her hands.

"Oh God," Merribelle cried, then remembering Lily sleeping in the back, clamped a hand over her mouth. "Stop the car, Tim," she said through her fingers. "We have to call the Sheriff, something terrible's happened." She did begin to scream then, hollow soundless screams when her husband quickly pulled over to the side of the road. He immediately took her in his arms, gently prying the phone away from her clenched fingers. When he'd read the text message he reset the screen, dialing a number from memory as he held his distraught wife against his chest.

"Sheriff Reed, please. Yeah Griffen, it's Tidwell. We got an emergency situation, here. You better grab your boys and head on out to the Bella Bloom property..."

Mae snapped the phone shut, sliding it back under the couch. She crawled as quickly as her body could carry her back to the spot where she lay when Richard had left the room. She closed her eyes and tried to breathe deeply, feigning another bout of unconsciousness. Moments later, she heard the toilet in the downstairs bathroom flush. The door opened wide with a squeak of protest, and Richard was back.

"Honey, you ready?" he called out giddily, nearly skipping over to her. "Let's go, Lily's waiting."

She lay there with her eyes still closed, fighting the urge to move. Her heart pounded so rapidly in her chest she wondered if it might just quit beating altogether.

Not before I get him away from Lily. She felt her mind beginning to drift away on a cloud, and she prayed she wouldn't slip back into unconscious for real again until she could at least get them as far away from the house as possible…

Suddenly, she felt his hands under her arms, pulling her roughly to her feet.

"Get up, wakey wakey. You got work to do." He stooped and lifted her over his shoulder, carrying her through the house and out the back door as if she were merely a sack of flour. Rain pelted them mercilessly as they traveled down the steep hill to his waiting car.

Despite her prayers, she continued to float in and out of consciousness anyway, though by this time the bleeding from her scalp had slowed nearly to a stop. When they were in front of his car he set her down on her feet; when she slumped to the ground, he snatched her up again by her collar, slapping her hard across the face.

"I said wake up, you stupid cunt!" He wrenched open the door, throwing her roughly inside before jogging around to the driver's side and jumping in.

"You'd better not be lying to me, Mae," he said, twisting the key in the ignition and gunning the engine. "If you're up to something, remember that in my world, there's worse things than dying."

Henry sat at the back of the bus depot, a bottle of beer in his hand. He sagged into his old dilapidated recliner, shifting around until he settled into the grooves his body had formed after occupying that same spot for years. He took a sip of the ice-cold brew and grunted satisfaction, reaching up and loosening the top button of his uniform shirt. Feeling around the inside of the recliner, he finally pulled out a universal remote, buttons of nearly every shape, color and function lined up in neat rows across the face.

"Let's see here," he muttered, pressing one of them. "Gene tried to teach me which one worked to turn on the television…" He pointed and waved it at the giant screen. When nothing happened, he slammed the remote down in frustration, getting himself up from the chair. "Damn fan-dangled satellite machin'rey," he grumbled, walking over to the TV to punch the ON button. "What the sam hell's the use?"

As he got up, a pair of headlights turned onto Main Street, dancing past the big picture window overlooking the Square. Still surly from his preoccupation with the television, Henry only glanced out the window, quickly looking away when the glare nearly blinded him. "Damn car lights. Can't you get your butts in gear and move along the street like the rest of us?"

The car idled there in the rain for some minutes, as if the driver were undecided about where he wanted to go next. Henry held a hand above his eyes and squinted as he stepped over to the glass, trying to catch a glimpse of the driver. When he was unsuccessful, he walked over to the coat tree in the corner and donned his red slicker.

"Folks seem to be gettin' lost all day today," he mumbled, opening the door and stepping into the storm. He walked into the depot parking lot. "Hey, Hey there!" he called, heading toward the car. "Hey buddy! Need help?"

As he got closer, he thought he recognized the vehicle as the same one that had been parked in front of the depot just that morning. The closer he got, the more he was sure it was one and the same. "I remember…" He pulled the slicker tighter around him. "That big city fellow with the face I couldn't quite place…"

Before he could reach the vehicle, the driver sped off, his tires spraying Henry with water from head to toe.

He didn't care all that much about it, though. If his eyes weren't failing him, he was positive he saw and recognized a passenger in the vehicle as well.

"Better get m' Bessie," he said, running back to the depot for his keys.

"What the hell is *this?*" Richard yelled, slamming his fist against the wheel. "Where the fuck are we?"

Mae sat across from him, staring out the windshield at the bus depot. Across the street, Henry was fast approaching in his familiar red rain slicker, waving his arms and calling out as he sloshed through the soggy parking lot. "I...I don't know," she stammered groggily, eyes never leaving Henry. "My head hurts so much, it's getting blurry—"

Richard's fist flew up from the steering wheel, smashing mercilessly into the side of her face. "Well, wake the fuck up! Bitch, you really want a headache, keep fucking with me. I swear, I'll make it so no one ever finds you."

The force of his fist sent her head straight into the passenger window, her right temple colliding with the glass so hard her ears began to ring.

"Richard, please!"

He grabbed her by the collar, shaking her so violently it ripped away from the rest of her shirt. "You take me to her now!" he bellowed at her. "No-more-bullshit!"

"Okay!" she screamed, pushing him away and collapsing into tears. "Okay," she sobbed. "Drive."

He stomped the gas pedal as Henry was closing in on the driver's side door, sending sprays of water in his face.

The car raced down the road leading out of town, propelling both of them toward an uncertain destiny. Mae continued to wipe away tears as she gazed at her rearview mirror, watching her last hope of survival rapidly disappear into the growing darkness.

Jasper reached the top of the muddy access road, pulling into the driveway. He glanced over at the house as he parked. Lights burned brightly on the first and second floors, giving the house a warm glow in the midst of the driving storm.

He pulled the hood of the jacket over his head, tucking the drawing back in his pocket. "You know a man's in deep when he risks the pouring rain to see his girl," he said with a smile, climbing out of the SUV.

He jogged over to the porch and rang the doorbell. He waited a beat, then pressed the button a second time. No shadows appeared on the other side of the door.

"Hello?" he called, knocking loudly as he glanced in the front window. The flames had burned out in the fireplace, striking him immediately as odd.

"That's strange," he muttered, jumping off the porch. He was in the process of checking the other ground floor windows when a rain of fists pelted him from behind.

"Rick! You sorry son of a bitch!" The unseen person gripped his back, acrylic nails digging through the thick jacket to his flesh.

"What the..." he bellowed, whirling to face his opponent. A petite shadow stood before him, a heavy object pointed in his face. "You're not getting anywhere near her, if I have anything to do with it. This is between you and me—"

"Whoa, whoa, wait a minute," Jasper interrupted, pushing the object away with ease. His probing fingers told him the woman was holding an industrial-sized flashlight.

"Who the hell is Rick? Who the hell are *you*, for that matter? I'm here to see Anne Marie."

The flashlight clicked on suddenly, blinding him. "Will you please turn that damn thing off me?" he backed up a step, holding an arm up to shield his eyes. "Look, I don't know who the hell you are or what your business is here, but you're wearin' my patience pretty damn thin—"

"Oh!" the woman gasped. "I'm sorry, I'm so sorry. You must be Jasper." The hand holding the flashlight reached out and grabbed his, shaking it furiously.

"And just who am I talkin' to, if I may be so impolite as to inquire?" Jasper asked sarcastically, taking his arm back and moving to the porch again.

The woman turned the flashlight on herself. "Dr. Deborah Barr. I'm uh...I'm a good friend of Anne Marie's." She climbed the porch steps behind him and stood with him near the door. "Look, I'm really sorry about attacking you. I thought you were someone else."

"Must be one mean son of a bitch for you to go attackin' blind in the dark like that." Jasper opened the screen door and kneeled down, fumbling with the lock a moment. He glanced up at her. "Shine that light down here while you chat, if you don't mind."

"Rick is her husband," she continued. "He's a detective. I was watching the house from my car on the main road, watching for suspicious anything, I guess. I had a strong feeling he might come here tonight looking for her."

Jasper stopped and planted his palms on his knees, staring up at her in disbelief. "Since evidently you didn't have sense enough to bring the law out here with you, I think you better help me get this door open," he said finally. "Lights are on but no one's home, as they say."

"It's complicated, Jasper, trust me." Deborah leaned in closer with the light. "The lock looks really old. If you ask me, I think we should just bust it in."

Jasper stood and shrugged, taking a few steps back. "Under the circumstances, I don't see a better solution." He turned his body sideways, aligning his shoulder with the center of the door. "Ready?"

Deborah nodded, moving down the steps. "Go ahead."

Jasper dropped his shoulder and rushed forward, hurling his bulk at the door. It gave easily under the force, opening onto—a mess.

"What the…" Jasper mumbled as he surveyed the scene, carefully making his way around upended furniture and piles of bloodied, broken glass. Deborah rushed in seconds later, stopping short beside him.

"Oh my God," she cried, covering her mouth. "We're too late. He's got her."

"Pull over, Richard."

He continued to ignore her; since the incident at the depot, he refused to speak except when asking for false directions and the occasional street name, which Mae was all too happy to give. Hours had passed since they'd left Beau Ciel in their taillights; cars were few and far between as they drove down the dark, desolate stretch of road.

The occasional flash of lightning revealed they were in swamp country; clusters of gnarled trees towered over the stagnant water, their branches weighed down with scarves of thick green moss. She shuddered, thinking of all the unseen predators lurking in the hidden places. She wondered what they would do to the unfortunate soul who ended up lost out here, stumbling around in the dark….

She eyed the knife laying on the dashboard in front of her husband, smears of her blood beginning to dry on the heavy blade.

It's now or never, she thought, gathering her remaining courage. *Now or never…*

She grabbed his shoulder. "I said, pull over."

He shook her off and clamped his fingers around her wrist, never once taking his eyes off the road. "I wouldn't do that if I were you."

She snatched her hand away and rubbed it, glaring at him. "You're not going to let me go, are you?"

When he didn't answer, her voice grew even louder, fear turning quickly to anger. "You never planned to let me go, did you?" She gave a harsh laugh. "Of *course* not, Mae, what was a dummy like me thinking? Detective Spencer never loses a case, right?"

She shifted in her seat, still glaring at the side of his face. "Look at me, you bastard. You owe me that at least."

"Settle down," he replied in a surprisingly mild tone, turning another corner. "You don't know what the hell you're talking about. Give me Lily, and I'm happy. All I want is what's mine."

"Oh yeah?" Mae countered, sliding closer to him on the seat. "What does Debbie have to say about that? She put you up to this? Huh? *Did* she? She's got you and now she wants my kid, too, is that it? 'Cause you know," she finished in a whisper, leaning so close her cracked and swollen lips almost touched his ear. "She's kind of like Barbie. That bitch gets everything."

Mae was off the seat in a flash, reaching for the blade. Before he could even turn to strike her again, she grabbed the knife and plunged it deep in his side with all her strength.

Richard's screams pierced her already ringing ears. He wrenched the wheel hard to the right, plunging the car into the dark water.

Henry sat behind the wheel of his beloved Caddie, perched on the edge of the seat. He'd hopped into her and followed the speeding car through the countryside, careful to hang back at a distance so as not to be recognized. He'd lost them a couple miles back and was driving in unfamiliar territory now, a private stretch of deserted swamp land that even he was afraid to go near after dark. The wipers swished water back and forth across the windshield. With no car in sight for some time, every passing second served only to increase his anxiety. He was certain he had seen Mae in the car, and just as certain the man with the cool shades was someone she wasn't too thrilled to see. If his gut was telling him right, she was in deep trouble, and probably running out of time.

He shifted the car into high gear. "Hold on, Junie," he said to the empty interior. "Hold on, honey, I'm comin'. You jus' give Henry another sign…"

Mae gave a loud cry as the hood slammed into the muddy water. She leapt from the car and landed on her shoulder, the soft moss carpeting the ground catching her fall. She lay there moaning in pain, trying to catch her breath. Richard was unconscious, his body slumped over the wheel of the sinking car, bleeding badly. Rolling over at last, she got to her knees, and then to her feet, praying they wouldn't give way. Surprisingly, she hadn't injured anything severely in the accident, though the cut to her scalp had begun to bleed again.

Dazed, she tripped over a fallen log just as she reached the edge of the swamp, tumbling down a short slope to the water's edge. Sharp branches and rocks scraped and bruised her skin as she climbed to her feet again and stumbled along the muddy ground. Crickets and cicadas chirped from the hollowed out trunks of trees, and alligators waded through the inky water, only their eyes visible on the surface. She held her arms out in front of her when it got too dark to distinguish one shadow from another, touching every tree she ran across and grabbing onto the lowest branches, taking measured steps. Some time later, she thought she saw light in the distance.

She stumbled on toward the source, leaving the protective shelter of the trees to climb another short slope. At its crest, she stood and peered through the hanging moss. A small shack stood across the way, the corrugated tin roof illuminated by light from a single watt bulb swinging from an orange extension cord. A footbridge constructed of wood planks jutted out over the water.

"Somebody," she called louder, taking the planks two at a time. "Somebody!" she finally shouted, breaking into a dead run. "Somebody help me!" She was across the bridge and at the front door in seconds. "Help, please," she panted, leaning on the door and banging it with her fists. "Please, anybody, open up. I'm hurt, a man's trying to kill me..." She slid to the ground, drawing her legs to her chest. She lay there shivering against the door in the cold rain, once again slipping into unconsciousness.

Henry braked suddenly, pulling the Caddie to the side of the road. He stared through the windshield. "That's my girl." He grabbed a heavy flashlight and got out, switching it on. Even from this distance, he could see the vehicle was half submerged in water, the front end stuck in peat dirt two feet thick. When he got closer, he saw the passenger door flung wide open. Jogging over to it, he raised the light and shined it in the interior. It was completely empty.

Henry carefully ran his hand along the steering wheel and pulled it away, examining his fingers in the light. *Blood.* It was all over the seats and smears of it covered the windows; small pools of it had begun to congeal on the floor.

"Oh, Junie," Henry whispered, wiping the blood on his trouser leg. "I jus' hope I'm not too late."

Mae opened her eyes again, immediately rolling over and coughing up water that had collected in her mouth as she'd lain passed out against the door. She tried to pull herself up to her knees, then grabbed the back of her head. The bleeding had stopped again, though her head still felt as if a chorus of hammers and anvils were sounding between her ringing ears.

"Come on, Mae, don't give up," she told herself over and over, using the doorknob to climb to her feet. "You don't get help soon, you're gonna die out here."

She dragged herself to the edge of the bridge, slid off it into the shallow mud. "And what would happen to Lily?" she questioned aloud as she limped around the side of the shack, searching for something strong enough to break one of the high windows. "How would she go on without you?" Not finding anything useful, she hobbled back around to the front, climbed back onto the bridge. "She needs you, Mae. She's just a baby, and she's been through so much. She's just a little girl, and—"

Before she could finish the thought, a hand snaked out of the darkness, closing around her throat.

Richard squeezed with everything he had left, lifting her off her feet. The tips of her sneakers scraped feebly against the wood before he brought her back down, slamming her hard against the planks. He staggered, and then bent to his knees, holding onto the wooden railing. Blood still poured from the wound in his side; big drops of it splashed onto her face.

Mae lay there writhing and clutching at her throat, swallowing cold air and rain together in thick gulps. There wasn't enough air to breathe, let alone scream…yet she found the strength to scream anyway, rolling onto her stomach and crawling away from him. "Help me, somebody! Please, he's going to—"

She made it only a few feet before he was behind her again, dragging her back down the planks by her ankles. "NO!" she screamed again, clawing at the wood. The nails ripped down to the quick, splinters of wood tearing the pads of her fingers to bleeding shreds.

"Somebody, PLEASE!"

He flipped her over onto her back again, once again straddling her with his knees. When she continued to fight, he sat down hard on her chest, pinning her beneath him and knocking the wind from her lungs. Seemingly possessed by an eerie calm, he reached into his pocket and pulled out the bloody knife. He seized it in both hands, raising the blade high over his head as if he were a priest, offering her body up to the gods as a sacrifice. "Bitch…"

Mae shut her eyes. Only Lily flashed through her mind.

When she heard the first shot, she thought she was dead, believing her husband had at the last second thought better of it and somehow switched his knife for the .38 special he always carried with him.

When she heard the second, she felt the oppressive weight suddenly lift off her chest, allowing her to breathe again.

When she heard the third, she screamed, using her feet to push herself away. She opened her eyes to see his lifeless body fall backward, sliding into the black water with hardly a sound.

She tried to keep moving, but found her own body had used the last of its strength. She covered her face with her hands and just lay there, sobbing uncontrollably. After a while, her thoughts began to spin again, the perception of her surroundings beginning to blur around the edges. She heard footsteps on the bridge above her, then felt sinewy arms lifting her from the wet planks.

"Henry," she said softly, drifting away.

She came to again in the front seat of the Caddie. Henry was sitting behind the steering wheel, a Remington rifle laid carefully across his lap. When he realized she was awake, he gave her a weak smile, though his eyes remained unreadable. He stroked the top of her head. "Don't you worry, Junie. I called Merribelle, an' she's got the ambulance comin' on its way. Jus' hold on, it won't be much longer."

She reached for his hand. "Henry," she whispered, "you saved me. How did you know where he'd taken me?"

He shook his head. "He come into the depot earlier, lookin' for you. He wore cool shades an' had a big city attitude, tried to pass himself off as an insurance agent." He shrugged. "Soon as he hit the door, I felt in my gut somethin' wasn't right, I jus' couldn't quite put my finger on it...but I recognized him an' the car tonight in the parking lot. When I saw you on the other side of him, that's when I knew." He shifted uncomfortably on the seat, turning to stare out the windshield. "I got my keys, jumped in m' Bessie, and followed you on out here the rest of the way."

From somewhere far off, sirens began to sound.

Henry remained silent, still staring out the windshield at nothing.

"What is it, Henry?" Mae asked. "Something's bothering you, I can feel it."

"Probably the Sheriffs'll be out here 'rectly, too." He picked the rifle up and examined it, testing the weight of it in his hands. "Never had to shoot a man before, in all the years I ever lived, even in the military." He brought the Remington to rest on his lap again with a sigh. "I have to warn you, Junie. If those Sheriffs go to huntin' around an' find that man's body all shot up like it is, they likely to throw me in jail."

Mae tried to sit up in the seat. "Henry, no! They can't do that. I won't let them. I'll tell them everything. I'll..."

He held a finger to his lips. "You be quiet now, y' hear? Don't go gettin' yourself all riled up 'bout things don't really concern you. Now I shot the man with m' own hands, an' I ain't none sorry 'bout it. I'm prepared to take responsibility for m' actions—"

The sirens grew louder.

Mae grabbed his arm. "But you didn't shoot him, Henry."

Henry stared at her incredulously. "See here, you done gone an' stressed 'till you done twisted yourself up in a delirium fever."

"I never saw you shoot him," she repeated stubbornly. "It was an accident, he just fell in."

The sirens grew louder still, and lights could be seen in the distance.

"Junie—"

"I *said,* he just fell in." She sat back on the seat, closing her eyes in exhaustion. "If and when they ever find the body, I'll be sure to tell them something different."

They sat together in silence until the ambulance finally arrived, followed closely by a fleet of police cruisers. The sound of the sirens was deafening, now; together, the vehicles flooded the car with their flashing multicolored lights.

"Put your gun away, Henry," Mae said, swinging her legs out of the car. As soon as they spotted her, a pair of EMT's leapt from the ambulance and started running, stretcher and emergency equipment in hand. "You won't be needing it anymore."

EPILOGUE

Mae lugged a plain cardboard carton into the room, tossing it onto one of the kitchen chairs. She picked up her masterpiece and held it one last time. The images that had flashed through her mind so long ago had emerged at last as pure perfection. A broiling desert sun slipped beneath the cover of distant mountain ranges, painting the desolate landscape in shadows of blush and purple. Her fingers lovingly caressed the canvas, tracing familiar images on the grainy surface as they had done so often before. Rows of cactus stretched their prickly arms toward the heavens; clusters of sagebrush blew this way and that. At the center of the twilight scene was her beloved waterfall.

Mae smiled, her index finger following the path of raging water from a cleft high in the rock to a bubbling spring far below. Here, the waters formed the crystal silhouette of a woman with head thrown back, arms raised high in triumph. The piece, "Desert Oasis," had been the toast of the night at *A Day In Her Life*, her first gallery show. It garnered rave reviews from all who'd attended, and along with a few of her earlier pieces, was currently en route to a gallery owner in New Orleans, who enjoyed her collection so much he'd purchased some of it at twice the asking price, to the dismay of others waiting eagerly in line to place their bids.

Giving it a final glance, she carefully wrapped the canvas in soft sheets of foam, then placed it in the cardboard carton. As she was rummaging through her purse for the pre-printed label and postage she'd bought, a cable news station blaring from a portable radio on the counter caught her attention.

"In other news, the city of Philadelphia virtually came to a stand-still at noon today as the memorial for Detective Richard F. Spencer got underway. A decorated officer known best for his arrest of Saturday

Night Special killer Ronald Mangus, Detective Spencer became the focus of nation wide attention when his wife, local television producer Ella Mae Spencer, abducted their six-year-old daughter and fled their home. Their mutilated bodies were later discovered at Elysium State Park; the details of their deaths were never publicly disclosed.

"In a strange twist, in the weeks following the tragedy, Detective Spencer himself became the subject of a national search when he was reported missing by his homicide partner, Detective Peter Blake. By analyzing recent credit card transactions, authorities were able to trace his last known whereabouts to Beau Ciel, Louisiana, a rural town outside Metairie Parish, near New Orleans. A rental car bearing some of his personal affects was discovered on the edge of a swamp just outside the town. Authorities believe it is there the detective may have met an unfortunate fate. Though they've vowed to continue their search, experts say the proliferation of alligators and other indigenous wildlife would make it nearly impossible for his body to ever be found and identified…"

But you didn't shoot him, Henry. It was a terrible accident, he just fell in…

Deep at the bottom of her purse, her cell phone chirped. Startled, she dropped it on the floor, the contents sliding in every direction. She dropped to her knees and plucked the phone from the mess, pressing the SEND button. "Hello?" she answered quickly, trying to disguise the trembling in her voice. She listened and frowned deeply, face clouding over with concern. After a couple of seconds, she nodded grimly. "All right, I'll be there soon."

She flipped the phone shut and set it on the table above her, beginning to feel along the floor for her belongings. As she retrieved them one at a time, shoving them roughly back into the purse, an ice-cold hand settled on the nape of her neck. Mae froze, chills rising on her spine. *Is he dead, Henry, is he really dead? It was an accident. He just fell in…*

She jumped up, whirled around…and was immediately arrested by a set of lips, pressed gently against her own. *Jasper.*

Instantly, her body relaxed. She closed her eyes, allowing him to pull her into his embrace. When they parted, she smacked her lips, smiling up at him. "Lemon pie, my favorite."

"I know." He grabbed her hand and pulled her to him again, tossing the purse on the table. "Thought I'd oblige myself and sneak a taste of Merri's pie when no one was looking."

"Hey!" She punched him on the chest playfully. "I thought this party was for me! You know, in *my* honor?"

"Oh yeah, I got it," he grinned, gesturing at the carton's contents. "What a wonderful way for a woman to celebrate her newfound success in the city. Hidin' out in her kitchen, crawling around on the floor…" he peeked in the box, folding back a layer of foam wrapping. 'Desert Oasis' huh? That one sold like hot melted butter at a pancake parade." He winked. "Seems that fancy pants gallery owner Lancaster sure took a liking to you, moment you stepped in the door wearing that dress."

"Dress?" Mae stepped back and folded her arms, eyeing him questioningly. "I'm sorry, what dress would that be, Dr. Jasper?"

"Oh, *you* know," he nodded approvingly, gaze traveling slowly up and down her form. "The red one." He moved toward her again, arms circling her waist easily. He lowered his head, his lips so close they tickled her earlobe as he spoke. "I distinctly remember slipping you out of that number just last night…"

Mae giggled. "Don't be silly, he's a friend of a friend. If Mrs. Smith hadn't judged my work good enough to invite him down for the showing, I'd still be the best kept secret in Beau Ciel." She gestured to the few articles still scattered around the room. "Now, if you don't mind, I'm up to my eyeballs here. Can't you see I dropped my purse?" She crouched down to pick up a pair of prescription wire rims much like those given her one night by Alyssa at Victory House, the night her life was transformed forever. When she stood up again, Jasper was waiting, a tiny gift wrapped box sitting in the middle of his open palm.

"Here. You must have dropped this, too."

"What on earth…" She took the box and held it up to her ear, giving it a couple of good shakes. "I told you, no presents."

"Don't talk, just open." He leaned against the counter, shoving his hands in his pockets. "Time's gettin' away from you. Take too long, and you'll miss everything." He began to stroke his chin, staring thoughtfully up at the ceiling. "But *hey*, if you do, maybe I can talk Merri into giving me the rest of that pie to take home after all…"

"Ha! You wish," Mae laughed, ripping the bow and paper off the box. She balled them up in one hand, preparing to toss it his way as she carefully opened the box with the other.

"Oh," she gasped, the ball of paper quickly forgotten. "Oh, my goodness…" She was staring down at a platinum engagement ring, a trio of white diamonds set elegantly in the center. She clamped a hand over her mouth and shook her head as she continued gazing down at it, finally shutting her eyes against the tears that threatened to fall. "Jasper…"

He left the counter and went to her, taking her in his arms again. She forced herself to look at him. "We talked about this. You know I can't, not right now…"

"I know," he whispered, stroking her face tenderly.

"It's not that I don't ever want to, it's just that today…I'm not saying no forever, I don't want you to think that—"

"I don't," he smiled, giving her another kiss. He leaned his forehead against hers, their faces so close their noses touched. "I won't lie to you, A.M. I'm ready, though I don't want to cause you any more pain by asking again." He nuzzled her nose. "Keep it, anyhow. Keep it and wear it on your right hand, like this…" He took the ring from the box and held her hand in his, caressing it a moment before sliding the band onto her fourth finger. "Wear it that way long as you like. When you feel the time has come…" he slid the ring off her right hand, placing it on the fourth finger of her left, "do this, and I'll know you're ready, too."

"What if it takes a long time?" she asked solemnly, staring deep into his eyes.

He shrugged as he put the ring back on her right finger, and she laced her arms comfortably around his neck. "I was told by a wise lady once that when a man finds a wife, he finds a good thing." He held his hands up in a defensive gesture when she scowled, punching him in the chest again. "No old flames this time, A.M." He chuckled. "I promise."

"Where's my baby?" she murmured, pulling him close again.

"Outside, with the kids." He reached into the back pocket of his jeans, producing a colorful party favor. "Noise maker, for you," he said, holding it out to her. "She sent me in here to tell you to get your tooshie out there and blow on this."

Mae laughed. "*Tooshie?* She's growing up so fast."

Jasper glanced at his watch. "If we don't get this party started soon, we're gonna be eatin' in the middle of a mean downpour. Checked the news right before I headed over here. Weather guy says rain's on the calendar today for sure." He went over to the window and looked up, eyeing the thickening clouds. He shook his head, suppressing a smile. "Tim shoulda known better than to set that grill up out there on a day like today."

Mae checked her own watch. "Oh my gosh," she cried as she snatched her purse up and raced around the room, shoving the last of the spilled articles inside. "I've gotta go, I promised someone I'd be somewhere." She disappeared down the hallway a moment to retrieve a denim jacket.

"So they call you out of the blue like that now, huh?" he smiled proudly at her when she returned.

Mae smiled, shrugged. "Guess so. It's my first time."

He pointed to the lapel of her jacket. "Aren't you forgetting something?"

Mae glanced down at herself, then back up at him. She frowned, slowly shaking her head. "Not that I know of."

Again, he reached into his back pocket, this time producing a photo ID badge. Mae took it from him and read the name: Anne Marie Croft, Peer Counselor I.

She grinned. "How did you get this?"

"I can pick things up, too, can't I?" He winked again. "Found it on the floor by the counter when you were busy with your gift."

"You are the gift." She was leaning in to kiss him again when she heard the screen door slam against the frame.

"Hey guys," Merribelle called when she entered the room, shivering. "Whew, much colder out there than I thought it was gonna be." She wrapped the gray sweater she wore tighter around her. "A lot of good this flimsy thing is doing me today."

Jasper smiled down at Mae, dropping his hands at his sides. "You know Merri," he sighed, "I was just saying the same thing before you popped up."

"Oh my goodness," she replied, glancing nervously from one face to the other. She held up a hand in apology. "I didn't interrupt anything, did I? You think I'd have been raised polite enough to knock, even in my own sister's house—"

"You worry too much, girl," he chuckled, waving her off. "It's no deal. Matter of fact, I'm glad you're here. 'Cause what I *really* want to know is…" he lowered his voice to a conspiratorial whisper. "How's Tim doin' with those ribs? He said he had it covered when I was on my way in." He left Mae's side and approached her, resting his hands on her shoulders. "Truth be told, Merri," he said solemnly. "Could the man actually use some help out there?"

Merribelle bit down on the inside of her cheek to suppress a laugh, trying her best to return his solemn gaze. "Oh I don't know, Jasper. There's lots of haze and smoke flying around out there. He may just be that bad off, after all. All's I know is he sent me in here to grab some paper plates after I told him the children are gonna fall dead in the yard if he doesn't feed them any time soon."

Jasper nodded grimly. "I'd better be on my way, then. I know where I'm needed." He zipped the navy parka he wore and stepped out the door.

Merribelle turned to her sister, laughing. "You've got a good one in that man, girl. Don't you even think of giving him up anytime soon."

Mae glanced out the window and smiled, watching him bound down the porch steps into the yard. "I'll do my best."

Merribelle gasped, reaching for her right hand. "And where on earth did this pretty little bauble come from? So *that* must have been what I was interrupting."

Mae groaned, turning to rummage in one of the cupboards. "Don't start with me again, Merri. I told you. I'm not getting married anytime soon, so you can just forget your dreams of planning a big summer wedding—"

Merribelle waved her off impatiently. "All right, all right, I'm over it." She crouched down, opening one of the cabinets nearest her. "Where on earth are your paper plates?"

Mae crossed to the far side of the room, quickly searching through the contents of another cupboard. "Don't think I have any," she said, shutting the door at last. "Lily must have used them all."

Merribelle started toward the door. "I'd better get on down to the Square before Tim gets through, then. The grocery mart closes in an hour."

Mae shook her head, stepping into the hallway. "You don't have to go all the way down there just for paper plates when I've got a ton of real ones right here."

"But those are Grandma Lily's," Merribelle said, following her across the hall to the dining room. "She only ever brought those out for special occasions—"

"And today we're celebrating one of the most special occasions of my life. I don't think she'd mind," Mae replied, reaching into a mahogany china cabinet in the corner of the room. She pulled out a stack of ivory plates, turning to the doorway where her sister still stood. "You gonna come over here and help me with these, or what?"

Merribelle edged her way around the dining table and walked up to her, arms outstretched. "Like I always used to say when we were kids: Remember, this was *your* idea."

The two of them spent the next half hour laughing over pleasant childhood memories, stacking plates and cups side by side on the polished mahogany table. Merribelle giggled, placing a handful of silverware atop a set of desert plates. "Remember the day Momma whipped you for flushing our goldfish Ernie down the toilet? I think we were on summer break, and she and Daddy were planning to take us down to the ocean for the weekend—"

"Yeah, yeah," Mae interrupted, closing the cabinet door. "It was an experiment. I thought if I went through with it, I'd be able to retrieve him from the water and bring him back home without either of them knowing the better of it." She shrugged when her sister grabbed her side and turned away, consumed by peals of laughter. "What? I was like, seven? How the heck was I supposed to know?"

Merribelle leaned against the wall, hands still on her sides. "Oh, Mae. I'm so glad you came back home, I missed you so much." Her smile faded. "For so long, I thought I'd never see you again, especially after the way you shot out of town so quick after Grandma Lily's funeral."

Mae pulled one of the dining chairs away from the table and sat down. "You know, after everything I've been through, I can honestly say that was probably one of the most difficult days of my life. I was so scared back then, just terrified. She was my safe place, my protection for so long…" her hand floated through the air. "Then one day, she was gone."

Merribelle took a seat across from her. "Protection…you mean from Daddy…"

Mae sighed, dropping her head. "He hurt me really bad, Merri. Did things to me no man has any business doing to a child. He'd stay up late with me, follow me into my room while you and Momma were sleeping, and he'd…"

Merribelle reached across the table for her hand, waiting patiently until her sister's fingers rested on her palm. "It's okay, honey. We don't have to talk about it anymore if you don't want to."

Mae raised her head, looked her in the eye. "He always sang to me, you know? I never knew why. Some stupid song, always the same one." She wiped a tear from her cheek. "Maybe in some sick way he thought it would comfort me, help me to get through…."

"And Momma knew all about it the whole time?" Merribelle's hand tightened on hers. "That doesn't seem possible, Mae. She would have done something—"

"She did." Mae wiped away another tear with the sleeve of her jacket. "She threw me out of the house the day I told her. It was my fifteenth birthday, I remember it so well…" she went on to tell her about the scent of lemon cake mix, the shards of blue glass on the kitchen floor, their mother's acrylic nails digging into her flesh, the vicious fight in the hallway.

When she finished her tale, Merribelle continued to sit silently, wiping tears of her own. "I'm so sorry Mae," she whispered when she was finally able to gain her composure. "I should have been there for you, I was supposed to be there."

After a moment, Mae got up and went to her, wrapping her arms around her tight. Merribelle was pleasantly surprised, eagerly returning her sister's embrace.

"You're here now, Merri," Mae whispered, leaning her head on her shoulder. "That's all that really matters."

The two women stepped onto the porch ten minutes later, a stack of expensive china in each of their arms. Streamers were everywhere. Ribbons of pink, yellow, blue, green and white hung from shrubs and tree branches, an explosion of color. Confetti and matching balloons lay strewn everywhere on the grass. Music thumped from colossal speakers on either side of the porch. The smell of barbeque drifted through the air, wafting into Mae's nostrils with each breath. She glanced over at the corner of the yard where Tim was flipping slabs of meat. Jasper stood next to him, chatting away as he wrapped ears of corn with aluminum foil and arranged them carefully on the grill. Plumes rose and billowed around them as they rocked to the beat, smoke so thick she could hardly see their faces.

"Keep it up, Tim," she called, shouting over the music to be heard. "You're doing good things. Fire department coming anytime soon?"

He glanced up and grinned, holding his tongs up in victory. "Aw, girl, you won't be hollerin' like that when my secret sauce gets up on these ribs n' down on your plate in a few minutes!" He used the tongs to point to the tall white hat cocked on his head. "You must *read* and *heed* the sign, my dear. It says to 'Kiss the Chef,' not 'dis him."

"Jasper!" Merribelle yelled as the screen door slammed shut behind her. "I thought we sent you out here specifically to help this poor man get dinner on the table before nightfall! What happened to that?"

Jasper smiled, holding his hands up in a helpless gesture. "Did what I could. You like corn?"

"Men," she sighed, turning to her sister. She shook her head. "It's times like this I think I might have been better off with that puppy I wanted instead. They're easier to train, and when they get on your nerves you can just send 'em on out to the doghouse without the neighbors lookin' twice."

Mae stared at her, smile playing at the corners of her mouth. "You tried to send Tim out to the doghouse, huh?"

Merribelle rolled her eyes. "Never works, he always seems to find his way back in."

Mae giggled and walked to the edge of the porch, glancing up at the bank of heavy clouds slowly moving in off of the horizon. "So much for a perfect Beau Ciel day. You still think this is a good idea?"

Merribelle shrugged. "Honey, don't ask me, this is Tim's deal." She shifted the stack of plates to her other arm. "At least we'll have a place to run for cover if things get too bad. You're still a good swimmer, right?"

Mae laughed. "That is not funny, Merribelle. Let's get these plates on over to the table. My arms are killing me."

"Momma!" Lily shrieked, waving wildly. "Hurry up!"

She turned to see her holding onto one of the fence pickets as she chatted with her cousin Kyra, struggling for balance on a pair of pink roller skates.

Kyra turned and wheeled up the front walk to greet them as they descended the steps. "Hey, Momma." She pointed to the china in her arms. "Wow, nice plates. Auntie," she said to Mae, "what's taking you so long? We've been waiting for you, like, *forever.*" She tossed one of her braids off her shoulders, rolling her eyes dramatically. "I made sure Momma brought you your skates, did she tell you? They're right over there by Henry." She pointed past the gingham covered picnic table to the tree swing in the garden. The skates dangled there from the seat by their strings; Henry was busily working away nearby, digging around a small tomato patch he'd planted recently at the edge of the yard.

Gathering up the courage, Lily finally pushed away from the front gate, spinning herself in a wobbly circle with arms outstretched. "Momma, come on! You said you'd skate today!"

Just then, Ben came running around the side of the house, followed close behind by Isaiah.

"Mo-om!" the younger one cried, "Ben took my Psychic Nun-Chuk Ninja action figure!" They raced through the yard, weaving past the girls, the table, the garden, the grill. "He won't give it back!" he screamed as they ran around to the other side of the house. "Mom, make him give it back!"

"Boys, stop it!" Merribelle yelled as she and Mae crossed the yard, plunking plates and silverware down on the tablecloth. "You settle down or I'm taking that ugly thing from you both!" When they didn't answer, she bellowed, "I'll make it mine for good, I swear!"

Mae set the stack of desert plates at the end of the table, then walked over to her. "Don't worry, they'll cool down."

Her sister sighed, hands on her hips. "Yeah, but will I?"

Mae laughed, slipping an arm through hers. Together, they walked toward the shimmering fountain in the garden. "So, Miss *Anne Marie*," Merribelle smiled. "How's it feel to be an overcomer *and* an overnight success?"

"Didn't think I'd make it," Mae answered when they were standing in front of the bubbling water. She glanced around to see if anyone was within earshot, lowering her voice. "For a while there back in that swamp, it didn't look so good…"

Merribelle turned to her. "God's smilin' on you, honey," she said, taking her hand again. "Don't you ever forget that. You're not a victim anymore, you're a survivor. He brought you through to the other side, and you lived to tell the tale."

"Thanks to you," Mae replied, "and Henry." She turned to the tree swing. "Hey, Henry!" she called. "How's my favorite guy?"

Henry chuckled as he stood up from his work, resting a hand on the trunk while he massaged a muscle in his lower back. "What was takin' you so long in that house, girl? If I'm still your favorite after all *that* time, why don't you get yourself on over here quick an' give your guy a big hug, then?"

Mae stepped over rows of budding tomatoes, right into his arms. "Feels like home," she sighed, resting her head on his chest.

Henry pulled away, looking down at her carefully. "You all right now, huh?" he whispered. "You ain't lettin' them newscasts get to you?"

She shook her head. "You saved me. I'll never forget what you've done…"

"Hush, girl." He laid her head on his chest again. "He's gone for good, an' he ain't comin' back. That's all the world really needs to know for now."

"Momma!" Lily cried again.

"Honey, I'll be right there!" She turned back to the two of them. "Guys, I hate to do this, but I got a call in the house a while ago, and I have to go meet someone."

"Well, can't it wait?" Henry asked, dusting the soil off his pants.

"Who was it?" Merribelle asked, frowning.

"Serena." Mae gave a slight nod, shoving her hands in her jacket pockets as a cold breeze began to settle in, sending balloons and streamers in every direction.

The sisters exchanged a long glance. "No, Henry, I'm afraid she's got to go see about this one," Merribelle said finally, taking his hand. "Come on over to the table, I'll get your place set. Dinner's almost served, if we can convince the 'chef' over there to put some food in our bellies before we end up drenched and freezin' out here."

Mae approached Lily at last as her sister led Henry over to the picnic table. She was holding on to the pickets again, moving her legs back and forth in a scissor-like motion.

"Hey, honey," Mae called out, "What are you still doing over here?"

"Waiting for you to put your skates on and skate with me," she replied, eyes cast to the ground. "I didn't want to start without you."

Mae crouched in front of her, taking her hand. "Oh, honey, you don't have to wait for me. Kyra's here. She wants to skate with you, too."

"But if you put your skates on, then we can all three skate together." Her face brightened. "Hurry, Momma! Go get your skates on real quick so we can—"

Mae squeezed her hand. "Honey, I know I promised I'd skate with you today, and you know I always say it's important to keep your promises, right?" Lily nodded, doing another scissor kick on the wheels. "Well," she continued, "today someone needs me, and I have to go and help them. Remember how important it is for us to help people who need us?" Lily nodded again. "So that's why I have to break my promise to you. But I give you my word," she said, taking her child's face in her hands. "I give you my word we're gonna skate together, okay? Do you believe me?"

Lily stared at her a moment. After a while, she finally nodded. "When will you be coming back?"

"Soon as I can, I promise." She reached for her daughter, hugging her close. "Know how much I love you?"

Lily giggled in her arms. "More than the stars and the moon?"

Mae watched her get up and grab onto one of the pickets again. She smiled, tugging on a strand of her hair. "More than the stars and the moon."

"Hey, Kyra!" Lily turned and yelled up the walk at her cousin. "I'm ready now!"

Kyra had been sitting on the porch steps, looking bored; when she saw her, she stood up on her wheels and grinned, waving her over. "Come on, then! You can do it!"

Slowly, very slowly, Lily wheeled around and took a step. Then another. Yet another and she was off, rolling up the brick walkway. "Momma!" she screamed in delight. "Momma, look at me! I'm doing it!"

"I see!" Mae yelled, clapping her hands. "That's my girl!"

Jasper passed her on the walkway, giving her a high-five. "All right, Lilybug. Keep it up!" Spotting Mae standing there at the gate, he jogged up to her just as the first waves of thunder rolled across the sky. "Let me walk you to your car."

"No, thanks." She shook her head. Then I'll never want to leave."

He scratched his head, smiling sheepishly. The wind was picking up; Tim's hat flew off his head. He jumped up from his chair by the grill and chased it wildly around the yard, a cry of dismay escaping his lungs when it snagged on one of the bushes, ripping to pieces. "You comin' back soon?"

Mae laced her fingers through his. "I'll do my best."

"I know you will."

Mae walked over to the sedan and unlocked the door. "I'll give you guys a call later to make sure you're all still present and accounted for." She pointed up at the darkening sky. "Don't want to come back and find out any of you floated away from me." She got in and started the engine.

Early the next morning, she sat on the porch steps of Bella Bloom, cradling a hot cup of herbal tea in her hands as she watched Lily skate up and down the walkway. A pen and yellow legal pad sat atop one of her knees, the first draft of a letter scrawled on the pages in neat script. Though yesterday's storm had squashed her celebration with uncharacteristic fury, sending those closest to her scurrying indoors with plates of soggy barbeque, it had passed over the area quickly, leaving a clear dawn in its wake. She had been out here since the first rays of sun could be glimpsed on the horizon, mulling over her not so distant past, as well as the events of the night before.

She closed her eyes. Miranda Murchinson flashed through her mind. A twenty-three-year-old, normally pretty blonde woman who'd been beaten nearly to a pulp by a husband who believed their brand-new baby just *couldn't* be his. After all, the woman had mentioned, face streaming with tears, their baby girl had dark eyes and jet black hair; his was sandy brown. She didn't look a thing like him...

Mae still saw her face clearly, as if she were standing back in the tidy little kitchen at Victory House. Both eyes were swollen and had already begun to change color. Her upper lip had been busted in three places. One of her arms had been secured in a makeshift sling. With her good arm, she rocked the tiny infant, her body so sore and bruised she was hardly able to lift a bottle to her mouth. Mae had fed the baby for her, made a pot of black coffee for the two of them, and had spent the rest of the night sitting with her on one of the living room sofas, comforting and counseling the grieving mother. She prayed Miranda would accept April's invitation to remain at Victory House as long as she needed; Mae looked forward to spending more time with her in the near future.

She opened her eyes and stared off into the distance, tapping the legal pad against her leg. She'd gone straight up to bed when she came home, but after only a couple hours of sleep, had found herself wide awake again. She'd lain there under the pile of tangled bedding, staring up at her ceiling for hours. Light filtering through the bedroom windows and a phone call from Jasper had eventually led her downstairs and out here, to face the beginnings of a brand new day.

She glanced at the legal pad, setting the cup of tea down next to her. She picked the pen up again and twirled it absently through her fingers, reading the letter a final time:

Deborah,

Sorry it's taken so long for this letter to finally reach you. I'm sure you'll understand when I say every wounded thing under the sun needs its time to heal, and it seems I am no exception. I've stared out the windows of my home many a day, watching the seasons tumble over each other as if by magic, and you want to know something? I will never cease to be amazed at the fact that everything around us is constantly dying, just so it can be reborn again. Perhaps this letter is my rebirth, my way of rejoining a world that refused to stop turning, even when I felt as if my own had come to a screeching halt.

I thought I was going to die that night in the swamp. I was ready to give up my spirit, let it go the way of my praying angels before Henry showed up. In one night I saw more armed men gathered there than I've ever seen in all my years of being married to Richard...

Sorry, I had to pause for a moment. Even now it's difficult for me to think of him without wanting to bolt the door to my room and crawl under the bed. My therapist says it's completely normal for me to experience such a powerful backlash of emotion. I tell her I sometimes lay awake all night, crying into my pillow so Lily won't hear... but she says that's all right, too. She tells me everything I do is all right; I wonder if she'd tell me it's perfectly all right to hear his voice calling to me from the shadows beyond my bed, to wake from a dead sleep and see rivers of blood running down the walls? She'd probably lock me up and throw away the key, right? Yeah, that's why I've chosen to keep that particular "backlash" to myself for the time being...

Thank you so much for the gifts and flowers you sent right after the "incident." I was in and out of consciousness for what seemed like forever, but whenever I'd open my eyes and look around, those beautiful sprays were laid out right where I could see them. I was never happier to see so much color... it gave me strength, I think. It gave me a reason to keep my eyes open, besides the fact that Lily and Jasper were sitting right next to me, smiling and holding my hands.

Jasper. He is something else, more than I ever expected or imagined. Could we call it love? Let's not go that far just yet. I see it in his eyes, though, whenever he looks at me, while we're playing with Lily or just hanging out together on the couch. He'll suddenly stop whatever he's doing, walk over and start twirling a strand of my hair. I don't know where he learned such a silly habit, but I've come to realize what it means over time. Yes, he's brought the M word up in our private conversations, but he knows not to press the matter. Whenever he starts getting sentimental, I just squeeze his hand gently and move on to the next subject. He knows it'll be a long while before I can even begin to think of the future—it's enough for me to get through the day...

Congratulations on your recent engagement, by the way. I know someday Malcolm (or "Big Mac," as you like to call him) will make a wonderful father. I'm really happy for you guys; I'm crossing my fingers, wishing you all the best. Just remember that when the time comes, being a mom is the one job you can never quit. That kind of love takes over your mind and heart, and it can lead you straight into forever...

I've got to go now. Lily's been begging me to try out the new skates she and Merri picked out for me the other day. Roller skating? Haven't been on a pair of wheels in years. But I'm willing to give it a try once more—I'm hoping in time I'll be able to give everything in my life another try. I'm still searching for all that I've lost over the years, but the people around me every day—the Henry, the Merri, the Jasper, and especially the Lily in my life have shown me I don't have to depend on finding all those things again; I can plant new memories and harvest new happiness as long as the world itself keeps dying away to begin anew.

Good luck in life, Deborah. My greatest hope for you is that you, too, will give in to happiness. Love the life you're living and appreciate all you've been through. Don't be afraid to have joy as a welcome visitor in your life, as Jasper always likes to say. I've learned the hard way that people need to be forgiven in order to be set free, to be at peace, and I hope this letter has given you some of the peace you've sought desperately for so long. Perhaps there'll be a place in time when we'll call each other friend once more, but until then I ask only that you give your own life another chance. Who knows? Maybe happiness will find us for good this time around, if we let the past go the way of the dead. Ah, to be able to open the door wide, let it all come rushing in...

Always,

Anne Marie

"Come on, Momma, you're such a slowpoke!"

Mae set the pen and pad aside. She glanced up in time to see Lily beckoning to her from the front gate, the pair of brand-new vanilla-colored skates resting beside her. "Jasper's coming. Hurry *up*! We're gonna be late for the park!"

"Be right there, sweetheart," Mae called to her. She spotted the green SUV coming up the hill, spraying flecks of mud in every direction. She sighed, leaning back on her palm as Lily practiced skating figure 8's on the brick walkway. Droplets of water from a nearby tree landed on her as she turned this way and that, glittering in her hair like diamonds beneath an immaculate blue sky.

This is good, Mae thought as the SUV came to a stop in front of the house. *This is what good really feels like.*

She closed her eyes and smiled, turning her face up to the Louisiana sun.

ABOUT THE AUTHOR

Born and raised in the heart of California's Central Valley, **I. L. Goodwin** began a love affair with books at the tender age of five while living in Madera with her eighty-one-year-old grandmother, a wise Southerner and third-generation survivor of domestic violence. During those lazy summer afternoons spent listening to her grandmother's timeless wisdom, the desire to chronicle the experiences of strong women burned deep within her heart. The death of her own mother years later at the hands of a violent partner allowed what was once held captive to finally be released on paper. At age thirteen, she wrote her first full-length manuscript, and several years later completed *A Perfect Place to Pray*, her debut novel. She currently resides in Stockton, CA and is hard at work on her next novel. Please feel free to send author questions and comments to templegrl79@netzero.net.

2006 Publication Schedule

January

A Lover's Legacy
Veronica Parker
1-58571-167-5
$9.95

Love Lasts Forever
Dominiqua Douglas
1-58571-187-X
$9.95

Under the Cherry
  Moon
Christal Jordan-Mims
1-58571-169-1
$12.95

February

Second Chances at Love
Cheris Hodges
1-58571-188-8
$9.95

Enchanted Desire
Wanda Y. Thomas
1-58571-176-4
$9.95

Caught Up
Deatri King Bey
1-58571-178-0
$12.95

March

I'm Gonna Make You
  Love Me
Gwyneth Bolton
1-58571-181-0
$9.95

Through the Fire
Seressia Glass
1-58571-173-X
$9.95

Notes When Summer
  Ends
Beverly Lauderdale
1-58571-180-2
$12.95

April

Sin and Surrender
J.M. Jeffries
1-58571-189-6
$9.95

Unearthing Passions
Elaine Sims
1-58571-184-5
$9.95

Between Tears
Pamela Ridley
1-58571-179-9
$12.95

May

Misty Blue
Dyanne Davis
1-58571-186-1
$9.95

Ironic
Pamela Leigh Starr
1-58571-168-3
$9.95

Cricket's Serenade
Carolita Blythe
1-58571-183-7
$12.95

June

Cupid
Barbara Keaton
1-58571-174-8
$9.95

Havana Sunrise
Kymberly Hunt
1-58571-182-9
$9.95

2006 Publication Schedule (continued)

July

Love Me Carefully	No Ordinary Love	Rehoboth Road
A.C. Arthur	Angela Weaver	Anita Ballard-Jones
1-58571-177-2	1-58571-198-5	1-58571-196-9
$9.95	$9.95	$12.95

August

Scent of Rain	Love in High Gear	Rise of the Phoenix
Annetta P. Lee	Charlotte Roy	Kenneth Whetstone
158571-199-3	158571-185-3	1-58571-197-7
$9.95	$9.95	$12.95

September

The Business of Love	Rock Star	A Dead Man Speaks
Cheris Hodges	Rosyln Hardy Holcomb	Lisa Jones Johnson
1-58571-193-4	1-58571-200-0	1-58571-203-5
$9.95	$9.95	$12.95

October

Rivers of the Soul-Part 1	A Dangerous Woman	Sinful Intentions
Leslie Esdaile	J.M. Jeffries	Crystal Rhodes
1-58571-223-X	1-58571-195-0	1-58571-201-9
$9.95	$9.95	$12.95

November

Only You	Ebony Eyes	Still Waters Run Deep –
Crystal Hubbard	Kei Swanson	Part 2
1-58571-208-6	1-58571-194-2	Leslie Esdaile
$9.95	$9.95	1-58571-224-8
		$9.95

December

Let's Get It On	Nights Over Egypt	A Pefect Place to Pray
Dyanne Davis	Barbara Keaton	I.L. Goodwin
1-58571-210-8	1-58571-192-6	1-58571-202-7
$9.95	$9.95	$12.95

Other Genesis Press, Inc. Titles

A Dangerous Deception	J.M. Jeffries	$8.95
A Dangerous Love	J.M. Jeffries	$8.95
A Dangerous Obsession	J.M. Jeffries	$8.95
A Drummer's Beat to Mend	Kei Swanson	$9.95
A Happy Life	Charlotte Harris	$9.95
A Heart's Awakening	Veronica Parker	$9.95
A Lark on the Wing	Phyliss Hamilton	$9.95
A Love of Her Own	Cheris F. Hodges	$9.95
A Love to Cherish	Beverly Clark	$8.95
A Risk of Rain	Dar Tomlinson	$8.95
A Twist of Fate	Beverly Clark	$8.95
A Will to Love	Angie Daniels	$9.95
Acquisitions	Kimberley White	$8.95
Across	Carol Payne	$12.95
After the Vows	Leslie Esdaile	$10.95
(Summer Anthology)	T.T. Henderson	
	Jacqueline Thomas	
Again My Love	Kayla Perrin	$10.95
Against the Wind	Gwynne Forster	$8.95
All I Ask	Barbara Keaton	$8.95
Ambrosia	T.T. Henderson	$8.95
An Unfinished Love Affair	Barbara Keaton	$8.95
And Then Came You	Dorothy Elizabeth Love	$8.95
Angel's Paradise	Janice Angelique	$9.95
At Last	Lisa G. Riley	$8.95
Best of Friends	Natalie Dunbar	$8.95
Beyond the Rapture	Beverly Clark	$9.95
Blaze	Barbara Keaton	$9.95
Blood Lust	J. M. Jeffries	$9.95
Bodyguard	Andrea Jackson	$9.95
Boss of Me	Diana Nyad	$8.95
Bound by Love	Beverly Clark	$8.95
Breeze	Robin Hampton Allen	$10.95

Other Genesis Press, Inc. Titles (continued)

Broken	Dar Tomlinson	$24.95
By Design	Barbara Keaton	$8.95
Cajun Heat	Charlene Berry	$8.95
Careless Whispers	Rochelle Alers	$8.95
Cats & Other Tales	Marilyn Wagner	$8.95
Caught in a Trap	Andre Michelle	$8.95
Caught Up In the Rapture	Lisa G. Riley	$9.95
Cautious Heart	Cheris F Hodges	$8.95
Chances	Pamela Leigh Starr	$8.95
Cherish the Flame	Beverly Clark	$8.95
Class Reunion	Irma Jenkins/John Brown	$12.95
Code Name: Diva	J.M. Jeffries	$9.95
Conquering Dr. Wexler's Heart	Kimberley White	$9.95
Crossing Paths, Tempting Memories	Dorothy Elizabeth Love	$9.95
Cypress Whisperings	Phyllis Hamilton	$8.95
Dark Embrace	Crystal Wilson Harris	$8.95
Dark Storm Rising	Chinelu Moore	$10.95
Daughter of the Wind	Joan Xian	$8.95
Deadly Sacrifice	Jack Kean	$22.95
Designer Passion	Dar Tomlinson	$8.95
Dreamtective	Liz Swados	$5.95
Ebony Butterfly II	Delilah Dawson	$14.95
Echoes of Yesterday	Beverly Clark	$9.95
Eden's Garden	Elizabeth Rose	$8.95
Everlastin' Love	Gay G. Gunn	$8.95
Everlasting Moments	Dorothy Elizabeth Love	$8.95
Everything and More	Sinclair Lebeau	$8.95
Everything but Love	Natalie Dunbar	$8.95
Eve's Prescription	Edwina Martin Arnold	$8.95
Falling	Natalie Dunbar	$9.95
Fate	Pamela Leigh Starr	$8.95
Finding Isabella	A.J. Garrotto	$8.95

Other Genesis Press, Inc. Titles (continued)

Forbidden Quest	Dar Tomlinson	$10.95
Forever Love	Wanda Thomas	$8.95
From the Ashes	Kathleen Suzanne	$8.95
	Jeanne Sumerix	
Gentle Yearning	Rochelle Alers	$10.95
Glory of Love	Sinclair LeBeau	$10.95
Go Gentle into that Good Night	Malcom Boyd	$12.95
Goldengroove	Mary Beth Craft	$16.95
Groove, Bang, and Jive	Steve Cannon	$8.99
Hand in Glove	Andrea Jackson	$9.95
Hard to Love	Kimberley White	$9.95
Hart & Soul	Angie Daniels	$8.95
Heartbeat	Stephanie Bedwell-Grime	$8.95
Hearts Remember	M. Loui Quezada	$8.95
Hidden Memories	Robin Allen	$10.95
Higher Ground	Leah Latimer	$19.95
Hitler, the War, and the Pope	Ronald Rychiak	$26.95
How to Write a Romance	Kathryn Falk	$18.95
I Married a Reclining Chair	Lisa M. Fuhs	$8.95
Indigo After Dark Vol. I	Nia Dixon/Angelique	$10.95
Indigo After Dark Vol. II	Dolores Bundy/Cole Riley	$10.95
Indigo After Dark Vol. III	Montana Blue/Coco Morena	$10.95
Indigo After Dark Vol. IV	Cassandra Colt/	$14.95
	Diana Richeaux	
Indigo After Dark Vol. V	Delilah Dawson	$14.95
Icie	Pamela Leigh Starr	$8.95
I'll Be Your Shelter	Giselle Carmichael	$8.95
I'll Paint a Sun	A.J. Garrotto	$9.95
Illusions	Pamela Leigh Starr	$8.95
Indiscretions	Donna Hill	$8.95
Intentional Mistakes	Michele Sudler	$9.95
Interlude	Donna Hill	$8.95
Intimate Intentions	Angie Daniels	$8.95

Other Genesis Press, Inc. Titles (continued)

Jolie's Surrender	Edwina Martin-Arnold	$8.95
Kiss or Keep	Debra Phillips	$8.95
Lace	Giselle Carmichael	$9.95
Last Train to Memphis	Elsa Cook	$12.95
Lasting Valor	Ken Olsen	$24.95
Let Us Prey	Hunter Lundy	$25.95
Life Is Never As It Seems	J.J. Michael	$12.95
Lighter Shade of Brown	Vicki Andrews	$8.95
Love Always	Mildred E. Riley	$10.95
Love Doesn't Come Easy	Charlyne Dickerson	$8.95
Love Unveiled	Gloria Greene	$10.95
Love's Deception	Charlene Berry	$10.95
Love's Destiny	M. Loui Quezada	$8.95
Mae's Promise	Melody Walcott	$8.95
Magnolia Sunset	Giselle Carmichael	$8.95
Matters of Life and Death	Lesego Malepe, Ph.D.	$15.95
Meant to Be	Jeanne Sumerix	$8.95
Midnight Clear	Leslie Esdaile	$10.95
(Anthology)	Gwynne Forster	
	Carmen Green	
	Monica Jackson	
Midnight Magic	Gwynne Forster	$8.95
Midnight Peril	Vicki Andrews	$10.95
Misconceptions	Pamela Leigh Starr	$9.95
Montgomery's Children	Richard Perry	$14.95
My Buffalo Soldier	Barbara B. K. Reeves	$8.95
Naked Soul	Gwynne Forster	$8.95
Next to Last Chance	Louisa Dixon	$24.95
No Apologies	Seressia Glass	$8.95
No Commitment Required	Seressia Glass	$8.95
No Regrets	Mildred E. Riley	$8.95
Nowhere to Run	Gay G. Gunn	$10.95
O Bed! O Breakfast!	Rob Kuehnle	$14.95

Other Genesis Press, Inc. Titles (continued)

Object of His Desire	A. C. Arthur	$8.95
Office Policy	A. C. Arthur	$9.95
Once in a Blue Moon	Dorianne Cole	$9.95
One Day at a Time	Bella McFarland	$8.95
Outside Chance	Louisa Dixon	$24.95
Passion	T.T. Henderson	$10.95
Passion's Blood	Cherif Fortin	$22.95
Passion's Journey	Wanda Thomas	$8.95
Past Promises	Jahmel West	$8.95
Path of Fire	T.T. Henderson	$8.95
Path of Thorns	Annetta P. Lee	$9.95
Peace Be Still	Colette Haywood	$12.95
Picture Perfect	Reon Carter	$8.95
Playing for Keeps	Stephanie Salinas	$8.95
Pride & Joi	Gay G. Gunn	$15.95
Pride & Joi	Gay G. Gunn	$8.95
Promises to Keep	Alicia Wiggins	$8.95
Quiet Storm	Donna Hill	$10.95
Reckless Surrender	Rochelle Alers	$6.95
Red Polka Dot in a World of Plaid	Varian Johnson	$12.95
Reluctant Captive	Joyce Jackson	$8.95
Rendezvous with Fate	Jeanne Sumerix	$8.95
Revelations	Cheris F. Hodges	$8.95
Rivers of the Soul	Leslie Esdaile	$8.95
Rocky Mountain Romance	Kathleen Suzanne	$8.95
Rooms of the Heart	Donna Hill	$8.95
Rough on Rats and Tough on Cats	Chris Parker	$12.95
Secret Library Vol. 1	Nina Sheridan	$18.95
Secret Library Vol. 2	Cassandra Colt	$8.95
Shades of Brown	Denise Becker	$8.95
Shades of Desire	Monica White	$8.95

Other Genesis Press, Inc. Titles (continued)

Shadows in the Moonlight	Jeanne Sumerix	$8.95
Sin	Crystal Rhodes	$8.95
So Amazing	Sinclair LeBeau	$8.95
Somebody's Someone	Sinclair LeBeau	$8.95
Someone to Love	Alicia Wiggins	$8.95
Song in the Park	Martin Brant	$15.95
Soul Eyes	Wayne L. Wilson	$12.95
Soul to Soul	Donna Hill	$8.95
Southern Comfort	J.M. Jeffries	$8.95
Still the Storm	Sharon Robinson	$8.95
Still Waters Run Deep	Leslie Esdaile	$8.95
Stories to Excite You	Anna Forrest/Divine	$14.95
Subtle Secrets	Wanda Y. Thomas	$8.95
Suddenly You	Crystal Hubbard	$9.95
Sweet Repercussions	Kimberley White	$9.95
Sweet Tomorrows	Kimberly White	$8.95
Taken by You	Dorothy Elizabeth Love	$9.95
Tattooed Tears	T. T. Henderson	$8.95
The Color Line	Lizzette Grayson Carter	$9.95
The Color of Trouble	Dyanne Davis	$8.95
The Disappearance of Allison Jones	Kayla Perrin	$5.95
The Honey Dipper's Legacy	Pannell-Allen	$14.95
The Joker's Love Tune	Sidney Rickman	$15.95
The Little Pretender	Barbara Cartland	$10.95
The Love We Had	Natalie Dunbar	$8.95
The Man Who Could Fly	Bob & Milana Beamon	$18.95
The Missing Link	Charlyne Dickerson	$8.95
The Price of Love	Sinclair LeBeau	$8.95
The Smoking Life	Ilene Barth	$29.95
The Words of the Pitcher	Kei Swanson	$8.95
Three Wishes	Seressia Glass	$8.95
Ties That Bind	Kathleen Suzanne	$8.95
Tiger Woods	Libby Hughes	$5.95

Other Genesis Press, Inc. Titles (continued)

Time is of the Essence	Angie Daniels	$9.95
Timeless Devotion	Bella McFarland	$9.95
Tomorrow's Promise	Leslie Esdaile	$8.95
Truly Inseparable	Wanda Y. Thomas	$8.95
Unbreak My Heart	Dar Tomlinson	$8.95
Uncommon Prayer	Kenneth Swanson	$9.95
Unconditional	A.C. Arthur	$9.95
Unconditional Love	Alicia Wiggins	$8.95
Until Death Do Us Part	Susan Paul	$8.95
Vows of Passion	Bella McFarland	$9.95
Wedding Gown	Dyanne Davis	$8.95
What's Under Benjamin's Bed	Sandra Schaffer	$8.95
When Dreams Float	Dorothy Elizabeth Love	$8.95
Whispers in the Night	Dorothy Elizabeth Love	$8.95
Whispers in the Sand	LaFlorya Gauthier	$10.95
Wild Ravens	Altonya Washington	$9.95
Yesterday Is Gone	Beverly Clark	$10.95
Yesterday's Dreams, Tomorrow's Promises	Reon Laudat	$8.95
Your Precious Love	Sinclair LeBeau	$8.95

Order Form

Mail to: Genesis Press, Inc.
P.O. Box 101
Columbus, MS 39703

Name _____
Address _____
City/State _____ Zip _____
Telephone _____

Ship to (if different from above)
Name _____
Address _____
City/State _____ Zip _____
Telephone _____

Credit Card Information

Credit Card # _____ ☐ Visa ☐ Mastercard
Expiration Date (mm/yy) _____ ☐ AmEx ☐ Discover

Qty.	Author	Title	Price	Total

Use this order
form, or call
1-888-INDIGO-1

Total for books _____
Shipping and handling:
  $5 first two books,
  $1 each additional book _____
Total S & H _____
Total amount enclosed _____

Mississippi residents add 7% sales tax

Visit www.genesis-press.com for latest releases and excerpts.